The Duke's Heart

A Sweet Victorian Romance

Marina Pacheco

Marina Pacheco

Get all my short stories for FREE!

Building a relationship with my readers is one of the great things about being a writer. Sign up for my no-spam newsletter that only goes out when there is a new book or freebie available, at: www.marinapacheco.me

Contents

Chapter One

Well here I am, lord and master of all I survey, Felix thought, 10th Duke of Morley, and finally in complete control of my land and my money.

'It's a gratifying turnout,' Aunt Lavinia said as she returned to Felix, after having guided one of the guests to a comfortable chair.

'Do you think so?' Felix said as he gazed at the collection of ancients his aunt had gathered for his birthday. Aside from his enormous uncle Marmaduke, working his way through a plate piled high with delectable morsels, he doubted any of the rest were under the age of 50. There were also only about a dozen people invited. The numerous plants, emerald green wallpaper, thick Chinese silk carpet and deep velvet curtains overwhelmed them almost to obscurity. A life-sized portrait of his grandfather, the 8th duke, had more life than the rest combined and seemed to glare disapprovingly at his grandson from the opposite wall. It all added up to an uncomfortable experience.

'It would have been nice to have a few younger people, and more people in general. I would like to widen my circle of acquaintances.'

Felix had lost the particular battle of meeting more people years ago. But he couldn't resist saying something now as he leaned back in the green leather wingback chair he always used. It provided support without making it too obvious that he needed it. The chair was next to the fire that was burning brightly. An ornate screen embroidered with a Chinese style dragon was pulled in front of the fire to protect him both from direct heat and from any smoke that might escape the chimney. His aunt wafted her fan at it to blow away any additional wayward wisps.

'It would be far too dangerous for your heart.'

It was what she always said as a clincher in any argument they ever had. Felix suppressed a sigh as he watched the flames. He wished his cousin Arthur could be here. Arthur was in India now, pursuing what would doubtless be a great career in the civil service. His cousin Percy had also promised to drop in, but as he was a member of the Horse Guards and a prized guest at any of the season's many parties, he was in high demand. Felix even wished his female cousins, ensconced in the nursery upstairs, could join them and add some liveliness to the party.

As it was, all he had were the most elderly of his relatives, carefully selected by his Aunt Lavinia to ensure that none of them overexcited him. She had clearly given this as her strict instruction to all the guests. As a result, they had all approached him with some trepidation. They wished him well upon achieving his majority and then retired a little distance away to continue a hushed conversation amongst themselves.

Felix was left with his aunt who stood to his right, like a guardian angel, one guest said. She was undoubtedly a guardian. The second sister of his father, the daughter of a duke and a formidable woman. Aunt Lavinia had taken it upon herself to raise Felix when his father died in a hunting accident. None could doubt her dedication to keeping him alive. But try as he might, Felix couldn't see her as an angel.

Arthur had recently sent him some photographs of life in India. He'd taken to his new hobby of photography with enthusiasm. One of the photos was of a rhinoceros, with an amusing anecdote about trying to shift this immovable creature from the railway tracks it had decided to sleep on.

Felix was forcibly struck by the idea that his aunt was like a rhinoceros. It didn't help that she had a rather prominent nose. Today she was dressed in a deep green many-layered velvet dress. It had a bustle that only served to emphasise her already ample bottom and her impressive counterbalancing bosom.

Felix stifled a sigh and flicked at some imaginary dust on his knee. He'd had no great expectations for his party, but he'd dressed in his best grey morning suit all the same. It fitted him to perfection as was to be expected. Felix had the services of the best tailor in London after all. He'd been pleased with how he looked, slim but, he thought, elegant. Felix was fair-haired and was considered handsome. As he had a title and great wealth, he was never sure if those compliments were genuine. What was true, was that he was very pale. It was due to a combination of ill health and seldom venturing outdoors. It emphasised his grey eyes and his dark eyebrows a bit more than he liked.

The door at the far end of the room swung open. Instead of Chivers announcing a new guest a tall, handsome man with a similar aquiline nose to his aunt's but with friendly eyes and a generous, smiling mouth strolled in. He was dressed in his full green and black Horse Guards regalia that would be enough to take the shine off anybody else in the room.

'Percy,' Felix said with relief as he made to stand up.

'No don't,' Percy said as he rapidly closed the gap, his hand held out in greeting. 'Happy Birthday, Felix, old fellow.'

'You came,' Felix said beaming up at Percy as he took his hand in a firm grasp.

'I wouldn't miss your birthday for the world, old boy.'

'Indeed,' Lady Lavinia said. 'I can't tell you how happy it makes me see you achieve your majority, Felix. Lord knows many was the time when I feared you'd never live to see this day.'

'And yet, here I am, Aunt,' Felix said irritated that she'd decided to join in a conversation he wanted to have just with Percy.

'Thank the Lord. Still, we mustn't tax you, which is why I have only arranged this modest little get together. We don't want you getting overexcited, do we?'

'There isn't much chance of that,' Felix said as he cast his eye over the assembled gathering.

'They are a thoroughly boring collection, Aunt Lavinia,' Percy said, not bothering to lower his voice. 'Where did you dredge them up from? I don't recognise the half of them.'

'They are all family, and are all aware of Felix's delicate condition.'

'Delicate condition be damned. You'll bore him to death at this rate!'

'How can you say that, really, not in front of Felix.'

'Oh, I don't mind. I like it when Percy is frank.'

'He is a good deal too frank most of the time, but there, we'll not argue. It will spoil a perfectly pleasant afternoon.'

'Indeed. Now if you don't mind, Aunt, I'll return to my room.' Felix wanted a proper conversation with his cousin, and he'd not be able to do it here.

'Are you all right? I didn't mean for today to tax you, but you are looking a bit pale. Shall I get Chivers to bring your chair?'

Somehow his aunt always found the most irritating things to say. 'No, it's fine. If Percy is so good as to offer me his arm, I will be quite safe.'

'The chair would be better. You shouldn't strain yourself unnecessarily and the walk from your room-'

'Percy will accompany me,' Felix said and gave his cousin a meaningful look which thankfully he understood.

'I will ensure no harm comes to him, Aunt, you have my word,' Percy said, as he took Felix by the elbow and gave him a gentle lift.

'I really think-'

'Aunt Lavinia, you will upset him more if you fuss, you know that.'

'Yes, of course, you take care of him.'

'You know I will,' Percy murmured as he walked Felix out of the drawing room, and the footmen swung the doors wide to let them pass. 'Where to now, your grace?'

'Oh Good Lord, please no, not you too,' Felix said.

'Well? You have reached your majority. So, even if I wasn't bowing and scraping before, Aunt Lavinia made it clear to the family that you are now in sole command of your life, your house and all your lands.'

'You weren't paying close attention to what she's been saying if that's what you think you heard. She has already informed me that she and Uncle Marmaduke will remain in this house to act as my support, as they have for so long.'

'I may not be as observant as you, but I did notice that,' Percy said as they completed the short walk across the hall to Felix's rooms.

Due to his condition, they were on the ground floor. The room was oak-panelled as it had once been a library. Percy manoeuvred Felix around his large four-poster bed to the area he'd turned into an informal sitting room. It contained a large comfortable Chesterfield sofa and a couple of armchairs set in the alcove before his window. A fire burned at the far end of the room and did much to cheer the place that was heavily wrapped with deep blue velvet curtains and a thick blue carpet, all designed to ensure the room kept its occupant warm.

Percy helped Felix to sit and said, 'You should send them off with a flea in their ear. You no longer have to put up with Aunt Lavinia's overbearing ways.'

Felix loved his cousin for his forthright pronouncements. He wished he could be as plain-speaking himself. 'The devil of it is, I do need them, Percy.'

'Nonsense, you're an intelligent man. You're far more bookish than I am or than your aunt and uncle are. You may not be able to go about in the world, but you are better read than most, and you know all about your land. I've seen you going through the estate records, you're meticulous.'

'Which is possibly more than Aunt Lavinia knows.'

'You should tell her. You should take charge.'

Felix smiled up at Percy and said, 'Perhaps I will.'

'And I shouldn't nag at you, or I'm no better than Aunt Lavinia. Now tell me, do you wish me to the devil too, or did you just want to get away from all your ancient relatives?'

'It was rather a dismal gathering and sometimes my condition... it gives me all the excuse I need to leave.'

'Well, it has to give you some advantages, after all.'

'Indeed, just as long as I don't use it too much.'

'I doubt you will. So... can I interest you in a game of chess?'

'With pleasure, but not before you pour us a couple of brandies.'

'Brandy? Really?'

Felix was pleased that he could still surprise Percy on occasion.

'I have a stash in the bureau, with a couple of goblets.'

'Is that wise?'

'Are you going to mollycoddle me too?' Felix said, trying to laugh off what could turn into an argument.

'Of course not, don't know what I was thinking. I must have been channelling Aunt Lavinia for a moment.'

'What a terrifying thought.'

'Perfectly,' Percy said with a shudder.

He opened the door of an ornately carved, dark lacquered bureau and pulled out a cut-glass decanter and two matching goblets. He poured a short measure for himself and put a stingier amount before Felix who gave him a quizzically arched brow in return.

'I know, but humour me.'

'Just as long as you keep it our secret.'

'No blabbing to Aunt Lavinia, you have my solemn oath. Now, for the chess, and while we play, you can tell me your plans. Even if they don't include the ousting of your aunt.'

'It would be cruel of me to do it, Percy,' Felix said and moved his spindly side table which held his chess set, already laid out, to be between him and Percy. 'Aunt Lavinia couldn't have looked after me more assiduously if I was her own son.'

'She hemmed you about with more doctors than I have ever seen. But I always felt she was protecting the title and the family name more than she was protecting you.'

'What a shame she never bore a son of her own.'

'Just as well for you, she didn't, old boy, or she'd have been hastening your demise instead of keeping you alive as her life's project.'

'Now you do her an injustice. She is very proper. She would always have upheld me as the duke, even if she did have a son.'

'I wouldn't be so sure, but as the matter is purely academic, I shan't argue with you over it. Now pick,' Percy said, closed his hands about a black and white pawn, put them behind his back for a moment and then held out two fists.

'Left,' Felix said.

'Black, I go first.'

Percy turned the board so that his cousin had the black pieces before him. 'Do you have any idea what you will do next?' he said as he pushed his first pawn forward.

'I shall get a new valet.'

'Why's that? Do you want somebody who'll dress you more snappily? Because you've always been a very neatly turned out fellow. There's no-one of my acquaintance who is better dressed.'

'Really?' Felix said and felt a flush of pride.

'Would I lie to you?'

'I have the time to read the fashion magazines and the funds to indulge my passion. I call it my little indulgence.'

'That and the brandy, eh?'

'Precisely,' Felix said and after a moment's deliberation slid a black pawn up to meet Percy's.

'So, why the new valet?'

'For no other reason than that Grantley is getting old. He is more tired than I am these days. I have spoken to him and agreed on a suitable pension.'

'You have?'

'A far too generous pension as far as Aunt Lavinia is concerned. But, as you have said, I am the master of my own funds now, and I have chosen to reward Grantley for his loyal service. Other than my aunt, nobody has done more to keep me alive. I will miss him.'

'So you waited till you could retire him properly, did you?'

'I made my announcement of Grantley's pension last night at supper.'

'I suspect it didn't go down well.'

Felix smiled up at his cousin as he took a sip of his brandy, then swirled it around in his glass and said, 'I was accused of being irresponsible. Aunt Lavinia feared that next, I would gamble away what remained of the family fortune.'

'What twaddle!'

'She apologised straight away and then spent the better part of the evening trying to get me to change my mind.'

'But you stood firm, well done! None knows better than me how persistent aunts can be.'

'Indeed and then... then she announced that it was time I married.'

'What?' Percy gasped and stared at Felix, who kept his eyes resolutely on the board. 'She didn't!'

'Apparently, it is now imperative that I produce an heir. The sooner, the better.'

'Lest you totter off this mortal coil and leave the house of Peergrave headless? No, she can't do that to you.'

Felix had dreaded telling Percy this news because of the reaction he'd get. He hadn't been mistaken.

'On the contrary, she has already made a list of suitable young women and intends to introduce me to the first of those fair hopefuls on Monday morning.'

'Monday?'

'And then every morning until the end of March by which time, she informs me, I will have met every eligible young female in the land.' Felix smiled at the thought and at his cousin's dismayed face. He hoped he'd eventually see the humour of the situation.

'March! But it's only January now. That sounds like hordes of young women.'

'And one assumes that they must all be interested in a title and a fortune. For never having met me, they can have very little interest in making my acquaintance.'

'But no, Felix, this is intolerable!'

'It is peculiar certainly and, one can't help feeling, a little backward in this day and age.'

'An arranged marriage!' Percy was so exercised by the idea that he jumped up and strode to stare out the window. 'It's 1864 not 1764 for God's sake!'

Felix laughed and said, 'It's arranged matchmaking at any rate. I, apparently, will have the final say in which young lady I decide to marry.'

'It's a farce. If it weren't your future happiness, we were discussing I'd find it positively comical. But we are considering your future, and this is no joking matter.'

'But, Percy,' Felix said and hoped his cousin might understand and come round to the idea. 'How else will I meet an eligible young lady?'

That pulled Percy up short. He went back to his seat and examined Felix more closely than was comfortable. 'Do you want to get married?'

'I have considered it. I wouldn't be human if I didn't wish... I'm just not sure it would be fair on any young woman. Besides, why would any of them want to marry me when there are dashing men like you in the world?'

'Dashing but penniless.'

'Are you?'

'I'm fine. I have sufficient for my needs, don't concern yourself with me.'

'And plenty of women interested in you too, no doubt?'

Percy seldom mentioned women to Felix, and he wondered whether that was for his sake or a lack of interest on Percy's part. He suspected the former.

'Women go crazy for the uniform you know,' Percy said and actually flushed. 'So it's hard to gauge whether it's me or the notion that is attractive to them. Fortunately, my lack of fortune soon has them, or more frequently, their mothers hurrying away.'

'I sometimes wish you could inherit,' Felix said, surprised by his cousin's sensitivity to the subject of women. He'd always assumed he was not easily hurt by rejection.

'I wouldn't be human if I hadn't considered inheriting, but we are very distantly related you and I. We're third cousins at best. We only know of our cousinly relationship because my family made sure to maintain a connection to a duke. We bask in your reflected glory, but my own family is modest, to say the least.'

'And yet you are my favourite cousin by far.'

'It will cheer my parents no end to hear that. Now, don't change the subject. We were discussing nuptials. You have no need to fear what the young women will think of you. You're a good looking fellow, a natty dresser as we have already agreed, and very charming. There is no reason they wouldn't take to you.'

Felix was embarrassed as well as pleased by the description.

'I am also an invalid incapable of leaving my own house, and when I consider lovemaking... I fear it as much as I long for it.' Felix shook his head. 'This is a stupid conversation, think no more of it. My party tired me more than I realised and is making me maudlin. Perhaps I should take a rest.'

'An effective way of bringing any confidences to a close but I won't challenge you on this. You do look pulled. However, if Aunt Lavinia's matchmaking is too much of a trial send for me, and I will put a stop to it.'

'You are very kind, Percy, but there is no need to worry. I know how to manage my aunt.'

'I hope so, just don't let her wear you down.' Percy stood, held out his hand and added, 'I would have won this match, you know?'

'I will leave the board untouched and when next you visit you can prove it.'

Felix's gaze remained fixed on the door after his cousin left. His reaction was what Felix had feared. His cousin supported him in most things and encouraged him to take his own path whenever it conflicted with his aunt's wishes. But, in this matter of a wife, it appeared Percy didn't think he was up to it which was profoundly depressing. He couldn't tell his handsome and robust cousin how lonely he truly felt in his life. It wasn't manly to reveal how very much he wished he could have somebody who loved him. Felix wasn't sure that was even possible, but he hoped it was.

Percy's inclination after taking leave of his cousin was to go back to Horse Guards. But he was so outraged by Aunt Lavinia's plans for his cousin that he felt compelled to say he piece. In fact, he was so outraged he got to the drawing room doors and threw them open before the footmen could open them for him.

He wished his entrance had gained him more attention, but it was only Aunt Lavinia, now seated in the chair Felix had vacated, who looked up. That was fine. She was the one he wanted to speak to anyway.

He marched up to her, steeling himself for an argument.

'I'm off, Aunt Lavinia,' Percy said in strident tones. It wasn't what he'd intended to say.

'Really so soon? I thought you and Felix would be closeted away for longer.'

'Even if you disapprove of that?'

'You tire him, and sometimes you fill his mind with so many impossible things. He wishes he could be like his tall, fit, dashing military cousin, and we all know that is impossible.'

That's as maybe, but it wasn't me tiring him today.'

'It can't have been the party; I made sure it wasn't too exciting.'

'And you excelled at that. No, it wasn't the party. It's your plans for Felix's future and this determination that he should get a wife.'

Aunt Lavinia looked about hastily to ascertain that they weren't overheard and said, 'Sit down, Percy. I can't talk with you looming overhead.'

Percy wanted to maintain his position of dominance but realised it would look foolish and might also result in this conversation being overheard which Felix wouldn't like. So he did as ordered.

Aunt Lavinia leaned towards him, lowered her voice and said, 'You know it's high time he did. I would have got him married earlier still, but Doctor Morton advised against it. He hoped that with age, Felix might strengthen but sadly, that hasn't come to pass.'

'So now, despite his health, you have decided he must wed.'

'The line must go on, Percy. Otherwise, all my struggles and sleepless nights will have been in vain.'

'My God, the line won't come to an end. Have you forgotten Arthur?'

'My oldest sister has been given strict instruction to never let her son think that he may one day become the duke. It would be entirely inappropriate.'

'No, it wouldn't. Noble houses have frequently continued the male line via female relatives. It is a perfectly acceptable tradition.'

'Well, it isn't acceptable to me. I have no wish to usurp Felix's rightful claim. He can, and he will have a son,' Aunt Lavinia said and sat back in her chair as if the discussion was over.

'My God. Do you care nothing at all for Felix? Is the succession all you think about?'

'Of course not. I have nursed Felix since he was a boy. I wish him nothing but the best. Only I can't change the facts, and I have a higher duty to answer to. I have to ensure the Peergrave line continues.'

'You would be well served if he died while trying to fulfil your wishes. Then all your scheming will come to nothing. The only reason I don't wish for that is that I care for Felix and I don't want him to die.'

'I don't want him to die either, but the family needs an heir at least and preferably two.'

'Aside from being astonished by your optimism, how do you know Felix's condition won't transfer to his children?' Percy said. It was a question that had always bothered him, but he'd never dared ask.

'No Peergrave has suffered from such a thing before. All the doctors assure me that it isn't hereditary. In fact, we are confident it was the fever his mother contracted halfway through her pregnancy that caused the defect in his heart.

'Ophelia was ever a delicate, drooping young thing. I don't understand what Alex saw in her, really I don't. She never did recover from the fever. I don't know which was more devastating for Ophelia, the lingering illness or the knowledge that she had somehow damaged her child in the womb. Whatever it was, she succumbed only a few short months after Felix's birth.

'The duty to care for the child then fell to my brother and after Alex's untimely death to me. So you see, I have kept him with us, and I have considered all the risks.'

'I'm not sure you have considered all the risks,' Percy snapped and hastily looked around the room again, he'd spoken a little too loudly. Fortunately, most of the remaining guests were now dozing or looking suitably befuddled.

'Possibly,' Aunt Lavinia said. 'But you know as well as I that at some point all young men think of marriage. You would be a fool if you thought that Felix wasn't already considering it before I broached the subject. What's more, this way, I can make sure he meets a decent young woman. Heaven only knows who he would meet if he used you as his guide.'

'Clearly, I have no hope of convincing you otherwise. I just pray that we don't all come to regret this,' Percy said, stood, gave his aunt a brief bow and swept away.

It was a shame he couldn't repudiate her completely. She was right, Felix was considering marriage already. The thing was, trapped as he was in his home, he had no hope of meeting anyone other than those his aunt invited to the house. Percy thought it might be an idea to introduce a few other women. He chuckled at the reception that would get from Aunt Lavinia.

Honour stepped out of the carriage, straightened her inky black skirt and looked up at the imposing white mansion she was soon to call home. It was an exceedingly fine building that formed part of a crescent of identical houses. It rose to three stories and also had a basement seen just below pavement level. Each house had a run of three steps up to their large black doors. Each one had identical chubby columns holding up the roof to form a vaguely classical looking portico.

If it weren't for the number of the house, 17, neatly signposted in shiny silver on the door, Honour wouldn't have known she was exactly where she needed to be. Her heart gave a flutter of mingled fear and hope as she took a resolute deep breath.

Then she didn't move. Should she go ahead of the footman who'd been sent to meet her at Waterloo station? He was still helping the coachman get her trunk down. It was rather a small affair, but the two men were struggling with it. She supposed London men weren't as strong and capable as the men of her father's regiment.

That thought caught her unawares as the most vivid image of her father resplendent in his red captain's uniform rose before her eyes. She resolutely blinked her gathering tears away and told herself firmly that dwelling on the past would do her no good. It was all change for her from here.

Father's death had come as a shock, especially as it hadn't been the result of a battle. Honour had suddenly found herself orphaned and with no means of support. She'd always feared what might happen as he'd been on enough battlefields for that to be a distinct possibility. Still, she'd never really believed, deep down inside, that he would die. Honour supposed that was why she'd done so little to secure her own future. She'd assumed she'd always be with him and with the regiment.

As a single female, without a guardian, that became impossible. The Colonel had been very good though and allowed her to stay on until she could find an alternative. To do that she had to work her way through her father's papers. Honour was surprised by all the communications he'd kept with a family he assigned to the devil whenever he was drunk.

The letters were universally the same, her father asking for money or support from his family and a chorus of denials from them. She was shocked to discover that he'd also written to her mother's side of the family upon her death and tried to find one of them to take Honour in. That had met with an equal wall of denial.

Still, she was orphaned now and without means to support herself. So Honour wrote to all of them once again. She offered herself as an able-bodied woman who could support their households in whichever way they might need. She'd met with the same denials as her father had.

Honour had begun to fear she'd never be able to leave South Africa when she'd received a letter from Lady Isolde Giddings. It was written on lavender paper and liberally sprinkled with a perfume that tickled Honour's nose and sent her into a fit of sneezes. The letter was so out of the ordinary that Honour read it as she dabbed at her eyes and blew her nose.

Honour was thrilled to discover that Lady Giddings was a direct cousin. She was the only daughter of her mother's younger sister. She was also only two years younger than Honour herself but, according to her letter, in desperate need of a chaperone who wouldn't be beastly. It was an odd choice of words to use, but Honour was so relieved to have this invitation that she wasted no time in letting Lady Isolde know that she was on her way.

Sergeant Major Bruin, her father's bosom companion, and a man Honour looked up to as an uncle, secured her passage on a ship back to England. He'd found a group of girls who, suddenly motherless, were being shipped home. Honour was to act as their temporary chaperone.

She'd left them in tears at a boarding school for young ladies in Southampton. The place was so dismal that she was doubly thankful that her father had decided to keep her with him when her mother died. It couldn't have been an easy decision.

It was a short trip from there by train to London. She'd occupied her time gazing out at the wintry countryside that flashed by and sketching her first impressions, as an adult, of England. It was so different to what she'd grown accustomed too, first the warm green fields of India followed by the red earth and tan grasslands of Africa. In England, a wintry grey sky dominated everything, even the surprisingly green fields and the leafless dark purple woodlands that bunched in the creases of the rolling hills.

'Are you ready, ma'am?' the footman said as he dropped her trunk with a click on the ground by her feet.

Honour took a quick gasp of air at the thought of meeting her relatives then pushed her fear aside. There was no reason to be afraid.

'Let's go in,' she said with a bright smile.

The footman ran up the steps ahead of her and rang the doorbell vigorously. It took an anxiously long time before a butler slowly opened the door and looked Honour and the footman up and down as if they were total strangers. Honour expected that for herself but she was surprised the butler didn't seem to know the footman.

'This is young Miss Seaborn,' the footman said loudly to the butler. 'And I'll be needing a hand with her trunk.'

'Miss Seaborn, please come in,' the butler said, giving her a ponderous bow. 'I am Thompson.'

'Thank you,' Honour said. She realised that Thompson was on the elderly side. What she'd taken as unbending aloofness appeared merely to be shortsightedness as he peered closely at her as she stepped into the house.

It was pleasantly modern with straw-coloured satin curtains that complemented the warm stone interior. A curving staircase dominated the space.

'I won't have it!' came an elderly female voice from the landing above.

As Honour looked up, a stout woman stomped down the stairs, her voluminous grey skirts swishing.

She cast Honour a seething look as she reached the ground floor. 'I take it you're my replacement,' she snapped.

'I beg your pardon?' Honour said, but she was ignored as a carpet bag came flying over the bannisters, narrowly missed both women, rolled to the front door and hit it with a thump.

'Leave! I won't miss you,' a younger woman shouted from above.

A vision of loveliness followed the voice, flushed and breathing heavily as she looked down into the entrance hall. It had to be Lady Giddings. She had cool ash-blonde hair and a face that looked like it had been carved from marble, except it was a deep pink at the moment. Her blue eyes were large and sparkling with rage.

'You're a frump, and you keep getting in the way,' she shouted. She realised the woman wasn't alone and smiled abruptly. 'Honour? Honour Seaborn?'

'Yes,' Honour murmured as she glanced at the older woman who was staring daggers at her.

'You've arrived, how wonderful!' Isolde said and ran downstairs. She was wearing a sky blue dress that fanned out about her as she bundled into Honour and wrapped her in a hug.

Honour was overwhelmed by the same perfume that she'd smelled on the letter, this time mixed with the soft muskiness of her cousin.

'Lady Giddings?' she said as she disentangled herself from the embrace.

'She is,' the older woman snapped. 'I thank God she is no longer any concern of mine.' She swooped down on her carpet bag, said, 'I expect the rest of my luggage to be sent to the hotel,' and slammed out of the house.

'Good riddance,' Isolde said and, much to Honour's surprise, poked her tongue out at the door. 'Ignore her, she's my great aunt Gloria and a less glorious woman you have yet to meet.'

'I hope I wasn't the cause of her leaving,' Honour said.

'Oh, don't worry about her. She was quite, quite intolerable,' Isolde slipped her arm into Honour's and said, 'Come on upstairs. I'll show you to your room.'

CHAPTER TWO

F elix sat in his armchair, his feet propped up on an ottoman ordered all the way from Turkey. Felix liked it because of its blue leather cover that was tooled with a paisley pattern. It looked exotic as well as being a comfortable footrest. He had the latest edition of The Gentleman's Magazine open on his lap. He'd lost interest in it and was gazing out of the window instead.

A few years ago he'd had the high walls that surrounded the house reduced to waist height and the rest replaced with railings so that he could at least have a view of the garden square across the road. The trees in the square were leafless at this time of year, but still more interesting than a wall. The terrace houses that lined the other three sides of the square were more modern than his house and very genteel, as befitted the homes of a square that was graced by a ducal mansion. Felix's house took up the entire north side of the square. It included a curving driveway that led to the front door. A covered portico ensured that guests didn't get drenched in the short walk from their carriage to the double front door.

'Master Thomas Poole, your grace,' Chivers announced and pushed an anxious-looking young man into the room before shutting the door firmly behind him.

Poole was of slim build and medium height with blue eyes and straw-coloured hair that was a bit on the long side. It looked like he'd wet and brushed his hair before answering Felix's summons. He had rosy cheeks and the tan of somebody who worked outside. Poole was also wearing a waistcoat with the horizontal stripes in the duke's livery that indicated he was outdoors staff. All the indoors staff had red and gold vertical stripes.

'Your grace!' Poole gasped and flung himself forward into something resembling a bow as his knees bent trying to kneel.

Felix suppressed a smile, now was not the time to show amusement, it would only embarrass the young man further. Besides, he wanted to see what he thought of the lad, and that would require that Poole be as much at ease as possible.

'Master Poole,' Felix said. 'Please, take a seat.'

'Oh, I couldn't possibly, your grace.'

'Ah, but I would like you to. You see, we need to have a talk and I won't strain my neck simply to uphold the proprieties. So, you will have to sit down.'

'Yes, your grace, if you order it,' Poole said and looked about frantically, his eyes growing rounder and rounder.

'Here, your grace?' Poole said, his hand on the cushion of the chair set opposite Felix.

'Please.'

'Yes, sir, thank you, sir,' Poole said and perched ramrod straight on the edge of his seat.

'I understand you have recently joined my staff,' Felix said in what he hoped was a friendly tone of voice.

'Yes, your grace. I started this January,' Poole said and grimaced, tried to turn it into a smile and then smothered all expression.

'And your father worked in the stables before you?'

Felix knew this to be a fact. He'd thoroughly researched Poole before deciding to interview him. He was just asking questions he knew the lad would know the answers to so that he could put Poole at his ease.

'Yes, your grace, father worked in the stables, as my grandfather did before him.'

'I understand they have both died.'

'Fever carried dad off, old age did for grandad.'

'So you stepped into the breach, did you?'

'Somebody has to look after the family. My mum does what she can, but it's been hard for her.'

Poole was looking steadily more confused and anxious. Still, he was going to have to weather this interview for a bit longer because Felix needed to know what he thought of the lad. Poole was a significant change from Grantley and Felix wondered whether he'd be able to adapt to the change. In all honesty, he wondered whether either of them could adapt to what would be a massive change for both of them.

'Do you enjoy being a stable hand?'

'It's fine, thank you, your grace.' Poole said, and his face became even more mask-like.

'Is it indeed?' Felix said. This was the true test of Poole. This was where Felix would discover how truthful he was. He disliked dishonesty, even when it was for good intentions. 'I understand you labour under something of a disadvantage.'

'I... I do?'

'Chivers tells me that you are afraid of horses.'

'Oh no, your grace, I don't mind them, honest.'

'I wouldn't mind if you did. I find horses rather intimidating myself.'

'Oh,' Poole said. 'Well... they are very big and prone to bucking and kicking.'

Score one to Poole, Felix thought. Now onto the rest of the questions. 'Tell me, what do you make of London?'

'It's very fine.'

'Is that all?'

'There's plenty to see, but I haven't had a chance to look around. I've only spent a day walking down the Strand. It was full of the greatest swells I've ever seen.'

'Well-dressed were they?' Felix murmured.

'Oh, your grace, you have no idea. I've never seen anything to equal them.'

'Mmm, so you like watching people and fashion do you?'

'A bit,' Poole said, colouring up in embarrassment.

'Tell me, Master Poole, do you enjoy your job?'

'Enjoy? It has to be done.'

'That is true, but I imagine if you aren't keen on horses, it must be something of a trial.'

'My family rely upon me, your grace. I can't let them down, so I face my fears, and I carry on.'

'What if you could do something else?' Felix said, watching the lad even closer. Poole simply looked confused as he shifted uncomfortably on the edge of his seat.

'I can't, sir. I don't have any other skills.'

'Training could be provided.'

'Begging your pardon, your grace, but I'm too old for an apprenticeship, meaning no offence, sir.'

'None is taken, Master Poole. I am rather talking in riddles, I suppose. Part of that is because I am sounding you out and partly I am still making up my own mind.'

'Oh,' Tom said, but it was clear he had no idea what was going on.

That was fair enough, Poole could have no notion of why Felix was questioning him. It would be beyond his wildest expectations. He looked like a sensible, honest young man who looked after his appearance, despite the slight whiff of the stables. It was obvious he's scrubbed his face and hands and put on clean clothes when he was summoned for this interview. That spoke of one who tended towards tidiness.

'I asked to see you,' Felix said, 'Because when I asked Chivers whether we had any fastidious dressers amongst the staff, he mentioned you. He appears to be right. You are very neatly dressed for a stable boy.'

'I try my best, sir.'

'And when you talked about the Strand you mentioned the well-dressed people.'

'It was just an observation, your grace.'

'Indeed, but many's the boy who wouldn't notice such a thing at all.'

'Yes, sir,' Poole muttered.

'Do you like my suit?' Felix asked.

'Yes, your grace.'

'What do you like about it?'

'It's a nice grey, and it looks smooth and shiny, which is... nice.'

'I agree,' Felix said, and this time he did smile.

Poole might not be able to recognise silk yet, but he did have an eye for fabric.

'I beg your pardon, your grace, I didn't mean to be forward.'

'Not at all, you were answering my question. How could I possibly be offended?' Felix paused at Poole's hastily smothered dubious expression and murmured, 'I have a very privileged position, sometimes it means I miss the harsher realities of life. So I will put your torment at an end, Master Poole and come to the point. I am in need of a new valet.'

'Yes, sir?' Tom said and looked like a man who would love to help but had no idea how he could.

'I am proposing you take up that position,' Felix said nonchalantly, watching Poole even more closely.

Poole gasped and said, 'Me, sir! But... but I know nothing about being a valet and, and I-'

'Stop. You will be trained. Grantley will take you in hand.'

'Your current valet, sir?'

'He has been my most devoted servant for my whole life. His final service to me before he retires is to train his replacement.'

'Your grace, it's too great an honour. I'm not qualified, and I don't even know if I can, I-'

'Master Poole, I am not conferring upon you a marvellous promotion. Disabuse yourself of that notion straight away. You will be aware that I am far from robust, and for all we know I'll drop

dead a day from now. Even if I don't, and you receive your full
and proper training and step into Grantley's shoes, this job is
far from wonderful. I will need you to be at my side day and
night. As I rarely leave my rooms and even less frequently leave
my house, you will be trapped inside with me.

'I try not to be a tedious drain on my staff, but I rely upon
them. I will rely upon you more than any other master might. I
am also a severe disappointment to anyone who wishes to shine
upon the London stage for I never venture out onto it.'

'I don't understand,' Tom said.

'Most valets live to send their masters out on the town looking
their very best. What is the point of dressing a man to a T only
to have him stay indoors and your handiwork never seen? At the
very least, you will develop no reputation beyond these doors.
Which means you won't have every gentleman of the land trying
to lure you away with offers of better pay.'

'But you are a duke.'

'And aside from a prince and a king, the very pinnacle of
service, yes. I am glad you have already assimilated that fact.
But I fear for a true artist it is something of a soul-destroying
experience to have your art go unseen. You are not a valet yet, so
you don't understand what I am saying, but you will learn.

'The only advantage I can offer you in this position is that
you will be well trained. Upon my death, you will have a letter
of recommendation with which you will be able to find decent
employment as another gentleman's gentleman. At that point,
you may well be able to shine.'

'Yes, your grace.'

'So, what is it to be? Would you like to swap the stables for my
dressing room?'

'Yes, your grace,' Tom said and blushed bright red all the way
to the tips of his ears.

'That was very sudden, Master Poole, are you so certain?' Felix
said, amused by the young man's embarrassment.

'It's a big step up, your grace, and I am very grateful for it and to you for considering me and... no horses.'

'Very well,' Felix said and rang a bell picked up from the table at his elbow.

'Your grace?' Grantley said as he stepped into the room and bowed.

The contrast between Felix's old valet and the young man who would soon be his new valet was stark.

Grantley was dressed immaculately in a black suit, and not a hair was out of place on his thinning pate. He bowed very slowly and remained stooped even as he straightened up again. It confirmed in Felix that he'd made the right decision to retire Grantley.

'This is young Master Poole, Grantley. He has accepted the position and is ready to start learning.'

'Very good, your grace,' Grantley said as his gaze flickered briefly over the stable lad. 'Please follow me, Poole.'

'Yes, sir,' Poole said as he leapt up, hesitated before Felix, gave another quick bow and hurried after Grantley's retreating back.

Poole's mind was buzzing as he followed the valet into a dressing room that was bigger than the house Poole had grown up in. The opposite end of the room was dominated by a gilt-framed mirror. It had a dressing table pulled up before it that held a collection of white pottery jars and gold stoppered glass bottles as well as a hairbrush and razor blade. To one side was a porcelain bowl and jug and three white towels stacked one upon the other. To his left was a cupboard without doors that was filled with row upon row of suits, shirts and trousers. Shoes that had all been polished till they shone formed a serried rank along the bottom shelf. On his right was a chest of drawers and beyond that, a narrow, neatly made-up bed.

Tom gave a shiver of anticipation. This was to be his new place of work, and it was almost impossible to believe.

'It's nothing like the stable, eh?' Grantley said.

'No, sir.'

Grantley nodded, looked Tom up and down and said in a soft dry voice, 'Feathers will be ruffled and no mistake.'

'Will they?'

'Do you have any idea how many footmen have been watching me wondering when I'll shuffle off so that they might have a chance of inheriting my job?'

'No, sir.'

'Well, probably all of them,' Grantley said as he took a charcoal grey coat out of the cupboard and brushed the shoulders. 'Not that they or you would have been my choice. His grace would have done better to take on an established valet. He should have gone for someone from another noble house who has already made a name for himself. But that's his grace for you. He might look mild-mannered, but he does what he pleases.'

'He does?'

'Never doubt it,' Grantley said, hung the coat on a peg by the door and took out a matching pair of trousers. 'Now, the first thing we have to do is get you clean and out of those clothes. You've washed, but you still smell of the stable and no more vertical striped waistcoats for you. No horizontal stripes either, you will have a suit like mine.'

'Yes, sir,' Tom said, and a thrill passed over him. His change in fortune was only now starting to sink in.

'I suppose you being young and inexperienced is just what appeals to his grace. He'll be able to mould you to suit himself, and he knows I'll train you to his tastes as well. An older man would be more set in his ways.'

'Yes, sir.'

'Grantley, from now on I am Grantley, and you are Poole, do you understand?'

'Yes, si- Grantley.'

'And from now on, Lord love you, you are part of the upper servants. You will eat with us in the servants' dining room, and you will recall your station at all times and not fraternise with the lower servants, is that clear?'

'Yes, Grantley.'

Grantley nodded and took out a pristine white shirt. Each action was precise as he selected the clothes. 'You have been catapulted into an extremely privileged position, and it's going to take some getting used to. Not to mention all the people you have leapfrogged over who won't forget it in a hurry.'

'No?'

'Ignore them. You can do that now. The only person you will answer to in this house, once I am gone, is his grace. The rest can go swivel.'

Tom blinked to hear Grantley use such vulgar language and was even more astonished as he gave a self-satisfied smile.

'Get used to it, boy. You will have to develop a thick skin and arrogant attitude if you are to survive the equally high handed senior staff. And, in time, you will grow accustomed to each other. Thankfully, by then, it will no longer be my concern.'

'Where will you go, Grantley?'

'His grace has settled a house and a pension on me. It will provide a very comfortable living, and it has to be said it came as a surprise. Masters, on the whole, neither care nor notice the ills and ailments of their staff. But his grace did and without so much as a by your leave to Lady Lavinia. Everyone might think she is sole mistress of the house, but they're mistaken. His grace gave me leave to retire. Not to some poxy cottage on his estate either, for he knows I am no country bumpkin. No, he got me a house in Stepney.'

'That was very generous of him.'

'I've earned every brick, boy, and well he knows it, but you're right, it was generous. Many is the man I've seen dismissed without a penny when he could no longer work. I thank God his grace isn't one of those.'

'No.'

'Not that you'll have a similar fortune, mind you. You'll outlive his grace by decades. Truth be told, I thought I'd outlive him too. At this rate he may just outlive me,' Grantly murmured as he opened a drawer and ran his fingers over a row of silk ties.

'Is he really that unwell?'

'Do you think any man would choose to never leave his house? He is as careful as may be, and Lady Lavinia is too. She may be an overbearing, managing woman, but nobody can doubt she has kept his grace alive. With my help, mind you, and from here on in with yours too.'

'Yes, Grantley.'

'His grace has a weak heart, as you'll know. What you probably don't know is what that means.'

'No.'

'He tires very easily,' Grantley said, selected a grey tie with a red stripe and hooked that up with the rest of the clothes he was taking out. 'Even standing up can be too much of a strain on his bad days. We usually support him when he walks to make it that little bit easier for him. He has a bath chair, a contraption with wheels, but he doesn't like to use it. On occasion, he has no choice.

'Sometimes, his heart causes him pain. He tries not to show it, but on occasion, he'll cry out. He also gets breathless, and if he's standing and his lips or his fingernails start turning blue, you must get him to sit down immediately. If he doesn't, he'll likely keel over.'

'Die?'

'Not yet, so far. His grace just faints. On occasion, he faints for no obvious reason either. The best thing to do for him then is to get him into bed and raise his legs. That gets the blood flowing back up to his heart. For the most part, it is best if he stays still and rests.'

'Oh,' Tom said and fought not to show how shaken he was by the news.

'Not quite such a great thing being his valet now, is it?'

'I will do my best for him all the same.'

'As we all do. The only other thing I'll tell you now is that his grace is more susceptible than most to colds and fevers. To keep him safe nobody with so much as an itchy nose is allowed near him or his quarters. All the staff know this, but on occasion, some silly housemaid will come in and make up his fire when they are under the weather. They should be banished immediately, and everything they touched must be washed down.'

'Oh, so that's why Chivers asked me so many questions about my health before he brought me here.'

'Precisely. You will learn more of this in time. For now, I've had this truckle bed brought up,' Grantley said, took out a pair of grey socks and placed them on the dresser. 'Most valets sleep in their master's dressing rooms. I have a room just through here, and once I move out, you can take it over. Up till then, you have the dressing room.'

'All right.'

'Have you ever slept on your own, Poole?' Grantley said, raising his head a bit more so he could look him in the eye.

'Never, my family all slept together in the cottage, and since coming to town, I've slept with the other stable lads.'

'You'll get used to it. Because of his grace's condition, he tends to sleep a lot. It means you will have time on your hands, but you need to stay close and alert in case he needs you. I play solitaire to while away the hours, no doubt you will find something similar to keep yourself busy.'

'Yes, sir.'

'Other than that, your duties are to dress and shave his grace and to maintain his quarters in neat order. Maids will make beds and clean the rugs, but you need to pack away books and articles of clothing. You will also have to clean all of his grace's clothes.'

'Don't the maids do that?'

'Can you imagine what his grace's clothes would look like after they'd been pummelled and scrubbed by a maid?' Grantley said with a shudder. 'They would ruin them, absolutely ruin them. The silk suit he has on this morning wouldn't survive a single wash, and as for ironing? No! They might think they know what they're doing, but they don't. I will show you how to launder and iron all of his grace's clothes,' Grantley said and gave a nod of satisfaction at the outfit he'd gathered for the duke.

Chapter Three

It was pitch black when Honour woke, but her travelling clock read 7 am. It was something she was going to have to get used to again, the long dark winter nights in England. Now, she needed some time to get ready for the day's activities.

Sunday had been taken up entirely by Isolde who insisted on her sitting in the drawing room so that she could tell Honour why she was needed. She was thrilled, she'd said, to have the company of somebody her own age. Honour was pleased and relieved that she could be of assistance. She quickly realised that Isolde required no support in conversation. In fact, she hardly paused in her monologue and spent the time informing Honour of all the activities she was engaged in.

It transpired the reason Isolde wanted her as a chaperone was that it was the start of the season and the busiest time of the year for any young lady. Honour knew about the season, of course. She'd read about it every year in the papers, and the colonies had also had their own, scaled-down, version of it.

The aim was to find a husband. Then, once married, to take part in the festivities in winter before returning to the country estate in the summer. As a result, every day was jam-packed with activities. It sounded to Honour like Isolde was at the centre of every party and event in London and enjoying it thoroughly.

Honour stretched, got up and pushed the curtains aside to look out onto a back courtyard obscured by drizzle and swirling smog. The door to the servants' quarters below swung open and flickering light spilt onto the paved ground. A servant hurried outside, worked the pump energetically, filled up a bucket and then hurried back into the warm house.

In a little while, that water would be sufficiently heated and brought upstairs for the master and two ladies of the house to bathe. That was an unaccustomed luxury for one who had grown up living under canvas.

A hesitant tap at the door signalled the arrival of Doris. She was the young woman Isolde had decided should be Honour's maid. Isolde had been horrified when she'd learned that Honour didn't have one.

Until yesterday she'd been a mere kitchen servant. Her change in fortune had clearly flustered her, but she was willing and a welcome support to Honour.

'Good morning, miss,' Doris said bobbing a couple of curtsies. 'Are you ready for your hot water?'

'I am indeed, thank you,' Honour said.

'I'll tell the others,' Doris said and hurried away.

Honour didn't have to wait long before another tap heralded the arrival of a steaming bucket of water that was decanted with great care into her basin by Doris. She turned around and beamed at Honour and then her face faltered.

'Would you be needing help washing up, miss? Because I'm not rightly sure I know how to do that, but if you show me, I'll help all I can.'

'Truth be told, I've never had a maid, so I'm not sure what you should be doing at this point either. However, I am perfectly able to bathe myself. In the meantime, would you lay out my riding dress please.'

'Of course, miss. I spent hours yesterday ironing all your dresses they were that creased from being in your trunk for so long.'

'I was very grateful for that too,' Honour said as she slipped out of her nightdress.

'I suppose you'll be going to all the parties with Lady Isolde.'

'I will, indeed.'

'Miss Gloria complained all the time about all the gadding about. She said she barely slept since she came to this house. She was a complaining one though. I'm sure you'll have a lot more fun, miss,' Doris said beaming at Honour.

'I hope so,' Honour said. She was used to a rigorous life, but even she was astonished by the reserves one needed for the season. She wasn't surprised that Isolde's aunt had hardly slept.

'What will you be doing today?' Doris said as she reached into the cupboard and groped about for Honour's riding boots, emerging triumphant after a few seconds.

'As I understand it, we will be heading to Hyde Park for a ride first thing this morning. After that, we have a breakfast party although I'm afraid I have already forgotten the name of the hostess. After that more riding, followed by lunch and an afternoon concert, then on to a charity bazaar, a couple of visits to friends of Lady Isolde's, dinner, opera and a ball to round the night off. Lady Isolde tells me she usually gets home around three in the morning.'

'That she does,' Doris said nodding sagely. 'My, but that does sound like an awful lot of activity.'

'It does, doesn't it?' Honour said. 'And I'm going to have to hurry if I'm not to be late.'

She finished bathing and scrambled into her clothes while Doris went to fetch her tea and toast. That would do to sustain her till the breakfast party.

The clock was chiming a half of eight when Honour arrived in the hall. Isolde got there shortly afterwards and examined Honour closely.

'It's lucky you have a riding outfit,' Isolde said. 'I don't think I have anything I could lend you that would fit.'

'We did quite a bit of riding out on campaign,' Honour said although she wondered about the comment. She and Isolde were of a similar height and build. 'Although I didn't think I would be doing much riding in London and did contemplate leaving the dress behind.'

'Good thing that you didn't,' Isolde said. 'Well, come on, we don't want to be late. There is a gentleman I am cultivating. He is an earl, so I don't want to keep him waiting.'

Isolde looked triumphant as she spoke. Honour supposed she had a right to be pleased as an earl would be a great catch indeed.

The two ladies stepped out into the fine drizzle. They hurried to their horses that were stamping impatiently while a couple of grooms held them ready and waiting. Isolde was providing her with a horse, and it looked to be a little on the old side. Honour didn't mind and gave the old lady a pat on her nose before she mounted. The tiny droplets of water on the horse's shaggy chestnut coat soaked through Honour's glove. She'd forgotten all about how drenching a fine mist could be. She'd also forgotten how the English seemed not to notice what to her was quite an irritation as the water speckled her face.

Isolde set off to the park and Honour nudged her horse into action so that the two of them could ride abreast.

'The earl is Lord Overbrook,' Isolde said, her mind already focused on the coming meeting. 'He's quite old. I believe he is a year or two older than my father, but he is excessively wealthy. I have heard that women have been laying siege to him for years, but he has never shown any interest in any of them until I came along.'

'He's older than your father?' That came as a surprise to Honour.

She'd only met Lord Giddings briefly the previous day. He was ensconced in his study poring over the newspaper and gave Honour a distracted murmur of welcome. This apparently suited Isolde who was equally vague about why Honour was visiting. Honour had an uncomfortable feeling that she was engaged in subterfuge and that it wasn't proper to be such a young chaperone to her cousin. Then again, some ladies went about with their equally young maids, so maybe it was all right.

'Do you want to marry someone so old?'

'I don't mind,' Isolde said with a shrug as she led her horse down a wide lane that opened out onto Hyde Park. 'I will be content as long as I have plenty of money for jewels and pretty dresses and I am allowed to go to as many parties as I want.'

'What about being in love?'

'Love?' Isolde said with a laugh. 'I suppose that is something you would consider. After all, your mother ran off with a military man against her parents' wishes. But, look where that got her.'

'I believe she was happy,' Honour said and fought to hide how much she was hurt by Isolde's comment.

Isolde didn't notice. She was already scanning the horsemen dotted about the entrance to the park looking for her earl.

'I tell you what, Honour, you'd do well to find a husband for yourself. Otherwise, I don't know what you'll do. Once I'm married, I won't need a chaperone.'

'Oh, I hadn't really considered...' Honour petered out because she wasn't being listened to anymore. Isolde had spotted her quarry and urged her horse into a leisurely canter.

Honour followed along behind, her mind in a whirl. She hadn't really thought beyond finding someone to stay with in England. She hadn't realised how temporary that might be. Now Honour had the horrible realisation that she had to find another position quickly.

Marriage had also been the furthest thing from her mind until Isolde mentioned it. Could she get married? Was that even possible for a penniless orphan? Which man would be interested in her, especially when she was accompanying her beautiful and wealthy cousin.

'Ahoy there!' Isolde cried and pulled up beside a tall thin middle-aged man astride a handsome grey horse. His face was heavily lined, and, though it was difficult to tell because of his top hat, Honour suspected that he dyed his chestnut locks.

'Why, if it isn't Lady Giddings,' the man said with a smile that did nothing to warm his eyes.

'Lord Overbrook, it's so good to see you again,' Isolde said, flashing him a charming smile.

'It is always a pleasure to see you, and looking so rested and refreshed this morning.'

'I had all of Sunday to recuperate,' Isolde said, remembered Honour and waved her hand at her. 'My cousin, Honour Freeborn.'

The earl gave Honour a slight nod then dismissed her from his mind as he turned back to Isolde. 'Would you do me the honour of riding with me this morning?'

'But of course,' Isolde said, and her horse sidled and skipped as if she too were delighted.

Just then a tall young man trotted up to the group, his eyes shining as he bowed over his horse's head and said, 'Lady Giddings. Your presence here has brightened up what was, till now, a gloomy Monday morning.'

Isolde laughed and said, 'Lord Hounslow, how sweet of you to say so. You must join our party.'

The earl looked put out by the suggestion but didn't naysay it. After a brief introduction where Lord Hounslow paid Honour as little attention as the earl had, the two men took up position to either side of Isolde. They left Honour to take up the rear.

It gave her a chance to size up Lord Hounslow who was probably in his very early twenties. He had soft features, big hands, narrow shoulders and wide hips that made him look a bit unbalanced. He was clearly in awe of Lady Giddings and recited a couple of poems he'd written in her honour. She laughed and praised him for his genius but made equally sure to keep the earl engaged too.

Honour's brief consideration of marriage died on the spot. She was utterly ineligible. She would have to consider what other activities a single woman alone in the world could take advantage of. The two that came to mind was either being a governess or a housekeeper. Neither role appealed, but she realised with a sinking heart that her options were limited.

Felix gazed at himself in the mirror. The dawn light spilling in from the window made him look pale and haggard. To banish that dismal thought, he glanced up at Poole who was carefully clipping his nails under Grantley's hawk-like supervision. It was only Poole's first day, but Felix was satisfied that he'd made the right choice.

It was another disapproved of by his aunt. She held off scolding him only because he'd told her last night over supper and she'd said, 'I want you at your best tomorrow so I'll say nothing more on the matter.'

Well, he wanted to be at his best today too. He was more frightened than he'd expected for the day. He was usually so cloistered that he couldn't recall having met any young women other than his awed and hushed cousins.

They, after their first meeting, had been given strict instructions not to tax him. It meant they gazed at him with anxious round eyes, had nothing to say, and didn't demur when they were shooed away again. He often wished he could get to know more people.

He especially wanted to meet some of the rather dashing heroines he'd read about in the racier books Grantley got for him. They were books Aunt Lavinia wouldn't have approved of and was therefore blissfully unaware of. Felix wondered whether the women he read about from Dickens to the Bronte sisters were anything like the young ladies he was about to meet. It seemed to him that life was more prosaic than in a novel. He also feared that any feisty heroine would find him a very dull dog indeed.

That was the crux of the matter. He was afraid he would be a disappointment. No doubt, the mothers of all the young women his aunt had lined up had their eye on his title and his money. But the daughters would have to be social climbers of the highest order if they were willing to settle for him rather than for any other healthy young man to be found on the town.

'All done, your grace,' Grantley said as he ran a brush over the shoulders of the suit.

'Thank you, Grantley, and with half an hour to spare,' Felix said, checking the clock on the mantelpiece.

'Would you like Poole and me to accompany you to the drawing room right away?'

Now that was the question. Felix needed to be there early so that he wasn't out of breath when his first caller arrived. But if he did venture to the drawing room, he'd have to sit with Aunt Lavinia while he waited. Felix wasn't sure he could pay her sufficient attention, distracted as he was with nerves. On the other hand, he couldn't focus enough to read. Even the newspaper had proved impossible this morning.

'I may as well set off,' Felix said and hoped his nerves weren't too obvious to his valet. Grantley had looked after him since he was a boy, so no doubt he knew exactly what he was thinking.

'Poole, you support his grace on his left, I'll take the right,' Grantley said.

He grasped Felix by his elbow and gently helped him to stand. Poole was somewhat more forceful but careful enough that a stern look from Grantley was sufficient warning.

'Here we go, your grace,' Grantley said as they headed for the dressing room door. 'If I might say so, the blue suit looks very well on you. I'm sure the young lady will be impressed.'

'I hope so, Grantley,' Felix said and felt dizzy just speaking. God but this was going to be more of a trial than he'd feared.

'Felix, so you're up,' Lady Lavinia said as he walked into the room.

'As you see,' Felix said as he looked his aunt over. She was always fastidious, but even she'd taken more care in her dress than usual. She was resplendent in a deep red, many-tiered dress.

'You'd better sit down and gather yourself. Lady Curtis and her daughter will be with us shortly.'

'Of course,' Felix said as his men guided him to his wing-backed chair.

He rested his head against the back and hoped he didn't look like he was feeling faint. He didn't want his aunt to notice, but his heart was beating frighteningly fast in his chest. It was nerves, but it always made him fear it was something more serious.

'I am gratified that you have made a special effort to look your best today,' Lady Lavinia said.

'Why wouldn't I?'

'That is a fair question, I suppose. At least we are in agreement that you must have a wife.'

'It remains to be seen, however, if any young woman would have me.'

'My dear Felix, judging by the number of acceptances I have received from my invitations, you are quite the catch of the season.'

'But for all the wrong reasons.'

'The reasons need not concern you. No doubt you suspect some of our young ladies of being gold diggers. It is a sad reflection on our society that you are bound to be right with a few of them. However, I have trawled Who's Who and ensured that only young women of impeccable breeding have been invited. I have no doubt that one of them will be a perfect match.'

'Do you think so?' Felix spoke more for distraction than for any chance that his aunt could convince him, least of all dispel his fears for this day and the days to come.

'I guarantee that you will find somebody you may esteem. Just as I found my dear Marmaduke, who is the very model of a perfect husband.'

'Quite true, Aunt,' Felix said.

As his uncle Marmaduke seemed interested only in the quality and quantity of his food and paid his wife and nephew scant regard, Felix felt depressed to contemplate a similarly bloodless marriage. He wondered how his aunt could appear content by it. As the union had produced twelve daughters, he supposed it couldn't always have been such a distant relationship as the one he observed every day over the dinner table.

'Lady Curtis has arrived, your grace,' Chivers announced holding the door open. 'With her daughter, Miss Flora Curtis.'

Felix froze for a split second as the two ladies walked into the room and examined them closely, eager to catch sight of his first potential bride. He was disappointed. The girl was far too thin and dressed in a gingham checked dress that didn't quite fit her.

He heaved himself to his feet and said, 'Lady Curtis, Miss Curtis, welcome.'

'Your grace, so good of you to invite us,' Lady Curtis said. She surged forward, her hand outstretched. 'My daughter has been all atwitter to meet you. She has been so eager she could scarce catch a wink of sleep last night. Isn't that so, my pet?'

Miss Curtis coloured to a bright red and murmured, 'Mama, please,' before she took Felix's hand in a very light grip.

He smiled down at her, surprised that she appeared even more uncomfortable than he felt, and kissed the tips of her fingers.

'I hope you will both feel comfortable. Please allow me to introduce my aunt.'

'Oh there's no need for that, your grace,' Lady Curtis said. 'Lavinia and I have been friends for years.'

'Have you indeed?'

'We have,' Lady Lavinia said. 'Now why don't we all sit down and have a comfortable chat while Chivers fetches in the tea. I am very interested to hear how Flora is enjoying her first season in London.'

'Oh... it's very nice thank you, Lady Lavinia,' Flora said as she coloured up again and then subsided into silence.

'Flora has had a wonderful season so far.' Lady Curtis settled on a broad settee and patted the space beside her which her daughter obediently occupied. 'We have been to a ball almost every night, and any number of activities and rides. Flora is a particularly enthusiastic horsewoman.'

'Is she? Well, it sounds like she is settling into the London scene splendidly then.'

'Are you very fond of dancing, Miss Curtis?' Felix said.

Flora was about to speak when her mother cut in and said, 'She is enjoying it at the moment. But she is a very good and obedient girl and knows married life is a far quieter affair.'

'I see.'

Felix examined Flora discreetly. She looked acutely embarrassed, and his heart sank. How was he going to get to know any young woman if their mothers were always present and determined to get their daughters successfully married?

'Flora is also a very accomplished pianist,' Lady Curtis said. 'Would your grace care to hear her play?'

'By all means,' Felix said as his gloom increased.

Now there really would be no opportunity to engage Flora in conversation. He wondered whether he'd be able to do so even if they were the only two people in the room. She seemed a shy girl. He had a good imagination but couldn't conjure up an image of Flora dancing gaily at a ball. She was, however, the kind of girl who would like horses, that he could believe.

Poole sat on the edge of his chair and looked around the kitchen. It should have been a comfortable place for him with its shiny white tiled walls and state of the art range over which hung a selection of sparkling copper pots. He'd eaten here every day since he'd arrived. He'd been very impressed by how modern it was as a kitchen and had enjoyed the banter of the massed servants.

It was different now. Mrs Grayson, the head cook, had barely spoken to him before. Why would she, she was one of the upper servants? Now she was beaming up at him with her plump, reddish face in a most unaccustomed way.

'There we go, a nice cup of tea,' Mrs Grayson said as she poured out a cup each for Poole and Grantley. This would also have been unheard of before. 'The girls also baked some biscuits for his grace and their party, and you may as well try them. If I'm any judge, they'll mostly be sent back down untouched. His grace doesn't have an appetite at the best of times, and no young lady seems to eat anything these days.'

'You forget Lady Lavinia and her friend Lady Curtis,' Grantley said.

'All the same, there's sufficient for a biscuit for each of you. Now,' Mrs Grayson said, settling down beside them and giving her own cup of tea a vigorous stir. 'How is his grace faring?'

'Give it a rest, Mrs Grayson, it's only day one.'

'It's the most exciting thing that's happened in this house in years. I wonder which young lady he'll choose.'

'I have no idea, but I'll tell you this, it's unlikely to be the first one he meets and probably not the waif we saw going in.' Grantley bit a biscuit in half and sent crumbs flying as he spoke.

'You saw her? What is she like?'

'We were crossing the hall when they arrived. She's a somewhat uninteresting blonde and a bit sallow. On top of that, while she was dressed in the height of fashion, it was a poor choice. The dress didn't suit her.'

'So?'

'His grace would never marry a frump.'

'He is always very neatly turned out, that is true.'

Tom listened to their conversation in silence as he nibbled on an excellent shortbread biscuit. The quality of food the upper staff received stunned him. They ate as well as the lord and master of the house. He had nothing to add to the conversation and knew better than to get involved anyway.

Grantley had apparently accepted him without question, but the rest of the staff were less accommodating. There was stiff propriety at the dinner table the night before. Beyond being introduced to everyone before they all sat down to eat, nobody made any attempt to engage him in conversation.

The footman, Danby, walked in and said, 'Grantley, the half hour is nearly up. Mr Chivers said her ladyship gave strict instructions that each visit was to be limited to half an hour.'

'I am more than capable of keeping the time for myself, Danby, your intervention was quite unnecessary,' Grantley said.

'Maybe, but Poole over here is just a stable lad and has no clue as to the proprieties.'

'That is why I am training him,' Grantley said in a glacial voice. 'And while we're about it, Danby, I heard you fancied yourself my replacement. Let me tell you why you would never have been chosen, whether Poole was here or not.'

'Why is that, Grantley?'

'Because your tie is crooked.'

'So?'

'It is always crooked.'

'So?'

'Poole, would you care to enlighten Danby?'

'His grace notices things like that. You don't care enough about your appearance, and his grace does,' Poole said. He was surprised to be pulled into the conversation and even more surprised that he knew the answer.

'And that is why Poole was chosen over you. He's only spent twenty-four hours with his grace, and he already knows what he likes. You, Danby, would never have picked that up.' Grantley gave the slightest of bows on that remark, stood and left the kitchens at a stately pace.

'Thank you,' Tom said as he followed him out. 'Danby threatened to give me a thrashing if he ever caught me alone. He is convinced that the job should have gone to him.'

'And you know why it wouldn't. But you be careful, young Poole. Danby is ambitious and having missed out on my position no doubt he now has his eyes on Mr Chivers's job.'

'Is he likely to get it?'

'Chivers doesn't confide in me, as I don't confide in him, but I doubt he has any plans of retiring anytime soon.'

'And if he did?'

'Danby wouldn't get that position for much the same reason he wasn't invited to be a valet. He is slovenly, and he is lazy. He will always try and find somebody else to do his work for him, or not work to his best ability. As I told you before, his Grace knows more about what happens in this house than you could possibly imagine. He'd never promote Danby.'

'That went very well,' Lady Lavinia said once their guests had been shown out.

'Do you think so?' Felix said. He was overwhelmed with disappointment and couldn't see it in a positive light.

'Of course, I do. Flora was a very prettily behaved young woman who felt exactly as she ought on all the topics of the day.'

'She agreed with her mother the whole time. How can we possibly know what she actually thought?'

'Now, Felix, don't be tiresome. Of course a young woman is going to agree with her mother. She has been properly brought up and will echo the sentiments of her parents. Besides, she played the piano very prettily.'

'I thought it lacked passion,' Felix said despite himself. It was stupid to argue with his aunt, she would never agree with him anyway.

'She was a little nervous, that's all. It comes from being invited to meet a great peer of the realm. Your uncle and I are accustomed to treating you like any other person, but for others, it is a great honour to meet a duke. I thought it showed becoming modesty in young Flora that she didn't throw herself at you upon your first meeting.'

'Mmm, well I can't say I'm in any hurry to meet her again either.'

'She is only the first, Felix. There is no need to get in a mood from this one meeting. There will be plenty more. If Flora didn't appeal, I'm sure one of the others will.'

'I'm sure you are right.'

Felix was relieved that Grantley and Poole appeared which put an end to the conversation. His mood was despondent and talking to his aunt wasn't going to lift it. He had to find some distraction.

'The newspaper please, Grantley,' Felix said once he was safely back in his room. He replaced his jacket with a less restricting velvet smoking jacket and settled on his sofa.

'Very good, your grace, shall I also bring up some lunch?'

'No, I don't feel like it.'

'Begging your pardon, sir, but you hardly touched your breakfast either. Are you sure I can't tempt you to a light lunch? Nothing fancy, just a little boiled chicken perhaps?'

'I don't want it. What you can do is pour me a brandy, and don't be stingy about it.'

'Are you sure that's wise, your grace?'

'Just do it!' Felix snapped.

He picked up the paper and gave it a fierce shake to open out the pages which he held up so that he couldn't see Grantley's, no doubt offended, expression.

'Your brandy, your grace,' Grantley said and put the glass down with a firm click. 'Is there anything else you'll be needing?'

'No, just go.'

Felix was sorry that he was so rude. He didn't like himself when he behaved this way, but he was damned if he was going to unbend either.

'Very good, your grace,' Grantley said.

Felix didn't need to lower the paper to know he was bowing himself out at his most punctilious. He didn't dare look in case his valet's offended expression made him regret his actions even more and apologise. Felix didn't want to apologise. At the moment he felt a baffling sense of rage and the unnerving wish to burst into tears.

He put the paper down and reached for the brandy. As usual, he'd been given less than a tot. He sighed deeply, he supposed that was for the best. At the moment, all he wanted was to drink himself into a stupor. With his heart that would likely kill him.

Not for the first time, he wondered if that might not be for the best. What kind of a life did he lead anyway? He was cooped up in his rooms day after day, always wondering when he went to sleep whether he'd wake in the morning. He was so tired all the time that he felt wiped out after the briefest of walks and half an hour spent with visitors.

He shook his head to clear it. So far, if he was brutally honest, his expectations had been met. The visit had been taxing, the girl was insipid and the mother overbearing. He shuddered at the very idea of having her for a mother-in-law. He had learned how to manage Aunt Lavinia to a degree. If he had two such forceful women in his life, well, it didn't bear contemplating.

Felix gazed at the paper, but he wasn't taking in the contents. His eyes scanned each line, but he'd reach the end of a paragraph and realise that he had no idea what he'd just read. So he reread it, with the same result. Felix was just contemplating the third attempt or sneaking another brandy when his eye was caught by an advert.

He leaned closer. The advertiser obviously only had limited funds for the advert was brief, and the font was tiny. All the same, he could make out the words, Hieronymus Testwood, Inventor. No request too big or small. If you need it, I can invent it. Followed by an address in the East End.

Felix reread it. He wanted to meet this man. Maybe it was his name, or that he called himself an inventor, but he was curious. In the past, his aunt would have talked him out of meeting anyone who was possibly, no probably, disreputable. But he suddenly had a yen to find out more about this Hieronymus Testwood.

He laughed out loud. He felt like a child doing something naughty. He was rebelling against his aunt and the stifling search for a wife. He had a crazy idea that he'd ask this man to invent a machine that found him his perfect woman. Failing that, it would be a diversion to keep his mind off something that had become a dreary duty after only a single visit. The problem was he couldn't see it getting any better.

He reached for the drawer of his writing table and pulled out a sheet of paper. He only hesitated for a moment before he began writing. If he was quick about it, this Hieronymus Testwood would receive his letter in the third post today.

Chapter Four

H ieronymus,' Emma shouted through the workshop door, 'there's a letter for you, my darling.'

'It's probably just a bill,' Hieronymus said as he carefully fixed a tiny screw to the backplate of a sewing machine. It was so demeaning that he, an inventor, was being used to repair existing machinery. Still, as Emma said, they needed the money to feed the family.

'No,' Emma said. 'It isn't a bill.'

'How do you know? Have you opened it yet?'

Hieronymus scrabbled about his workbench looking for the screw he'd only just set down upon it but which had now, inexplicably, vanished.

'It's addressed to you, so I haven't opened it.'

'Don't be silly, darling, open it.'

'Hieronymus, I really think this is one you should open yourself.'

This was such a surprising response from his darling wife that Hieronymus put down his tools and wiped his hands clean.

'If you keep interrupting me I can't earn any money.'

'Here,' Emma said and handed over a large, pristinely white envelope.

'Good heavens, look at the thickness of the paper.'

'With an embossed crest on it.'

'Do you recognise it?'

'I've never seen anything like it before. And if you turn it over you'll see it's been closed with a seal.'

'Do you think it's something official?' Hieronymus said.

He wracked his brain to try and work out whether he'd ever done anything that might bring him to the notice of the powers that be.

'There's only one way to find out, you have to open it.'

'You're right, of course, it just feels a bit... well, a bit sacrilegious to destroy something so perfect.'

'Go on, I can hardly stand the suspense anymore,' Emma said.

'What is it?' Edward, their eldest son, shouted and ran over.

'No, tell me,' Diana said, standing on tiptoes so that she could get a better view of the letter in her father's hand.

'Quickly, before we even wake the baby,' Emma said.

Hieronymus tore open the envelope and pulled out the single sheet of paper. 'Look at this, the crest has gold embossing.'

'But what does it say, darling?'

'*My Dear Mr Testwood, I am writing in response to your advertisement this morning in the Times. I am very interested to hear about the work of an inventor. I would be grateful if you could call upon me at your earliest convenience. However, if you are ill in even the slightest degree, please put off your visit until you are entirely recovered. I have a sensitive constitution and cannot risk seeing visitors in anything but their physical prime. Yours sincerely, Felix Peergrave, Dux.*'

'Peergrave Ducks, what an odd surname,' Emma said.

'No, it isn't his surname, that is, Peergrave is, I think the Dux is Latin for duke.'

'A duke wrote to you? Don't be ridiculous!'

'No? Well, what about this crest then? Or the fact that he's used a whole embossed page of paper for a really short letter? We can tear off the bottom half of this and use it ourselves, the same with the envelope.'

'A duke wrote to you!'

'And there you were laughing and telling me my advert would come to nothing.'

'A duke! What could he possibly want?'

'I don't know, but I intend to find out.'

'But Hieronymus, you don't have a thing to wear, at least, not something smart enough to go before a duke.'

'Emma, this is my one chance. Whether I have to beg, borrow or steal, I must have a decent suit for tomorrow.'

'Tomorrow!?'

'Well, he did say at my earliest convenience. While I'd like nothing better than to go tearing down there tonight -'

'Where is there?'

'Belgravia.'

'Lord love me, you can't go to Belgravia. The police will have you marched away in no time as a vagabond.'

'I'll be fine, I'll just show them my letter. Besides, I won't look so out of place, there's bound to be plenty of tradesmen about.'

'Well... if you are to visit a duke, and I remain to be convinced about that, we have to find you a decent suit. You will have to take a bath too, first thing tomorrow morning!'

Felix emerged from his second visit of the week feeling twice as despondent as the previous day. On the whole, he decided, he preferred young women who played the piano to those who inflicted their self composed, truly dreadful, poetry upon their audience.

This one had more self-confidence. Still, she was brazen and, Felix felt, had only come for the opportunity to read her poetry to an unsuspecting victim. Felix very much doubted that she was interested in marrying him. In fact, he wondered whether Miss Carlin was interested in marrying anyone at all.

It wasn't going to be him, at any rate. He doubted he could have taken very much more of her overblown and oddly forced rhymes.

Grantley and Poole had just got him back to safety in his room when Chivers appeared.

He bowed deeply and said, 'There is a personage by the name of Hieronymus Testwood here to see you, your grace.'

'Good heavens, is there indeed?' Felix said. He'd clean forgotten about his hastily dashed off note of the previous day.

'Do you want me to send him away, your grace?'

'That bad, mmm?'

'He had the good sense to come to the tradesman's entrance. Even so, if he hadn't arrived brandishing your letter, I would have sent him off with a flea in his ear. As it is, he's been sitting in the kitchen for the best part of half an hour. He arrived just as your lady visitors were shown in.'

'Well, then he has been very patient. Send him up, Chivers, along with a plate of sandwiches. I suddenly find my appetite has returned.'

'Sandwiches for the both of you, your grace?'

'I can hardly eat alone in front of him, and I'm far too famished to wait.'

'Very good, your grace, I'll bring him up,' Chivers said and made it seem that he was perfectly happy to comply with the order. Felix wondered whether that was true.

'Are you sure about this, your grace?' Grantley said. 'After the morning you've had?'

'Believe me, Grantley, after the morning I've had this is exactly what I need. Unless of course, this inventor is as tedious as my recent, unlamented poetess.'

'He's an inventor, your grace?'

'So he claims. I am curious to discover what that means, exactly.'

'This isn't one of your little whims is it, your grace? You know how Lady Lavinia doesn't like those.'

'Well I'm not going to tell her, Grantley, are you?'

'Mum's the word,' Grantley said and stepped back as Chivers reappeared with Danby carrying a tray of food and trailing a young man dressed from head to toe in black.

'Hieronymus Testwood, your grace,' Chivers said.

The man's suit was so tight it emphasised how very skinny he was. He whipped off his black bowler hat to reveal a shock of curly dark brown hair. He was also considerably younger than Felix had expected, but he liked the man's face. It was honest and open.

'Thank you, you may all leave now,' Felix said. 'Not you, Mr Testwood,' he added as Testwood looked like he was about to back out of the room too. 'Please take a seat.'

'Here?' Testwood said.

'That's right.'

Now that he was nearby, Felix could examine the man more closely. He had clearly taken a great deal of care about his appearance. He'd scrubbed his face so hard it shone and his clothes, though threadbare, were clean. In fact, if he wasn't mistaken, they were also still a little damp. No doubt they'd been washed the night before and hadn't entirely dried by the morning.

'Thank you for coming. I wasn't sure that you would.'

'I wasn't sure you'd let me in,' Testwood said frankly, looking around and absorbing everything with an expression of wonder. 'I've never been inside a duke's house before.'

'I imagine it's a rarity for the majority of the population,' Felix said. 'Would you like a sandwich? Please help yourself.'

'Oh no, I couldn't possibly.'

'Why not? Tell me, Mr Testwood, how did you get here?'

'I walked.'

'All the way from the East End?'

'It isn't so far.'

'Perhaps not for you, but it would be an impossible journey for me. Either way, you must be hungry by now. So please, do help yourself. I'm sorry I can't offer you a beer, but you are welcome to the lemonade. It's what I have prescribed for me.'

'Prescribed?' Testwood said. 'So you are not teetotal?'

'No, I'm not teetotal. I have a weak heart.'

'I see, is that why I was to stay away if I was ill?'

'Exactly.'

'Your butler grilled me about that. He made sure neither I nor any of my family is currently ill. We're all fine.'

'I am relieved to hear that,' Felix said, watching the man. He looked nervous. Evidently, a lot was riding on this meeting for him. 'Tell me, Mr Testwood, what does the life of an inventor consist of?'

'I create things, your lordship, anything you like.'

'Really? So if I asked you to make me a mechanical heart to replace my defective one you could come up with something, could you?'

Felix had no such hopes, but he was curious to see what Testwood would say. As it was the man's face fell.

'That would be very difficult, your lordship. I doubt anyone could do that yet. Maybe one day but, advanced as we are, I don't think it's possible yet.'

'Thank you for your honesty, Mr Testwood. Many's the man who would have offered to do that for me if I was just to bankroll them.'

'They would be lying too, never trust someone who offers you the moon.'

'But perhaps a journey to the moon might be acceptable?'

'A journey to the moon?'

'You have not heard of the French author Jules Verne?'

'No, your lordship, I haven't.'

'It's a great pity he isn't translated into English very much or very well. His stories are highly enjoyable, and in one, he describes an expedition to the moon.'

'I fear that is also something I can't do as yet. But perhaps that is more feasible than a mechanical heart. You see, all you would need for getting to the moon is a suitable craft. Maybe some sort of a massive balloon or collection of balloons.'

'Ah, Mr Verne proposed something like a cannon and that the craft is fired from it.'

'Does he? That's interesting. It would have to be a massive cannon though, and if it were to shoot something straight up into the sky, it would require a tremendous amount of gunpowder.'

'So, something that will have to wait while our inventors iron out the technical difficulties,' Felix said, feeling happier than he had in days. There was nothing he liked better than new inventions and ideas, and it appeared Testwood was the same. 'So tell me, Mr Testwood, if you don't do ambitious engineering projects, what do you do?'

'Well, your lordship -'

'Correctly speaking, I'm a grace, not a lordship.'

'Pardon?'

'Dukes are addressed as your grace, not your lordship.'

'Oh, I beg your pardon. I didn't mean -'

'It's no bother, I just thought I'd mention it. Now please, tell me what it is you do for a living.'

'I try to make people's everyday lives easier, your grace. For that reason, I've redesigned the mangle, so it squeezes more tightly, thus getting more water out. But it takes less effort for a woman to turn it.'

'I see, and is that popular?'

'It is with those who can afford it. I'm afraid most of the people in the East End need their money for food, not for labour-saving devices. Although I did create a mechanical messenger service for one of the warehouses at the dock that is proving to be very popular.'

'And if I were to ask you to invent something for me, how would you go about doing that?'

'There's one of two ways, your grace. Some clients already have an idea of something they want, maybe a brighter lamp, or one which uses less gas. Anyway, I look at the current item and work out how I can make it better. The second way I do things is to watch somebody. I see how they live, and suggest inventions that could make their life easier.'

'Such as?'

'Well... I once made a wooden leg for a sailor that had a ball socket where the ankle should be. It helped him walk more easily, although he had to keep repositioning his wooden foot. That's something I'm working on fixing. For you... it depends on how you live, and what would be a help.'

'How would you work that out?'

'The best way would be to spend some time with you. Then I could come up with some suggestions for useful gadgets.'

'But I have servants that can do my every bidding.'

'Forgive me, your grace, if they were sufficient I doubt you'd have wanted to meet me.'

'Maybe I just like novelty.'

'I can see that, and maybe you really want that mechanical heart. As I can't deliver that for you I'm just wasting your time now.'

'Not at all,' Felix said and examined the man again. Testwood wasn't very much older than Felix was himself, and here he was trying to convince a duke that he could be helpful so that... what? 'Do you have a large family, Mr Testwood?'

'I have a wife and three children. My eldest is a boy who's five.'

'So you have a burgeoning family to support.'

'I wouldn't have it any other way, your grace. My family mean everything to me.'

'Do they?' Felix said. The man seemed sincere, more than that, his eyes softened as he spoke about his family. 'And you can support them on the money you make from inventions can you?'

'It's a precarious career. I make most of my money doing repairs on anything that breaks down. But I want to do more. We are in a great age of invention, exploration and scientific discovery, and I want to play my part.'

'Be a new Isambard Kingdom Brunel?'

'Not exactly. Brunel went in for the epic, tube trains and massive ships. I'm a bit more modest. I seek to make people's day to day lives easier.'

'I see. Do you have any projects in development at the moment?'

'I have a few plans but don't have the funds to build the prototypes yet.'

'Well, I'll tell you what, Mr Testwood, why don't you observe me for a little while and see what you can do to make my life easier. I dare say you think the life of a duke pretty easy already, but putting that aside, demonstrate to me how you work. If we get on, I may consider investing in your other inventions.'

'Oh... you'll... you'll pay me for this first work, this observation and generation of ideas?'

'I imagine I would have to, not so? Otherwise, you'll doubtless have to keep popping off to earn some actual money.'

'Oh... yes. That is, thank you, your grace.'

'Not at all. I'll tell my man of business to provide you with the necessary funds. When can you start?'

'Straight away if you like.'

'Don't you have anything you need to finish off first?'

'I can do that in the evenings, your grace. Please rest assured, your wishes will come first.'

'Perhaps, but there is no need to rush. You finish off your current work and come back to me... shall we say Monday?'

'I'll be here, Monday, first thing. Thank you, your grace!'

CHAPTER FIVE

Honour gazed in a distracted way at the skirt of her grey dress. She'd spent her limited free time making it and was pleased by how it had turned out. It was a simple dress, as befitted her situation, and had only a darker grey piping to provide any ornamentation.

She'd decided this morning that it was time to move from the deep mourning of her black dress to this slightly less oppressive shade. But in the dim dining room of her cousin Isolde's house, where the heavy lace curtain blotted out what little light came from the wintry grey dawn, the shade of the dress did little to lighten her mood.

'Honour, Honour, look!' Isolde shrieked as she ran into the dining room.

Honour wasn't in the mood for conversation. Still, she'd already learned that her cousin neither asked about nor considered her feelings.

'What is it?' Honour said.

'The newspaper.'

'You've been reading the newspaper?'

'Oh, I know, only for the gossip. But never mind that look here!' Isolde said, stabbing at a headline with an ink-smeared finger.

'*Duke of Morley in Search of a Bride...* oh.'

'Yes, yes, read on, it gets better.'

'One of the richest men in England is in search of matrimonial bliss. The twenty-one-year-old Right Honourable Felix Vivian Alexander Decimus Peergrave, 10th Duke of Morley, Earl of Chestermere and Pembleton, has started receiving young ladies at his house in Belgravia with a view to finding a suitable match. The duke is relatively unknown, as a heart condition has made him a recluse in his home. Still, it appears now that he has decided it's time to set up his nursery.'

'To think I didn't want to meet him, Honour! At least… I was only curious to see inside a ducal mansion. His aunt is quite frightful, you know, and I suspect he is the same and bedridden which wouldn't suit me at all.'

'So you said at the time you received the invitation,' Honour said as she continued to scan the article. After its opening lines, the rest was just a mixture of fawning over a duke and trying to guess who was visiting. 'It says he has visitors lined up to the end of March.'

'Does it really?' Isolde said. 'Well, that doesn't matter. I will sweep him off his feet, and after our visit, he will cancel all his others.'

'Do you think so, Isolde?'

'But of course. Every man I meet falls instantly in love with me. I have already turned down a dozen offers of marriage. It will be the work of moments to get this duke to fall in love with me too.'

'But why would you want to?'

'Because he is rich, Honour, and powerful, why else?' Isolde said as she finally sat down and stared into the distance, sunk in a pleasant dream of her future.

Honour was appalled. It was shocking to realise that although Isolde was the most ridiculously perfect woman, her character didn't match her glorious looks.

In the few days that Honour had been living with Isolde, she'd already learned that her cousin was only concerned about her own comfort. Honour wished this duke would give Isolde a rebuff. The men she'd met at the teas, balls and concerts had all disappointed her by falling at Isolde's feet and adoring her.

Isolde was no fool and cultivated every one of them. But she'd been looking for more and so far had not succumbed to a single proposal. Perhaps the duke would be the one she finally accepted.

'What of his heart condition?'

'What of it?' Isolde said. 'If he's thinking of marriage, it can't be that bad. I only hope the real reason he's a recluse isn't that he's hideous. I couldn't bring myself to kiss a hideous man.'

'You may be getting a bit ahead of yourself.'

'And you hope I will trip up,' Isolde said with a knowing smile. 'But you wait and see, if I want to, I will have this duke.'

Felix was exhausted. He lay still and tried to relax, but his face was already pulled into a mask of contracted muscles. His shoulders were bunched tight, and it took superhuman effort to open his eyes. He blinked into the gloom. It felt later than usual. Evidently, Grantley had left him to lie in.

He groped for the bell by his bedside table and gave it a ring and then his arm dropped. He didn't have the energy to pull it back under the covers. It was cold too. Had the fire gone out or was it his circulation this morning?

'Good morning, your grace,' Grantley said, with Poole standing behind him looking worried.

He'd not seen his employer in such a state before, Felix thought. He wished it were otherwise. There was nothing he could do about it, and the lad needed to learn before Grantley could go off. It was mornings like this when he wished the old man would never retire.

'A little help please, Grantley,' he murmured.

'Of course, your grace,' Grantley said. 'Poole, I'll lift his grace. You plump up his pillows and pull in a couple extra so that he may sit upright.'

'Thank you,' Felix said as, the operation done, he was gently placed back on the pillows.

'Would you care for some breakfast, your grace?'

Felix didn't really care for anything at the moment but felt it best not to say so. It would only lead to fussing so he said, 'Just something light, and stoke up the fire would you please; I'm cold.'

'Very good, your grace. Poole will bring your dressing gown.'

'Fine,' Felix said.

So Grantley thought he wasn't up to getting dressed today. He was probably right. He didn't even feel like he could sit up properly at the moment.

He lay back and closed his eyes and tried not to pay attention to the thump, thump thump of his heart. It felt uncomfortable today, and his breathing was more laboured too. Dear God if this was what five days of visitors did to him, he dreaded to think what it would be like to be married.

A light tap at the door signalled the arrival of breakfast and Chivers walked in holding the tray.

This was so significantly out of the usual that Felix said, 'What is it?'

Chivers set down the tray and said, 'Her ladyship has ordered that you not see the newspapers today.'

'She's done what? Why the devil not? And you, since when did you obey her ladyship over me?'

'The thing is, your grace... she may be right on this occasion.'

'Good heavens, what can possibly be so bad that I'm not allowed to see it?'

'Well...'

'You're just going to have to give it to me now. Or I'll fret myself all day wondering what the devil you're all hiding from me.'

Chivers sighed and said, 'I was afraid of that. Very good, your grace, I'll bring in the papers. Just please, don't blame me if you don't like what you see.'

'Why on earth would I blame you?'

'Because if I didn't bring them to you, you might remain in blissful ignorance,' Chivers said. He headed for the door and the waiting Danby who handed over the papers.

'That is highly unlikely now,' Felix muttered.

'Indeed, your grace. On the other hand, you could leave the papers and their gossip-mongering and focus instead on this letter from Sir Arthur.'

'Arthur's written?' Felix said and instantly cheered up. He always enjoyed Arthur's letters with his detailed descriptions of India.

'It's an unusually thick letter. It must have cost a fortune to post.'

'Indeed it must, thank you, Chivers, but it can wait. I have to know what the newspapers are saying first,' Felix said and slipped the letter into his dressing gown pocket.

Percy, like everyone else, had seen the news. It prompted him to put off heading straight to Horse Guards Parade, and he detoured to Belgravia. When Percy wasn't sure of Felix's condition, he usually stopped in on Grantley first to check that it was all right to visit. Today he tapped at Felix's dressing room door with more trepidation than usual.

But he hid that when Grantley opened the door and merely said, 'Morning, Grantley, is my cousin up to a visit?'

'Not to anyone else, Captain, but you might be just what he needs.'

'Blue devilled is he?'

'I'm afraid so, and as I feared all his visitors have tired him out.'

'Has he seen the papers?'

'He has, there was no way we could have hidden it.'

'And?'

'Hard to say, sir.'

'Well, I'll go see him then, no need to announce me,' Percy said, closed the door and walked along the corridor to his cousin's room.

There was no need for Felix to know that Percy was checking up on him before visiting. Felix was seated at the sofa by the window staring outside. He was still in his dressing-gown, and a half-read newspaper lay on his lap.

'Hello, old fellow,' Percy said. 'I see you've read all about yourself.'

'Percy,' Felix said, 'what a delightful surprise. And looking very dashing in your uniform.'

'I'm on my way to Horse Guards but thought I'd drop in and see how you are doing.'

Percy pulled a chair over and examined Felix. He was pale and had darker than usual shadows under his eyes.

'Was it the article that prompted the visit?' Felix said. 'I can assure you it isn't half as bad as I feared when everyone was running around trying to hide it from me.'

'It's the first time you've been written about though, isn't it?'

'And I didn't enjoy it. I feel so inadequate, this invalid who has to have young women visit him because he can't go out and about to meet them.'

'I wouldn't fret about it. The gossips will move on tomorrow, and it will be forgotten in under a week.'

'I'm sure you are right. I can't help wonder, though, how the news got out.'

'In London?' Percy said grinning from ear to ear, 'During the season where every day is filled with activities and gossip. My dear man, I'd have been amazed if your wish to marry had remained a secret. I'm sure every invited mama and their daughter has shared the news with their closest confidants, and they with theirs, and so on, and so forth. I doubt this newspaper is even breaking news to most of society.'

'I see, I hadn't realised that would happen.'

'You might not have, but Aunt Lavinia should have known. However, it can't be helped,' Percy said. 'So tell me, how has the last week been?'

'Perfectly dreadful.'

As Felix was smiling, it worried Percy less. Then again, his cousin was good at pushing things aside and not dwelling. 'What have they done?'

'It isn't so much the young ladies as their mothers. All are intent on making sure their daughters snare this rich, titled catch,' Felix said and twitched the newspaper. 'I have felt more like someone auditioning vaudeville acts than a man meeting prospective brides. Every last one of them has demonstrated their creative talents. I have been sung to, had pianos played and sat through half an hour of quite the worst poetry I have ever heard.'

'You poor fellow. But the young ladies, what did you make of them? Were there any great beauties?'

'Not a one. I'm not necessarily looking for a beauty, just someone I could feel comfortable with, but these young women... well.'

'Someone you could feel comfortable with?' Percy said. 'Come now, Felix, surely you want a little more than that.'

'At the rate I'm going, I'll be settling for considerably less.'

'No, don't do that. For God's sake, you deserve some happiness. Only marry a woman you truly love. You don't have to find a bride before the end of March. Please, promise me you won't propose to anyone just because you feel you have a duty to the family name.'

'How am I going to find this woman, Percy? I barely got two words out of all my recent callers. I have no idea as to their characters or whether I would like them or not. No, actually, I know I couldn't tolerate the poetess.'

'Well, that's a start. As for the rest, keep them in mind, nobody falls in love upon their first meeting. Some of the girls who come to visit will spark an interest, and at the end of March you can decide which of them you'd like to meet for a second time.'

'So that I may be safely married by the end of June,' Felix said on a laugh.

'Don't be absurd, who said that?'

'Who do you think?'

'Aunt Lavinia,' Percy said, shaking his head. 'She is impossible.'

'She wants me married before we go back to Morley for the summer.'

'Don't let her rush you. You can't possibly find somebody in such a short space of time.'

'Why not? The London season runs until June, in that time hundreds of marriages are agreed.'

'Maybe so, but plenty more are acted upon more slowly.'

'What if I don't want to wait?'

'Felix, honestly there is no hurry.' Then a horrible thought struck him, and he said, 'Is there? You haven't had bad news from your doctor, have you?'

'I never get good news from him, but no, nothing untoward has happened.'

'Then what's the rush?'

'I don't know, a certain restlessness, I suppose. A general sense of dissatisfaction. Lately, I have found myself looking at that box of postcards you gave me quite a lot.'

'Ah, I often wondered about the wisdom of doing that. I was young and rather obsessed with female anatomy at the time.'

'And you acted upon your obsession too.'

'Foolishly. Amorous adventures can get a fellow into a lot of trouble.'

'The thing is, Percy,' Felix said looking down at the newspaper as a blush tinged his cheeks, 'I have never had an, er, adventure and I... I really would like to.'

'All the same, don't rush things, please. I don't want you regretting a moment of madness for the rest of your life. I have always felt sorry that you've had to endure Aunt Lavinia for all these years. Don't get yourself attached to another such joyless woman.'

'It won't be as bad as all that,' Felix said and slipped his hands into his dressing gown pocket. 'Oh,' he said and drew out a thick envelope, 'I clean forgot Arthur's letter.'

'Arthur's written to you?'

'He writes all the time and most vividly. I've told him that when he gets back, he should publish a memoir,' Felix said as he slit the letter open. 'Photographs!' he said, beaming as he flicked through them. 'Look, he's been hunting tigers.'

'And getting fatter,' Percy said as he took the proffered photograph. It was good to see Arthur looking well, but he was sorry, once again, that Felix only got to see the world through other people's eyes. Here he was devouring these images and Arthur's letter from India taking it all in like someone with a great hunger. He had a yearning to know as much as he could.

'Even Arthur's thinking of marriage,' Felix said as he perused the letter. 'It must be something in the air. He tells me he is smitten by an Indian princess.'

'I doubt his mother would approve of that.'

'She is very beautiful though, don't you think?' Felix said, handing over a photograph of Arthur standing proudly beside a young woman.

'A bit too dusky for my tastes,' Percy said. 'I much prefer a pink English rose.'

Felix tilted his head and said, 'I think I prefer brunettes.'

'You don't know for certain?'

'I've never really thought about it much. Until Aunt Lavinia mentioned marriage, I tried not to think about it at all.'

'And now?'

'The best of the five I've met was a brunette.'

'That's hardly the best yardstick, Felix.'

'No I don't suppose it is, and actually, she was also the best dressed of the lot in a well-fitting dress and one that suited her colour.'

'Ha! I've just discovered your type. Brunette or blonde, dusky or fair, what you will always want is a woman who knows how to dress well.'

'You are probably right. I'm not sure I could be happy with an untidy, badly dressed wife. But, who can tell? Maybe Cupid's arrow will cause me to throw all my criteria out of the window.'

CHAPTER SIX

I f anything, Hieronymus was more nervous upon his return to the duke's mansion than he'd been on his first visit. That day he'd not seriously believed anything would come of it, although he'd hoped and prayed that it would. Now he had to prove his worth, and he wondered whether he could do it.

This time a mere footman took him to the duke's door. He assumed that was because he'd already been vetted and deemed acceptable, if not desirable.

'Am... am I too early, your grace?' Hieronymus said when he was shown into the duke's bedroom.

'Not at all,' Felix said as he looked up from his breakfast. It was laid out on a small table pulled in front of the sofa. 'The intention is that you get to know my habits so that you can discover which gadget I might need to make my life easier. For that, you have to see me from the start to the finish of the day.'

'That is how I work, yes, your grace.'

'Have you had breakfast?'

'Oh yes, thank you, your grace. I'm fine.'

The duke smiled at him in a vague, unconvinced way and said, 'Tea then.' He rang his bell, and when the footman reappeared, he said, 'Tea for Mr Testwood please, Danvers, and throw in a couple of Mrs Grayson's excellent biscuits for the two of us. I have a feeling I'm going to need them.'

'You are, your grace?' Hieronymus said.

'The hunt for a wife continues, as no doubt, you are aware. For that, I need to recruit my strength.'

Hieronymus felt himself flush with embarrassment as he muttered, 'Yes, I saw something in the papers.'

'I fear all of London saw that. I'm not accustomed to being the focus of every gossip in the land. Fortunately for me, I don't go out, so I shan't see the furtive glances and the whispers as I pass by.'

'No, your grace,' Hieronymus said, feeling on very uncertain ground. What on earth was he supposed to say?

'No matter,' Felix said. 'I have been thinking about your inventions, and it occurred to me that you should also talk to my valet.'

'Oh yes?'

'Grantley does everything for me. He has done since I was a boy. If anyone knows what I need, it will be him. At the very least, he should be able to recommend a few labour-saving devices that would make his life easier.'

'I will interview him then. That will be very useful.'

'After you've had the tea. Chivers will pour, won't you?' Felix said, smiling up at his butler. He'd just come in and looked to Hieronymus very much like he was intent on leaving the tea and making a fast exit.

'Very good, your grace,' Chivers said. He gave a stately bow, poured out the tea and then left the room looking quite unflustered.

'They'll not be keen on you for a while,' Felix said. 'But they will grow accustomed in the end and unbend.'

'Oh, er yes, thank you, your grace,' Hieronymus said.

It felt very strange to be sitting at a duke's breakfast table drinking tea. The man himself seemed to be enjoying the whole thing hugely if the glint in his eye was anything to go by.

'My programme for the day,' Felix said, 'isn't going to change very much. I usually wake around nine, have breakfast and get dressed.

For the foreseeable future, I will then make my way to the drawing room next door for my meeting with all the ah... prospective brides.'

'Yes, sir,' Hieronymus said, back to feeling awkward.

'After that, it's here for lunch and a rest. I spend most of the afternoon in my room reading and so on. Finally, it's out for supper in the dining room, which adjoins the drawing room. Everything is close by so that I can walk to it. It's the same reason my quarters are on the ground floor. This way, I don't have to attempt stairs.'

'I see.'

'I'm afraid it is all rather dull. You won't have to spend much time with me to see exactly what I do and what I'll need.'

'Are you ready to get dressed, your grace?' Grantley said emerging from the dressing room.

'I am,' Felix said with a sigh. 'I suppose I have to get on with it.'

'If you don't want to meet any more young ladies I can tell Lady Lavinia. You are looking very pulled, she'll understand.'

'You are being extraordinarily brave, Grantley, to face the wrath of my aunt, but no, it's fine. I will meet my next young lady. You don't happen to remember her name, do you?'

'I understand it's a certain Lady Isolde Giddings,' Grantley said. He came over and helped the duke to stand and then walked him, supporting his arm, to a dressing table in the next room.

Hieronymus watched closely. It appeared the duke needed aid when he walked. That was important information, as was the intelligence that he didn't walk very far at all. Hieronymus took out his little black book and pencil and scribbled a note to himself of this fact.

Then he took a proper look around the room. Maybe there was a walking stick or another device. Nothing obvious stood out. He'd have to ask the valet, but later. For the moment the man was working efficiently on getting the duke out of his beautiful dressing gown and pyjamas and into an elegant morning suit.

He reached abstractedly for the biscuit that had been placed by his cup of tea and took a nibble. Then a bigger bite, it was delicious and certainly appreciated as they were a bit low on money at the moment and he'd set off from home without breakfast.

'Poole, get out his grace's shoes,' Grantley said.

It drew Hieronymus back into the present, the duke was nearly ready.

'You can follow along to the drawing room,' Felix said. 'So you can see the process. Then you may as well retire with my valet and interview him.'

'Interview, your grace?' Grantley said.

'Testwood will explain everything,' Felix said. 'Now, shall we beard the lion in its den?'

'Are you sure you want to do this, your grace?'

'It's a bit late to cancel now. The young lady will most certainly have set off from home, and it would be the height of rudeness to turn her away at the door.'

'I'm sure she would understand, your grace.'

'No, we will do this,' Felix said and gave his valet a smile which clearly said he would not be budged.

'Very well, your grace,' Grantley said with a great sigh.

He nodded to Poole, who took the duke's left arm. The two men helped him out of his seat and started the walk to the drawing room. Hieronymus took up the rear, feeling very much out of place and followed their slow progress down the corridor. He was astonished that after such a short and supported walk, the duke sank into a high backed chair looking pale and out of breath.

'Felix?' Lady Lavinia said as she arrived, 'Are you sure you're up to this?'

'I'll be fine,' Felix said between deep breaths.

Her ladyship looked the duke up and down, and Hieronymus felt that nobody had ever looked more closely at another human being before. Surely this griffon-like woman would miss nothing. That was certainly true of him.

As her gaze lifted from her nephew, she paused and said, 'Felix... who is that... that man?'

'He is an inventor,' Felix said, and he smiled broadly.

Hieronymus wondered why the duke found the whole thing so amusing. He felt the urge to tuck tail and flee from this fearsome woman.

'I have asked him to do some work for me,' Felix said.

'You surely aren't paying him?'

'Of course I'm paying him. He's working for me.'

'But you haven't even mentioned him to me.'

'Well, let me present him to you now. Mr Hieronymus Testwood, Esq. Inventor. Mr Testwood, my aunt, Lady Lavinia Doubtless.'

'This is another one of your flights of fancy, is it?' Lady Lavinia snapped with the merest of cursory nods in Hieronymus's direction.

'Possibly,' Felix said and took a big gulp of air.

'Felix, are you sure you're all right?' Lady Lavinia said as she hurried to his side. All thoughts of inventors instantly banished from her mind.

'Time to go,' Grantley murmured and gave Hieronymus's elbow a tug.

'Oh, right,' Hieronymus said and hurried out after them. 'Is he all right?'

'Not really,' Grantley said and led the way down the corridor. 'But he's as determined as her ladyship to get a wife else he wouldn't be pushing himself in the way that he is.'

'I see. Is a wife a good idea?'

'You're married, aren't you?'

'Yes?'

'Do you think it's a good idea?'

'I love my wife and my children, but I'm not ill.'

'No? Well, many is the man, hearty or sick who has sought himself a bride. So it is with his grace, and that's not even mentioning the succession.'

'That's important for the higher-ups,' Poole said.

'Hark at you, barely five minutes of service and talking like an expert,' Grantley said.

'Um... where are we going?' Hieronymus said as they travelled down a passageway and some stairs.

'The kitchens for tea and biscuits with Mrs Grayson. This is our one moment of the day when we don't need to be in attendance, so we take a little break. Don't worry, we won't tell Mrs Grayson you've already had tea. Because, looking at you, I doubt you've had breakfast as you claimed.'

'I didn't want to-'

'It's no matter. His grace isn't a fool, though, and I doubt he believed you either.'

'All the same-'

'Best to be straight with him.'

'Really?'

'Always, as I've told Poole, most masters don't want the truth. They like to be toadied, but not his grace. He'll sooner turn you off without explanation than he'll sit and listen to a load of nonsense.'

'I see.'

'He knows his own mind, you're a case in point. There are not many nobles will have a scruffy inventor sitting around his rooms, never mind have you at his breakfast table.'

'I am aware of that. I've done work for far less august personages who never allowed me past the tradesman's entrance. I have to admit it was intimidating even though he was perfectly polite.'

'That's his grace for you. He likes to meet people and the stranger you are the better he likes it.'

'Oh, come now, I'm not strange.'

'You are to all of us,' Grantley said as he sat himself down at the foot of the long table that dominated the centre of the kitchen and gave a nod to Mrs Grayson.

She looked desperately like she wanted to find out who Hieronymus was. Still, through some code of servants, it appeared the valet had not given permission for her to join them. Her face settled into a disgruntled scowl, and with a tilt of her head, she signalled for a maid to bring over the tea and biscuits.

'Now,' Grantley said. 'You'd best tell us why his grace wanted you to spend time with us.'

'He wants me to create a few devices to make his life easier, and he thought you could help me work out what that might be.'

'Easier, huh?' Grantley said as he poured out the tea. 'Bit late for me, I've been breaking my back for his grace my whole life.'

'So what have been the hardest parts?'

'The hardest parts? That's when he nearly died, and there's no machine you can build to prevent that,' Grantley said suddenly far more severe. 'I wish you could.'

'But what precipitated those crises? Maybe I could do something that would take a strain away and make him safer.'

'Well, that would be something and no mistake. The problem is the duke is at most risk when he's agitated. Like with this damned search for a wife. It isn't so much the endless round of morning teas, it's the state he works himself up into. He doesn't go into high angst. You couldn't necessarily tell he's working himself up. But he is, and it's a strain on his heart.'

'And again, that isn't something I can help. But I can do things to help the duke physically. Like... like for instance, why do you have to support him when he walks. Can't he use a walking stick?'

'Walking sticks are for people with problems with their legs. It's no help to him if he gets dizzy, then he just keels over, stick or no stick.'

'What about a bath chair then?'

'He has one of those. We only use it when he's feeling too weak to walk, but he doesn't like it.'

'You aren't making this easy, are you?'

'If it were easy, we wouldn't need you.'

'I know what we could maybe use,' Poole said.

'You do?' Hieronymus and Grantley said in unison.

'Yes, don't look so surprised. This weekend his grace was so poorly he couldn't even sit up in bed. You had to help him up didn't you, Grantley? While we were holding him up, we also had to rearrange his pillows so he could lie upright. Well... maybe Mr Testwood could come up with some way that we could raise his grace in his bed without having to manhandle him quite so much.'

'An inventor, Felix, really?' Lady Lavinia said while she kept her hawklike gaze on her nephew.

'I thought it might be interesting.'

Felix was resting more against the chair than he wished he had to and he hoped his aunt wouldn't notice. Maybe the inventor would keep her distracted.

'What on earth can you find to interest you in a man dressed little better than a vagabond?'

'I suspect his suit is as far as his funds will stretch. Besides, it is always spotlessly clean. So while he looks shabby, at least he makes an effort.'

'I should think so too, the man would have to make a good impression if he is to wring money out of you.'

'His payment is a trifling sum. It won't make a dent in my funds.'

'So you said about Grantley and his house, but all these little things add up.'

Felix was conscious of a twinge of anger. It wasn't something he could afford today, so he pushed it down. 'I am fully aware of my financial situation. Rest assured that I won't fritter it away.'

'Very well, I won't argue. You are looking very unwell today. Maybe it wasn't a good idea to continue with these visits at such a pace. I shall review the young ladies I have invited and cull a few. Perhaps a meeting every second day would be better for you.'

'But only think what the papers would say then,' Felix murmured. 'Duke gets cold feet. And the young ladies who are put off might well complain vociferously to anyone who will listen.'

'That is immaterial. Your wellbeing is my only concern. The newspaper story was unfortunate, but it will blow over.'

'No doubt that is true,' Felix said. He grimaced as a pulse of pain flicked through his chest.

'Felix?'

'I'm fine. What is the time?'

'It's very nearly eleven. Lady Giddings should be here shortly.'

'No doubt with her charming mother in tow.'

'Oh, no, not Lady Giddings. Her mother died when she was quite young, and I don't know who her chaperone will be.'

'Oh,' Felix said and felt an immediate lightening of his mood. It was quickly dashed as he considered the alternatives. 'I dare say she has an overbearing aunt,' he murmured and was only just saved from his aunt's retort by Chivers's arrival.

'Lady Isolde Giddings and Miss Honour Seaborn,' Chivers announced and bowed himself out.

Felix hoisted himself to his feet and then stood stock still, stunned into silence by the vision of beauty who stared back at him. Never before had he seen a lovelier woman, and then she smiled.

'Your grace,' Isolde said, held out her hand, and curtsied.

'Lady Giddings,' Felix barely managed to croak as he kissed her fingertips.

'I was delighted to receive your invitation, your grace, although a little surprised for we have never met.'

'I'm glad you came all the same,' Felix said.

He was vaguely aware of another young woman standing behind this vision of perfection. By rights, he should say something to her too, but he was so bowled over he couldn't think straight.

'Miss Seaborn,' Lady Lavinia said, stepping into the breach. 'Welcome. I must say you are younger than I expected.'

'Oh, my dear Honour has been my lifesaver,' Isolde said, taking her cousin's arm. 'Until she came to live with us, I was accompanied by the least charming of my father's sisters. She was a dour old woman with no sense of humour at all! Honour and I have had the best of times since. Haven't we, my dear?'

'Oh yes,' Honour said with a slight smile and a glance around the room.

'You have suffered a recent bereavement?' Lady Lavinia said.

'My father.'

'Honour's father was a soldier,' Isolde said. 'Our mothers were sisters. Only mine married a Baron and Honour's married the first man she fell in love with who happened to be a penniless soldier. She was cast off by her family, who felt she'd let them down. So poor Honour had nobody to turn to when her father died. But I spoke to mine most firmly and insisted she should come and live with us. It's been perfectly delightful ever since.'

'That was very kind of you,' Felix said. He was feeling more overwhelmed than he had in anyone's presence ever before. 'Please, do sit down.'

'Thank you, your grace,' Isolde said and settled herself on the chair beside him.

It was considerably closer than any of his previous guests had sat, and a whiff of her perfume drifted over Felix. It was intoxicating.

'So... tell me Lady Giddings, is this your first season in London?'

He felt foolish asking such a question, or any question at all. Up until now, his Aunt had taken the lead cross-examining the mothers while the daughters sat demurely by.

'It is my first season,' Isolde said beaming at him. 'It is the most wonderful thing. I have never been to so many parties in my life and quite the gayest events they are too. I don't believe I have been to bed before three in the morning in weeks.'

'So you enjoy parties, do you?'

'But of course,' Isolde said with a warm smile. 'It is the most wonderful thing to meet everyone in London. I mean, I grew up here, and my father made sure I wasn't a complete mouse who took fright the moment she came out. But nothing can prepare you for the whirl of social engagements that the season brings.'

'I see,' Felix said, stunned into monosyllables. He was afraid that this wonderful, vital creature needed more excitement than he could ever provide.

'I enjoy the quiet moments too,' Isolde said as she laid her hand gently on his arm.

It felt like a jolt passed through him at her touch. He was also thrilled by her quick comprehension. 'Do you?'

'Oh yes, there is nothing more charming than an evening spent at home around the fire with a few choice friends.'

'I like that too,' Felix said.

What she described sounded like paradise, indeed. It was something he rarely did beyond a few comfortable evenings with Percy and Arthur. It opened new vistas though, and he liked the possibilities that brought. Maybe with Isolde, so stupid to call her Lady Giddings the name didn't suit her, he could develop a new circle of friends.

'Tell me, Lady Giddings,' Lady Lavinia said, breaking in on Felix's pleasant daydream. 'What do you do in your father's house?'

'In my father's house?'

'I understand your mother died when you were quite young. Did you take up her duties as you grew up? I imagine you must know a great deal about the management of a large house.'

'Well, I suppose so,' Isolde said with a laugh. It raised Felix's spirits just to hear it. 'But that must surely be of no interest to his grace.'

It wasn't. More than Lady Giddings' laugh, though, the fact that she didn't engage in boring chatter, or feel the need to ingratiate herself with his aunt, made Felix like her even more. All the other matrons had been at pains to show that their daughters could manage a ducal household.

'I have plenty of servants,' he murmured. 'No wife of mine would have to worry about managing the house.'

'I'm sure that is right,' Isolde said, giving him a warm smile of thanks. 'But if you must know, I am a passable seamstress. I know more than I should about horses, father is mad for them. And I could fend for myself should I have to deal with any tradesmen. My strengths, however, are in dancing and playing the piano. I am a charming hostess, although I know I am boastful to say so, but dreadful at poetry and singing. There, my full confession. Do I pass muster, your grace?'

'Oh yes,' Felix said, quite light-headed with all the emotion coursing through him. 'I am not fond of poetry either, at least, not the sort that is declaimed in drawing rooms.'

'I feel like you are speaking from experience.'

'A little.'

'Now would it be politic of me to press you for the name of your dread poet or should I refrain?' Isolde said with a conspiratorial smile.

'It would be best not to mention it.'

Felix was unable to stop the foolish grin spreading across his face. He'd not had this much fun in... well ever.

'That went very well,' Isolde said as she settled into her seat in their carriage and straightened her gloves.

'Yes, I suppose it did.'

Honour was disappointed, but not entirely surprised, that the duke had been so clearly bowled over by Isolde.

'He's better looking than I expected too. I mean, I hoped he wasn't some hideous creature hidden from the world for fear of what he looks like, but he's better than that. He's quite nice looking actually.'

'I thought he had a quiet dignity,' Honour said and looked out the window watching the houses pass by as the hackney rolled towards home.

'Well, of course, he had that, Honour, he's a duke. But he was also well... he could pass for handsome if he were a bit healthier.'

'He looked very tired.'

'True, and if he hadn't, I would have thought this whole tale about his heart might be nonsense. I say, you don't suppose he might have a weak mind too do you?'

'He didn't seem to.'

'You don't think so? At times he looked as if he didn't entirely understand me.'

'I think that's merely because you are outside his usual experience,' Honour said.

She kept to herself that the duke was so entirely swept away by Isolde that he'd been lost for words. She was already far too full of herself to be boosting her self-esteem further.

'The aunt didn't take to me though,' Isolde said. 'Although I dare say that won't matter.'

'No it probably won't,' Honour said and suppressed a sigh.

Lady Lavinia was a battle axe, anyone could see that. But it seemed to her that the duke would do what he pleased. That did surprise her. She might have thought that a sickly man brought up by a domineering aunt would have a more yielding disposition.

Lady Lavinia hadn't wasted time being polite either. She'd glared disapprovingly and said so many waspish things that even Isolde had noticed and that took some doing. At least, Lady Lavinia had taken a good measure of Isolde and didn't like what she saw. Equally clearly, although Isolde hadn't picked up on that, Lady Lavinia also looked to be at a loss about how she could turn her nephew away from what would surely be a disastrous marriage.

Honour couldn't, for the life of her, work out why she cared so much about the duke and his aunt's feelings. No, she was deceiving herself, she knew well enough. She'd hoped that Isolde wouldn't win the duke. She'd hoped that Isolde would suffer a setback and realise that not all men would fall down at her feet as she'd seen every man do day and night.

Instead, the duke was instantly smitten. She'd never seen a man who was more openly admiring of her cousin. Maybe that was because the other men were more worldly-wise and hid some of their feelings from Isolde. Even when the mainstream of the masculine world had decided it was not only acceptable but fashionable to fall at the feet of the glorious Isolde.

'I wonder when we will be invited back,' Isolde said.

'Do you think we will be?' Honour said and regretted the demon that provoked her to make the comment.

'Of course, we will,' Isolde said with a self-satisfied twitch of her shawl.

Honour was disappointed in herself to realise that she wouldn't mind meeting the duke again either. He might have been oblivious to her, but, for some reason, she felt a spark of curiosity about him.

'Time's up,' Grantley said, looking up at the clock on the kitchen wall. 'Chivers will be showing the visitors out, and we need to rescue his grace.'

'Rescue him?' Hieronymus said.

'Would you want to spend much time with Lady Lavinia?'

'I don't suppose so, no.'

'Come on then,' Grantley said, and the trio made their swift way back to the drawing room.

'Your grace, are you all right?' Grantley said as they arrived.

Hieronymus understood the question because the duke looked grey with exhaustion.

All the same, he smiled beatifically at his valet and said, 'I'm fine.'

'Perhaps a little nap then to regroup,' Grantley said and helped the duke out of his chair while Poole took his other side.

'That sounds good,' Felix murmured as he allowed himself to be supported out of the room.

Hieronymus took up the rear, watching the slow progress of the trio across the hall. It seemed to him that the duke was using his servants more than he had before the visit, and he was walking far more slowly.

'Ahhh!' Felix cried, clutched at his chest, fell, and curled up into a ball on the floor.

'Your grace!' Grantley cried, dropped to the duke's side and shouted, 'Chivers, get the doctor.'

Hieronymus was glued to the spot and thankfully, not needed. Chivers rushed off, and a pair of footmen ran to help Grantley and Poole who hoisted the duke and carried him to his room at pace.

'Felix, help is on the way,' Lady Lavinia said as she hurried to her nephew's side.

'It's all right, your grace, Doctor Morton will be here soon,' Grantley said, staring intently into the duke's face.

The duke looked to be in agony. He still clutched at his chest, gasping for air and stared panic-stricken up at his valet. Hieronymus felt that he should leave. This wasn't the place for an observer, and it was a gross invasion of privacy.

'I'm here,' a big man said as he surged into the room.

'Doctor Morton, thank God,' Lady Lavinia said.

'Everyone stand aside,' the doctor said. 'Felix, listen to me. I am here, and you are going to be all right.'

The duke's gaze flicked to the doctor, and he gave a quick nod. It appeared speech was beyond him.

'Shall I fetch some laudanum for the pain?' Poole said.

'What!?' the doctor roared. 'Who is this fool? Do you want to kill his grace?'

'No I- I-'

'Get out! You're in my way. All of you out. The only one I need is Grantley.'

Hieronymus didn't need more. He rushed for the door and was out before the footmen and an ashamed-looking Poole.

'You may as well go home, Mr Testwood,' Lady Lavinia said as she closed the bedroom door on the doctor and his patient.

'Is he going to be all right?'

'I don't know.'

Hieronymus realised that Lady Lavinia was scared. She managed to maintain her composure, but she really didn't know what was going to happen to her nephew.

'I'm sorry,' Hieronymus said and hurried away.

'Can't - can't breathe,' Felix gasped.

'It's all right, I'm going to help you with that,' Dr Morton said. He rolled Felix onto his side and started tapping him firmly on his back.

I'm going to die, oh God I'm going to die, Felix thought. Please, not not, not... 'It hurts,' he cried, he was so scared. Oh, God, please no.

'I will look after you,' Doctor Morton said. His calm voice just made it into Felix's mind. 'I will make sure you recover.'

Oh God, Felix thought, and tears oozed down his face. It hurt so much. It had never hurt this much.

'Help,' he whispered.

'It's going to be all right. I will stay with you every step of the way,' Dr Morton said. 'Now, I want you to hold my hand.'

It hurt, it hurt, he couldn't breathe, and it hurt and, why was his hand being squeezed? He couldn't breathe, why was his hand?

'Good, that's good,' Dr Morton said. 'Take deep breaths. That's it, in... out... in... out. You have to concentrate, Felix. Slow down your breathing. You're afraid, I understand that, but just listen to me. Do as I say and you will be fine.'

'Can't breathe,' Oh God, oh God, his chest was being crushed. He was going to die. He didn't want to die. Not now. Not now!

'I know it's difficult, but you have to calm down. Just concentrate on your breathing. Do you hear me, Felix?'

'Can't,' Felix gasped. Dr Morton, it was Dr Morton.

'You have to, young man. Hold onto my hand and breathe. Just concentrate on the breathing. Do it with me, in... out... in... out. That's good, slow your breathing. Don't panic. In... out... in ... out.'

'Grantley?'

'He's right here. Don't you worry about him,' Dr Morton said.

'Grantley help... can't breathe.'

'Now come, your grace, don't you trust me? You can you know? Haven't I pulled you out of similar scrapes like this before?'

'Ahhh!' Felix screamed as the pain grew spikes and shot through him.

'Dr Morton!' Grantley cried.

'It's all right, everything is going to be all right,' Dr Morton said.

Chapter Seven

Percy sat in the darkened room beside Felix's bed as he'd done on his visit for the last three days in a row. So far Felix had barely come round and had been incoherent in those brief moments when he did open his eyes. They were all terrified for him.

Percy wanted to shake him and bellow that he had to get better, damn it all. But he knew it would be futile. So instead, he put on a brave face for his aunt and the servants and pretended he was fine sitting beside someone who showed no sign of improving.

'Felix? Felix, can you hear me?' Percy whispered.

'Percy?' Felix murmured, and his eyelids fluttered open briefly.

'Thank God,' Percy said. 'Thank God, you recognise me.'

'Why... wouldn't I?' Felix said as he opened his eyes again and looked around vaguely.

'Because you haven't the last few times I came by.'

'Oh,' Felix said between gasps of air.

'Listen to me wittering on when I can see how much my visit is tiring you. I should go.'

'No,' Felix whispered and made a superhuman effort to open his eyes. 'Don't,' he said, and his hand turned over.

It was a gesture Percy hadn't seen in years, and it hurt him to see it now. Felix only ever clung to his hand when he was scared.

He took it in a firm grasp and said, 'Well, if it doesn't annoy you, I'll stay.'

Felix actually smiled at that, which came as a relief. But his breathing worried the hell out of Percy. He was puffing for air like a man who'd just run a hundred-yard dash.

'Can't marry,' Felix murmured.

'What?'

'Woman of my dreams... got so excited... collapsed.'

'The woman of your dreams?'

'Is...Isolde.... beautiful.'

'I see. Well if it's any consolation, you were looking peaky before her visit. Aunt Lavinia told me it looked like you had a spasm before you even met Lady Giddings. I wouldn't lay this at her door.'

'No?' Felix whispered.

'No,' Percy said firmly. 'So you liked her, huh?'

'Yes.'

'And it's not because she came unfettered by a mother?'

'Cousin... neat dresser.'

'Is that so? Aunt Lavinia said you hardly noticed her.'

'I was... very distracted,' Felix said and greatly relieved Percy with another smile. 'Why is it so dark?'

'Ah, that's not you, don't worry, your eyes aren't failing. That's your valet's doing. He's closed all the curtains and got the fire roaring away. He's convinced the heat will be good for you.'

'Oh,' Felix murmured, and his eyes drifted shut, but he maintained his grip on Percy's hand.

'Well?' Lady Lavinia said when Percy finally slipped out of Felix's bedroom.

'Good Lord, you startled me, Aunt, and so unlike you to be lurking in the hallway.'

'I'm in no mood for your games, Percy. You were in there a long time which I pray means that Felix at least knew you.'

'He did. We had a little chat.'

'Thank God! Did Grantley also get him to drink something?'

'He interrupted us to do just that, which exhausted Felix. But before you jump in and say it was necessary, don't. I know it had to be done.'

'Doctor Morton made it very clear that he must not be allowed to dehydrate.'

'And Grantley, with enthusiastic if not efficient assistance from Poole, did just that. I must say, Poole looks shaken himself.'

'I don't think he fully understood the gravity of Felix's condition till now.'

'Mmm,' Percy said and gazed thoughtfully at his aunt. Ah well, it had to be done and now was probably the best time. 'Could we have a word in private?'

'Certainly, come into my parlour,' Lady Lavinia said leading the way. 'Although I am surprised that you want to talk to me. You have always been a fierce ally of Felix's, but I am well aware you disapprove of me.'

'You treat Felix too much like a child, and he isn't, you know,' Percy said as he entered what was known to the family as his aunt's domain. The room was tastefully furnished but with a surprising amount of old fashioned chintz for one who seemed to have not an ounce of romance in her.

'I am aware that he isn't a child, but his life is precarious, and he must be protected.'

'I can hardly argue with you on that account now,' Percy said. 'And it's about his protection that I need to speak to you.'

'What is it?' Lady Lavinia said as she settled in an armchair.

'It's Lady Giddings.'

Percy sat down opposite his aunt, crossed his legs and leaned back into the chair, trying his best to look relaxed. He had to broach a delicate subject, and he couldn't show any weakness or Aunt Lavinia would dismiss him and his concerns.

'Did Felix actually mention her?'

'He did. He's... he's smitten.'

'Oh, dear Lord, I was afraid of that.'

'He didn't say anything before?'

'He hardly had a chance, not that he tells me anything. But I would have to be blind not to see how charmed he was by the... the-'

'Strumpet,' Percy finished for her.

'That may be a bit strong.'

'Gold digger then.'

'Am I to understand that you do not approve of Lady Giddings?'

'No, I don't. Really, Aunt Lavinia, what were you thinking, introducing Felix to a woman like that?'

'She comes from a good family,' Lady Lavinia said frostily. 'And the people I asked about her spoke highly of her.'

'Well, then they can't have been watching her very closely.'

'And you have?'

'Of course, I have. Lady Giddings is the most beautiful young woman to arrive on the scene this year. She has attracted men to her like moths to a flame. I'm not too proud to admit that I was one of them.'

'Really, Percy, you had your head turned by a pretty face?' Lady Lavinia said archly.

'Not just any pretty face. A paragon. And I'll tell you what, that young woman turned me down flat. She had no interest in me, and she wasted no time in making that clear. I was hurt, but not unduly so, and I've been watching La Giddings ever since. She is clearly after a man with wealth and a title for she flits ever upwards. The last person I saw in her snare was the Earl of Overbrook, and we both know how old he is.'

'And how wealthy he is,' Lady Lavinia said with a sigh. 'Oh dear, I was afraid of that.'

'Were you?'

'She was very charming towards Felix, but in a single-minded way. She may be good at wrapping men around her pretty little fingers, but she doesn't bother with the women. That, you know, is a mistake. If you are going to create the facade of a caring young woman, you need to extend it to all in your ambit. Otherwise, people will see through it. And, Felix, even if you don't think I realise this, is an observant man.'

'So what do we do? You can't forbid him from seeing her again,' Percy said relieved that his aunt was in agreement with him. That was so rare it was practically newsworthy.

'Good lord, no, forbidding the relationship will only make matters worse,' Lady Lavinia said and paused as Danby arrived carrying tea. She waved him away impatiently and poured the tea herself.

Percy waited till Danby had closed the door. No doubt the servants were all wondering what he was doing with Lady Lavinia and bringing tea was an obvious way of trying to glean information. 'Then we must delay things.'

'What do you mean?'

'You said yourself, Aunt, Felix is observant. We need to give him time to notice what we already know to be true.'

'No. We need to introduce Felix to more women.'

'That will be a waste of time. He won't be interested in meeting anyone else while he's infatuated. And it tires him out all those meetings which is the last thing he needs. We just need to slow things down. You can start by telling him you don't want a wedding by June.'

'Oh... he told you that did he?'

'Of course, he did. He wasn't opposed to the idea either. Which means you and I are going to have to work hard to make sure he doesn't propose to and marry Lady Giddings by June.'

'That isn't going to be easy.'

'We can start slowing things down immediately by stressing that he needs to rest. He got a big fright from this latest attack,' Percy said, took a sip of tea and then searched in vain for a space on the table beside him to place the cup. It was so filled with nicknacks; it was impossible.

'He isn't the only one to get a fright, and he isn't out of the woods yet. Dr Morton is very concerned for him.'

'I know, but I am going to proceed as if he will be fine and he will recover. But to Lady Giddings, I will make out that it will be a long and slow road and...'

'And what?'

'If that doesn't work, if she makes it clear she will marry him no matter what, then I'm going to have to be more underhanded to show her up,' Percy said as rather a good idea occurred to him. He just hoped his aunt would go along with it too.

'What do you propose?'

'If you aren't opposed... I might drop a few hints that I stand to gain should Felix die.'

'Why?'

'Because she might decide to play two games then. She may attempt to snare me and Felix at the same time and that, you know, Felix won't fail to notice.'

'It will expose her.'

'I hope so.'

'The only problem being you don't stand to inherit anything.'

'She doesn't know that. As long as you play along, we should be safe. The ploy might cause her to make a misstep. She isn't half as canny and worldly-wise as she thinks she is.'

'That is very underhanded, indeed.'

'And she isn't?' Percy said. It always surprised him how women rallied round one of their own. Even if they didn't like the lady in question.

'She is doing what any young woman gifted with beauty would do. She is ensuring she gets as much benefit as she can from it.'

'Nobody will blame her for that, but I still think Felix deserves someone kinder.'

'Heaven knows where we might find such a paragon.'

'What about the cousin?' Percy said and lifted his teacup off his knee, where he'd balanced it, and took another sip.

'She's a penniless nobody that Felix didn't even notice.'

'He told me she was a neat dresser.'

'Did he? Well, I suppose he must have noticed her then, even if he barely said a word to her.'

'Might she be worth cultivating?'

'What for Percy? She isn't even remotely eligible.'

'No, but she is always around her cousin, and that may be useful, don't you think?' Percy said and wondered whether it might not be worth giving the cousin a hand. But first, he needed to get to know her better.

CHAPTER EIGHT

Felix lay staring up at the canopy of his bed as he had done for the last couple of days. It never changed, and he was heartily sick of it.

'Right, that's enough!'

'I beg pardon, sir?' Grantley said starting from the light doze he'd fallen into as he sat beside the bed.

'I've had enough of lying around, Grantley. I want to get up.'

'Doctor Morton-'

'Be damned!' Felix snapped and struggled to get upright. 'If I stare at the top of my bed for one second longer, I will go quite crazy.'

'Your grace, please.'

'This isn't a request, Grantley it's an order.'

Felix felt so frustrated that he was riding roughshod over his staff, and he didn't care. He'd had enough of the mollycoddling, and the tiptoeing everyone was doing. It looked like it was going to have to be a battle as Grantley wasn't quite ready to comply.

Whatever he was about to say was cut short by a tap at the door, and Chivers stepped inside. 'Begging your pardon, your grace, but I let Mr Testwood know that you were improving. He's arrived carrying a rather large canvas bag and asking whether he can see you?'

'Show him in, Chivers, right away. I am so bored I'm about to fall out with Grantley.'

'Your grace,' Grantley murmured as Chivers bowed himself out.

'I'm sorry,' Felix said. 'I shouldn't have spoken about you like that in front of Chivers.'

'You're out of sorts, sir.'

'That I am. Now, I really do think I should be sitting upright for Mr Testwood. Don't you?'

'Mr Testwood is a harum-scarum inventor who, if you'll forgive me for saying so, your grace, can't be any good if he isn't making enough to feed himself.'

'I have always thought it a pity that only the wealthy have the wherewithal to fund exploration and invention. It must be a damned nuisance to have to tolerate the whims of a patron.'

'You're surely not thinking of taking that man under your wing are you, your grace?'

'That remains to be seen,' Felix said.

It was odd to be planning any distance into the future with his health so precariously in the balance. He supposed that was human nature, to look to the future, however uncertain it might be.

'Mr Testwood, your grace,' Chivers said as he opened the door for the man.

'Now see what your arguing has done,' Felix said. 'I'm having to greet a visitor lying flat on my back.'

'And you'll stay that way if I have any say in the matter,' Grantley muttered. He coloured as Felix raised an eyebrow.

'The privilege of an old retainer, Poole,' Felix said to the young man who'd appeared from the dressing room the moment he'd heard voices and was now standing anxiously beside Grantley. 'Don't ever consider speaking to me in that way.'

'No, your grace,' Poole said in wide-eyed dismay.

'Forgive me, Mr Testwood, we really shouldn't be bickering and leave you standing.'

'Oh... not at all, your grace,' Hieronymus said and gave a hasty bow.

'You appear to be heavily laden.'

'Well... I've been thinking while you've... you' ve-'

'Been indisposed,' Felix said with a wry smile. People found it so hard to speak to him when he was laid low. Then again, he couldn't blame them; he felt embarrassed and ashamed to be such a burden as well. 'And what have you been thinking about?'

'A way to help you sit up in bed. Grantley and Poole suggested that it might be useful.'

'I dare say it would. Is it a substantial contraption?'

'Not really just some rope, pulleys and a harness.'

Hieronymus put down his holdall and pulled back the flap to reveal a weathered rope and ancient wooden pulley.

'Did that set you back very much?' Felix murmured.

'Oh no, I borrowed them from a friend at the docks and promised to return them.'

'Did you?'

'Well, it might not work, your grace. You don't want to be spending money till you're certain it will actually do what you want it to do.'

'Very sensible, and what will it do, exactly?'

'The plan is to fit the harness around you and attach the pulley to the top of the bed. Then with not a lot of effort, a single man should be able to hoist you up.'

'That sounds vaguely alarming. Have you tried this contraption out?'

'I have your grace. Emma, my wife, has been hoisted successfully, not just once, but on every occasion.'

'Your wife?'

'Yes, your grace. I estimated that she weighs about the same as you, although she's shorter and plumper, so some adjustments will have to be made.'

'She didn't mind being your guinea pig?'

'Oh no, Emma's a good egg. She'll happily get involved in any of my projects.'

'That sounds nice.' Felix was much struck by the idea of a woman who was willing to be hoisted over and over again by a pulley. He couldn't imagine any of his relatives being that patient. 'And er... is that her corset you're using for the harness?'

'It is, your grace,' Hieronymus said flushing. 'No sense in spending money on a harness until we know it works.'

'Quite so, and your very accommodating wife allowed that too?'

'She did, your grace, although it was touch and go. Her not wanting her underwear being wrapped around a duke. She said she might curl up with shame should she ever meet you after this.'

'Well, you can tell her I am most grateful for her sacrifice.'

'I will and all,' Hieronymus said with a grin. 'That will please her. Now, it will only take a moment to set up. I practised that as well. I won't be long. That is... you don't mind me climbing all over the bed while you're still in it do you, your grace?'

'I don't see how else we can test your invention.'

'You could get out of bed and then in again.'

'Oh no, you would face a battle royal with Grantley if you tried such a thing. I will remain in bed. Then be hoisted effortlessly and without strain by my man once you are done.'

'It might be best if I do it the first time, your grace,' Hieronymus said.

He pulled himself up onto the end of the bed and started tying his contraption to the top of the bedpost. Felix felt a twinge of envy at the ease with which this man hoisted himself up and then clambered about the bed much like a sailor putting up the rigging.

'It isn't very attractive,' Grantley said with a sniff. 'And it reeks of fish.'

'Oh... yes. I hadn't noticed that, but now you mention it...' Hieronymus said. 'I'm sorry, your grace. I didn't realise.'

'It's quite all right. I assume if this experiment is a success, that you will take the whole contraption away and make a new one?'

'That I will sir, and it will also be less bulky and therefore won't look quite so bad on the bed.'

'Mr Testwood, if your hoist works I won't give a damn how it looks.'

'Well that's a relief,' Hieronymus said with a grin. 'Because I'm not sure how much I can prettify it. Now the final bit, your grace. I need to slide the harness under your back.'

'Go ahead.' Felix found himself at once excited and apprehensive. Surely this was a very minor thing they were attempting. There was no need to worry, and yet worry he did as Testwood pushed a bumpy corset under him. 'Not the most comfortable of operations,' he murmured.

'I'm sorry, your grace. I've just realised that Emma was helping me by arching her back.'

'Do you need me to do the same?'

'Your grace, no,' Grantley said. 'Please, don't tire yourself. I fear this experiment is too much.'

'Is it?' Hieronymus said and stopped midway through his attempt to inch the harness under the duke.

'No, it's fine, carry on,' Felix said and made an attempt at arching his back. He hoped nobody noticed how feeble it was. Grantley was already close to stepping in and stopping the whole thing on the spot, and any sign of struggle on his part would be all it took.

'There you go,' Hieronymus said. 'Now to do up the ties and attach the ropes to either end. I've made hoops by the shoulders. And done. Now the final bit. As you have no support under your neck, you need to hold yourself up. Will that be all right, your grace?'

'I'm sure I'll manage.'

'If this works to your satisfaction, I can make more of a brace to the back that can support your neck as well. But for now, I'll start to lift, and you tell me how it feels.'

'Your grace, please,' Grantley said. 'You're not even supposed to be sitting up, let alone being experimented on in this... this infernal contraption.'

'Is that right, your grace?' Hieronymus said.

'It's fine,' Felix said. 'Haul away, Mr Testwood.'

'If you're sure?'

'I am, now let's have no more delay.'

'Very good, sir,' Hieronymus said and began to pull on the free end of the rope he was holding as he stood beside the duke.

'Ah, I feel it,' Felix said as he was tugged very slightly upwards.

'The beauty of the pulley is that you can control the rate at which you rise, so there are no sudden jerks or heaving.'

'Very clever,' Felix said as he was pulled inch by inch ever more upright. 'I think, however, you need to do it a little bit faster so that Grantley can get that bolster he's hovering with under my back.'

'If you're sure, your grace.'

'Of course, he's sure,' Grantley snapped as he pushed past Hieronymus. 'And you're tiring him what with him having to hold his neck up.'

'I'm fine,' Felix said as he relaxed and let his head rest on the bolster.

'Another one, your grace,' Grantley said and tucked a cushion under Felix's head.

'Thank you,' Felix said. 'That is a handy contraption, Mr Testwood. I like it.'

'I also thought I could add a crane-like arm so that once you are upright, it can swing you out of bed.'

'Don't be preposterous!' Grantley snapped. 'If his grace can't get out of bed on his own steam, he is in no state to be up at all.'

'It's all right,' Felix said and patted Grantley's arm. The poor man was worked up to a frantic level of worry. 'I like the experiment, but my valet is right. If I can't get myself upright, I doubt I could move around even in the damned bath chair.'

'It's just a suggestion,' Hieronymus said.

'And a good one. I'm sure we will come up with uses for it other than getting me on my feet.'

'I'm glad you like it, your grace.'

'I do. I'll have Chivers take you to my man of business, Mr Forsyth. He will bankroll the acquisition of all you need for the production of a permanent hoist for my bed.'

'Thank you, I'm most honoured,' Hieronymus said and bowed as deeply as he could.

'Felix, you seeing people?' Percy said as he poked his head around the door.

'Good God yes, please come inside,' Felix said.

'What the devil is going on here?' Percy said with a good-humoured grin. 'You look like a marionette hanging in your bed.'

'In which case, meet my puppet master,' Felix said, waving in Hieronymus's direction. 'Mr Testwood is an inventor and is helping to make my life, and the lives of my staff, easier. Even if they don't entirely believe it yet.'

'Is that... is that a piece of women's underwear wrapped about your person?'

'It's temporary,' Felix said, amused by Percy's bemusement. 'Mr Testwood, please give me half an hour. Grantley can take you to my man of business in the meantime. You may as well get to know him. Grantley, take Poole along he should meet Mr Forsyth as well.'

'Very good, your grace,' Grantley said, gave his master a stiff bow and shooed Hieronymus and Poole out before him.

'He looks put out,' Percy said once the door was closed again.

'He's worried that I shouldn't be sitting up, but honestly, I couldn't take being flat on my back anymore.'

'You look improved but not quite up to par yet,' Percy said as he pulled up a chair and sat beside his cousin. 'Is it wise to exert yourself in this way, even if you are bored?'

'I will let Grantley lower me when he gets back and behave myself after that.'

Felix was irritated by Percy's concern. There was nothing worse than being told off for something when you knew you were wrong to be doing it.

Percy must have understood because he said, 'I'll not nag. You're a grown man, you must make your own decisions.'

'Thank you, now what brings you here?'

'Just dropped by to check in on you, old fellow. To make sure you aren't being hemmed about by fussy people driving you to distraction. Imagine my surprise when I discover you've found your own source of amusement,' Percy said and flicked one of the ropes holding Felix up.

'Mr Testwood is heaven-sent. I was particularly pleased to see him today. His invention may not be the finest you've ever seen, but he provides a distraction. And who knows, this contraption of his might just come in useful.'

'As long as it keeps you happy.'

'It keeps me diverted at any rate,' Felix said. 'Now tell me, what of the world outside?'

'There isn't much to tell, life continues on its weary path.'

'Oh,' Felix said disappointed that Percy had so little to say. Usually, he was very good at providing conversation. 'What of… what of Isolde Giddings?'

'You're still thinking about her, huh?'

'I haven't had much else to do. But, truth to tell, she feels like a vague memory or a… or a dream. She is very beautiful though, isn't she?'

'Oh yes, no doubt about that, a diamond of the first water.'

'Do you… do you see much of her?'

'She goes to pretty well all the activities of the season so, yes, I've seen her regularly.'

'Oh… do you go to many dances?'

'Well, you know… people like a man in uniform so I get invited to all of them. Some people are invited to these events for their status, their notoriety or their money. Soldiers get invited because of their fancy dress.'

'I didn't know. You don't mention parties very often.'

'Didn't want you to feel left out.'

'Is there much else of your life you don't mention?' Felix said, surprised at how hurt he was that his cousin had kept something from him.

'Not really. I tell you far more than I tell anyone else, friends or family.'

Felix nodded, of course, Percy had his own life, and he was foolish to wish he could be more a part of it. He sighed and said, 'I wish I could see a ball.'

'Well you do have a ballroom,' Percy said, and his smile faltered. 'No, ignore that. I wasn't giving you ideas. A ball would be far too much excitement.'

'You mean because I conked out after a mere week of meeting lovely ladies?'

'Aunt Lavinia is always scolding me and telling me your health is more precarious than I realise. I thought she was over cautious and I'm guiltily aware that I may have egged you on to do more than was wise.'

'And a ball would fall into that category?'

'Maybe it would. I'd certainly not recommend that you go to one elsewhere. That would be too much of a strain.'

'Probably,' Felix said and felt a black depression descending. To fend it off he said, 'Tell me about Lady Giddings, is she... is she looking well?'

'As well as ever. She doesn't change from one party to the next she is always hemmed about with admirers.'

'Then no doubt she has forgotten me already.'

Felix's depression deepened, but he wasn't really surprised. How could he stick in anybody's mind when he'd been in bed for over a week? He was surprised though by the way Percy hesitated and then shut his mouth.

'What aren't you telling me?'

'Nothing.'

'Don't do that, Percy, please. Don't try and protect me. I may be an invalid, but I can look after myself. At least, I am in control of my emotions.'

'All right, then I'll say that Lady Giddings is highly unlikely to forget you.'

'Do you think so?'

'Felix, you're a duke and an incredibly wealthy man into the bargain. Even if she'd wanted to, Lady Giddings is highly unlikely to forget that.'

'You think she's a gold digger?'

'I think any woman would be a fool, and seriously disingenuous, if she pretended your title and money didn't matter to her. Just as Lady Giddings is fully entitled to use her glorious looks to secure her future. After all, her looks are all she has. Her father's wealth won't be going to her but to a distant nephew.'

'I see.'

'What's bothering you?'

'I'm not sure. You're right, of course. I suppose I was just hoping for more. I mean, every person should use all at their disposal to better their lives. I just... I would hope that it didn't simply revolve around money. I wish that... if you didn't love somebody, and you found someone poorer, that you did love, that you'd opt for love rather than wealth.'

'You get that from all your novels, do you?'

'I suppose I do. Isn't the world like that?'

'Not entirely. People can be more calculating. But I will say this, if it was all about the money we soldiers would be the least likely to attract a mate, for we are not the best endowed financially. Yet plenty of my fellow comrades are happily married.'

'So there is hope.'

'You feel that strongly about her, do you?'

'It wasn't just her looks, Percy. She was so open and natural with me. She didn't put on airs and she... she didn't mind Aunt Lavinia. I don't want a wife who can't stand up to my aunt. It would only make her life miserable.'

'So you liked her character as well?'

'I did,' Felix said and found himself being examined more closely by Percy than he was accustomed to.

'Do you want me to talk to her?'

'Who? Isolde Giddings?'

'If I see her, I can let her know what happened to you and why you haven't been in touch. I doubt Aunt Lavinia has said anything to her so she must be wondering.'

'Do you think so?'

'I would wonder.'

'Please don't tell her I collapsed right after her visit. I don't want her to think it's her fault. I also... I don't want to give her a disgust of me,' Felix said. 'Do you think she'll be put off?'

'That I can't tell.'

'I would be. It's hypocritical, but I doubt I'd want to marry a sickly woman.'

'You don't think you'd enjoy comparing aches and pains, huh?' Percy said with a wide grin.

'I really wouldn't. Which is hardly fair and yet I am hoping I can attract a woman like Lady Giddings. It really is the height of arrogance.'

'You're only human, Felix, nobody can blame you.'

'No, but they couldn't blame a poorly woman either. They also wouldn't expect her to be able to secure a match unless she was also very wealthy. I have read about men marrying wealthy women purely for their money and seeing them into an early grave, the better to spend their inheritance. It always struck me as particularly cruel.'

'You're no fool. You keep your eyes and ears open, and you should be safe. Just don't... don't rush into anything, all right?'

'Do you think I'm capable of rushing?' Felix said as he pointed up at his new contraption.

'You know what I mean. Now I should take my leave for if I'm not mistaken Grantley is on his way back, and I'd rather exit gracefully than be booted out.'

Hieronymus rushed into his house to get out of the fine cold rain that blanketed London like a heavy mist and stamped his feet vigorously to get them to warm up. The walk from Belgravia was a long one and today a particularly cold one. Then he fished the leaflets he'd picked up from the Royal Society out of his coat pocket, removed his coat and shook it out over their small black stove. It sizzled as a spray of water droplets hit the hot plate.

'How was he?' Emma said as she handed her husband a towel. 'I assume you got to see the duke or else you wouldn't have been away so long.'

'He was... he was still very ill,' Hieronymus said and swept his wife into a warm embrace.

'Oh, what's that all about?' Emma said as he planted a kiss on her lips.

'I don't know. I suppose I'm just grateful to be alive and healthy and married to a wonderful woman.'

'Good heavens, all this from a visit to a duke?'

'I know, but... we always say it, money can't buy you happiness, and the greatest blessing is to have good health. But, Emma love, you really have to see it to understand. His grace... he was so fatigued and weak. I hoisted him up, and he struggled, I mean really struggled to get upright.'

'So the harness didn't work?'

'It worked perfectly. I mean, I didn't even think of providing the duke with a neck support, and I should have because it was a struggle for him to keep his head up. That... that's somebody who is very ill, and since it's his heart, he has no prospect of it ever getting better. Although I did solve one question that had been bothering me.'

'What was that?'

'The way the doctor appeared so quickly, I wondered how that was possible.'

'And?'

'It turns out he is part of the duke's household. He lives in the house and travels to the country with the duke when they make their annual pilgrimage from town.'

'At least he has the funds to do something about keeping himself safe.'

'Oh yes, and he's generous with it too. Look,' Hieronymus said, pulled an envelope out of his pocket and jingled it.

'Hieronymus, that sounds like a lot of money!'

'Payment for my time plus funds to buy the equipment I need. It was given to me by Mr Forsyth, his grace's man of business. He's as dry and uninviting as they come, but he didn't quibble. He had my payment ready for me, and very generous it was too. He gave me an advance on the goods I need to buy. I have to take in all the receipts but, Emma, we've got a good sum here. It's sufficient for our needs and a little left over.'

'All from the duke?'

'He pays well. As long as he continues to be happy with my work, I am confident that he will continue to be good for our family. That is... as long as he stays alive, and that by no means is certain.'

'You said he had an excellent doctor.'

'I did, but I also remember how scared everyone looked when he collapsed, including his grace. They didn't know whether he would live or die. So we need to save as much money as we can while we are getting it.'

'I understand.'

'He paid you a complement too as it happens,' Hieronymus said.

'Me? What could he possibly know about me? Have you been talking?'

'A little. The duke was very struck by the fact that you were willing to be my tester, but that wasn't it. When I helped him back down, he noticed the stitching on the harness and said I had a very neat hand. So I had to confess that the handiwork was yours and that you're a seamstress. He said that you were to be commended.'

'Did he?'

'Oh, yes. The duke knows what he's talking about too. He's very keen on fashion, has magazines about it in his room and stylish clothes.'

'And he didn't... he didn't mind that you used my corset?'

'On the contrary, I think he found it amusing. His cousin was outraged, but his grace wasn't. He's really very easy going, which is surprising for one with such precarious health. I've met other sickly people, and they're more pernickety. His grace is, well, he's serene.'

CHAPTER NINE

P ercy felt more on edge than usual when setting out to a ball. He was about to practice deception upon Lady Giddings, which he didn't much mind, but worse, upon Felix. It was clear Felix was smitten by La Giddings and no amount of telling him she was poison would have worked. No, Felix was going to have to work the woman out of his system by himself.

Percy prayed to God that he would. The worst possible fate could be his cousin marrying Lady Giddings and going to his grave never realising how little she cared for him. No, that wasn't right, the worst would be if he married her and then realised how shallow she was. If nothing else it might carry him off.

So, with those concerns, why the devil had he suggested to Felix that he'd talk to Lady Giddings? It was folly. He was, in effect, facilitating her path towards his cousin.

He should have kept his mouth shut. He should have kept Felix in the dark as to his partying habits and about Lady Giddings. He could then have mourned the loss of a love he never got to know and moved on, and with any luck, Lady Giddings would be safely promised to somebody else in that time.

Then again, perhaps not. Felix was still very unwell and more depressed than Percy had ever seen him. This latest attack had dented his confidence, but it would return. At that point, his cousin was more than capable of taking matters into his own hands. Hadn't he engaged that ridiculous inventor entirely off his own bat? He could do the same with Lady Giddings, start a correspondence with her and arrange a meeting without the rest of them knowing.

It was his right. He was, as Percy kept reminding Lady Lavinia, a grown man and one of considerable wealth. He also wasn't a fool. He knew his estate backwards, and understood business far better than Percy did.

He was just... he was vulnerable. Particularly to a beautiful and manipulative woman. That was something he hadn't come across before. He'd undoubtedly read about such creatures in his novels and the newspaper. Still, Percy doubted he could be brought to believe that Lady Giddings was one such woman.

Perhaps he was being unfair on her too. After all, she had spurned his advances. No worse, she'd laughed at his attempts and then turned her back on him. She'd been so blatant in letting him know he wasn't worth her time and that had stung. But maybe she was merely honest. She, after all, did have to snare herself the best possible match.

He would soon find out, he thought, as he strolled through the grand entrance of Lady Littleton's house and the footman announced his arrival.

Percy remained at the entrance examining the room. As with most parties, the house was filled beyond capacity, and all the doors were flung open wide. All the chandeliers were lit, and with the blaze above and the crush of people below, it was hot. It was so hot that the ladies in their satin and silk dresses were all fluttering their fans to keep themselves cool and prevent their makeup from running. The men looked equally hot and flushed, but even so, everyone was in high spirits. The hubbub of chatter nearly drowned out the music coming from the quintet sawing away at the far end of the ballroom.

'Ah, Captain Shawcross, welcome. It's so good to see you this evening,' Lady Littleton said as she hurried across the hall.

'Lady Littleton,' Percy said and delivered a deep bow. 'It is always a pleasure, and I see your party is already a great success.'

'It's a fearful crush. Heaven knows how I have managed to squeeze so many people in. But everyone seems to be enjoying themselves, so I am content.'

'Indeed, and while I have your attention, may I beg a favour?'

'Anything, Captain, is there a particular young lady you have your eye on?' Lady Littleton said with a twinkle.

'Am I so transparent?'

'Silly man, why do you think I hold this annual ball? I simply love matchmaking. Now come, tell me who I may introduce you to?'

'I was wondering if you might introduce me to Miss Seaborn,' Percy said.

'Miss Seaborn? I'm not sure I know that young lady. Do you think I invited her?'

'Well... she is the cousin of Lady Giddings and appears to be her chaperone these days.'

'Really? Good gracious! I hadn't realised. But honestly, Captain, are you trying a different approach to Lady Giddings? Most people ask for a direct introduction to the beauty. I doubt you'll fare better going via the cousin.'

'Oh, but I have already tried my luck with La Giddings and been turned down flat. I am told that her cousin is a pleasant young woman though,' Percy said and hoped he was right.

'Well, as your hostess I am honour bound to introduce you. It may take a moment for me to locate the young lady, but I shall return!' Lady Littleton said and dived into the crowd.

Percy pushed his way through to the refreshments, shouting greetings to all the people he knew as he went. For the first time ever, he wondered what Felix would make of this crush. A person needed to be robust indeed, to even make his way from one side of the room to the other.

Percy had a feeling Felix wouldn't like the multitude of people, the noise and the oppressive fug. He might find it interesting, but Percy felt that his cousin had a more reflective temperament. One that actually did prefer solitary contemplation to this roar of humanity.

Maybe that was why he was able to bear his quiet life. If his temperament was one of gaiety and the need to be continuously surrounded by a whirl of people, his existence might well have been unbearable for him.

Percy armed himself with a drink and turned to examine the people around him more closely. They were the usual group, debutantes dressed up to the nines watched by hawk-eyed mothers. An assortment of men, young and old, making eyes at all the ladies. Some of the girls were enchanted, excitement sparkling in their eyes. Others looked like little more than wilted flowers, girls struggling against the press of people and expectations.

He was just watching one particularly sorry looking specimen when Lady Giddings, resplendent in a pink satin dress, strolled into the room trailing men. A stripling who couldn't have been long out of the nursery was talking earnestly into one of her perfect ears. A far older gentleman, the Earl of Overbrook, strolled along on her other side. He had the complacent air of one who believed his conquest secure and was amused by the other men. Percy wished it were so, and feared that he was in a position to topple the earl's current position.

'Lady Giddings,' he said as he stepped up to the crowd and gave her a deep bow.

'Do I know you, sir?' she said, arching a brow at his temerity to introduce himself.

'We met at the Portmaster's ball. I am not surprised you don't remember me, it was a great crush too.'

'I'm sure,' Lady Giddings said, and her eyes flicked away, dismissing him.

Percy wasn't willing to let her go. He had to enact his plan now, while he had her ladyship's attention, faint as it was. It would be tedious to make a second attempt later.

'I was just discussing you with my cousin this morning. He was most struck by your beauty.'

'Your cousin?' Isolde said her brow creasing in irritation.

'The Duke of Morley,' Percy said lazily and watched the young woman all the more closely. It seemed she stiffened as Felix was mentioned.

'Your cousin is the Duke of Morley?'

'Indeed, he's been a little under the weather but is feeling much improved, so I paid him a visit.'

'He's been unwell?' Lady Giddings said and allowed the press of people to drive her closer to Percy so that they were now uncomfortably close to each other.

At least the advantage of being so close to Lady Giddings, Percy thought, was that fewer people would hear what he was saying.

'It's a consequence of his condition, I'm afraid. He's a bit up and down.' Percy hated saying that to anyone, but especially to Lady Giddings, who was now examining him with interest. Something he'd not experienced from her before.

'Is that why he's no longer receiving visitors?'

'I assume so, I didn't ask.'

'But all of London is talking about it. Lady Lavinia cancelled all his further engagements after I visited and that was ages ago, since then... nothing.'

Percy resisted telling the young woman she'd bowled Felix over. He didn't want to give her too strong an impression of impending triumph.

'As I said, his health is precarious. I warned Lady Lavinia not to put him under too much strain, but I'm afraid she didn't listen to me.'

'I see,' Isolde said. 'Do you think he'll be receiving visitors again soon?'

'I'm sure he will be shortly.'

'That's good,' Isolde said.

'Lady Giddings, you surely aren't interested in a broken-down young man,' Lord Overbrook drawled, already looking less confident.

'On the contrary, he was charming,' Isolde said, flashing the earl a broad smile. Then she turned her full attention on Percy, slipped her arm into his and said, 'Take me somewhere quiet, Captain. I'd like to learn more about your cousin.'

'Certainly.'

Percy wondered whether the young woman even registered his astonishment at her boldness. Or considered whether he might be put off by the way she'd gone from writing him off to draping herself over him. Evidently, her beauty so far had carried the day, and she was unaccustomed to setbacks. He prayed he wasn't leading Felix deeper into trouble with this young woman and that he'd be able to extricate Felix from this beautiful but selfish creature.

'Here,' Isolde said as they found an unoccupied chaise, newly vacated by a couple who headed off to dance. 'Shoo,' Isolde said to the men who'd followed and now formed a semicircle before her. 'Captain Shawcross and I need a moment of privacy.'

The men melted into the crowd, except for the stripling who hovered nearby scowling at the pair of them.

'You certainly have them under your power,' Percy said on a laugh. He had to be careful how he played things now and didn't want the young woman to sense any disapproval from him.

'They are all very sweet,' Isolde said. 'Now tell me. How is your cousin?'

'As I said, recovering.'

'And the stories are true, are they? He stopped receiving any female visitors after he'd seen me?'

So that was it, La Giddings had to know her effect on Felix. 'He collapsed shortly after your visit,' Percy said dryly. 'He was in no condition after that to receive any visitors at all.'

'But he is improving?'

'He is. It will be slow, though. You will have to be patient.'

'I'm sure he wouldn't mind a visit from me.'

Percy was so surprised he blinked at her. It appeared Lady Giddings' arrogance was greater than he'd realised.

'I suspect at the moment even you would not be welcome.'

Percy wondered whether it was possible to put La Giddings off at all. It didn't seem so, even though any young woman must surely think twice about visiting a man who was so ill. Perhaps it was time to put his second plan into action.

'A visit from me would cheer him up,' Isolde said. 'I'm sure it would help rather than hinder his recovery.'

'Honestly, m'lady, you can do what you like. I'm sure I don't mind.'

'You don't?' Isolde said and actually looked intrigued.

'Felix is my cousin, and I have a certain affection for him, but as you know, affection doesn't put food on the table.'

'I don't follow you?'

'Felix will leave a considerable inheritance.' Percy tapped the side of his nose, knowingly, bowed and said, 'I have taken up too much of your time. I wish you all good fortune in your chase of my cousin,' and with that, he took his leave.

Never had he felt more uncomfortable with an encounter. He certainly wasn't cut out for this work, and he wished it hadn't come to the point where he was forced to take such drastic measures.

'Ah, Captain, I've found you at last,' Lady Littleton said. 'It has taken some effort, but I have found the young lady you were after. I must warn you, however, that she is in mourning and therefore not dancing.'

'That's fine, Lady Littleton. I would still like to meet her. Call it curiosity on my part.' And that it was. Percy also fervently prayed that Miss Seaborn wasn't cut from the same cloth as her cousin.

'Well, here you are,' Lady Littleton said as she pulled Percy to the other end of the room. They stopped before a dark-haired young woman wearing a sombre but elegant grey dress. She was apparently watching the festivities with a great deal of interest, and a smile lingered on her lips.

∞

Even though it was past midnight, Honour was enjoying herself at the ball. The crystal chandeliers with their dripping candles sparkled brightly, and the musicians were the best she'd heard so far this season. It resulted in a crowd of happy people who laughed, danced and chatted around her.

She was relieved that as a chaperone, she could sometimes just sit and watch people. It saved her from the constant effort to make herself agreeable.

'Miss Honour Seaborn,' Lady Littleton said from a few yards away as she pushed determinedly through the crowd towards Honour.

She was followed by a handsome, dark-haired man in a spick and span Horse Guards uniform. Honour's heart sank. The first few times a hostess had arrived trailing a young man her heart had skipped a beat, relieved and pleased that she could attract someone. But her slim hopes were always dashed, and now she knew better than to expect anything.

'Allow me to introduce you to Captain Percy Shawcross of the Royal Horse Guards.'

'How do you do, Captain Shawcross?' Honour said, stood up and offered her hand.

'How do you do, Miss Seaborn,' Percy said and kissed her fingertips.

'Well that's my duty executed, my dears,' Lady Littleton said. 'I will now leave the two of you in peace.'

'I beg your pardon for that hasty introduction,' Percy said. 'But I was curious to meet you.'

'You were?' Honour said and hoped her resignation didn't show in her reply. 'Forgive me, sir but I don't know you. As you aren't in the same regiment my father hailed from, I can't work out how you even know about me.'

'Your father was in the army?'

'The 43rd light infantry,' Honour said.

'And now?'

'He died, which is why I have returned to England.'

'And to the home of Lady Giddings?'

'Ah,' Honour said. So they had come to the reason he'd sought her out, and he hadn't wasted any time getting to it either. 'Perhaps you would like an introduction to Lady Giddings, sir?'

'Do you get much of that? People using you to get to Lady Giddings?'

'A fair amount.'

'Well, I have met the fair creature, so no, I have no need for a further introduction. I wanted to meet you.'

'I can't imagine why, sir,' Honour said and felt a flicker of nervousness as she sat down and indicated for the captain to do the same. It got them out of the flow of the crowd who were continually pushing past and gained them a bit more privacy too.

'Because my cousin told me about you,' Percy said, and he sat down on the sofa but kept a respectful distance between them.

'Your cousin? I'm afraid now I am even more confused. You'll have to explain,' Honour said on a laugh. She felt like this captain was engaged in some light sparring, and that intrigued her.

'Felix Peergrave, the Duke of Morley.'

That revelation was such a surprise that Honour blinked at the captain and had to gather herself before she said, 'The Duke of Morley is your cousin?'

'He is.'

'Then, I am even more puzzled. I didn't think his grace noticed me.'

'Well, he did. He said you were a neat dresser and I can see that he was right.'

Honour felt herself blush at that comment and scolded herself forcefully for doing so. What did she care if the duke thought her a neat dresser? What did that even mean?

'It's very kind of you to say so, and good of his grace to notice.'

'Felix doesn't miss much.'

'Doesn't he?'

'Rarely,' Percy said.

Honour was seized with a sudden wish to get this man to warn the duke against Isolde. Maybe he could help someone she was feeling more warmth towards despite him barely noticing her. Or apparently noticing her sufficiently to mention her to a cousin. That was surprising. But no, she had only just met the captain, and it wasn't her place to say anything, leastways not something treacherous about her own cousin.

'Is his grace all right?' Honour said instead.

'Why wouldn't he be?'

'Forgive me if I'm being forward, but he looked unwell when Isolde and I visited. Since then nobody, that is, no young lady has been to see him, so I did wonder.'

'He fell ill shortly after your visit, but he is on the road to recovery.'

'When he will continue with the visits?'

'Not for a while, I shouldn't think. But he may resume them at some point.'

'I see.'

'Do you disapprove?'

'It is none of my business, but I do wonder at the wisdom of this quest to find a wife.' It was as much as Honour dared say.

'Felix is only human, Miss Seaborn. He, like all of us, would like someone with which to share his life, although he is also aware of how precarious his life is. At times, he questions what he is doing and hopes it is the right thing. But honestly, what else would you have him do? Especially with my aunt so set on him continuing the line?'

'Lady Lavinia Doubtless?'

'She cares about Felix, don't misunderstand me, but she is also anxious for the succession.'

'Then perhaps she should reconsider, for his grace can't be very robust if he has taken ill after little more than a week of visits.'

Honour was surprised that the captain would say so much about his cousin to a relative stranger. She'd got the impression that the duke was a private sort of man, judging by how little he'd said about himself when they'd visited. She doubted he'd want his cousin spreading gossip about him.

'I have told my aunt the same, and I hope she will listen to reason. Besides, my cousin may have found the woman of his dreams already.'

Honour gave him a sharp look, more shocked than she wished to show. Part of her had already suspected what the captain just said, but all the same, it felt like a blow. 'Isolde?'

'You seem less than pleased with the idea.'

'I suppose I shouldn't be surprised. I could see how struck his grace was by Isolde but maybe... maybe she wouldn't be best for his health.' It was as far as she could go in providing a warning and she regretted it instantly.

'You don't think so?'

'I mean, no woman would be if he needs to be kept calm for the sake of his heart.'

'You are probably right, but as I said, he is only human and... no never mind.'

'Please, tell me,' Honour said and put her hand on his arm. It felt shockingly forward, but she really needed to know.

'I probably shouldn't say this, but I feel I can trust you. Felix is lonely. He's surrounded by servants and cared for by my aunt, but he has precious few friends, and he could use a few more.'

'I see, well, maybe you should help him with that then, rather than with finding him a wife.'

'You know, that's a very good point, Miss Seaborn. I will set about doing just that.'

The Captain looked like he was about to expand on the topic when a very pregnant young woman pushed herself through the crowd and swooped down on him. She was dressed in a dark wine red dress that was the very height of fashion, and she nearly stifled the captain with a feather boa as she leaned down to give him a warm hug.

'Percy, just the man I was hoping to find,' she said with a wide grin.

'Celia, my dear, should you be at a party in your interesting condition?'

'Probably not but as Bellamy is away on business I have escaped from the house and am determined to have a little fun,' Celia said and looked meaningfully at Honour.

'I beg your pardon,' Percy said. 'May I introduce Miss Seaborn? Miss Seaborn, my cousin Lady Celia Bellamy who is apparently playing hooky this evening.'

'Don't mind him,' Celia said with a big lazy smile as she shook hands with Honour. 'Percy is always funning. Bellamy wouldn't mind terribly to hear I've come to this party. Besides, I am behaving myself and will make an early night of it.'

'Be sure that you do, miss,' Percy said.

Honour wondered if any husband would be relaxed about his wife being out of the house without him. It seemed that this young matriarch didn't give a fig either way and Honour warmed to her because of it. She appeared to be a woman who knew her own mind and acted on it.

'So, Miss Seaborn,' Celia said, 'How is it that you know this reprobate?'

'Oh, I don't,' Honour said. 'That is, we've just been introduced.'

'Miss Seaborn is a cousin of Lady Giddings,' Percy said.

Honour noted a slight stiffening of Lady Bellamy's face that she quickly schooled to give away nothing but polite indifference. She'd seen it on the faces of too many women to be offended. Honour suspected that if she wasn't related to Isolde, she might feel the same way as the other women.

'Your cousin is making a great impression upon London this season, Miss Seaborn,' Celia said.

'Yes,' Honour said, 'so it would appear.'

'Well, I hope you don't mind if I steal Percy away from you, but I must have a private conversation with him.'

'Must you?' Percy said.

'It is imperative!' Celia said.

'Of course,' Honour said, gave the two a curtsy and allowed the surging crowd to carry her away. She was sorry their meeting had come to such an abrupt end.

Percy watched as Miss Seaborn vanished into the crowd and said, 'That was hardly fair, Celia.'

'I know, but considering her relative I have very little wish to speak to Miss Seaborn,' Celia said.

She settled on the space lately vacated by Honour and fanned herself rapidly.

'Ah, so I was right, you don't like La Giddings.'

'No I don't, Percy. She has all the men trailing after like so many hungry dogs. She thinks she can snap her fingers and they'll all jump to her command. She's insufferable. Only you men are so dense you don't see it.'

'We, men?'

'Don't tell me you were making up to Miss Seaborn because you are actually interested in her.'

'Well no, I wasn't. But before you jump in with an I told you so, I will hastily add that I'm not interested in Lady Giddings either.'

'Then why on earth are you talking to her cousin?'

'It's a long story.'

'All right, well you can tell me, but not before you've spilt the beans on what is happening with Felix.'

'What?'

'Percy! Come now, he was in the newspapers. All of London knows he's looking for a wife but, typical of my mother, she never mentioned it to me. So when all the gossipmongers came calling at my house for tea, I had nothing I could tell them. Not one word! It was shameful. They all left my house thinking I was frightfully discreet, which couldn't be further from the truth.'

Percy burst out laughing and said, 'But, Celia, what do you think I can tell you?'

'Everything! I'll bet you knew about these plans before they got into the papers.'

'I learned of them at Felix's birthday party from which, incidentally, you were conspicuous by your absence.'

'I sent him a card,' Celia said with a guilty flush. 'That's how Felix and I communicate. He sends me cards on all major events, my wedding, Edmund's birth, and no doubt I will receive another when my second child is born.'

'Are you telling me that Felix has never even met young Edmund?'

'Well, of course, they've met. When Edmund was born, I took him everywhere and showed him to everyone. Felix was with my mother in the drawing room when I took Edmund round to meet mother.'

'Ah.'

'He was charming, actually. He refused to hold the baby. I think for fear he'd drop him, which I feared too so was rather relieved about, but he held his finger out, and Edmund grabbed onto it. Then he said he appeared a very healthy and happy baby.'

'And that was all?'

'Pretty much. Felix did pay Edmund more attention than any of the other gentlemen I showed my little treasure off to. But it was more curiosity than anything else, I think. He watched Edmund as if he were astonishing. Like he was some fantastical creature. And afterwards, he sent a gift for Edmund, a little silver rattle.'

'That was kind of him.'

'Yes, it was. Some people might say he was merely fulfilling a duty, but Felix isn't like that. He sent the gift because he wanted to.'

'I'm glad you realise that – most people don't.'

'Most people have never met Felix, so they wouldn't know one way or the other.'

'You two are of an age, aren't you?'

'We're practically twins. I was born a week before Felix. When Lord Peergrave died, mother transferred all her attention and energy to Felix and handed me over to nanny.'

'Do you resent that?'

'Good God, no! I always felt bad for Felix that he had my mother's undivided attention. It meant we girls could get on and do everything we wanted to. Nanny was a very kind woman, and after her, we had a series of governesses. We learned how to control them so they didn't cause us undue discomfort and nanny would always step in if they did try and harm any of her little chicks as she called us.

'Now enough of the interrogation. It's my turn. What is happening with this intention to wed? Why did it start, and why did it come to such an abrupt stop? Surely, that wasn't as a result of the news coverage?'

'It wasn't,' Percy said and looked around to make sure nobody in the crowd around them was listening in. 'Felix, as much as your mother, does want to get married. I don't like the idea or the execution of the plan, but neither of them would listen to me.'

'That is no surprise. So what happened?'

'Felix collapsed. I don't know if it was the strain of the visits or just a gradual deterioration in his health. It was touch and go for a while, but he seems to be on the road to recovery again. I'm surprised your mother didn't tell you about it.'

'She doesn't. Mostly because she doesn't think about us girls much at all. But also, I suspect, because Felix doesn't like his condition to be broadcast. So, does this mean the search for a bride will continue?'

'Ah, well... as to that... the last person Felix met was Lady Giddings.'

'No!' Celia gasped.

'You are quick to comprehend,' Percy said. 'I'm afraid he's smitten.'

'That's terrible news, Percy. La Giddings is heartless, absolutely heartless. She'll only be interested in Felix for his money and his title in that order. Somebody has to warn him.'

'It would be a waste of time, believe me, I know. I've been similarly bowled over by a woman and nothing anyone said at the time made the least impression.'

'So what are you doing? Why are you talking to the cousin?'

'Because I am trying to loosen La Giddings' grip and for that, I need to know as much as I can about her. Besides, Felix also noticed Miss Seaborn.'

'Noticed her? Of course, he did, he takes in everything.'

'He said she was a neat dresser.'

'So?'

'He likes that. It may be a small thing on which to pin my hopes, but it is something to work with.'

'Percy, there is no way Miss Seaborn can compare to her devastatingly attractive cousin.'

'She is pretty, though.'

'She is, but not in a stand out way and never when she's in the same room as Isolde Giddings.'

'She's all I have, Celia, and she did give me one good suggestion.'

'Good lord, you didn't tell her everything, did you?'

'Of course not. I don't know Miss Seaborn. I would never reveal my hand.'

'So how could she possibly offer a suggestion?'

'She thought Felix should have more friends, that's all, and she's right. He needs to get to know more people. That way, he has more to compare La Giddings to.'

'How are you going to do that? Especially when he has to avoid anyone who is feeling poorly themselves?'

'I'm not entirely sure, but you could help, Celia.'

'By doing what? I can't introduce him to new people. He'll think that very odd.'

'No, but you could visit. You could be a friend.'

Celia blinked at him and said, 'Be Felix's friend?'

'Why not?'

'I don't know. I suppose because I've never considered it. Mother didn't encourage it, and I don't expect she'd start now. Good Lord, Percy, we didn't even have our meals together for fear that we girls would either tire him or infect him with the multitude of colds that did the rounds of our nursery.'

'But you're a grown woman now. You are unlikely to either tire him or infect him with anything. He could use a couple of sensible women around him so he can see how you behave.'

'And provide a contrast to Lady Giddings?'

'I certainly hope so.'

'Mmm, I'll think about it, but I still don't think mother would approve.'

'Bring Edmund along. It would be good for Felix to get to know him better too,' Percy said. 'And now, I am going to escort you home for I'm sure your husband will not approve if you get home at three in the morning. Where is Bellamy anyway?'

'I honestly have no idea,' Celia said with a chuckle.

Percy shook his head at Celia's nonchalance as to her husband's whereabouts, but he wasn't surprised. Bellamy, some years Percy's senior, was a very austere man who was involved in some secret way in affairs of government. Percy had never really understood what Celia saw in the man. She was a fun-loving creature with an excellent sense of humour and a personality every bit as strong as her mother's.

After talking to Captain Shawcross, the party had fallen flat for Honour, and she was relieved when Isolde finally decided to head for home.

'What a marvellous party!' Isolde said as she sank into the carriage and put her feet up on the seat opposite.

'Yes, it was rather good.' Honour said, but she sensed Isolde meant more and she had an inkling of what it might be.

'I met the Duke of Morley's cousin this evening,' Isolde said. 'Apparently, the duke collapsed after I'd been to visit and that's why he never got back in touch.'

'So I heard,' Honour said.

It was as well the mystery had been solved for Isolde was growing unbearable with her constant checking of the post.

'I knew it had to be something,' Isolde said with a flick of her hair. 'His grace was bound to want to see me again.'

'Did his cousin say when he might be back in touch?'

'He didn't, but no doubt it will be soon. I said I could visit again but the cousin, Captain Shawcross, didn't think the duke was up to seeing visitors yet.'

'Captain Shawcross?' Honour said and pricked up her ears. It was unusual for Isolde to remember the names of men she wasn't interested in. 'Did you like him?'

'He was very dashing in his uniform, don't you think?'

'Really, Isolde? You, interested in a soldier?'

'Not just any soldier. He's with the Royal Horse Guards.'

'All the same, you've never been interested in a single military man the whole time I've known you. Let alone what you say about my mother running off with my father.'

'Well... well, Captain Shawcross is different.'

'Is he?' Honour said as she examined her cousin more closely. It was difficult to make out much in the dim light of the coach. 'In what way is he different?'

'If you must know, he stands to inherit.'

'Inherit what?' Honour said.

'From the duke. Can you imagine that, Honour? Can you imagine if Captain Shawcross inherited the duke's title and all his money? Then I could have a handsome, healthy husband as well as a title and great wealth.'

'You think the captain will inherit? What gave you that idea?'

'Something he let slip. It's of no great consequence.'

'Isn't it?' Honour murmured.

She found herself wondering what the captain was up to. She thought it highly unlikely that he was first in line to inherit from the duke. She would have to do some research into the family. He didn't seem the kind of man who would brag about an inheritance either, or be so feckless as to let anything slip.

It also made her wonder again why he'd sought her out. She had a feeling she was being sized up. But as the captain merely chatted with her and made no amorous advances, she was sure he wasn't directly interested in her. That made the whole lot more puzzling.

Surely it couldn't have been because of anything the duke said. Then again, what other reason would the captain have for speaking to her? She was frankly astonished that the duke had mentioned her at all. Aside from a slight acknowledgement of her presence, he'd hardly torn his eyes away from Isolde. Maybe the captain was right, and he did see more than people realised.

'I'm going to write to him,' Isolde said, breaking in on Honour's musings.

'Who? The captain?'

'No, silly, the duke.'

'Really? Why?'

'Because the captain thought he was still too unwell to receive visitors. I want him to know I'm waiting for him and that I'll be available at any time he wants.'

'But I thought you were now more interested in the captain.'

'Honestly, Honour, you're being very stupid this evening. I'm not going to marry a penniless soldier when there is a duke for the taking.'

'But-'

'Obviously, I'll make sure the captain falls for me as well and waits for me till the duke dies. If his health is as precarious as everyone says that surely won't take long. Then I can marry Captain Shawcross.'

'Isolde, do you even hear yourself when you speak like that?' Honour gasped. 'How can you be so cold? You are playing with the lives of two people!'

'Don't be such a prude. This is the way of the world. You should stop lecturing me and make more of an effort to find yourself a husband too. After all, you can't always live with father and me.'

'I am aware of that,' Honour said and switched her attention to the view outside the coach window. It was easier to have these kinds of conversations with Isolde if she wasn't looking at her.

'So what are you going to do?' Isolde said.

'I don't know. Maybe I'll become a governess.' It was the first time Honour had said it out loud, and it made the whole notion feel that much more real.

'A governess! How can you even say that?'

'I can't see many alternatives. I don't have your beauty or a dowry, and I haven't found a man I'd like to marry or who would like to marry me.'

'No, Honour! You can't think like that. You just have to make more of an effort to talk to men at all the events we go to.'

'No doubt you're right but, maybe it's too soon. I still miss my father, and I find it difficult to dredge up any interest in men just yet.'

'You should take a look at the soldiers. You obviously don't mind living with very little money or with the discomfort of travel. You would make an ideal wife for one of them.'

'Really, Isolde, now you're telling me I should do exactly what you condemn my mother for doing?'

'It's better than being a governess! How will I be able to tell people you're my cousin once I'm a duchess if you take such a lowly position?'

'The duke doesn't seem to mind that his cousin is a soldier, and they appear quite close.'

'It isn't the same thing. You have to make more of an effort.'

The problem was, Honour thought, even if she made an effort, men in search of a wife weren't interested in her. The thought of marrying a soldier, much to her surprise, also didn't appeal. It was an unsettled life continually moving from one military camp or battlefield to another. She'd seen the world that way. She'd lived on three continents throughout her childhood. Now she felt a yen to settle down.

She wanted to put down roots and find a place to make her own. That was unlikely as a governess. But she had no other skills, other than the ability to keep house and make things last longer than they usually would. She wasn't qualified for anything else.

She'd realised that, while she'd gained a great deal from her life on the road with the army, she'd lost an equal amount. She had very few friends. Most were the offspring of military men themselves and not in England. She had no connections in the country and precious few relatives.

She also had little in common with the young women she met who'd led very sheltered lives in their parents' homes. Their first real foray into the world was when they emerged into society to find a husband. It made Honour despair about finding her place in this world.

Chapter Ten

'Doctor Morton,' Felix said as he woke to find the doctor sitting beside him lit by the warm glow of morning.

'Good morning, your grace. How are you feeling?'

'Better, thank you. I assume Grantley told you I sat up yesterday?'

'He did, and he mentioned some infernal invention.'

'A hoist,' Felix said and couldn't suppress a smile.

'You're amused at your valet's alarm?'

'Not at his alarm, just his disapproval of anything new.'

'But you know that he was acting on my orders that you should not rise.'

'I do, and I am sorry, but I couldn't stay on my back for another minute. And I did lie down again after half an hour.'

'How did you feel then?'

'Fine.'

'Your grace, I've told you before, you have to tell me the truth. How do you really feel?'

'Weak.'

'Other than that?'

'Not much different to before.'

'You didn't feel dizzy or experience any pain?'

'No,' Felix said and watched his doctor watching him, gauging whether he was telling the truth.

Apparently, he accepted his patient's assessment and said, 'In that case, it's all right for you to start sitting up again. But, we will talk before you do anything more than that. You may not attempt a walk till I give you the all-clear.'

'Very well.'

'Mmm, on the whole, your grace, you are a very good patient.'

'I'm no fool, doctor; I know well enough you keep me alive.'

'I do what I can. Yours is the burden to ensure you follow my instructions.'

'Doctor Morton, can I ask you something?' Felix said. 'It's of a personal nature so feel free to turn me down if you don't wish to answer.'

'Ask, and I shall see.'

'I was wondering... whether you had ever been married?'

'Ah, well, no, I have never entered into matrimony.'

'Might I ask why? It isn't because you've been working for me, is it?'

'Oh no, nothing to do with that. Being taken on as your physician was something of a godsend really. It means I don't have to worry about finding lodgings or someone to see to my daily needs. As for a wife, well, I'm not really the marrying kind. It is not a state that appealed to me.'

'It didn't?'

'I am a creature who prefers his own comfort before anybody else's. If I had a wife and children, I fear I would be neglectful or resentful of their intrusion upon my quiet life.'

'Oh,' Felix said genuinely surprised at the doctor's description of himself.

'You feel differently,' Dr Morton said. 'Which is hardly surprising. I have always felt you are more warm-hearted than I am. You care for the people around you.'

'But you're a doctor, surely you care for people.'

'I care for my patients. But at the end of the day, I prefer to go to my rooms, close the door and settle in with a good book.'

'Which is why you join us so seldom for supper.'

'Most likely,' Dr Morton said with more of a grin than he was accustomed to giving.

Felix understood. Aunt Lavinia was hard work at the best of times but probably more so for a man who preferred his own company.

'Do you... do you think it is foolish of me to consider getting married?'

'Aaaah, well now, far be it for me to say, your grace.'

'But as my physician, you must surely have an opinion. Is it beyond my physical ability?'

'You are referring to procreation, are you?'

'In part. What is the point of being married if there is no intention to have children?'

'There are plenty of marriages where the marriage bed isn't shared, your grace. The one doesn't follow the other, but that isn't what you are asking, is it?'

'No,' Felix said but couldn't bring himself to be more explicit.

'I would say,' Dr Morton said, rubbing his chin as he considered. 'That if you were in a good state and proceeded with caution, that it would be possible. In your current condition, though, I wouldn't recommend it.'

'Do you think I can regain what I have lost and be able to go back to walking?'

'I don't see why not.'

'Do you think... that I got overexcited when I met Lady Giddings and that caused the attack?'

'I would say that was unlikely. It was an unfortunate coincidence, that's all. Although you were growing more tired from the visits so they should be reconsidered as well. I would say seeing so many strangers was more of a strain than coming face to face with a young lady who I have had described to me as the very pinnacle of perfection.'

'She is magnificent.'

'Well, then I can see no reason why you shouldn't continue to see her.'

'Thank you, Doctor, you have relieved my mind.'

'I only wish I could help you more, your grace,' Dr Morton said and stood to leave.

Grantley appeared the moment the doctor left the room and said, 'Your breakfast is ready, your grace, and Dr Morton has said we can return to solid food.'

'Thank God for that. He also said I can go back to sitting, so you may as well help me up straight away and get Chivers to bring in my mail.'

'Your mail, your grace?'

'Don't tell me I haven't had anything, Grantley, I find that hard to believe.'

'Well as to that, sir, I can't possibly say. Although Dr Morton did say, you were not to be overtaxed by having to deal with business.'

'My correspondence is always rather dry. I doubt it will provide even a flicker of excitement and I do need to know what is going on. Bring in the latest papers as well.'

'Very good, your grace,' Grantley said in his least encouraging tone of voice.

Felix didn't mind, at least he was taking back charge, and that felt positive. He hated when he was so ill that even his very light duties of managing his household and estate were delegated to somebody else.

'I think I'll see Mr Forsyth this afternoon too.'

'As you wish, sir, I'll let him know,' Grantley said.

Felix resisted commenting on the unspoken which amounted to, if you still feel up to it by this afternoon. He would tell on that one. In the meantime, he was looking forward to his first proper meal in an age.

Felix was rather pleased with his breakfast. Eating often felt like an effort, but today it was a rare treat. Mrs Grayson had outdone herself with the lightest fluffiest of scones on which he spread lashings of slightly salty butter topped with strawberry jam.

He was just sipping on a milky tea when there was a discreet knock at the door.

'Your post, your grace,' Chivers said and held out a salver with a modest pile of letters. 'I've also brought up all the newspapers and magazines of the last week so you might catch up on current events.'

'Thank you, Chivers, that will keep me busy.' Felix said as he put down his teacup. He paused and wrinkled his nose. 'What is that peculiar smell?'

'Ah, it's a letter, your grace,' Chivers said, keeping his face impeccably neutral. 'It appears to have been doused in perfume.'

'Good God, really?'

'It's the one in the lavender envelope, your grace,' Chivers said and bowed himself out.

'A perfumed letter,' Felix murmured as he reached through his pile of correspondence to get at this singular item.

He'd never received such a thing before, and he felt a delicious tingle of anticipation. His heart also thumped uncomfortably quickly for he knew who he wished it was from and hoped he wouldn't be disappointed.

He sliced the envelope open, ignoring the scent. He would consider that later. There was a thin sheet folded within. Felix opened it out, noting the trembling of his hand.

Dear Lord Peergrave, it started. Felix quickly checked the bottom of the page and his heart gave another frightened kick. Written at the bottom was, *yours in friendship, Isolde Giddings.*

'She wrote!' he gasped. It was such an unexpected thing, but he wasn't going to dwell. First, he had to see what it said.

Dear Lord Peergrave, he read. *Your cousin, Captain Shawcross, was kind enough to inform me last night that you are indisposed. I am so sorry to hear that and hope you will be feeling better shortly. It is a miserable thing to be poorly. If you wish for any support or entertainment while you are stuck in bed, please do feel free to call upon me. I am aware this may sound a bit forward as we have only just met. But I felt an instant connection with you upon that first meeting, and I hope you felt the same.*

Felix was so overwhelmed by the kind sentiment that he was quite shaken. He gazed out of the window for a moment, trying to regain his composure.

'She wrote,' he said as a feeling of great joy filled his heart.

He snatched up the envelope and gave it a deep sniff. It was too much and brought on a fit of sneezing which brought Grantley into the room trailing Poole.

'Your grace, are you all right?'

'I'm better than all right, Grantley,' Felix said through a stuffy nose. 'But I would appreciate a handkerchief.'

'Right away, your grace.'

'Then bring me paper and pen. I have a couple of letters to write.'

'Are you sure, your grace?' Grantley said as he handed over a hanky.

'I won't strain myself writing. I promise you.'

Felix opened his eyes and blinked up at the canopy of his bed. He hadn't intended to fall asleep.

'Felix?' Lady Lavinia said.

'What time is it?'

'Two o'clock. Would you like me to read to you today?'

'No I'm fine, thank you, Aunt,' Felix said and reached for his bell.

Grantley and Poole appeared immediately, and Grantley said, 'Would you like to sit up, your grace?'

'I would,' Felix said and winced as Poole pulled him upright. 'I'll be glad when Mr Testwood's hoist is ready,' Felix murmured. 'I hadn't realised up till then how uncomfortable it is to be manhandled. It's no fun for my people either is it, Poole?'

'Oh... it's no bother, your grace,' Poole said flicking an alarmed look towards Lady Lavinia.

'I'm not sure I like the idea of a hoist,' Lady Lavinia said, ignoring the valets as they bowed and effaced themselves.

'It is more comfortable.'

Felix was too tired to have an argument with his aunt today and so didn't bother making more of a case.

She must have realised it as she picked up the book on his bedside table. 'Are you sure you don't want me to continue reading to you?' But as she opened the book, the lavender envelope slipped out and drifted to the floor. Lady Lavinia reached for it and her nose wrinkled in distaste. 'Good heavens, Felix, what is this?'

'What does it look like?' Felix said with a slight smile.

'It smells like the inside of a lady's boudoir, and really... lavender?'

'It's from Lady Giddings,' Felix said, watching his aunt more closely. At the same time, he cursed himself for leaving the envelope where his aunt might see it. Now he was going to have to tell her the rest.

'Lady Giddings wrote to you?'

'She heard I was unwell and sent me a note wishing me a speedy recovery.'

'Did she indeed? That was very forward of her. No well brought up young woman should be sending unsolicited letters to a single man. It was unsolicited, wasn't it?'

'I didn't write to her. But I did ask Percy to let her know why she hadn't heard from me since her visit, should their paths cross. Apparently last night they did.'

'Well, I don't approve,' Lady Lavinia snapped.

Felix nodded and said, 'I've invited her for tea this Friday.'

'For tea? This Friday? But Felix, you know I won't be here on Friday. I've been telling you for weeks, I'm visiting my sister, Anne. I can't possibly rearrange. She and her husband are only in London for the day, and then they're heading off to India to see Arthur.'

'I didn't forget.'

'Felix! You did it deliberately? You made sure I would be out of the house before you invited that... that young woman to visit?'

'Don't be angry, Aunt,' Felix said. He laid his hand on hers, which still maintained a tight grip on the letter. 'You are a very forceful woman. I just wanted to give Lady Giddings a chance to talk to me and not have to constantly justify herself to you.'

'But you're still so unwell. How can you risk a meeting in your current condition?'

'I have written this morning to ask Mr Testwood to add an arm to the hoist he is designing for me. I have sent him extra money so that everything may be ready in time. He and my staff will hoist me into the bath chair. Grantley will then wheel me out to the drawing room. So there will be a minimum of strain.'

'I don't like it.'

'I'm sorry, Aunt, but I am going to go through with this.'

'Then I will cancel my visit with Anne and be here to make sure you are all right.'

'Don't do that. I know how much you have missed your sister. Don't lose this opportunity to see her just because of me.'

'I have to make sure you are all right.'

'I will be fine. If you like, I will have Doctor Morton on standby just in case.'

'No, I can't let you do this alone. I will see Anne at some other time.'

'Aunt Lavinia, please, you have to let me do this on my own,' Felix said but without much hope. His aunt was very worked up, more worked up than he'd seen her in a long time.

Then, much to his surprise, she nodded and said, 'Very well, if that is what you want.'

'You'll go on your visit to Aunt Anne?'

'I will, after all, I have no idea when I will see her again.'

'Thank you,' Felix said. It was so out of character for his aunt to give in that it made him wonder what was going on. 'As you will still be going to see Aunt Anne I hope you will take the present I have bought for Arthur with you. It's just a small token for his wedding so it shouldn't add unduly to their luggage.'

'I suppose you don't mind at all that he's marrying an Indian woman.'

'She's a princess from an extremely wealthy family.'

'I know, but she isn't one of us.'

'Arthur doesn't care, so far be it for me to say anything.'

'Anne isn't happy. She had her sights set on Lady Darlington's daughter. She's a very pretty blonde girl. You know Lady Darlington.'

'I believe we have met, yes,' Felix said. 'I thought her eyes protruded alarmingly. If her daughter is the same, I doubt she would appeal to Arthur.'

'She's a very well brought up young lady.'

'I'm sure that's true.'

'Well... we'll not agree. You are in a very contrary frame of mind today, Felix, so I think it best I leave you to rest some more.'

'Thank you, I believe I will take a nap,' Felix said.

He was surprised that his aunt was so willing to give in today. Usually, she would stay and try and convince him of the merits of Lady Darlington's daughter. For even though he'd agreed with her in the hopes of putting an end to the argument, they both knew he didn't really agree.

That would usually result in her going over all the person's good points until he called a halt and, when possible, made his escape. Maybe his latest attack had made her less willing to win her points. Or maybe, he looked worse than he realised and she was still being careful. Either way, it was curious behaviour on his aunt's part.

CHAPTER ELEVEN

H onour ran her fingers along the spines of a collection of books on a dusty shelf. Neither her uncle nor Isolde were great readers, and until she'd arrived in the house, she suspected none of the books had been disturbed in years. Her uncle only used the room as an office, and the desk he usually occupied was piled high with newspapers opened at the stock pages and heavily underlined. That was his passion.

As he was a negligent homeowner, his staff had deemed it safe to ignore the books. Honour had tried to get them to at least give the shelves a thorough dusting, but she had yet to succeed. As a poor relative, she was paid very little attention.

She now found what she was looking for. It was a somewhat out of date Who's Who, but it would be sufficient for her needs. She flicked through the pages until she came to the Peergraves and checked the line of succession.

'Are you ready, Honour?' Isolde said as she slammed into the library.

'I am.'

Honour snapped the Who's Who shut and slipped it back onto the shelf confident that Isolde wouldn't ask what she'd been up to.

'I've been looking everywhere for you and calling and calling. What are you doing in Daddy's library anyway?'

'Just looking something up,' Honour said. Then because she needed to divert Isolde's attention, she added, 'Are you really set upon wearing that red dress?'

'Of course I am. Why wouldn't I? It's my most beautiful dress and red suits me. Everybody tells me so,' Isolde said as she grabbed Honour's elbow and hurried her into the hall.

'All the men compliment you on that dress.'

'Well, it's a man we're visiting today.'

'One who dresses in simple but elegant fashion and your dress is... it's very showy.'

'My dear, Honour, you let me worry about his grace. I promise you he won't mind a bit.'

'Very well.'

'Besides you look positively dowdy in that grey dress. If anyone is going to be ignored, it will be you.'

'I am not the one the duke wants to see.'

'Also true, and I suppose it will be good to have you looking so sober. It might convince the duke's awful aunt that I, at least, have a boring chaperone. Now come on, I don't want to be late,' Isolde said and ran out of the front door to their carriage.

Honour straightened her hair, took a quick look at herself in the hall mirror and made her way outside at a leisurely pace. Until she'd started living with Isolde, she'd been considered an attractive woman. The soldiers at the balls she'd been to with father were always keen to dance with her.

Some were overly keen, but father had dealt with them. Only one firm talking to was ever required to keep them in their place. Here she was practically invisible. The men who did speak to her had all, besides Captain Shawcross, been trying to get an introduction to her glorious cousin.

She smiled a thanks up at the footman who held the coach door open for her and climbed inside. She'd barely sat down when the carriage pulled away and headed towards the duke's house.

Isolde talked non-stop in excited anticipation of their upcoming meeting. Honour paid her only half her attention with a murmured yes every now and then in the required places. The rest of her mind was bent on working out what Captain Shawcross was up to.

He'd plainly led Isolde to believe he would inherit from the duke. It was the kind of thing Isolde wouldn't have come up with on her own.

That was why she'd been examining the Who's Who. It told her that Captain Shawcross was so distantly related to the duke as to make their connection just one step closer than mere friends. So why had he lied?

He'd also spent time talking to her and sounding her out. Her father had always said a good soldier reconnoitres the ground before he goes into battle. She had the odd feeling that the captain was doing just that.

'We're here!' Isolde said as she hopped out of the coach then turned around to Honour. 'Quickly, tell me, how do I look?'

'Perfect, as always,' Honour said as she followed Isolde into the duke's house. 'Not a curl out of place.'

The butler was waiting and with no delay showed the ladies into the drawing room.

'Lady Giddings, Miss Seaborn,' the duke said as he turned to meet them but remained seated in what Honour realised with surprise was a bath chair. 'Please forgive me for not getting up.'

Honour was also surprised by how pale and drawn he looked and... and scared. His hand shook as Isolde hurried over, offered her hand and sank a curtsy to him.

'Your grace, I'm so happy to see you again.' Isolde smiled as she took his hand in both of hers and settled into the chair beside the duke. 'I was so very sorry to hear from Captain Shawcross that you were unwell.'

'That is very kind of you to say so.' Felix gently removed his hand from Isolde's grasp and held it out to Honour. 'Miss Seaborn, it's good to see you again too.'

'Oh... thank you, your grace.'

Honour found herself inexplicably flustered as she hurried forward. She took the duke's hand in a firm grasp, thought better of it and quickly let go. For some reason, this elicited a smile from him.

To cover her embarrassment, she said, 'Will Lady Lavinia not be joining us today?'

'Her ladyship is out visiting her sister,' Felix said, his amusement deepening.

'Oh, that was clever of you,' Isolde said reclaiming the duke's attention.

He looked thrown for a minute and said, 'Clever?'

'It gives us a chance to get to know each other better,' Isolde said with a winning smile. 'I'm sure Lady Lavinia is a very kind lady, but it is so awkward when our elders are in the room.'

'I fear it is,' Felix said with a surprised laugh. 'Although, you didn't seem unduly awed by her last time, Lady Giddings.'

'Well, I tried not to show it, but she is a very grand personage, isn't she?'

'She can be somewhat austere at times, but she has my best interests at heart.'

'Captain Percy Shawcross, your grace,' the butler said reappearing as the captain strolled into the room.

'Percy?' Felix said, an eyebrow raised in query.

'Blame Aunt Lavinia, old boy,' Percy murmured. He turned a broad smile on the room, bowed deeply and said, 'Ladies, it is a pleasure to see you both again.'

'Captain Shawcross,' Isolde said. 'What a surprise.'

'And a pleasure, I hope, Lady Giddings?'

'That remains to be seen, sir,' Isolde said with a laugh.

'If you're staying, Percy, you'd better sit down,' Felix said.

'Of course, old boy.' Percy's lazy smile lingered on his lips as he selected a chair on the other side of Isolde. 'So tell me, Lady Giddings, how did you enjoy the racing?'

'The racing?' Felix said.

'There was the jolliest party at Epsom Downs,' Isolde said turning sparkling eyes on Felix. 'Overbrook laid it on, and he must have invited half of London. Isn't that right, Captain Shawcross?'

'Oh, half of London at least,' Percy said.

Honour watched the conversation with deepening interest. The duke didn't look thrilled to have his dashing cousin, dressed in his military best, sitting in their midst. He looked the picture of health while the duke was still very unwell. And... the duke looked worried.

It wasn't just his cousin, Honour realised. He'd known he was taking a risk seeing Isolde so soon. Honour wondered why he'd done it. Why was he showing Isolde his worst side, especially when it was obvious he was desperate for her to like him?

She wished she could reassure him. She wanted to tell him that no matter what, Isolde was his for the taking. She just couldn't.

There were so many reasons. The most obvious being that you couldn't blurt out, 'Don't worry, Isolde wants your money and title. It doesn't matter what you look like or how ill you are. She'll make sure she gets your ring on her finger.'

She couldn't be that vulgar. Besides, she didn't want Isolde to have this man. He seemed a decent sort of person. He was smitten beyond sense, but he didn't deserve to have his life ruined by a heartless girl.

Maybe that was what his cousin thought too. Maybe that was why Captain Shawcross was doing what he could to salt the ground and prevent a marriage.

He seemed to be doing rather well at the moment. He dominated the conversation, bringing up events where he'd also seen Isolde. The captain drew Isolde into his conversation and left the duke without any way of joining in.

Isolde wasn't playing along though and gave the captain a playful slap on his arm. 'For shame, Captain, you can't keep mentioning parties, you'll bore his grace.'

'I'm sorry,' Percy said, looking at Felix. Honour felt like he was making a bigger apology than the obvious. 'What should we talk about?'

'I don't mind,' Felix said. 'You sound like your week has been a whirlwind of activities.'

'It has been quite a week,' Isolde said, taking the duke's hand. 'I can't tell you how happy I was that I couldn't go to the planned indoor picnic today because I was coming here instead. I am utterly shattered.'

'Now you're just being kind.'

'It's the truth, your grace, upon my honour. I couldn't face another party, not this week. I am even beginning to dream of the summer. Everyone returns to their estates in the country, and I can get some sleep. I doubt I've been to bed before three in the morning for a month.'

'Then you have great stamina.'

'Not at all. We all do it because we have to. I am sure half the young ladies are just praying some kind soul will propose so that we may settle down to a quieter life.'

Honour blinked at Isolde's blatant play, and the captain laughed and said, 'I fear you are exaggerating for my cousin's benefit, Lady Giddings. I, for one, love the season.'

'But some of us are more sober,' Isolde said primly.

'Are you sober, Lady Giddings?' Felix said. 'I get the impression you are enjoying yourself tremendously with your round of parties.'

'Well... they are fun, but as I said, they can get a bit much. Then it is nice to just meet up with a few close friends for a quiet morning.'

'I'm sure that is true.'

'And what is just as true is that it's been a long visit,' Percy said. 'I have strict instructions from Lady Lavinia to make sure his grace isn't tired out. So may I walk you ladies to the door?'

Honour stood up at that instruction. It was so much like the orders her father gave that she did it without thinking. Isolde looked put out and possibly inclined to argue the case. The duke, much to Honour's surprise, looked absolutely astonished.

So, his cousin was acting out of character, Honour thought. She was sure now that the captain was in a battle with Isolde. One where he was apparently willing to alienate his cousin to detach what he must think of as a bad match.

Honour was in agreement but only because she knew Isolde. She didn't feel like she'd learned very much more about the duke. He hadn't managed to get a word in edgewise this morning.

'May I come in?' Percy said when he returned to Felix's room after seeing the ladies out.

'Do I have a choice?' Felix said.

He was unaccustomedly angry with his cousin. He was also annoyed that he'd arrived when he was still attached to the harness. He was only halfway towards being winched back into bed, with Mr Testwood standing anxiously by watching the two valets operating the equipment.

'I'm sorry,' Percy said. 'But it really wasn't my idea. Aunt Lavinia insisted that as she couldn't be present I had to be, and you know how forceful she can be.'

'She can be very persuasive,' Felix said, in no way mollified.

'It was more than that. You know Aunt Lavinia doesn't like me. It was important precisely because she called on me. Me! She'd only do that if things were serious.'

'Mmm,' Felix said and waved away his staff. He was thankful that Testwood took the hint and left with them.

'What possessed you, Felix?' Percy said as soon as they were alone.

'What are you talking about?'

'Inviting Lady Giddings over when you look like this,' Percy said, throwing his arms out to encompass his cousin lying in his bed.

'I wanted her to know... I needed her to see me at my worst. I don't want any secrets. I don't want her to think I'm mildly ill, but can sit and walk around with ease. She needs to know the truth. That way if she decides... if she decides she couldn't stand that, she'll distance herself immediately. Better that she steps away now rather than that I fall for her, propose and then she sees me at my worst and decides she couldn't live with me.'

'And?'

'And what?'

'Do you think she will distance herself now?'

'I don't know. Maybe I would have a clearer sense if you hadn't come today. You distracted Lady Giddings and kept her so busy reminiscing about parties she hardly noticed me.'

Because it was too painful to look at his healthy cousin, Felix stared down at his blankets rubbing an edge between his fingers.

'Oh she noticed you, don't you worry about that.'

'What's that supposed to mean?'

'I was trying to distract her. Maybe keep her from seeing how very ill you looked today, but it was hard work. She kept trying to bring you into the conversation.'

'Do you think that means she likes me?'

'I'm pretty sure if you proposed she'd accept.'

'That isn't what I asked.'

'Well, it's all I can tell you.'

'You think she's a gold digger.'

'I think you could do better.'

'I love her.'

'You scarcely know her.'

'She's cheerful and bright and unfazed when she sees somebody ill. Lady Giddings is the most natural person I've ever met. She completely overlooks my illness and treats me like everyone else in the room, and I like that.'

'Fine, I'm sorry. I was heavy-handed this morning. It isn't my intention to fall out with you now. Let's just agree to wait and see, shall we?

'What if I decide to propose to her anyway, without yours and Aunt Lavinia's blessing?'

'That would be your choice, of course. Just don't do something life changing in a fit of pique, please.'

Felix closed his eyes. He felt dizzy, tired and more distressed by Percy's behaviour than he could stand. 'I need to rest.'

'Of course. I'm sorry, I shouldn't have treated you the way I have,' Percy said and gave his shoulder a squeeze.

Felix barely managed a parting smile as Percy left. Funny how the morning had not gone as planned. He'd played so many scenarios out in his head. From Lady Giddings being so shocked by his appearance that she refused even to join him, to her replaying a touching scene where she resembled Florence Nightingale. What he hadn't anticipated was the insertion of his handsome cousin who took over the gathering and left him with nothing to say. It was very out of character for Percy, and he felt deeply hurt by it.

He took a deep breath and said, 'I shan't be beaten.'

It was a phrase he'd used in his youth, and it felt childish to be resorting to it again. After all, he was a grown man now. He was a master of his own destiny. He could do as he pleased. The question was, what did he do now?

He had to calm down for a start, and consider things properly. This time he replayed the morning thinking more about Lady Giddings. She'd been charming. She was interested in him as much as in Percy and willing enough to humour both of them. It wasn't her fault Percy had barged in and dominated the conversation. Much as he didn't want to admit it, Percy was right, Lady Giddings had brought the conversation back more than once to include him.

That would seem to imply she was partial to him. The fact that she hadn't recoiled at the door was something else to be glad about. She'd sailed in the picture of delight to be seeing him again.

Her cousin hadn't been as blithely unaware. She'd looked at first shocked... no not shocked, dismayed possibly with a touch of worry. Who could blame her? He'd seen himself in the mirror and had to admit he looked haggard.

Still, it was nice that they'd both behaved like he wasn't some fragile being to be cosseted. In fact, they'd both treated him like they might any other visitor. That could be counted as a victory too.

He was probably far too used to the elderly relatives his aunt inflicted on him. They were more likely to tut over his parlous condition or tiptoe around him lest any sudden movement or loud noise caused him to suffer an attack. And if they weren't considering his health, they were discussing their own.

A large part of their conversation always revolved around their various diseases, aches and pains. They assumed that as Felix was ill, he would be interested in their complaints too. He wasn't.

It had been a relief to have visitors who didn't mention his health at all. It was one of the reasons he was so fond of Percy, he thought with a guilty twinge. He shouldn't hold a grudge. Percy, after all, had been acting on orders, even if he'd made a ham-fisted intervention. Now it was his turn to act, and he knew what he wanted to do.

He rang his bell, and as Grantley and Poole emerged, he said, 'Bring me that catalogue on my dresser please, Poole.'

'Are you feeling all right, your grace?' Grantley said.

'I'll do, thank you, Grantley. What's happened to Mr Testwood?'

'He went off home, sir. He was muttering something about another invention for you.'

'Was he indeed?' Felix said as he took the catalogue from Poole. 'Did he happen to mention what it was?'

'He didn't, not that I'm wanting to encourage him, sir.'

'You don't like the hoist?'

'We've never needed it before.'

'I dare say there are many things we take for granted these days that old-timers have said weren't needed before. We'll not make progress by avoiding the new,' Felix said flicking rapidly through the catalogue. 'I, for one, am glad. I like the hoist.'

'Very good, your grace,' Grantley said at his most neutral.

'Good man!' Felix said. It was as close as he could come to ribbing Grantley without offending him. 'Now, Poole, I have an errand for you.'

'You do, your grace?' Poole said looking very surprised, which earned him Grantley's discreet foot on his foot.

Felix pretended not to notice. 'I want you to go immediately to buy these two shawls, the red one and the grey one.'

'Ladies' shawls, your grace?' Poole said uncertainly.

'Gifts, Poole, but don't let the shop wrap them. Bring the wrapping paper back with you. I want to be sure of the shawls before we send them off.'

'Very good, your grace,' Poole said, executed a perfect bow, which Grantley was surely drilling him on, then hesitated.

'Now, Poole. Stop by Mr Forsyth for the money.'

'Yes, your grace,' Poole said, gave another bow and hurried away.

'Sit, Grantley,' Felix said.

'Your grace?'

'I want a chat.'

'A private one, your grace?' Grantley said and pulled a chair closer. He placed it an angle that would cause Felix the least strain to see him.

'I wanted to ask you about Poole. How is he coming on?'

'He's doing fine.'

'Just fine?'

'Truth to tell, I'm not the best judge, never having trained anyone in the role before.'

'No, I suppose that's true.'

'I had thought I might supplement my income training other gentlemen's gentlemen upon retirement, your grace, but now I'm not so sure.'

'That doesn't sound very restful.'

'Probably not.'

'Is the pension I've proposed insufficient?'

'Not at all, your grace, it's very generous. It's just... I've never not worked. I'm not sure I'll know what to do with myself.'

'You've always worked?'

'I started off as a bootblack, and I don't really remember life before that.'

'I never knew.'

'I don't mention it much. In fact, I doubt anybody in your household knows. Not that it's shameful or anything. Most people in service work their way up from something simpler.'

'Like Poole.'

'Indeed, he started off labouring in your fields, then into your stables, and finally a swift step up to here.'

'An inappropriate step?'

'You can do what you wish, your grace.'

'Yes,' Felix said. 'But locked away as I am, I sometimes miss the unwritten rules. It can cause difficulties when you break them. I don't wish to handicap Poole.'

'Well, it will be awkward for him having the household know of his humble roots. But as he's your valet, they won't be able to touch him, and after a few years it will hardly matter.'

'What would have been a more conventional route?'

'Mostly household servants become valets. I've never heard of them outdoors, making it to this position. Although some stable lads have made it into the ranks of the footmen but it's rare.'

'And how about you, Grantley? What was your next step after the bootblacking?'

'I became a footman. Then I was fortunate that I was working in a household where the eldest son was heading off to Oxford and needed a gentleman to look after him. The master of the house decided I'd be the best one for the job.'

'I see, so you went off to Oxford.'

'For five years.'

'Your young man became a don?'

'No, your grace. He was just a terrible student and kept changing his mind on what he wanted to study.'

'Ah, and you were his sole servant?'

'He lived in lodgings with a couple of friends. They shared a housekeeper, and each gentleman had a gentleman to look after him. I was fortunate that one of the other gentlemen was an actual valet.

I couldn't call myself that at the time. He had far more experience than I and was willing enough to impart his knowledge.'

'You didn't like your young man, Grantley?'

'You are astute, your grace. I'm afraid he was a rioter. He was always out on the town up to mischief. His dress was slovenly, and nothing I did could get him to smarten up. On top of that, he was more frequently drunk than sober.'

'Ah... I don't suppose you'll be so indiscreet as to tell me who he was?'

'I can't do that, your grace. Not that he amounted to anything so you'll not have heard of him anyway.'

'Then I'm happy to consign him to oblivion. Now tell me, how did you get away from him and land up working for my father?'

'I was offered a job by a minor nobleman while I was still at Oxford. He lured me away with the promise of more money and of living in London. I was tired of Oxford. It's a provincial little town over full of misbehaving students. This gentleman was also a natty dresser, and I yearned to put into practice all I'd been taught.'

'A big step up, then.'

'It was, but not as large as my next one. After a good number of years, by pure chance, your father once asked my gentleman who his valet was. He lured me away with the offer of even more money, and more importantly, the possibility of having an open purse when it came to buying his clothes. My then gentleman had a more constrained budget. It was an opportunity I couldn't let slip through my fingers.'

'Ah, were you with him long?'

'I started with him ten years before he was married, so yes, you could say I was.'

'Did you get on?'

'It isn't a requirement of the job, your grace, but yes we did. He was a lot like you, not high on the instep with the people around him.'

'More so with others?'

'He knew how to keep his distance. The thing with being a duke, especially a fabulously wealthy one, is that people are always trying to get close. Some for the reflected glory but most because they're after the money and influence. Your father was adept at keeping them all at a distance. He could depress pretension in even the most hardened of toadies.'

'Mmm, sometimes I'm glad my condition means I've never had to face people like that. Aunt Lavinia has kept them away very effectively.'

'She does her best.'

'Yes she does. Now tell me, after your high flying career, what made you give it all up to look after me?'

'Ah,' Grantley said and looked down at his hands clasped in his lap. 'I'm not entirely sure. I was shocked by your father's sudden death and in such a senseless accident. None of us could believe it for a while. And you were... you were hit the hardest by his death. I remember your face. You looked... lost.'

'It was the worst day of my life,' Felix murmured.

'Well, I felt I owed it to his grace, and to you, to stay and look after you. Fortunately, Lady Lavinia agreed that you needed a manservant and not just your nurse. And you know the rest.'

'I do, indeed. Thank you, Grantley. I'm sorry I never asked you any of this before. You've been a rock for me throughout my life, and I have been unforgivably ignorant about yours.'

'It's no matter, your grace. It isn't the way of the world for a master to know all about their servants. You have always known more than most about your people anyway.'

'It's my curiosity. I can't curb it, and my servants are the people I see more regularly than anyone else.'

Chapter Twelve

Honour lay in bed gazing at the sun-dappled ceiling and decided that she liked Sunday mornings. It was the only day of the week when she could lie in and have breakfast in bed, thereby avoiding Isolde and Lord Giddings. She rubbed along fine with Isolde as long as she wasn't talking about her conquests. But that was becoming such a frequent event that Honour found it increasingly tiresome.

It also exasperated her that Isolde had such success and never experienced a set back with any man. She hoped it would happen one day. Maybe Captain Shawcross would... Honour shook her head, she still didn't know what the captain was up to. He looked like a man determined to win Isolde at their meeting yesterday. Isolde had undoubtedly had that as her opinion on the coach ride home.

Lord Giddings was less of a trial. He was vaguely affectionate towards his daughter. And, as much as he gave her any attention at all, was in full agreement with Isolde that she would marry well.

Lord Giddings spent almost all his time buying, selling or thinking about shares. Honour had a suspicion that his obsession was akin to that of a gambler. Fortunately for Isolde, a man could lose less at stocks than at the gambling table, or so Honour had gathered.

A knock at the door drew her from her reverie. She recognised the pattern and really it was unlikely to be anyone else anyway.

'Come in, Doris,' she said.

'Oh, Miss Seaborn, look you have a parcel!' Doris said as she hurried to the bed.

'I do?' Honour said taking in the large brown paper wrapped square. 'Good heavens, who can it be from?'

'I don't know, miss, but Lady Giddings has one too, nearly identical in size and shape.'

'The mystery deepens then.'

Honour was uncertain how she felt about Isolde also receiving a parcel. Isolde would have been told the same thing by her maid, and she wouldn't be happy.

'Aren't you going to open it, miss?'

'Certainly,' Honour said and accepted the scissors from Doris.

With a snip she got rid of the string and then carefully eased the tape away and unfolded the neat wrapping.

'Oh, miss, it's lovely!' Doris breathed as a grey paisley shawl tumbled out.

'It is,' Honour said as she ran her fingers over the silky soft angora wool.

'Who is it from? Do you have an admirer, miss?'

'I suspect not, Doris. Not if the same gift was also sent to Lady Giddings.' Honour had a good idea of who the sender was. She searched through the folds of the shawl and found a gold embossed card. 'It's as I suspected, it's from the Duke of Morley.'

'Ooh, fancy getting a gift from a duke. That's ever so smart that is.'

'Mmm,' Honour said as she read the brief note. '*Dear Miss Seaborn, please accept this small gift as a thank you for your visit. I very much enjoyed the pleasure of your company and look forward to our next meeting. Yours, Felix Peergrave.*'

'Well, that's very prettily said. Fancy thinking this lovely shawl is a small gift,' Doris said.

'I expect to a duke, and one as wealthy as he is, it is no great thing to send such a gift. Now Doris, whatever you do, not a word to anybody else about this present.'

'But why ever not, miss?'

'I have my reasons, please, not a word.'

'As you wish, miss, but it's an awful shame, so it is. Now I've dallied long enough. I'll just pop off and fetch up your breakfast. You must be that hungry by now.'

'Thank you,' Honour said.

She ran her hand over the shawl again. It really was a lovely garment of a quality she was unaccustomed to having. The greys ranged from a dark charcoal all the way to something close to silver. It was also a kind gesture on the part of the duke. It made her like him all the more for it.

Their meeting had been an odd affair, Honour thought. She couldn't understand why the duke had agreed to meet Isolde when he was unwell. Was he so smitten that he couldn't bear to wait any longer?

He clearly still admired Isolde greatly, and his eyes lit up when he looked at her. He, more than most men, looked awestruck when he spoke to Isolde. It was as if he could scarce believe such beauty existed, let alone that said beauty was interested in him.

She had to say this for Isolde, she was made of stern stuff for she ignored the duke's illness and treated him like she might any other man. That had worked. It pleased the duke.

If it hadn't been for his cousin's arrival, the duke would have had a delightful visit. As it was, he'd practically been side-lined. It said much about his character that he'd not made a performance about that.

He'd accepted his cousin and tried his best to engage in polite conversation. He'd never once lost his temper even when his cousin was trying his best to charm Isolde in front of him. A tactic that would never work, for Isolde, was very clear about who she wished to marry.

She might be overconfident about marrying the duke. Still, she wasn't so foolish as to show a preference for another man in front of him. Honour supposed she'd best get used to thinking of the duke as a suitor. Especially if he was sending gifts.

It was a shame, really, because she found she liked him. She'd not expected to. Her father had brought her up to be suspicious of the great and the good, and you didn't get much higher than a duke.

He was also sickly and smitten by Isolde. That would, under normal circumstances, have put her off as well. But he'd noticed her.

This time she knew it for sure. The duke had seemed pleased to see her too. It wasn't as great as his pleasure at seeing Isolde, but he was pleased. He'd not treated her like an indigent relative to be ignored, but somebody to be included in conversation when he managed to get a word in edgewise.

'Honour, did the duke also send you a gift?' Isolde called as Honour left her room.

'Oh, yes,' Honour said as she steeled herself for the coming conversation. There was an accusatory tone to her cousin's voice. 'It was very kind of him.'

'Very kind?' Isolde snapped. 'What was it?'

'A shawl,' Honour said trying desperately not to annoy Isolde. 'A simple grey shawl.'

'A grey shawl? Really, he sent you something grey?'

'He probably chose it to match my dress. I was wearing grey yesterday after all.'

'I suppose you were. His grace sent me a shawl too, but mine's red and has a gold thread running through it. It matches my dress perfectly. And he sent a very gratifying card with it. He said he enjoyed my visit and hopes I will repeat it soon. What did your card say?'

'Less than that. He just thanked me for the visit.'

'Oh... well, I suppose that's all right then.'

'I'm sure he only sent me a gift out of politeness.'

Honour wondered whether she should push past her cousin, who was blocking the corridor or just stay where she was. She was uncomfortably aware that a couple of maids were hovering near the stairs with the express aim of listening in.

'You're probably right. The duke was being polite, but he'd better not make a habit of it. Especially when he starts sending me diamonds.'

'Diamonds, Isolde?'

'If he's serious about making me his wife he's going to have to show it with far more than a shawl. Overbrook has already sent me a pendant with a solitaire diamond. Maybe I should tell the duke that when we next meet.'

'I wouldn't, not like that.'

'Of course, not like that. But I may well hint, you know. I must make him show me he's serious.'

'There's no doubt he's serious,' Honour said. 'He was so anxious to see you and so worried about what you'd make of him that he looked nervous.'

'So you said yesterday. But if he loved me as much as you think he does he'd have sent me more than a shawl,' Isolde said. 'I wonder how ill he is too. I don't think there's time to waste. I have to get him to propose as soon as possible.'

Felix sat on his sofa with his feet propped up on a contrasting green cushion. He had a newspaper in his hands, but his mind was far away. He wondered whether Lady Giddings had received his gift yet and whether she liked it.

He hoped she liked it sufficiently well to send him another scented lavender letter. That thought made his pulse quicken, and he hastily shook his head to clear it and tried to focus back on the paper.

'Lady Bellamy is here, your grace, and asking if you're receiving visitors,' Chivers said providing much-needed distraction and, even more, rather a surprise.

'Lady Bellamy, really?' Felix said then gathered himself.
'Certainly, yes, show her in.'

'Here, your grace? Not the drawing room?'

'Is there some reason it shouldn't be here?'

'The thing is, her ladyship isn't alone.'

'She isn't?'

'She has young master Edmund with her, your grace. You
might not want a young boy in your rooms.'

'I don't mind about that,' Felix said, as he folded his
newspaper and put it on the side table.

He was altogether more surprised that Celia was visiting him
at all than worried about admitting a child into his rooms.

'He might have a sniffle, your grace,' Chivers said ponderously.

'Then I doubt Lady Bellamy would let him anywhere near me.
Now come on, man, don't keep my guests waiting.'

'Very good, your grace,' Chivers said and bowed himself out.

Felix had only moments to wonder why Celia wanted to see
him when she swept in trailed by Edmund. It was funny how
she simultaneously looked like her mother and didn't. At least
Felix's heart didn't drop when she walked in, as it did whenever
her mother arrived.

'Felix, I'm so glad you could see us. I hope we won't be
too much of a bother,' Celia said as she took his hand. Felix
experienced a momentary whiff of perfume, then Celia pushed
her son forward.

'Little Edmund. You'll scarcely recognise him since the last
time you saw him.'

'No, indeed, he has grown. He's quite a sturdy little lad, er...
how old is he now?' Felix said, examining the boy with his curly
blond hair and face that looked surprisingly like a painting of
a cherub. He was wearing a sailor suit in navy blue that looked
comically charming on one so young.

'He's just turned three,' Celia said. She put her son on a chair
opposite Felix and pulled another one to be beside her son which
she eased herself awkwardly onto.

'You look pulled, my dear,' Celia said. 'Are you sure we aren't an imposition?'

'Not at all. How are you? You look... you look well.' Felix said because, despite her condition, Celia was dressed in the height of fashion in a brown velvet walking dress trimmed in sky blue.

'I look as fat as an overstuffed pillow,' Celia said on a giggle. 'My second child is due any day now.'

'I didn't know, I'm sorry.'

'No need to apologise. I'm not at all surprised that mother hasn't said anything to you about it. She has ceased to regard the arrival of grandchildren as anything but a commonplace.'

'Ah,' Felix said uncertain of what else he could say. 'Celia is... is everything all right?'

'Yes, of course it is.'

'The thing is, you don't usually visit me.'

'No, well I just dropped by to see the girls. I thought, as I was here and not trailing some diseased child, I'd come and see you too.'

'You came to see the girls?'

'I do from time to time, just to keep an eye on them, you know. I make sure they're all happy.'

'And are they?'

'Pixie, the twins and Grace are.'

'Pixie? You mean Prunella?'

'Only mother calls her Prunella. She hates the name. The rest of us call her Pixie.'

'I didn't realise.'

'No reason why you should. Juliana, on the other hand, is in a strop. She was expecting to come out this season, and she's livid that mother postponed it so that she could find a bride for you.'

'I didn't know Aunt Lavinia had done that. Tell her I'm sorry, would you?'

'Tell her yourself,' Celia said. 'You do live in the same house after all, and I'm about to have another baby of my own. I won't have time to come running around to soothe Juliana's lacerated feelings.'

'Do you think she'd want to have an apology from me?'

'Honestly, unless you accompany that apology with the presentation of a wildly handsome and eligible man, I doubt Juliana will be mollified.'

'Then, I believe I will continue in my current manner.'

Felix's mind boggled when he considered trying to calm an outraged girl.

'That's probably wise, all things considered. I doubt you'd want to put up with a tearful tantrum at the moment.'

'Is she miserable? I don't want her to be unhappy.'

'That's a very kind thing to say,' Celia said giving him a disconcertingly direct look. 'Mother doesn't care two tuppences about how Juliana is feeling. But no, she isn't desperately unhappy, just thwarted at the moment. She needed somebody she could vent her full frustrations to.'

'And that was you this morning?'

'It was.'

'Mmm,' Felix said, still at a loss to explain why Celia was here. He was also distracted by his nephew, who was sitting very quietly on his chair. 'Is Edmund all right?'

'Yes, of course, why wouldn't he be?'

'He just seems very quiet.'

'That's because children given the honour of sitting with their elders must know how to behave. They should be seen but not heard. Edmund is a very good little boy and has learned his lesson.'

'It must be dreadfully dull for him,' Felix said gazing at the little boy who was watching him back with an alarmed expression.

He supposed it was uncomfortable to be sitting with what to him was a total stranger. He rang his bell and Poole and Grantley appeared immediately.

'Grantley, do you happen to recall where my animal collection is?'

'I will find it, your grace,' Grantley said executing a bow that added a greeting to Celia.

'Your animal collection?' Celia said.

'Something to entertain Edmund.'

'But his training, Felix.'

'I'm his cousin, and he's in my room. It's exceptional enough not to set a precedent, don't you think?'

'This from you who is so obedient.'

'I'm not really,' Felix said. 'Just more quiet from necessity.'

'A trait mother encouraged with gusto. I remember how she came down on Arthur and Percy whenever they got too rowdy, not to mention us girls.'

'She was doing what she believed was best. But Edmund is fine, isn't he?'

'So the doctors tell me.'

'Then, please, allow him to play a little here. I really don't mind. It's better than having him sit so quietly,' Felix said as his gaze flicked across to his nephew.

'The animals, your grace,' Grantley said reappearing from the dressing room with a battered tin box.

'Here, see if he likes them,' Felix said and handed the box to Celia.

'Good God, they're made from silver, Felix,' Celia said as she prised the lid open and removed the tissue from what turned out to be a lion.

'Somewhat ostentatious, I know. They were my father's and my grandfather's before him. They've become something of a family heirloom. I didn't notice their worth as a child, though, and I doubt Edmund will care either.'

'Well... if you're sure?'

'Of course.'

'Here, my dear,' Celia said as she lifted her son off the chair and made a space for him on the floor. 'This is a rather fine collection of animals your cousin has given you to play with. Say thank you.'

Edmund examined his cousin with a wide-eyed gaze and whispered something incoherent. Felix was happy enough to accept that as thanks and smiled down at the boy. He was the first child he'd seen in a while, well actually since the last time he'd seen Edmund as a baby.

'He's a little shy amongst his elders,' Celia said. 'But then most children are at this age.'

'Are they?'

'Oh, yes. I've seen it many times, with the girls at first, and now with my son and the children of friends. I hadn't realised till Edmund though, that little boys were just as shy as little girls. It's been strange having a son for, shyness aside, they are quite different to girls. But look at me wittering on about children. It can't possibly be interesting to you.'

'I wouldn't say that,' Felix said watching Edmund remove his animals from their tissue paper wrappings.

'Most men aren't interested. Even Bellamy tells me I bore him if I go on too long about Edmund. But then he's fully engaged in affairs of state so I can understand how children might be less interesting to him.'

'I suppose so. He's prospering then is he, Bellamy?'

'He's very senior in something top secret now, so he can't speak of it. It leaves us with very little to say to each other over the dinner table.'

Felix was still trying to work out why Celia had come and now wondered whether she wished to unburden herself about an unhappy marriage. It would be odd if that were the case for they knew so little of each other.

'Are you... unhappy?' Felix asked cautiously. Heaven knew what he would say if she admitted to being discontent with her lot.

'Who me? Unhappy? No, why?'

'It's what you said about Bellamy, I wondered...'

'Oh no, I'm perfectly content. Bellamy is a good man and a good father. He's also passably good looking, and when we do go to parties, he acquits himself well. The rest of the time he's a tolerant man who lets me do exactly as I please, which suits me very well. I have far more freedom as a married lady than I ever did living in this house.'

'So... forgive me, Celia, I don't mean to be rude, but, why the visit?'

'Ah, well,' Celia said with a laugh, 'that's Percy's fault.'

'Percy, what has he been up to?' Felix said and felt a tingle of suspicion.

Percy seemed to be meddling a lot in his life at the moment, and that was out of character.

'I ran into him at Lady Littleton's ball and had to interrogate him on this whole business of you getting married.'

'You did?'

'What you probably don't know, Felix, and I should tell you, so you are forewarned, is that I'm a frightful gossip. The whole thing about you in the newspaper, and then you vanishing for a time, got people curious. As a relative, they came to me to find out what was going on. Rest assured that as I knew nothing, I had nothing to tell.'

'I see.'

'And I won't ask you how it's going either. That way, I will have nothing to inadvertently give away.'

'So you haven't come for information then?'

'It's so unlike me, but no, I haven't.'

'Now I'm even more confused.'

'I came because Percy said you could use a few more friends.'

'He did?'

'I told him that was ridiculous, and furthermore that we have nothing in common. But that isn't quite true, is it?'

'That it's ridiculous, or that we have nothing in common?' Felix said and found himself intrigued.

'We do have things in common. We have mostly grown up under the same roof, with mother ruling both our lives.'

'That is true.'

'We really should be closer. But mother saw to it that we weren't.'

'She had her reasons. She was trying to keep me safe.'

'I'm not saying they were bad reasons, but it has left us more like strangers than anything else. I know all my other cousins better than I know you. You and I were never even left alone together to get to know each other, mother was always there.'

'Well, when you put it like that, I suppose it's true. And I am aware that your mother gave me more attention than she gave any of you.

I have always been sorry about that. I have tried to point out the unfairness of the situation to her, but she always brushed it aside.'

'Good Lord, Felix, I didn't want any more of her attention. Thank goodness she didn't listen.'

'Really?'

'Do you like her attention?'

Felix blinked at Celia, so surprised he couldn't think of a thing to say for a moment.

'She can be very forceful.'

'And you are frightfully polite. No, as I said to Percy, we were all relieved that mother spent more time with you than she does with us. I bear you no grudge. In fact, I have frequently felt sorry for you and did try to get mother not to smother you the way she does.'

'Oh... well, thank you. I am accustomed, though.'

'You are a veritable saint.'

'Not really.'

'More than I could be. Do you know that mother and I have had many lacerating encounters? Fewer now that I am married and no longer under her roof. But, my dear, the number of arguments we've had.'

'That I have heard. Your mother mentioned it once when she arrived very flustered and red-faced in my room. As for the rest, the servants talk, you know.'

'No doubt they do. So you see, I don't mind that. But Percy is right, it's a shame that we don't know each other better.'

'So you are remedying that?'

'Would it be so terrible if we were to be friends?'

'Not at all but I don't have any women friends. I'm not entirely sure I know what we would talk about.'

'Anything at all, children, for instance. I could teach you a little about them.'

Celia waved her hand at her son, who was contentedly moving his silver beasts around the floor, making all the appropriate sounds as he did.

'Or I can bring you the latest gossip. I'm a veritable mine for that. I know most of the stories behind what gets into the society pages. It's a lot juicer than they make out, believe me. Or we could talk about women, as you're now venturing into the world of matchmaking. I can be a lot more helpful than any others of your acquaintance when it comes to women.'

'Could you?'

'Believe me, Felix, we women understand each other. Men get bowled over by a pretty face, and they don't know or want to know what lies beneath. To them, it is an unfathomable mystery, but we women see all. It's no mystery to us. We can always tell if things will turn out well or badly.'

'Percy told you about Lady Giddings did he?' Felix said as a spark of anger flicked through him.

'He did.'

'And you, what? Came to warn me off? Clear the path for Percy?'

'Clear the path for Percy? Good Lord, what makes you think that?'

'Because he came to visit yesterday when Lady Giddings was also here. He made a pretty obvious play for her attention.'

'Did he? Well, that was stupid and pointless. Lady Giddings has no interest in Percy.'

'Doesn't she? She laughed at everything he said.'

'And there you have it. You men really don't understand. Lady Giddings, along with any well brought up young lady, will laugh and admire anything that comes from a man's lips. It's merely politeness.'

'She didn't mean it?'

'I wasn't there, so I have no way of knowing. If I had been, I would have been able to tell if she was genuinely amused or merely being polite. As would any other woman in the room.'

'Her cousin was also there.'

'Miss Seaborn?'

'You know her?'

'We met at Lady Littleton's. And yes, as her cousin is always around Lady Giddings, she would be able to tell you too. But you surely aren't going to ask her, are you?'

'Why not?'

'What a male question! Because she's penniless and completely reliant on the kindness of her cousin. You can't ask her to betray that trust.'

'By which you assume, Lady Giddings was merely being polite. Why do you think that?'

'Well, as you like plain speaking, Felix, I'll tell you. Because Lady Giddings would never marry a soldier, no matter how well set up he was. And Percy doesn't even have that distinction.'

'You also think she is after money.'

'Of course she is, we all are. Why do you think I married staid but wealthy Lord Bellamy rather than dashing Captain Roberts?'

'There was a Captain Roberts?'

'Believe me, Felix, every young woman has a Captain Roberts. That handsome, adventurous young man who'll sweep you off your feet and give you a life of high adventure and passion. But it's nothing other than a pleasant daydream. When a young woman considers things in a more dispassionate light or has their mother do it for them they realise that the sensible but boring man is really much safer.'

'So you have no regrets?'

'I'd be lying if I didn't sometimes dream of what might have been. But my dreams are tempered by the fact that Captain Roberts died last year in the middle of some gruesome battle.'

'Oh! I'm sorry to hear that.'

'As was I, especially as it proved mother right. I hate to ever admit that.'

'No,' Felix murmured. 'I often feel the same.'

'Do you? Well, that's marvellous. I never knew.'

'We should have spoken before,' Felix said on a laugh. He'd never had such a delightful conversation with Celia. 'Maybe Percy's right; it would be good to be friends.'

'It's a shame mother kept us apart for so long,' Celia said, smiling at him.

'She'd be surprised to see us now.'

'And disapproving of the fact that I brought Edmund. That is particularly why I chose a Sunday morning to visit when I knew she'd still be in bed.'

'She doesn't want me to get to know Edmund?'

'Aside from her belief that all small children are plague carriers? No, she didn't want you to know each other well. It's her way of trying to depress pretension.'

'The inheritance?'

'She has always made it clear to Bellamy and me that we should not expect Edmund to inherit your title or consider himself your heir. There really was no need for her to worry about that though,' Celia hurried on. 'Bellamy is a wealthy man from an excellent family and more than able to provide for his children.'

'Not to mention that Arthur stands in his way,' Felix said. 'I suspected some of the reason you didn't visit was that you didn't want to look like you were after the title for your son.'

'I really am not, although, say what I like, mother never believes me.'

'For her, it's a very great prize.'

'And it isn't for you?' Celia said, giving him a very searching look.

'I don't really care. I mean, I know I have my wealth to thank for being alive. A poorer man could not afford to have a doctor living in his house, keeping him safe. But honestly, I wouldn't mind if Arthur or Edmund took over from me. They are still family and the succession would be safe.'

'But if not for an heir, why the search for a bride?'

'Why do you think?' Felix said with a laugh to cover his discomfort. 'The obsession with an heir is entirely your mother's.'

'And you?'

Felix sighed as he said, 'I live buried in this house, or the few rooms I use of it. I escape through books and periodicals. I feel incomplete, not a full member of this world. I only read about experiences that everyone else takes for granted, a ride in the park, going to the opera, a shopping trip. I can accept that I will never experience most of that. But it would be nice to know what it's like to... to be married.'

'To be married?' Celia said with a quizzically raised eyebrow.

'To be loved and to love. I would really like that,' Felix said and felt his skin prickle along his hairline to admit this to anyone.

'I understand,' Celia said. 'Mother has really done you a disservice the way she brought you up. She shielded you too much. I also realise now that you, like me, have never had any love from her.'

'Your mother is driven by duty. It doesn't leave much room for anything else.'

'It doesn't.'

'But you got married. You have a child and a second on the way, and you have changed. You are far more grown-up than when we last met.'

'Do you think you should grow up?' Celia said with a laugh. 'You always seemed very grown-up to me. You've had very little choice in the matter.'

'Not grown-up enough.'

'Because you haven't experienced love?'

'It's a part of the reason.'

'Be warned, Felix, love is a tricky emotion. That's why the Captain Roberts of this world are so dangerous.'

'They are?'

'He was so handsome and dashing and so sure of himself that I burned like a fire for him.' Celia flushed as she spoke and her fingers brushed along her leg leaving lines in the velvet. 'My every waking moment became a dream about seeing him again and what I would say to him when I did.'

'Oh,' Felix said uncomfortably aware that he felt exactly the same about Isolde Giddings. He was reluctant to hear more.

'I can't say how things would have worked out with him though because mother intervened. For which I may never be able to forgive her. She introduced me to Bellamy, who was far too old, as I thought then. He was also far too quiet, although he had more self-assurance than the captain. You have that same quiet assurance. It is something I envy in you. Anyway, I didn't love Bellamy, not then. But I have grown to love him. It's a quiet love. There is no fire, but there is a deep and abiding passion. He is my safe harbour. I trust him, and I rely upon him, and I'm glad he isn't Captain Roberts.'

'You're warning me off Lady Giddings.'

'I'm saying, be careful. You are going to marry this person and be tied to them for the rest of your life. So choose wisely.'

'The rest of my life won't be that long. What would it matter if I had a burning passion for the last part of it?'

'Oh, Felix! Don't talk like that. I wish so much more for you than something superficial.'

'That is very kind of you to say,' Felix said with an attempt at a laugh. 'But you know, I have accepted my lot and am now trying to get the most out of it.'

'I do know, and I've tired you with my visit. I'm sorry. It wasn't my intention. I thought I might just divert you for a bit, not delve so deeply into your life.'

'I'm glad you came. And now that we have had a chance to meet without your mother, I hope you will repeat it.'

CHAPTER THIRTEEN

Honour hurried down the road, enjoying the brisk walk despite the smog which the fine drizzle was doing nothing to dispel. London stank of coal smoke, manure and human beings living far too close to each other. Still, it was better than the stink of Calcutta. The lack of sanitation plus the blazing Indian sun had created a smell that could fell a horse. She shook her head to dispel the memory and glanced back to make sure Doris was still with her.

'Where are we going, miss?' Doris said. She was out of breath already despite the short distance they had travelled.

'I'm going to an employment agency,' Honour said. 'And, Doris, not a word about this to anyone.'

'An employment agency, miss, but surely… you aren't after a maid are you, miss? I have been trying me best.'

'I'm not after a maid, don't worry. No… I'm after a job.'

'Surely not, miss. You don't have to work.'

'I'm afraid I do. The moment Lady Giddings is married, I will have to leave.'

'Couldn't you stay with his lordship?'

'That would be extremely inappropriate, Doris. Lord Giddings couldn't keep me in his house without his daughter nor, I fear, would he want to.' Honour had come out early so that she didn't have to tell Isolde what she was up to. But despite the hour, there were so many carts and carriages that it felt life-threatening every time she crossed the road. She paused now at the kerb and looked left and right, waiting for a gap in the traffic.

'Come on, Doris,' she said and hurried across.

'What about your other relatives, miss?' Doris said.

She half skipped every now and then to keep up with Honour but remained slightly behind. It was impossible to walk two abreast here because of the crush of shoppers and men about their business.

'None of my other relatives wants to have anything to do with me, I'm afraid. A young woman without means is nothing but a drain upon her family. It's for this reason that I have to find work to support myself.'

'But you're such a fine lady and beautiful as well. Even if none of the men notices what with all being smitten by Lady Giddings.'

'I'm a poor bride for any man who should also be looking to better his lot with a union.'

'Well, it's plum crazy.'

'It's the way of the world, I'm afraid.' Honour looked down at the paper clutched in her hand and up at the facade of shop windows. 'We're in the right place, I just don't see... ah, there it is,' Honour said and hurried to a discreet door halfway down the road.

A bell rang as she stepped inside closely followed by a wide-eyed Doris. 'This looks very posh, miss.'

'That's the whole idea.' Honour crossed to the austere young woman dressed in black who stood at the counter examining them and said, 'I'm Honour Seaborn, Mrs Pirbright is expecting me.'

The young woman examined her ledger, then said, 'This way, miss, your maid can wait here.'

'Fine, thank you,' Honour said and shooed a reluctant Doris to the row of chairs by the door.

Then she hurried after the young woman into a room which held six desks at which were sitting six equally austere looking women. A couple of them had clients already. Honour was led to the largest desk in the room, and a thin, elderly woman who had her iron-grey hair pulled into a tight bun.

'Please sit down, Miss Seaborn, and tell me how I can help you today?' Mrs Pirbright said.

'Well,' Honour said and took a deep breath. She couldn't believe how nervous she felt now that she'd come to this point. 'I'm looking for employment. I thought I could be a governess or a housekeeper.'

'I see. Do you have any experience in either role?' Mrs Pirbright said and looked her up and down over her half-moon spectacles.

'I kept house for my father till he died. He was in the army, and we moved around a lot. I constantly had to set up a new house in whichever country and city we found ourselves. I got very good at it. I also managed the household budget, which was challenging at times. My father could be... careless with his salary.'

'And the governess role?'

'I'm good with children, and I can teach them all the basics, reading, writing and arithmetic. I'm also good at drawing and passable on the piano, so I would be able to teach the younger ones in the family.'

'Mmm, you may be a bit too young and pretty to be taken on in most homes. Those with young families have wives who have to have a care for their husband's roving eye. Households with older boys in it have to worry about the boys too.

'Surely there must be some suitable placement?'

'Do you prefer the idea of being a governess? It seems to me you have more experience as a housekeeper.'

'I'd prefer to be a governess,' Honour said. Governesses were considered above housekeepers in the social hierarchy and were more integrated into the families they served.

'Do you have any references?' Mrs Pirbright said.

'Not yet, but I will be able to get them. My cousin, Lady Giddings, will give me a good reference as will her father, I'm sure. There are a couple of other noblewomen I've met since being in London who have said they would sponsor me.'

Honour watched Mrs Pirbright all the closer. She was using Isolde's title shamelessly, but she had to. She had to get as much advantage as she possibly could from her connection. Fortunately, Mrs Pirbright looked impressed.

'Where are you living at the moment, Miss Seaborn?' she said in a considerably softened tone.

'I'm living with Lady Giddings, but that is a temporary arrangement until her ladyship is married.'

'Your family can't support you?'

'They could, but I would rather not throw myself upon their mercy.'

'I see. Is Lady Giddings likely to be married soon?'

'I would say very soon.'

'Well... I shouldn't think we'll have any difficulties placing you, Miss Seaborn. Let me go through our books, and I will then send you a list of our current suitable clients for you to peruse.'

'You won't do that now?'

'It will take some time, but don't fear, we have never let any of our ladies down. I will have the list delivered to your home address.'

'Right, well... thank you,' Honour said.

'It won't be easy, you know,' Mrs Pirbright said suddenly. 'It's a very different life. Not everyone can adjust.'

'I don't really have a choice, Mrs Pirbright,' Honour said, gave her a tight smile and a nod and took her leave.

Honour took her time going home. She detoured to a tea parlour after her meeting at the agency and treated herself and Doris to a sticky bun each. Then she'd taken the longer route home that took them via a park. It was next to empty, dripping and cold. She might have lingered there all the same, but Doris had started shivering, so she thought it best to return home. It surprised her all the time how much less robust the people of London were. Nobody in her father's company would have found a bit of strolling around London tiring.

All the same, Honour couldn't delay any longer and headed back. She hesitated as she got to the front door. Going inside would mean the end of her adventure. She wondered why she disliked this house so much. Nobody had actually been unkind to her.

How much worse would it be as a governess? Would it be worse? She supposed what she hated most about the house was Isolde's terrible behaviour, her self-centeredness was breathtaking. Even taking her in hadn't been out of kindness but expediency. Isolde wanted a chaperone she could ignore.

'And she got that in me,' Honour murmured.

'What's that, miss?' Doris said.

'Mmm? Oh, nothing, ignore me,' Honour said and rang the doorbell.

'Miss Seaborn,' the butler said. 'Welcome home.'

Honour set to pulling off her gloves when a shrill, 'No, no no!' came from the landing above followed by the sound of shattering glass.

'Good heavens, what's happened?'

'Ah, Lady Giddings has come down with the influenza, Miss Seaborn,' Thompson said. 'And she is quite distraught.'

'Oh dear, she did mention a ticklish throat last night. I'm sorry it has got worse. I'd better go and see her,' Honour said and got a beaming look of approval from the butler. They hid it most of the time, but the staff always dreaded one of Isolde's tantrums.

'Where have you been?' Isolde muttered as Honour arrived to find her sitting in bed looking glum.

'I went out for a walk. I'm afraid I'm not used to being indoors as much as I have been since returning to-'

'Never mind that,' Isolde snapped. 'Look at me, look at me!'

'You look fine,' Honour said. In fact, Isolde looked glorious wrapped in a frothy dressing gown with her hair tumbling across her shoulders.

'Well, I don't feel good. My head hurts, and my throat is burning, and I just know it's going to get worse and today of all days.'

'Ah yes, Overbrook's ball in your honour.'

'How can I not go? After he made such an effort. It's going to be such a fancy ball at his house which is said to have one of the largest ballrooms in London. This is so utterly, utterly unfair!'

'Perhaps you'll feel better by this evening,' Honour said as she poured her cousin a glass of water and held it out to her.

Isolde ignored it and said, 'No, I won't be better, I know I won't. I never get well quickly from the influenza. Besides I can't let him see me looking this haggard.'

'Does it really matter? You've set your sights on another man after all, and you did say Overbrook was a bit of a bore.'

Honour put the glass of water down on the bedside table within easy reach and pulled up a chair. Clearly, her duty for today was to cheer Isolde up.

'He may be a bore, but he's rich, and so far no woman has ever been able to get him to marry her,' Isolde said. 'That is a challenge, and one I will win.'

'But what if he asks you to marry him? What if that is his intention for this evening?'

'I don't think so, not this evening for he hasn't spoken to papa.'

'Maybe he wants to ask you before he approaches your father. Maybe he wants to make sure you would be receptive.'

'How could he doubt that I am?'

'Isolde! I thought your intention was to marry the duke.'

'Only if he lives. I'm not altogether convinced he'll live long enough to propose.'

'So you plan to string Overbrook along till you are certain you have the duchy in the bag?'

'Maybe.'

'Mmm, what if... what if the widowed duchess doesn't get a substantial inheritance?'

'What do you mean?'

'I mean, if you don't have children with the duke, you might find yourself widowed and without a substantial provision. Ancient families like the Peergraves have very rigid entails. I wouldn't be surprised if everything will go to the next male heir. If that isn't a son of yours well… there may not be very much for you at that point.'

'You mean it would all go to Captain Shawcross?'

'Or whoever the male heir is.' Honour didn't want to complicate this conversation by adding in her doubts about the captain.

'So unless I have a son with the duke I will get nothing?'

'I expect there will be some settlement for his wife, but I wouldn't pin my hopes on it being a large one.'

'So I'll have to get pregnant?'

'That is usually what wives are for Isolde, to perpetuate the family name. I have heard some very unkind gossip that Lady Lavinia is pushing the duke into marriage because all she cares about is the succession.'

'Where have you heard this gossip?'

'At practically every event of the season that we have attended.'

'I haven't heard that.'

'I doubt the gentlemen that surround you would tell you anything at all about their love rivals.'

Isolde's eyes narrowed as she considered this. 'So you hear more gossip than I do?'

'It's the women who do the gossiping, Isolde, and you have never been interested in speaking to them.'

'And they say the duke must have a son?' Isolde said and nibbled thoughtfully on the end of her finger.

'They say that's the only reason he is contemplating marriage.'

'Do you believe that?'

'I don't think it's his only reason, no.'

'What do you think his reasons are?'

Honour had met the duke twice now and had the opportunity to study him without fear of being noticed. 'I think he's lonely,' she said, knowing Isolde wouldn't understand.

'Lonely? Why would he be lonely? He lives in a house full of people.'

'All the same,' Honour said. 'It is possible to be surrounded by people and still be lonely.'

Isolde stared at her in incomprehension then lost interest. 'I don't want to have a child, not straight away. Children ruin your figure.'

'Once you are married, you won't have much say in the matter unless you intend to bar your husband from the marital bed.'

'I don't want to have this conversation,' Isolde said. 'I'm ill. I don't want to have you being so mean spirited and gloomy. You're supposed to cheer me up. And I've just remembered something else, if I'm ill, I won't be able to see the duke. Remember what that horrible Lady Lavinia said when she first invited me to meet the duke? She said nobody with influenza, or so much as a cough would be allowed anywhere near him.'

'Yes, I remember.'

'So now that's two gentlemen I won't be able to see!' Isolde wailed. 'I hate this, I hate it, I hate it, I hate it.'

'I'm sorry, Isolde,' Honour said and thought she'd best get used to tantrums. She was going to have to deal with a lot more of them once she was a governess. 'What can I do to make it better?'

Chapter Fourteen

G rantley, is the drawing room free this morning?' Felix said, looking at his valets via the mirror as Poole and Grantley finish dressing him by brushing the shoulders of his blue suit with a lint brush. It felt good to have got to the point where he was up to dressing properly again.

'I believe it is, your grace, but I will check with Chivers. I understand Lady Lavinia is out visiting her dressmaker this morning.'

'Ah yes, she mentioned something about that yesterday. Well, then I'd like to spend some time in the bay window. My view of the garden is starting to bore me, I'm hoping there will be more happening on the street.'

'There isn't much, your grace. It's cold today, so them as can are staying indoors.'

'Ah well, at least there will be different dripping, leafless trees to gaze out at on the square.'

'Very good, your grace,' Grantley said. 'I will get Chivers to build up the fire there.'

'Ah yes, it has a considerably larger fireplace, that will be nice,' Felix said and paused as Chivers's familiar knock came from the bedroom.

'I'll go,' Poole said with a quick bow.

'It's the wrong time for a visitor,' Grantley said, checking the dressing room clock.

'Perhaps it's Mr Testwood. We haven't seen him for a while.' Felix was proved right as Poole returned trailing Mr Testwood.

'With a huge parcel,' Felix said. 'Good morning, Mr Testwood.'

'Your grace,' Hieronymus said and gave a deep bow.

'You have something new for me?'

Felix always enjoyed surprises and Mr Testwood had so far delivered at least one good one.

'Something I hope you will like, your grace,' Hieronymus said and pulled the brown paper off his parcel to reveal a cane rectangle.

'What is it?'

'I call it a walking frame, your grace. Grantley told me you can't use a walking stick to aid you as it will be no good should you suffer a dizzy spell. But this frame stands on its own, and you can lean heavily on it without it toppling over.'

'Very interesting, Mr Testwood. Did you use your wife as your guinea pig for this project too?'

'No, your grace.' Hieronymus said with a broad grin. 'I tried it out on Old Pete, my neighbour, who is extremely unsteady on his feet. He attempted walking with two walking sticks, and even that didn't help him, but the frame did. He liked it so much he's asked me to make him one too.'

'Then I shall try it straight away,' Felix said.

'Here you are, your grace,' Hieronymus said and placed the frame in front of Felix. 'You can also use it to get onto your feet.'

'Are you sure about this, your grace?' Grantley said.

'It's worth a try, Grantley. And you'll be at the ready should I need you, won't you?'

'I'm not letting you out of my sight with that contraption.'

'Here we go then,' Felix said, gripped the golden bamboo frame and pulled himself upright. 'Quite solid. It only wobbled slightly. But how do I walk when it's in my way?'

'Just like a walking stick, your grace, you lift it and push it forward,' Hieronymus said. 'That's why I used cane for the manufacture. I tried it in metal first, but it was too heavy.'

'Ah yes, I see,' Felix said as he took a step forward, lifted the frame placed it ahead of himself and took another step. 'It will take a bit of getting used to, but I like it, thank you, Mr Testwood.'

'It looks like it's a bit low for you, your grace. I need to make you a slightly taller one.'

'Perhaps just a couple of inches higher, yes,' Felix said. 'But certainly a success.'

'It leaves Poole and me without anything to do, you grace,' Grantley said.

'I wouldn't be so sure of that. Somebody still has to carry my books and periodicals, not to mention simply trailing along in case something happens.'

'Very good, your grace.'

'And Poole can open the door for me. That is a bit awkward with this frame.'

'Yes, your grace,' Poole said as he hurried to obey.

'What a sight we must make, me accompanied by three men all for a short journey to the drawing room,' Felix said as they crossed the hallway.

'Not at all, your grace.'

Grantley rearranged the furniture so that Felix could get at the pile of reading material they set on an elegant, spindle-legged table beside his green wing-backed chair. In the meantime, Poole moved a palm tree so that it didn't block Felix's view of the outside.

'Good to see you up and about again, your grace,' Chivers said appearing at the drawing room door. 'Is there anything I can provide?'

It was a question that got both Poole and Grantley to stiffen considerably.

Felix suppressed a smile lest he further offends his valets. 'Yes, you can, thank you, Chivers, send somebody in to build up the fire and, after that, please invite Miss Juliana to have tea with me.'

'Miss Juliana, your grace?' Chivers said with only a flicker of surprise.

'Yes, that's right. Do you think Mrs Grayson might prepare something a little special for us, maybe some tea cakes?'

'I will find out, sir,' Chivers said and removed himself at a stately pace.

'Miss Juliana, your grace?' Grantley said the moment the butler was out of earshot. 'Is that wise?'

'If any infections are doing the rounds of the nursery then I'm sure Miss Juliana will remain there. Otherwise, I see no reason why I shouldn't have her visit.'

Felix inflected his voice with the tone he used when he wished no further discussion on a matter.

It worked because Grantley gave an accepting nod and said, 'Is there anything else, your grace?'

'Not at the moment, thank you. Mr Testwood, I like your walking frame, yet another helpful invention. I look forward to seeing the next one. Do you have anything more planned?'

'I have a couple of thoughts, your grace,' Hieronymus said and pulled a pamphlet out of his pocket as he perched on the edge of the seat opposite Felix.

Felix waved his valets away, and they left on a bow, but he hardly noticed as he took the pamphlet from Testwood. 'It's from the Royal Society.'

'Yes, your grace. I attend their public talks whenever I can, and I found this demonstration particularly interesting.'

'You attend the talks?' Felix said and suppressed a twinge of envy. 'I have a subscription to their journal. It is always full of fascinating discoveries.'

Felix turned his attention to the leaflet that had a heading proclaiming a demonstration on how to compress air. The name of the man who would be giving the presentation, one Thomas Andrews, was printed below in slightly smaller print and below that was a description of the proposed experiment.

'Did he succeed?'

'He did indeed, your grace, and a most impressive event it was too.'

'Fascinating,' Felix murmured. 'But I don't understand why you're showing this to me.'

'Well, I wondered...' Hieronymus said and petered out.

He looked like he was uncertain of what to say next so Felix said, 'If you are concerned you may touch on a sensitive matter, Mr Testwood, don't worry. I'm sure it isn't half as bad as you fear.'

'It's about your attack, your grace, and something Grantley mentioned. He said that sometimes you turn blue and it looks like you can't get sufficient air.'

Felix was astonished that Testwood had made the leap that he evidently had as he said, 'Do you think compressed air may provide a solution?'

'I think the extra air might be a help.'

'Yes, I suppose it's possible,' Felix said examining the inventor. He looked embarrassed and as close as they were sitting to each other Felix could also see that, although he'd shaved, some hairs had not been cut as short as others, and in places, he'd grazed himself. Felix shook that thought away. Now was not the time to be distracted.

'That is an astonishing leap, Mr Testwood, from compressing air to providing it for a person, but I am curious to test it.'

Testwood flushed with pleasure and looked relieved that he wasn't being rebuffed.

'If I have your permission, your grace, I would like to approach Mr Andrews and ask him if I can work with him and his condensing mechanism.'

'By all means. I will write you a letter explaining everything, that should help smooth your path.'

'Thank you, your grace,' Hieronymus said. 'I'm sure that will be a great help.'

'Not at all, my only regret is that I won't be able to visit the natural philosopher with you. I look forward, however, to hearing all about your meeting.'

'Thank you, your grace,' Hieronymus said and flushed with pleasure as he bowed himself out.

Felix was glad he'd made Testwood so happy. He wished he was so far improved that he could walk without any aids, but that was still beyond him. In the meantime, having a walking device, and the promise of a very intriguing compressed air device, pleased him. It gave him more autonomy.

He gazed out at the street that had only a few people hurrying by, all carrying umbrellas to protect from a steady rain. Then he turned his attention to the fire, it had been stirred to life and fed more coal, and the flames were jumping about brightly. It did much to warm the room both physically and by adding more cheer.

So long as he didn't look up at his grandfather overhead. He'd never liked the painting and couldn't understand why the old man had wanted such an austere pose of himself. Family was such a complicated thing. He wondered what it would be like to have one. Well, maybe not a family, but a wife at least.

An image of Isolde Giddings came forcibly into his mind, and for a moment he hoped Juliana would not visit so he might dwell more on what might be. He shook that thought away. It would be better to focus on something more attainable for the moment.

He felt oddly daring to have issued his invitation. Heaven alone knew why. It had taken a visit from Celia to make him realise that he could see the other girls if he wished to.

He'd never really thought much about them before. They were the silent creatures who were sometimes allowed at the dinner table, but who, good manners dictated weren't allowed to speak unless spoken to. As their mother and father weren't that chatty, and Felix had grown up with next to silent meals he too wasn't accustomed to making small talk so had never tried to engage them either.

He, therefore, had no idea what pleasant company they might be if their mother wasn't around as he'd discovered with Celia. And despite what he'd said to her, it preyed upon him that Juliana was put out. He wanted to make it up to her. It remained to be seen whether she'd let him.

'You wanted to see me?' Juliana said as she stepped warily into the room.

'Ah yes, Juliana please come in, sit down,' Felix said and examined his cousin more closely than he had before. She was a plump, big-boned girl who already took after her mother. Fortunately, her soft brown curls did much to soften her face, and she appeared to have a sweet disposition. It made him feel worse about upsetting her.

'Mother isn't here?'

'I understand she's at her dressmaker's so, I assume she will be away for the rest of the day.'

'Have I done something wrong?' Juliana said, lingering by the door.

'On the contrary. I believe it is I who have wronged you.'

'You have?' Juliana said the picture of confusion.

'So I've been told but, please, join me at the window. I've ordered some tea for the two of us.'

'Just the two of us?' Juliana said and came into the room but still looked suspicious. Her schoolgirl gingham dress made her look far too young to have considered a come out. Felix supposed that was the magic of clothes. In something more sophisticated, Juliana would no doubt look older.

'We've never had the chance to chat have we?'

'You and me? Chat?'

'Certainly, why not?'

'I don't know,' Juliana said as she finally sat down at the edge of the chair opposite Felix and examined him with dawning curiosity. 'Mother said we'd make you sick.'

'But you don't have anything contagious, do you?'

'No.'

'Do any of the other girls?'

'Nobody's even got the sniffles.'

'There you are then, no need to worry.'

'Mother will be furious.'

'If she is, it will be at me. You don't need to worry.'

'All right,' Juliana said and sat back in her chair, all concern evaporated.

'So now,' Felix said and wondered how he was going to phrase this. 'I understand, er... that you expected to come out this year.'

'Oh yes, I did!' Juliana said suddenly recalled to her reason for a grudge. 'And it's your fault that now I have to wait till next year. This after I absolutely starved myself and didn't even eat plum pudding at Christmas.'

'You starved yourself? Why?'

'To get a thin enough waist, of course. Because I'm plump and gentlemen don't want plump women, but I can't help it. Pixie is skinny and has a tiny waist, but I don't, and so I had to diet. I've been training with a corset for months and months and very nearly got to a 22-inch waist.'

'Did you?' Felix said, stunned by this narrative.

'I did, only it was too tight, and I fainted. Nurse came running in and made Pixie loosen the ties.'

'That was probably just as well.'

'I suppose so, but I've never been able to get down to 22 inches again.'

'I don't think it's that important,' Felix said.

'Don't you? Because you're a great swell and mother says you know everything about fashion.'

'Does she?'

'She does, and that she wouldn't take advice about her dress from any other man.'

'Did she say that indeed?' Considering that Juliana seemed to be a chatterbox Felix held off saying that he couldn't actually recall ever giving Lady Lavinia any advice on her clothes. 'Tell me, Juliana, how old are you exactly?'

'I've just turned seventeen. And don't tell me that's too young for I'll bet you've met plenty of young ladies who are my age and have already come out and Celia got married when she'd just turned 18, and although I think Bellamy is frightfully old, Celia likes him.'

'Tea, your grace,' Chivers said and opened the door so that a pair of footmen could put down the trays bearing the teapot and the plate with the tea cakes.

'Thank you, Chivers,' Felix said.

'Tea cakes?' Juliana said.

'Yes, I'm sorry about that,' Felix said and waved Chivers away. 'I didn't realise you were dieting.'

'Oh, I'm not anymore,' Juliana said and reached for a teacake. 'There isn't any point now.'

'I see.'

'Would you like me to butter a teacake for you?'

'If you would be so kind.'

Felix found himself wondering how old Isolde Giddings was. She seemed older and more worldly-wise than his cousin. He also found himself wondering how old Miss Seaborn was. Perhaps she was a year or two older than Lady Giddings. She seemed more mature and self-assured.

'Tell me, Juliana, have you ever left the nursery?'

'Of course I have. Mother didn't want any of us to be totally green when we came out. The most exciting thing I've been to was the squire's ball up at Morley.'

'Ah yes, Aunt Anne makes sure the squire's ball is the highlight of the festive season.'

'It was very jolly,' Juliana said and proceeded to nibble on her teacake. 'Of course, I knew everybody there because they're all our neighbours. So I had heaps and heaps of people to dance with. Although they were only the local boys and mother wouldn't dream of allowing me to marry any of them.'

'I dare say she wouldn't,' Felix said.

'Pixie came along too, and she was ever so popular with the boys. That was another reason I wanted to come out this year and not next because next year Pixie will also come out. Then there will be two of us at the balls and all the men like Pixie more than me.'

'Do they?'

'Yes they do. They always say things like, oh Pixie you're so beautiful, and you're so lively and such great fun, and they never say things like that to me.'

'What do they say to you?'

'They say, very pleased to meet you, Miss Juliana. Would you care for a dance and then... then they ask me questions all through the dance about Pixie!'

'That hardly seems fair,' Felix murmured.

'Well it isn't, and I do love Pixie. Honestly, I do, but I did so much want to come out without her.'

'I understand, but why couldn't Pixie wait till the year after next?'

'Because then she'd be far too old. Only nine months separate us, you know?'

'I was aware of that, yes.'

'So if Pixie had to wait two years before she came out, she'd be nineteen, and that's practically on the shelf.'

'Is it indeed?' Felix said and let Juliana hold forth on her own. She needed very little coaxing.

Felix found himself wondering where Juliana and Celia got their chattiness from.

'Juliana, my dear,' Lord Doubtless said as he poked his head around the door. 'You have taken up enough of your cousin's time. I believe you should thank him and run along.'

Felix was astonished to see his uncle and to hear him giving orders.

'Of course, father.' Juliana gave Felix a quick curtsy, said, 'Thank you for the tea, it was lovely,' and swished out of the room.

'May I come in?' Lord Doubtless said.

'Please do,' Felix said and waved his hand at the chair Juliana had recently vacated.

'That's a bit small for me,' Lord Doubtless said and eased himself onto the sofa instead. It creaked as it took his weight, and he gave a great sigh and looked around. 'How are you feeling, my boy?'

'Much improved thank you, Uncle Marmaduke.'

Felix wondered what would come next. His uncle was the man of fewest words he'd ever met.

'Good, good,' Lord Doubtless said, looking around again. 'Don't take this the wrong way, Felix, but it's never a good idea to marry a cousin.'

'Marry a cousin?' Felix said blankly, and then realisation dawned. 'Juliana? No uncle, you misconstrued. I merely wanted to apologise to Juliana for making her wait for her come out. Celia told me she was upset about that.'

'Ah, then I apologise too. The thing is, you've never taken an interest in the girls before.'

'I haven't really been encouraged to.'

'True. Lavinia has kept you separate, sometimes for good reasons and sometimes not. How did you find Juliana?'

'She's a nice girl.'

'Ah,' Lord Doubtless said, and his lips twitched a smile. 'She is sweet but not bright. My girls have been born on either side of the fence. Some like Celia and Pixie are sharp as knives, the others are... nice but dim.'

Felix had no idea what he could say to that. His own experience with Juliana seemed to bear his uncle out. He also found it interesting that his uncle knew Prunella preferred to be called Pixie.

His uncle appeared to understand and said, 'You are also bright. You should marry a clever woman. Some men like vacuous wives, but you aren't one of them.'

'I believe you are right,' Felix said. 'Although my experience is limited.'

'You'll get there. In the meantime, I'm glad to see you're taking matters into your own hands. Lavinia had found husbands for five of our girls, she, therefore, thinks she knows how to find you a wife. She is mistaken. It is not the same for we men. It is not for a mother or an aunt to find us our life's companion.'

'I am aware, sir.'

'And you know your own mind and will do exactly as you please. You have taken some of the reins already with that business with your valet, and I'm sure you will continue.'

'You approve?'

Felix was surprised. His uncle, after all, had said nothing when Aunt Lavinia objected so strenuously when he'd first announced his plan.

'It was generous.'

'Too generous?'

'You can afford the pension, and there is no doubt that Grantley deserves a reward for his devotion. Other employers might have fabricated some infraction and stripped him of his pension altogether. I disapprove of such money grubbers.'

'I see.'

'I also disapprove of leeches, and I am aware that to many my family and I might appear in that light.'

'I don't follow you, sir?'

'We have lived in your home, both your houses, as if they were our own. I have taken over a room to be my library in this house, and my girls pretty much occupy the entire third floor.'

'It was hardly by choice, sir.'

'There is always a choice, Felix. Your aunt felt she needed to keep you safe and alive after her brother's death, but even so, it could have been done differently. Do you know that initially, I suggested you move in with us? I have a perfectly nice house in Mayfair.'

'I didn't know.'

'Your aunt felt it would be better for you not to be moved out of your home. She wanted to disrupt your life as little as possible and thereby cause the least distress and strain to you.'

'I see.'

'I have had tenants living in my house ever since. But I want you to know that when you set up home for yourself, with your wife, that we will move out.'

'You will?'

'It would be inappropriate to stay, and what's more, we would be in your way.'

'Would you?'

'Can you imagine trying to have a comfortable supper at home with your wife with your aunt and me sitting at your table?'

Felix had considered that of course, but assumed he'd have no option so simply gave his uncle a noncommittal smile.

'Your aunt will resist. She fears what will happen if she isn't around, but I believe you will manage fine.'

'Do you?'

'You are more resilient than you give yourself credit for.'

'Really?' Felix was still so shaken by his latest brush with death that he had a hard time believing his uncle.

'My boy, we have all been in hourly expectation of you dying since the day you were born, and you turned blue. And yet, here you still are having reached your majority.'

'Not without mishap, sir.'

'I'm not saying it's been easy. You've been surrounded by doctors and carers your whole life, and they have helped, no doubt about that. But sometimes they hinder you too. Fear of what might happen holds you back.'

'It hasn't always been my decision,' Felix said with a slight smile.

'Your aunt can be very forceful, but you go your own way when you see fit. Having reached your majority, I see you doing things to your liking, and it is good.'

'I'm glad you approve.'

'Ha! You don't care what I think, boy, but all the same, I am proud of you.'

'You are?' Felix said, considerably surprised.

'I think of you as the son I never had.'

'You've never said that before, sir,' Felix said more astonished by the moment. His uncle had hardly seemed to notice him his whole life.

'I liked your father. We were old friends. I was very sorry when he died. I could never measure up to him in your affections though, and I'm not the most demonstrative of men either. But yes, I am proud to have you as a nephew.'

'Oh... thank you, sir.' Felix said. 'Did you know him very well?'

'We were friends for years, met at Oxford, long before either of us was married.'

'I never knew.'

'Not the sort of thing I'd tell a boy.'

'But now I am grown up.'

'Yes you are.'

'Do you know... do you know why he never remarried after my mother died?'

'Huh, now there's the question. Do you feel he should have done more for his succession than leave it in the hands of one sickly child?'

'It seems he had less care for the succession than my aunt does.'

'That is certainly true. By the time you were born, Arthur was already a couple of months old, and your father didn't see a problem with the title passing to one of his nephews. Although he always prayed you would survive, and you know how hard he worked to keep you alive.'

'Yes, I remember.'

'You know he was considerably older than your aunt, don't you?'

'Yes, he had a brother who died and two sisters between them.'

'Exactly, yet he got married at more or less the same time as Lavinia and I, so quite late even for a man.'

'Are you saying he wasn't the marrying type?'

'Honestly, Felix... he wasn't that interested in women at all.'

'Oh?' Felix said and examined his uncle closely. He was a hard man to read, but Felix sensed he was concealing something. 'Are you saying his interests lay on the other side of the blanket?'

'I never asked, and he never told. As far as I could see, he was largely celibate and spent more time with you than anyone else once you were born.'

'Ha, how strange,' Felix said. 'I never even considered that option.'

'Of all the things to know about your father, that is the least important.'

'I suppose you're right.'

'Now I have overstayed my visit and will leave you to rest. If you want a chat perhaps... about women, my door is always open.'

'Thank you, Uncle Marmaduke,' Felix said and watched as his uncle heaved himself out of the sofa and headed back to the fastness of his study.

'What a strange conversation!' Felix said to the empty room.

Still, it had given him something to think about. The future. It wasn't something he dwelled on.

He was always loath to make plans for himself in case they were thwarted. But his uncle had a point, once he was married, it would be odd for his aunt to stay in the house. He'd never considered that, and it gave him a little frisson of excitement and fear.

He would be free of Aunt Lavinia and able to live his life without her constant meddling. He felt bad that losing her could make him so happy. At the same time, it was frightening. She did look out for him all the time with a focus of effort far beyond his own. What would he do if she was no longer around to keep him alive?

'You'll have to do it for yourself,' he murmured.

It wasn't as if he would be entirely alone. He'd still have Dr Morton and Grantley... well for a while anyway and he was training Poole, and Chivers and... And he would have his wife.

Was it fair to place such a burden on anyone? Would Isolde Giddings be willing or even able to do such a thing? Whether she would or wouldn't, he didn't like the idea of placing such a burden upon anyone, least of all any woman who married him.

It left him feeling profoundly uncomfortable to contemplate that. How did you say to any woman, thank you for marrying me. Aside from the usual duties of a wife, you will also be expected to help keep me alive. It wasn't fair. He couldn't ask that of anyone.

A light tap at the door was followed by Percy who said, 'May I come in?'

'Percy!'

'Chivers said you've had a busy morning, so if another visitor is too much just tell me to go away.'

'No come in, sit,' Felix said, thrilled to see him.

Percy was ruddy-faced from the cold outside, and he stopped before the fire to warm his hands.

'So am I forgiven?'

Felix couldn't understand the question for a moment then remembered that he was supposed to be angry with Percy.

'I had forgotten.'

'Then I shouldn't have dredged it up again, I'm sorry.'

'It's all right.'

'You're looking much improved, and I hear you're back on your feet too.'

'With some assistance,' Felix said with a wave in the direction of the walking frame.

'That won't be for long.'

'I hope not.'

'Still blue devilled about it, huh?'

'Pondering the future and whether it's fair to ask a wife to look after me.'

'It is, so long as you are honest with them. When it comes to Lady Giddings, you have been perfectly honest. The question might also be, would your wife be capable of looking after you?'

'You don't think Lady Giddings could?'

'I don't know. I was being more general. Some women are like Aunt Lavinia, very capable and practical. They can hold themselves together in a crisis. Others are more fragile and liable to go into a dead faint at the least sign of trouble.'

'I hadn't thought of that. The thing is... Uncle Marmaduke said they'll move out when I marry, and I hadn't even realised that might happen let alone considered how I'd get on without them.'

'Do you think they would? I can't see Aunt Lavinia giving up her life's project just because you're married. She's not likely to let a mere wife get in her way,' Percy said, as he flicked his coat-tails up so that he wouldn't crease them and settled on the sofa.

'No,' Felix said. 'But I got the impression that my uncle would make her leave. I think he can be every bit as implacable as she can.'

'Really? We are talking about the same man? Uncle Marmaduke, who barely speaks and then only to remind everyone that it's time for a meal.'

'We've just talked. It's probably the longest conversation I've ever had with him. I think he wants to move out and go back to his own home. I got the impression he's never been happy with the situation.'

'It's a bit late saying that now though, isn't it?'

'Apparently, it's time. I can look after myself and have started taking the reins of power.'

'Well, he's not wrong about that.'

'So why am I so nervous about my next step?'

'What next step?'

Felix took a deep breath and said, 'I want to hold a dinner party.'

'A dinner party?'

'There's no need to look quite so surprised.'

'I'm sorry, Felix, but you've never done such a thing before.'

'I am painfully aware of that, and of the fact that I don't have a lot of people I can invite.'

'So why do it?' Percy said, pulled over an ottoman and rested his long legs on it, one elegant black boot crossed over the other.

It struck Felix that he was playing for time. But at least he was also giving the idea a fair hearing. 'Because I'd like to have a small party. I want to see what it's like and also... I want to invite Lady Giddings to something other than sitting for half an hour with an invalid.'

'I see.'

'You're at the top of my list of guests.'

'Along with Lady Giddings.'

'Of course, and Miss Seaborn. I also thought I'd invite Celia and her husband, and Aunt Lavinia and Uncle Marmaduke, naturally.'

'And I begin to see your problem.'

'Indeed,' Felix said. 'It isn't much of a party, and I don't know who else I could invite. It's a pity Arthur is so far away. It would be wonderful to have him and his Indian Princess in attendance.'

'Considering how Aunt Lavinia feels about that union, it's probably best that they are safely far away.'

'She told you, did she?'

'Thankfully only in passing.'

'I can come up with two more girls, Juliana and Pixie.'

'Pixie?'

'You possibly know her as Prunella.'

'No, I don't think I do.'

'Ah well, she's another of Aunt Lavinia's daughters and one I am curious to get to know better. I owe you thanks for that by the way. I had no idea how different Celia is without her mother around. I have decided to get to know all the girls better too. I just have to wait for a time when Aunt Lavinia is away.'

'Lest she bans any meetings?'

'Exactly, I might be able to do as I please these days, but as their mother she is within her rights to keep them from me.'

'Something she has been doing your whole life and theirs.'

'I'm afraid so, and also why I have so few male friends.'

'She very nearly banned Arthur and me too, I remember that.'

'I never knew how that got overturned. Now I begin to suspect Uncle Marmaduke may have had a hand in it. Either way, I thank God for it. But it did mean, especially as I never went to school or university, that I never met any young men other than family members.'

'Well, as it happens, I've been thinking about that too.'

'Ah, Celia did mention that you thought I needed more friends.'

'I've always thought that, but as you said, Aunt Lavinia was very good at keeping everyone at bay. Now I feel I can introduce one or two of my friends to you without fear that they will be barred.'

'I would like that.'

'Then I shall introduce you to Bertram Foley, Lord Hounslow, we were at school together, and he's a thoroughly good egg.'

'I believe you have mentioned one or two of the larks you got up to in the past. I should like to meet him.'

'You'll like him, but we still need another man if we are not to be outnumbered by ladies.'

'Perhaps Celia can suggest somebody. I'll ask her when I send her an invitation.'

'Good, that's settled then. When is your dinner party to be held anyway?'

'Not very soon, I'm afraid. Celia has just delivered her second child, so I doubt she is in the mood to go out.'

'She's had the baby?'

'A girl. She named her Felicity.'

'Did she indeed?'

'She said she hoped her illustrious uncle will smile upon her.'

'That was a nice gesture on her part, Felix.'

'It was.'

'Fine. So no sooner than a fortnight which, come to think of it is probably just as well.'

'Is it?' Felix said.

'Indeed, for the gossip of the morning is all about the Earl of Overbrook's ball and how it fell dreadfully flat.'

'Why? What happened?'

'I have mentioned that Overbrook is keen on Lady Giddings, haven't I?'

'You have,' Felix said and his heart gave a kick of fright. What was this all about?

'Well Overbrook made a great show of holding this ball in Lady Giddings' honour. Most people assumed it was going to herald an announcement of engagement.'

'Did you think that?' Felix said. 'And why do you have quite such a look of unholy glee on your face?'

'Because Lady Giddings didn't turn up. She sent profuse apologies. Apparently, she's been laid low by influenza.'

'It could be true.'

'Whether it is or isn't, Felix, it left Overbrook with egg on his face and in a terrible mood for the rest of the party.'

'But if it is true, I won't be able to see Lady Giddings for a fortnight at the very least either.'

'I'm afraid so.'

'Well I suppose that gives me time to plan and prepare, as well as get myself back to walking without assistance.'

'That's it, and I'll get to considering who else I can introduce to you.'

Chapter Fifteen

F elix was feeling inordinately excited about his dinner party. The wait had been interminable, but now the night was finally here.

'You look very smart, sir,' Grantley said as he put the finishing touches to Felix's hair.

'Do you think so?' Felix said, examining himself gravely in the mirror. He'd never worn full evening dress before, and he quite liked the stark black and white look of it.

'None will be smarter than you tonight, that's a certainty.'

'How about you, Poole, what do you think?' Felix said.

'Very stylish indeed, your grace,' Poole said as he paused in putting away the discarded clothing.

'Good,' Felix murmured and watched Poole more closely. He'd come along in leaps and bounds, and this evening he was behaving like the perfect valet full of decorum and looking unflappable. He'd have to congratulate Grantley on that.

Which gave him a twinge of regret. If Poole was nearly ready to take over, then Grantley was that much closer to leaving, and he didn't want that. He switched his attention to Grantley and examined him as closely as he could via the mirror. These days he always looked tired. It wouldn't be fair to keep him on much longer.

He dismissed such melancholy thoughts and stood up. 'May as well go to the drawing room, the guests will be arriving soon.'

'Are you sure you want to do this, your grace?' Grantley said.

'I am certain. I am quite looking forward to it as it happens.'

'You won't stretch yourself too far though will you, sir? You've only just got back to the point of walking under your own steam again.'

'I will pace myself, Grantley, I give you my word. Now I'd best go before I get the same speech from you that my aunt gave me when I first proposed the dinner.'

'Your grace!' Grantley said, giving him his most pained look.

'Well if you don't wish to be compared to an old woman you'd best not behave like one,' Felix said with a grin. 'Now come along.'

He forced himself to take a slow walk even though he wanted to charge through the door and hurry on to the party. He was more excited than he could believe possible. It gave him a little frisson of pleasure each time he considered it.

It was such a foolish thing to be so excited over a mere dinner. Still, Felix felt like he was taking another step into ordering his life more to his liking. He was also looking forward to meeting new people and of course, to seeing Lady Giddings again. The thought of spending an evening with her came close to taking his breath away.

He suddenly understood why young ladies got giddy with excitement over their coming out and the parties that lay before them. He'd also started making even grander plans, but he had to be careful. He couldn't get too carried away. First, he had to see if he could cope with this evening. After that, he could decide whether he might do something bigger.

'Felix, let me take your arm,' Lady Lavinia said as he entered the drawing room and she hurried over to him.

'No, it's fine, thank you, Aunt. I can make it to the chair without assistance.'

'If you're certain,' Lady Lavinia said and hovered beside him as he made his slow way to his chair. He'd contemplated using a different one, without quite such a substantial backrest but then thought better of it.

'You're looking very nice, Aunt.'

'Oh... do you think so? I was beginning to regret the green satin.'

'It suits you very well,' Felix said and looked about the drawing room. He'd never seen it lit with so many candles before. It wasn't just the chandeliers that were lit, there were also several candelabras placed strategically about the room. All in all, it looked perfect. Just as he'd planned.

'How do you feel?' Lady Lavinia said, bringing him back to the conversation.

'I feel fine... I'm enjoying the anticipation.'

'And you're certain you want Juliana and Prunella at this dinner?'

'But of course, especially now when Percy is bringing Lord Hounslow and Celia is bringing Professor Antrobus. We can't have more gentlemen than ladies.'

'But we don't know these two men. They could be rakes. I put nothing past Percy.'

'I'm sure they will be fine, Aunt Lavinia, particularly Professor Antrobus. I understand he is a friend of Bellamy's.'

'Well, then he is probably all right, but Lord Hounslow?'

'I looked him up in Who's Who. He comes from a good family. I'm sure you'll find nothing to dismay you in him. Now, shall we invite Juliana and Prunella down? I'm sure they are longing to be released from their quarantine.'

'It was for their own good. We couldn't have them mixing with the little ones if they were to be certain of making it to the dinner.'

'All the more reason to release them. They have put up with quite a trial to enable them to come to this little party.'

Felix glanced at his uncle as he spoke and he could swear he saw a spark of amusement in his eyes at the exchange, but as usual, he didn't get involved.

'Very well, I will tell Chivers to bring them down,' Lady Lavinia said. 'It would probably be best if they did arrive first. It will give them time to calm down before the first guests arrive.'

'I'm not sure they will if they are feeling any more excited than I am.'

'Felix, you must remain calm, remember what Dr Morton has told you. You are to avoid too much excitement.'

'I'm all right, Aunt,' Felix said and smiled at her to further reassure her.

It was probably a futile gesture. His aunt would never be reassured enough over a plan she'd damned as foolish from the moment she'd heard about it.

'Miss Doubtless and Miss Prunella,' Chivers announced as he opened the door to let in the two ladies who arrived with a sparkle in their eyes.

Felix could see now why Juliana didn't want to appear with Pixie. She was a slim girl with arrestingly large brown eyes. She was pretty rather than beautiful, but she had armfuls of character.

'Cousin Felix,' she said as she gave him a curtsy. 'Thank you so much for inviting us. Juliana and I are ever so glad to be here.'

'Well, I hope you will enjoy yourselves. It is by necessity a somewhat quiet affair tonight.'

'It will be wonderful,' Juliana said. 'I just know it.'

'And you will behave, both of you,' Lady Lavinia said at her most quelling.

'Oh, we will, Mother, I promise,' Juliana said as she hurried over to her mother and clasped her hands. 'You'll see.'

Felix noted with interest that Pixie didn't bother trying to reassure her mother. Instead, she stayed beside Felix and gave him a big conspiratorial smile. He liked it at once. She clearly went her own way and wasn't overly cowed by her mother.

'Lord and Lady Bellamy,' Chivers announced.

'Ah, the family are all here first,' Celia said as she made her way to Felix. 'That's good. How are you feeling this evening, Felix?'

'Very well thank you. More to the point, how are you?'

'I am recovered, thank you.'

'We are surely not going to be discussing childbirth over dinner, are we?' Lady Lavinia said. 'That would be most inappropriate.'

'Not over dinner, Mother,' Celia said. 'But Felix sent a very kind christening gift for Felicity, so I don't think he minds a little talk about children.'

'Not at all,' Felix said and held his hand out in greeting to Bellamy. 'It's been a while. I understand you have been very busy these last few years.'

'I have indeed, your grace,' Bellamy said. 'It's good to see you again.'

'Thank you. I don't suppose you could tell us some of what you have been involved with?'

'I'm afraid not. It's of the most sensitive nature and not a conversation that will interest the ladies.'

'I wouldn't be so sure of that, my dear,' Celia said. 'But I'm afraid he is a perfect civil servant, Felix. My husband won't divulge a thing, not even to his wife.'

'Most especially not to my wife,' Bellamy said, and his lips twitched a brief smile.

'You know me too well, my dear,' Celia said.

'Captain Percy Shawcross and Lord Hounslow,' Chivers said as he ushered in the two gentlemen.

'Felix!' Percy said, 'How are you, old fellow? Allow me to introduce you to my friend Bertram Foley, Lord Hounslow.'

'Your grace, it is an honour to meet you,' Bertram said as he executed a deep bow.

'How do you do?' Felix said as he took in a plump young man with a pleasant soft face. Lord Hounslow was a surprise. He'd expected all of Percy's friends to be lean, athletic, military men and Lord Hounslow certainly didn't fit that category. 'Percy tells me you two met at school.'

'That we did, your grace. We were the two worst pupils in our year, or so the headmaster kept telling us. I'm afraid I have never been much of a scholar.'

'Bertram is being modest,' Percy said. 'He's a dab hand at poetry.'

'Poetry? Is that so?'

'I dabble, your grace. I have no illusions of being the next Wordsworth.'

'He does write some damned funny rhymes through, Felix, you'll enjoy them.'

'Perhaps we can prevail upon Lord Hounslow to entertain us with a few poems after dinner,' Lady Lavinia said.

'Oh, well as to that, Lady Lavinia, I don't know,' Bertram said blushing profusely. 'Percy has rather overblown my ability.'

'Nonsense, I'm sure they will be delightful,' Lady Lavinia said. 'Now allow me to introduce you to everybody else. It is something of a family gathering tonight with three of my daughters in attendance.'

Felix felt as though he should have been irritated by his aunt's high handedness. Strictly speaking, as the host it was his duty to introduce the guests to one another, but this way he got to watch the people instead. He was delighted to note that Percy appeared quite struck by little Pixie.

'Professor Anselm Antrobus,' Chivers said and guided an astonishing man into the room.

He was tall and loose-limbed and with a shock of red hair and a bushy red beard. While he was nominally sporting black tie and clothes of good quality, he'd apparently thrown them on at random.

'Antrobus,' Bellamy said, 'Allow me to introduce you to everyone. Anselm is a Don up at Oxford for most of the year where he teaches philosophy. But every now and then he is enticed down to London.'

'And as rarely, Belly visits me in Oxford,' Antrobus said giving everyone a bow. 'But an invitation from a duke, that's something new for me. Thank you for it, your grace.'

'You're very welcome.'

Felix wondered why on earth Celia had brought this man along. He would have to waste no time in asking her, as soon as he could manoeuvre her into a quiet corner for a chat. Now all that remained was to wait for Lady Giddings. He sincerely hoped she wouldn't cry off.

'Lady Isolde Giddings and Miss Honour Seaborn,' Chivers announced and Isolde swept into the room, assimilated all the people, spied Felix and gave him a radiant smile.

'Your grace, it's wonderful to see you again. And, as you'll note, I am wearing your lovely shawl.'

'So I see, Lady Giddings and I'm delighted to see you again too.'

'I'm only sorry it's been so long, but I've been laid low with a terrible cold. Honestly, I could hardly move for days.'

'I'm very sorry to hear that.'

'I'm fully recovered now, never fear,' Isolde said, directing a pointed look at Lady Lavinia. 'And I'm ready to enter into any entertainment you have arranged.'

'We will be having a quiet night,' Lady Lavinia said, 'I don't want Felix stretching himself too much.'

'I'll be fine,' Felix murmured but felt acutely embarrassed as everyone gave him a more appraising stare. 'Perhaps, now that everyone has arrived we should go into the dining room?'

'Certainly,' Lady Lavinia said and led the way, much to Felix's annoyance.

'Oh, how splendid,' Celia said as they stepped into the dining room. 'Felix, you have transformed this place.'

'I thought a bit of decoration might make more of the evening and elevate it from the commonplace.'

Felix was thrilled by the entranced looks on the ladies' faces. They appeared thrilled by the glittering array of sparkling silver cutlery and crystal glasses and the bouquets he had arranged in the centre of the table and which filled each corner of the room. The glossy green porcelain vases were brimming over with violets, ivy, holly branches with their bright red berries and white hellebores. It helped to soften an otherwise austere room. He suspected his grandfather had something to do with the original decoration as it was simple and, to his eyes, spartan. Maybe, if he were going to use it for dinner parties more often, he'd get it redecorated.

'It looks wonderful,' Celia said. 'Where did you get all these flowers at this time of the year?'

'I had people scouring the markets for them.'

It had taken Felix days to plan the dinner from the decoration to the exact dishes for the meal. He just hoped the seating arrangement would be as successful. He'd placed Lady Giddings to his right and Percy as far away from her as was possible so that they wouldn't be able to converse easily. What he hadn't taken into account was the effect Lady Giddings had on all men. Lord Hounslow appeared to know her and blushed each time he looked at her and Professor Antrobus was stunned by her. Unfortunately, he'd put Antrobus to Lady Giddings' right.

'Please, do sit down,' Felix said and lowered himself into his seat. He was pleased he'd managed to stay standing for as long as he had, but he was in desperate need of relief now. Once seated, he watched his guests as they hunted for their names on the table.

'Ah, now we're all settled,' Percy said, rubbing his hands together enthusiastically. 'What surprises are you going to tantalise our tastebuds with this evening, Felix? I'm guessing you've expended as much effort on the menu as you have on the decorations.'

'I hope you'll enjoy it. The theme is food from around the world.'

'That sounds like a challenge,' Antrobus said. 'And I like a challenge.'

'Do you?' Felix said.

'Oh yes, that's why I went into philosophy. It's like a giant puzzle of the human heart and mind.'

'I suppose that's true,' Felix said.

'No doubt about it, the heart and the mind.'

'Must it be both?'

'This is an argument we've had before,' Bellamy said. 'I've always maintained that philosophy is the epitome of logic. It removes emotion and considers the facts in a cool and calm way.'

'My dear fellow, I keep telling you human beings are incapable of removing emotions from their thought process. We are fundamentally creatures of heart. It is nonsensical to even pretend we can remove that element of our life experience from our deductive processes.'

'Do you really think so?' Isolde said, turning her wide blue eyes on Antrobus.

'Without a doubt, Lady Giddings. In fact, you are the perfect subject to make my case for me. No man could fail to be moved by your lovely face. A philosopher would have to be made from stone to contemplate anything to do with you in a purely logical way.'

'But a philosopher would be wise to try,' Bellamy said dryly.

Felix was surprised by that. Clearly, his lordship was warning his friend off. Had Celia primed her husband and told him all about Lady Giddings? He supposed she must have, especially if she really was an inveterate gossip. And Bellamy was trying to make sure his friend didn't muscle in which was good of him but Felix felt he should be able to hold his own.

The problem was, now that she was sitting beside him, he couldn't think of a thing he could ask her. It was especially tricky when the conversation had kicked off on philosophy.

'I think the world would be a sadder place without emotion,' Isolde said and gave Antrobus a glittering smile.

'Then I have found a champion,' Antrobus said grinning back. 'It is always a pleasure to find a like-minded traveller on the road to knowledge.'

'What do you think, your grace?' Isolde said, turning to Felix. 'Do you think philosophy should be ruled by logic or by the heart?'

'Well...' Felix said. 'I believe we should strive for an answer uncluttered by emotion. But I suspect Professor Antrobus is right. It is difficult for man to completely remove emotion from the equation.'

'You have an interest in philosophy, your grace?' Antrobus said, looking surprised.

'Felix has an interest in everything,' Percy said. 'I doubt I know a better read fellow.'

'It isn't like I have anything else to do,' Felix murmured.

'All the same, philosophy is not for the faint-hearted,' Antrobus said. 'Tell me, your grace, which of the philosophies do you tend towards? Are you more of a romantic, or are you a strict utilitarian?'

'I suppose, due to my circumstances, I lean towards the utilitarian. I am especially fond of Bentham's very logical way of looking at the world and applying that which provides more pleasure than pain as a way of measuring what is good and valuable.'

'Ah a Benthamite, how fascinating, especially for one of such august standing in society. Forgive me if I offend you, your grace, but the extremely wealthy often don't give a damn about the poor and by extension, the happiness of others. With Bentham, that does need to be taken into account.'

'We are not all cut from the same cloth.'

'So you are a philanthropist, are you?'

'I try in my own small way.'

'Felix is actually a very generous person,' Celia said. 'Now, perhaps we can move onto the mundane for I fear I can't hold my own in a conversation about philosophy.'

'I bow to your wishes, Lady Bellamy, but I would enjoy taking this further at some point, your grace. Bellamy was right when he said you would surprise me.'

'Why would he surprise you?' Isolde said. 'What a very odd thing to say.'

'I come burdened with my own opinions, mostly formed from what I have seen before. I'm afraid, up until this evening, men of high rank have always seemed rather vacuous. It's as if their rank and wealth relieve them of the need to think. They merely move from one entertainment to the next, and that rarely provides them with the stimulation one needs to sustain a healthy inner life.'

'Oh,' Isolde said blinking up at him.

'I have been rude, I beg your pardon, Lady Giddings and, your grace. Bellamy chides me on it frequently.'

'Not at all.' Felix was uncertain whether to be amused or angry and wondered why Celia had introduced this man into his life. 'I should like to explore philosophy further with you on another day, Professor Antrobus. I don't believe I have ever discussed it with anyone before.'

'There's nothing like a thorough rummage in the bowels of philosophy for passing a cold winter's day. It always leaves me feeling quite invigorated.'

'But not fed,' Lady Lavinia said meaningfully.

'Of course, forgive me,' Felix said and nodded to Chivers, hovering by the door.

'Oh, how delightful!' Isolde said as footmen proceeded to lay out a fantastic spread.

It included a massive mould of a castle-shaped jelly filled with vegetables sliced and laid out like flowers in the aspic, roasts, freshly baked bread, an assortment of sauces and vegetables and some beautifully decorated pies.

'I especially love jellies.'

'I'm glad to hear that,' Felix said with a laugh. 'I must confess I find them unnecessarily complex, but chef loves to make them and has certainly excelled herself this evening.'

'They're beautiful, like edible jewels.'

'Well please, begin,' Felix said.

He helped himself to the plate of chicken with a light curry sauce that was placed, by design, nearest to him. He'd carefully chosen the dishes he was able to eat. They were somewhat blander than the delights he'd arranged for his guests but spread amongst the rest so that nobody would realise when he only ate from a few of the plates.

He just hoped that his aunt wouldn't notice the curry sauce. He was rather partial to it, but she believed anything foreign to be dangerous for his health. If it wasn't for the fact that he'd placed her at the foot of the table, she might have tried to prevent him from partaking.

'You really are spoiling us, your grace,' Isolde said. 'I've been to hundreds of parties this year, and this is by far the best dinner I've attended.'

'That's because the other hosts have been nip purses trying to save money,' Celia said. 'In fairness, it is costly to cater properly, and not everybody has Felix's budget.'

'If you can't afford to do it properly you shouldn't do it at all,' Isolde said. 'When I am a hostess I will make sure to only provide the best. Don't you agree, your grace?'

'I'm sure every host or hostess tries to put on the best entertainments they can provide,' Felix said. 'But I am glad this one meets with your approval, Lady Giddings.'

'Oh, it does, especially as I have been pining to be out and about again. Honestly, I am a terrible patient. I detest being cooped up. The only consolation is that I have everyone at my beck and call. Poor Honour has been sitting by my bedside reading to me every day.'

'Have you, Miss Seaborn?'

Felix examined her more closely. She was dressed very simply in a grey dress and yet she had a quiet dignity about her. She looked surprised to be asked a question but didn't hesitate in her reply.

'It was a trifling service,' Honour said.

'She is too modest, your grace. Honour is a saint. And I'm afraid I was an ungrateful wretch getting her to fetch and carry. At least I also had my maid and several footmen to help, and I feel less guilty about them. After all, that's what they're paid for.'

'I suppose so,' Felix said.

'You must know what I mean,' Isolde said. 'For you have the same, I'm sure. And I hear you pay well over the market rate for your servants so they can't complain if you make exacting demands.'

'I try not to,' Felix said rather thrown by Isolde's remarks.

'But surely that's why you pay them more.'

'I'm surprised that what I pay my servants is a topic of conversation for anyone other than my man of business and me.'

'My father mentioned it. He said it affects the going rate and pushes up what it costs others to hire servants.'

'Oh,' Felix said and suppressed the urge to tell Lady Giddings' father to go to hell. It was probably best he wasn't in attendance.

'You have so surprised his grace he's at a loss for words, Lady Giddings,' Professor Antrobus said. 'I take it from your remarks that you aren't greatly concerned by the plight of the working classes.'

'I didn't say that,' Isolde said. 'But my father's servants aren't really the working class, are they?'

'I don't know what else you could call them,' Professor Antrobus said and proceeded to expound on the position of servants.

The rest of the table split into smaller conversations. Each person at the table turning to talk to the people to their left or right. Felix watched them for a while, catching fragments from everyone. Percy and Lord Hounslow were having a spirited argument with Pixie who was chatting back most animatedly. He found himself wishing he could join them because they appeared to be having such fun. He turned to Miss Seaborn, who gave him an enquiring look and a friendly smile.

'Miss Seaborn, might I ask you a question that has perplexed me for a while now?'

'Of course, your grace, although I can't imagine what light I might shed on something that has you puzzled.'

'It has to do with you. If my question is too personal, please feel free to tell me to mind my own business.'

'Oh... well please, ask, and then I shall see.'

'I was wondering... Lady Giddings mentioned you'd gone to live with her upon the death of your father, by which I assumed your mother had predeceased him.'

'My mother died when I was seven.'

'Seven! And yet you remained with your father?'

'Ah, I see. You are wondering why I wasn't sent back to England upon my mother's death.'

'It does seem a trifle unusual.'

'I have come to realise that, but at the time all I knew was that I didn't want to be separated from my father. He didn't have many options either. None of my family from his side or my mother's were willing to take me in. The only other choice was to send me to a girl's boarding school which he refused to do. So he said there was nothing for it but for me to stay with him.'

'That must have been very difficult for you.'

'It wasn't really. I suppose because it was all I'd ever known. As I grew older, I gradually took over the running of my father's household, and we managed very well together.'

'So you went everywhere he went?' Felix was astonished to discover that this quiet young woman had such an exotic history. 'Even into battle?'

'Never into battle, but certainly quite nearby. I have been billeted in towns that have been shelled, but thankfully not too often.'

'What did you do at those times?'

'I made myself as useful as possible. Mostly by helping distribute food to the local inhabitants or working in the hospital tent.'

'That is very brave of you.'

'Not really. I was surrounded by soldiers and soldier's wives who treated every challenge and hardship as a commonplace, so I did too.'

'So... did your father die at war?'

'He didn't. He was bitten by a poisonous snake in South Africa when he was out scouting for a new campsite for the regiment. I was told he died before his comrades could get him back to the infirmary.'

'I'm very sorry.'

'Thank you, it was a wrench. I half expected to lose him whenever he went out to battle, but I admit it came as a shock to lose him when we were living through a quiet spell.'

'I don't think we ever expect to lose our parents, do we? It was a shock to me, too, when I lost my father.'

'I gather that wasn't recent.'

'No, I was seven, like you with your mother. Yet it still feels raw.'

'Yes,' Honour said.

'I'm sorry, this isn't a good topic of conversation for dinner. But please, tell me, you must have travelled a great deal.'

'I have visited three continents. I travelled across Europe down to Crimea, then overland to India. We stayed there for quite a few years before we were sent by ship to South Africa.'

'How amazing to have lived so much in such a short space of time. Your diaries must provide tales aplenty.'

'Not as much as you might imagine,' Honour said with a laugh. 'I'm afraid I'm not a great diarist. But I do like sketching. I have filled several books with my impressions of all the places I've visited.'

'You have pictures?' Felix said, 'How wonderful. I would love to see them.'

'That's very kind of you to say so, your grace.'

'No, I mean that sincerely, Miss Seaborn,' Felix said as he placed his hand on her arm for emphasis. 'I would really be delighted if you'd show me your sketches and tell me all about them.'

'Oh... well... I suppose I could send them over.'

'Ah,' Felix said. 'I suspect without your explanations the pictures wouldn't be half as meaningful.'

'I doubt...' Honour said and trailed off as she looked towards her cousin.

'It's no matter,' Felix said, but he wondered how he could he find a way that the two of them could meet so Miss Seaborn could show him the pictures. 'Perhaps one day.'

'Certainly,' Honour said.

'Did I hear that you have been to South Africa, Miss Seaborn?' Bellamy said, turning to join in the conversation.

'I was there until a few months ago.'

'Where were you based?'

'For the most part in Cape Town.'

'How did you find it?'

'The town itself was small but comfortable. The scenery, however, was breathtaking. To our back, we had the Table Mountain, and at our feet, the ocean. I have never been anywhere more beautiful.'

'And the people?'

'The usual mixture you find in the outposts of the empire, soldiers, bureaucrats, merchants, explorers and the local people. In Africa, that is a great diversity of black and brown tribes as well as the Boer nations.'

'I understand the African women don't wear much in the way of clothes,' Professor Antrobus said, breaking off what had seemed a very intense conversation with Lady Giddings.

'They tend to go topless, yes,' Honour said. 'It quickly becomes a commonplace, however.'

'How savage,' Isolde said. 'Surely it is an insufferable temptation to all the men in the town?'

'As I said, you grow accustomed, the men too. The women don't seem to be unduly molested.'

'How can that be when here we are so careful to keep everything covered to preserve our modesty? I find it hard to believe that such a blatant display of female flesh doesn't result in debauchery.'

'I can only relay what I saw,' Honour said.

'And as usual, Antrobus has homed in on the point most likely to cause argument,' Bellamy said. 'Well done, my friend. But if you don't mind, I'd like to ask Miss Seaborn more about the political situation.'

'What could she possibly know?' Isolde said. 'She was only a soldier's daughter.'

'Anyone immersed in a culture will get a sense of the politics around them, Lady Giddings.'

'If there is anything I can tell you that will help, m' lord, I will certainly try,' Honour said.

'You aren't interested in the affairs of Africa are you, your grace?' Isolde said.

'I'm interested in almost everything, Lady Giddings,' Felix said as he turned to speak with her. He felt a twinge of regret to not hear what Bellamy wanted to know from Miss Seaborn. 'I believe my tastes may be described as eclectic.'

'Well, I don't care to know about what happens in the overseas territories. It's tiresome when people go on about them.'

'So what are your interests, Lady Giddings?'

'I like to talk about people, and events, definitely events. I had a wonderful ride yesterday in Hyde Park. There was such a crush of people, and some of the men were positively ogling me.'

Felix was struck by the thought that Lady Giddings rather liked to be looked at. 'I imagine that was an uncomfortable experience for you.'

'Oh, I don't mind. One has to expect it, after all.'

'But not necessarily like it.'

Lady Giddings flashed him a dazzling smile and said, 'It's just the way men are. They can't help it.'

'I see, well I apologise on behalf of my sex.'

'Don't be silly,' Isolde said with a gurgle of a laugh that was the most charming thing he'd ever heard. 'It wasn't your fault.'

'No, but I often find myself wishing men behaved better towards women.'

'Do you really? And what would you do if I were your wife and men were ogling me? Would you be frightfully jealous?'

'Quite possibly,' Felix said and felt that he was being manoeuvred into a position he wasn't ready for yet.

'Only quite possibly? Your grace!' Isolde said and gave him a playful tap to his hand. 'What am I to make of that?'

Felix, much to his surprise, realised that Lady Giddings was flirting. He was at a loss to know what to say, never having had anyone flirt with him before.

'I suppose it's a bit of a letdown, Lady Giddings, but I'm afraid I would never be in a position to fight other men off on your behalf.'

'Oh,' Isolde said and blinked in surprise. She rallied quickly enough and said, 'I dare say it doesn't matter.'

'I'm relieved it doesn't bother you,' Felix said. 'Let's not dwell on that. Tell me some more about yourself instead. Have you always lived in London?'

'Have you been looking me up, your grace?'

'Mmm?'

'Most people think I grew up in the country on my father's estate. Everyone just assumes a lord has a country estate.'

'Guilty as charged. I looked your father up. In my defence, I look almost everybody up.'

'So you know I'm a Londoner born and bred. I'm proud of it too. I've visited friends in the country from time to time and found it deadly dull. There was nothing but fields and cows and yokels who just stared whenever I went past, and mud. It's impossible to walk anywhere in the country without getting covered in mud.'

'So what did you do when growing up, for entertainment in London?'

'Shopping mainly, I love shopping, and riding in the park. I was also taken along to any number of museums, galleries and to the library, of course. It was all very improving.'

'Did you go to school?'

'I had a governess. She was a sour-faced old bat who never had a kind word for anyone. I got rid of her as soon as I could.'

'It sounds a little lonely,' Felix said. 'If you were schooled at home and don't have any siblings.'

'I didn't mind. I have always been able to do pretty much whatever I wanted.'

'I see. How about reading, do you have any favourite authors?'

'Oh no, I like fashion magazines, sometimes I read something serialised in the periodicals, but for the most part, I don't remember the names of the authors.'

'I don't bother with the names either,' Professor Antrobus said, joining the conversation. 'A great deal too much is made of authors.'

'But without authors who would provide us with the entertainment and improving works we have?' Felix said.

'A fair point, although I have heard that there are no original tales left and that every story is one of 12 redone over and over again.'

'There are common themes to be sure,' Felix said. 'But the variety of how they are put together is what keeps it interesting.'

Felix was exhausted, and as the meal wound down, he was wondering how he could get away without bringing the party to an end or making too much of his exit.

'Ladies, shall we leave the gentlemen to have their smoke?' Lady Lavinia said as she rose from the table.

This was his opportunity. Felix heaved himself to his feet and said, 'Ladies and gentlemen, I'd like to thank you for coming this evening, and I hope you don't mind if I retire at this moment. Please do carry on without me.'

Percy rose to his feet and said, 'Thank you, your grace. It was a thoroughly pleasant evening.' He came over to Felix, as the rest of the guests murmured their thanks, and said in an undertone, 'Want a little support?'

'Not yet,' Felix said, gave a nod and a smile to everyone and started on his slow walk to the door.

'Ladies, please follow me,' Lady Lavinia said.

For once Felix wished he could thank her for providing this cover as the women got up and moved to the drawing room while he made his way to the corridor.

The moment the door closed behind him, Percy took a firm grip on his elbow and guided him to his room. 'Are you sure you're all right?'

'I'm just a little tired, nothing to worry about,' Felix said as a wave of dizziness overtook him and he stumbled.

'Felix!'

'I'm all right, really,' Felix said. 'I just need to rest.'

'Should I get Dr Morton?'

'There is no need, Grantley will look after me,' Felix said as he struggled to keep a clear head and on his feet.

'Grantley, his grace needs you,' Percy said as Grantley, hearing voices in the hall, popped his head around the door.

'Your grace, I knew it was too much. Poole, help me,' Grantley said. 'It will be all right Captain Shawcross, we'll look after him now.'

'He's right,' Felix said as he noted Percy gearing up to argue. 'Please Percy, will you stand my deputy and make sure everyone has a pleasant evening. I'd hate for the party to end early just because I've left.'

'I'll do that, never you fear, now you really must rest.'

Chapter Sixteen

Honour woke early. She hadn't slept much after the dinner because it had given her so much to think about. It was quite the most invigorating evening she'd ever spent. It was also a group of people she would never, under normal circumstances, have a chance of meeting. It was still astonishing to her that she'd sat between a duke and a diplomat.

As she couldn't sleep and a cool grey light seeped into the room indicating the arrival of the dawn, she got out of bed and hunted for her shawl. Remembering she'd left it in the parlour, she flung on a dress and went to fetch it.

She turned from retrieving her shawl to discover her cousin curled up on the sofa.

'Oh, Isolde, you're up. Did you even go to bed?'

'Not yet,' Isolde murmured. 'That Professor Antrobus, he was a strange one, wasn't he?'

'Most unconventional, yes,' Honour said and sat down opposite her cousin. She'd never seen her this reflective before, and her curiosity got the better of her. 'Did he catch your fancy?'

'Don't be silly. He is a pauper. Why would he interest me?'

'It just seemed to me last night that you enjoyed his company.'

'It doesn't matter, though, does it? I'm going to marry the duke.'

'Even if you don't want to?'

'Who says I don't want to?'

'Forgive me, Isolde, but it didn't look like the two of you enjoyed your conversations, and you kept turning back to the professor. And after the duke left, you appeared to have a better time.'

Isolde shrugged and said, 'The duke is boring, but at least he's sickly so I wouldn't have to spend much time with him. I could leave him at home and go out to meet people.'

'But why marry him at all? You even seem to prefer Overbrook to the duke.'

'Overbrook is more normal. The duke is just... he's odd.'

'I didn't think he was odd. A little on the quiet side, but interested in other people. That, you know, doesn't usually follow with the wealthy or the ill.'

Isolde gave her a suddenly arrested look and said, 'You like him!'

'He treats me like an equal, not the hired help. You have no idea how rare that it, so yes, for that I like him.'

'Oh really, and now you're trying to make me go after a penniless professor. Well, I'll never be so foolish, so don't you even think you can have the duke for yourself.'

'Isolde, don't be silly. I have no such ambition. I just said he was kind to me, that's all. Usually, I'm put down at the bottom end of the table at dinners or surrounded by elderly aunts and the least popular guests. It was a rare treat to be at the head of the table.'

'He put you there because he wanted to have me at his right hand. Don't you think otherwise, for you'd be wrong.'

'I know. I guessed he put me there because, not having been to other dinner parties, the duke doesn't know that chaperones don't have to sit near their charges. All I'm saying is that then he could have ignored me and he didn't.'

'And you made sheep's eyes at him instead of knowing your place and keeping quiet!'

Honour felt as if she'd been slapped. She always knew Isolde's thoughts were all about herself, but it hurt nonetheless for her to come out and say it. Honour gave Isolde a tight smile, stood and said, 'I'm sorry you felt that way. Now I'm running late so I'll leave you to your sulks.'

'Late for what? Who are you going to see? You can't just go out visiting people without telling me.'

'I did tell you, weeks ago. I'm going to meet with an old friend of my father's, Sergeant Major Bruin. I've known him since childhood, and he's only back in the country for a little while. We are going for tea and little chat, so you have nothing to worry about.'

'So you say.'

'Honestly, Isolde, you are by far the prettiest of the two of us. Do you really think any man is going to give me the time of day when he knows he could have you?'

'No, of course not.'

'There you are then,' Honour said.

Having slightly mollified her cousin, she hurried from the room before she could come up with any other objection.

'Come along, Doris,' she said to her maid lurking in the corridor. 'We're going to have to hurry, or I fear we'll be late.'

Honour was grateful for the walk and the brisk wind as she stopped outside the George Hotel. It had distracted her from the unpleasant conversation she'd had with Isolde. It would be even better when she met Sergeant Major Bruin and was further distracted.

Right on cue, she heard a loud voice boom, 'Honour Seaborn, as I live and breathe, you get lovelier every time I see you, girl!'

She looked up the stairs to the hotel entrance and felt a tug of sadness and pleasure to see a large portly man beaming down at her. Everything about him said army. From his immaculate, bright red jacket, to his majestic sideburns and whiskers now liberally sprinkled with grey.

'Sergeant Major Bruin, still flattering every young woman you come across, are you?' Honour said, and she hurried up the stairs, holding both hands out in greeting. It reminded her so forcibly of her father to see this big man that it hurt.

He gave her hands a squeeze and said, 'How are you holding up, old girl?'

'I'm fine.'

'Your cousin's treating you well, is she?'

'Well enough,' Honour said, pushing any complaints away. It wasn't seemly to moan, and the sergeant major couldn't do a thing about it anyway.

'Come on into the hotel. I'll get you a nice cup of tea and a tea cake, and you can tell me all about it,' Bruin said as he ushered Honour and Doris towards the hotel sitting room. It was a large room and dotted about with groups of chairs and sofas. Despite the early hour, quite a few guests were present, chatting or reading the papers. A high proportion appeared to be military men.

'Thank you,' Honour said as she looked about. 'It feels strange to be here.'

'Brings back memories, does it?' Bruin said.

'Father and I stayed here once, but that feels like a lifetime ago.'

'Aye, it's a military favourite and no mistake. It's where I always stay if I can get out of barracks.'

'Which you have apparently succeeded in today.'

'I have indeed because I convinced my CO that I have pressing personal business.'

'Have you?'

'Ah, we shall see,' Bruin said, tapping the side of his nose knowingly. 'But first, let me get you some refreshments. We can wait to be served, but I know the staff here so I'll expedite matters,' Bruin said and hurried away.

Honour sighed with relief as she sank into her chair. It was good to be here, amongst her people. She felt comfortable in this dining room, surrounded by men in uniform.

She hadn't realised how much she felt like a fish out of water until this moment. She understood these men. She could easily have a conversation with any of them without difficulty. She knew their trials and triumphs for she'd lived many of them herself.

'Miss Seaborn, good heavens, what brings you here?' a hearty voice said behind her.

Honour swivelled around and said, 'Captain Shawcross, I could ask you the same question.'

'I'm here to catch up with a couple of friends who are back from campaigning in India.'

'Well, as it happens, so am I. At least, I'm meeting with an old family friend and bosom mate of my father's.'

'Is he also late like my lot?'

'Not at all. But as he was a supply sergeant for many years, he is always trying to rustle up a better deal than one finds on the menu.'

'Ah, I know the type. Might I join you for a moment then?'

'Please do.'

'Thank you,' Percy said and sprawled on a chair without drawing it closer to Honour. 'How did you enjoy last night?'

'I had a delightful evening, thank you. Have you seen his grace this morning by any chance?'

'Not yet, too early.'

'I wondered, he looked fatigued by the time he retired.'

'I'm afraid so, but I believe he enjoyed himself.'

'I'm glad to hear it.'

'Are you?'

'But of course. It clearly meant a lot to him that it went off well.'

'You're very observant, Miss Seaborn.'

'Not really. You'd have to be particularly dense not to spot his grace's nervous energy.'

'Did Lady Giddings notice?'

Honour gave the captain a measuring look then checked on Doris to make sure she wasn't paying them any attention. Thankfully Doris was gazing about the hotel in awe and seemed oblivious to them.

'Now why would you ask me something like that?'

'Curiosity, I suppose. Your cousin was the guest of honour after all.'

'Not very obviously.'

'No, Felix is subtle that way.'

Honour took a deep breath, wondering whether she was about to be too bold, then threw that consideration to the wind and said, 'Might I give you a hint, Captain Shawcross?'

'A hint?'

'Forgive me if I've misread the situation, but it seems to me that you have been making my cousin the object of your gallantry.'

'If you're warning me off, Miss Seaborn-'

'No, that is... I get the impression that you aren't actually that fond of her. Which could mean only one thing,' Honour hurried on so that she couldn't be interrupted, 'You are trying to draw my cousin away from the duke.'

'And if I was, Miss Seaborn?'

'Well... last night his grace arranged for you to be far apart. That meant he got to speak to my cousin uninterrupted, and she...' Honour dropped her voice so as not to be overheard, 'I really shouldn't be this disloyal but, she can be her own worst enemy. She said a few things last night that I don't think your cousin liked.'

'Is that so, Miss Seaborn?'

'Distraction and competition can sometimes backfire, sir.'

'But what if I want to marry your cousin?'

'Do you really think that's likely?'

To her relief, Captain Shawcross laughed and said, 'You're almost as knowing as my cousin, Miss Seaborn. Now I do believe that large military gentlemen laden with a heaving tray is your host and I should take my leave.'

'Who was that?' Bruin said scowling after Captain Shawcross's fast retreating back.

'An acquaintance of the last few weeks.'

'He's not making eyes at you is he, Honour?'

'Would it matter if he was?'

'Well, that is to say... your father wanted more for you.'

'I'm afraid with my eccentric background, straitened circumstances and lack of connections I would be lucky to attract anyone like Captain Shawcross.'

'The Horse Guards like to give themselves airs, but they're no better than the rest of us.'

'I know, it's no matter though. I am looking for employment and am confident I will be able to secure a post as a governess soon.'

'No! Honour no, surely not a governess. What's wrong with staying with your cousin? It was a bit of good fortune that her taking you in.'

'So it seemed,' Honour said giving Doris a quick glance to see how closely she was listening. Thankfully she was still distracted by her surroundings.

Bruin understood though and merely said, 'I see.'

'Never mind me, though. What are you up to? What brings you to London?'

'We're in transit, heading off to Guyana for what I have been reliably informed will be a very relaxing time.'

'It's about time. The 43rd has been to some of the most dangerous places in the world.'

'Aye, that's so.'

'How long will you be in London?'

'Would you believe a whole month? They're giving the lads a chance to go home and see their families, those that want to anyway.'

'That will be nice for them.'

'And as you know, those of us without families while away the time seeing the sights of London.'

'I remember. Those were good days.'

'They were indeed,' Bruin said and glanced across at Doris. Then he leaned closer and whispered, 'I say, do you think we could speak in private?'

'Of course,' Honour said. 'Doris, would you be a dear please and pop outside for a periodical. Here's the money for it.'

'Of course, miss,' Doris said and hurried off.

'Well, she looks like an arch conspirator,' Bruin said with a grin.

'She has something of a romantic disposition and has jumped to the wrong conclusion, I'm afraid, but it will serve us well enough. Not that I can see why you need to speak to me in private.'

'Well, the thing is,' Bruin said and fingered his collar. 'I promised your father that if anything happened to him, I would make sure you were all right.'

'And I am.'

'Well no, miss, not if you're contemplating life as a governess you're not. What kind of a life is that for a spunky young lass like you?'

'It's the way life sometimes goes.'

'It's wrong and that business I hinted at, well... Miss Seaborn, would you do me the honour of marrying me?'

'I beg your pardon?' Honour said as she blinked in confusion at the sergeant major.

'It's my duty to keep you safe, and I give you my word as my wife you would want for nothing.'

'Oh, Gerald,' Honour said and put her hand over the sergeant major's. 'That's very kind of you, but quite unnecessary. Besides, I've had enough of traipsing around the world in military camps. I'd rather be a governess in England if truth be told.'

'Well, I see... um... well. The offer stands, my dear. If you ever need me, in any way, I'll see you right.'

'You are the sweetest man to have made the offer. I do believe, as a confirmed bachelor, that you have just done the most heroic thing of your life. But there really is no need to fling yourself on the fires of sacrifice for me. I'm more than capable of looking after myself. My father made sure of that.'

'He did and all, but you did as much for him. No man was better looked after than your father, and so we all told him.'

Felix lay propped up in bed with a book on his lap, but he wasn't reading. He closed his eyes and listened to the thump, thump, thump of his heart. Much as he tried to ignore it, there were times when he just needed to know. Not that feeling his heartbeat told him anything.

So he forced his attention elsewhere, to the dinner and Lady Giddings. She was as beautiful as ever. When she arrived, he felt a thrill pass through him to see her again but then... sitting with her in the sociable setting of the dinner table she was different. She was out of kilter, her opinions were... they didn't chime with his own. He replayed their conversation in his mind, and they jarred, and he didn't know what to make of it.

A tap at the door pulled him from his reverie, and Percy stuck his head into the room. 'Chivers tells me you aren't up for visitors, if that's so send me away.'

'No, come in. I could use the distraction.'

'You look peaky today.'

'Just tired. Dr Morton has given me the all-clear though.'

'And you're sure-'

'Tell me what happened after I left last night,' Felix said brushing away Percy's concerns. He didn't want yet another conversation about his health. 'Did people stay long?'

'Another couple of hours.' Percy pulled up a chair and settled beside the bed.

'Is that good?'

'It's about the average, so yes, it was good.'

'And?'

'Do you want the gossip?'

'Isn't that normal?'

'Oh yes, post-party gossip is what it's all about. Who got on with who, who fell out, any insults traded, all of that.'

'So what is being said about my dinner?' Felix said and leaned forward in his bed.

'That it was a good one,' Percy said and pushed Felix gently back against his pillows.

'Come on, Percy, don't toy with me, please. Tell me what I missed.'

'Not a whole lot to tell, old boy. You made certain of that by putting me at the boring end of the table with Aunt Lavinia. I'm not sure I will ever be able to forgive you for that.'

'I would apologise but for the fact that you, Hounslow, Juliana and Pixie seemed to be having a better time than those of us at the head of the table.'

'It was a laugh, that's for certain and, here's a tasty morsel for you, I believe Hounslow was quite taken with Juliana.'

'Really? I thought he fancied Lady Giddings.'

'He's been following her ladyship for weeks, but Hounslow has no illusions to his own beauty and seems to have decided that he doesn't stand a chance with her. Which was sensible of him. So he resolved to have a good time with everyone else and got to know the girls, and I swear by the end of the evening he was quite smitten by Juliana.'

'Did he tell you that?'

'He didn't have to, I mentioned he's a great rhymester, didn't I?'

'You did.'

'Well, Aunt Lavinia asked him to do a turn after Lady Giddings played the piano. Usually, he composes these amusing couplets. It has the lads rolling on the floor with laughter. Last night though, they were all little love sonnets. Not bad by half, just not funny, and not terribly popular with Aunt Lavinia. She could see which way things were headed.'

'What about Juliana? What did she make of the poems?'

'She liked them but rather like any girl would like soppy, romantic stuff. I swear she doesn't have a clue that they were aimed at her or that Hounslow has fallen for her.'

'So what will he do?'

'Gird his loins and talk to Aunt Lavinia I expect, see if he can visit with Juliana.'

'Astonishing,' Felix murmured. 'Fancy Juliana gaining a beau from just one evening, and she hasn't even come out yet.'

'It's no bad thing really, Hounslow is a good egg. Aunt Lavinia should be happy enough if they decide to get hitched. Not that that's why I invited him along, but there you go.'

'Yes, indeed,' Felix said.

'Celia's gambit didn't work out half as well.'

'Celia's gambit?'

'I'm pretty sure she invited Professor Antrobus for Pixie.'

'You are? But why?'

'Probably because she was trying to match one clever person with another. I must say Pixie is as sharp as a knife. She runs rings around her sister, Juliana. Celia kept trying to get Pixie and Antrobus to talk, but neither was particularly interested in the other.'

'No, Antrobus was altogether more interested in Lady Giddings,' Felix said and wondered why that admission didn't irritate him more than it did.

'I'm afraid so,' Percy said. 'She has that kind of effect on men.'

'Yes, I noticed. The thing is... Lady Giddings seemed rather struck by Antrobus too.'

'You noticed, huh? Well, of course, you did, you notice everything. I wouldn't worry about it, though.'

'Why not? Because you think her a gold digger? Someone who doesn't care for anything but money?'

'I never said that.'

'No, you didn't, you've scrupulously avoided doing so. But you've also flirted with her.'

'Not last night,' Percy said and flushed.

'No, not last night.' Felix didn't want an argument with Percy, not today, not ever really. 'I got the impression, actually that you were rather struck by Pixie.'

'Too observant by half, coz,' Percy murmured. 'But you know, I'm no Lord Hounslow. Aunt Lavinia would never countenance one of her daughters marrying a mere soldier.'

'Did you like her that much?'

'She's a taking little thing. I'd like to get to know her better. Then again, it would probably be best to put her out of my mind and concentrate on my job for no good ever came from mooning over what you can never have.'

'Mmm,' Felix murmured. 'My problem is the exact opposite, or perhaps not. While I have money and rank my health would or should make any mother wary of marrying her daughter to me.'

'Oh, I think most mothers would be more than willing to see past your frailty and look with great favour upon your wealth. The daughters might feel different, but not all of them.'

'What a lowering thought.'

'Possibly not, at least you can get the woman of your dreams.'

'Maybe,' Felix said. 'But enough of this talk, what did you make of Antrobus? Have you ever seen a more astonishing man in your life?'

'He is quite the eccentric isn't he? Until I figured out that he was supposed to be a suitable candidate for Pixie I couldn't for the life of me work out why Celia had introduced him to you.'

'I wondered whether she just wanted to introduce me to an oddity. Then I realised that he's an old friend of Bellamy's from their university days, and he has no patience for fools.'

'A friend of Bellamy's huh, well, well. Do you think you'll want to meet him again?'

'Possibly, but not perhaps, until I have resolved the issue with Lady Giddings.'

'Your mail, your grace,' Chivers said after a respectful knock at the door.

'Good heavens that's a lot,' Felix said.

'That will be because of the party last night,' Percy said. 'They'll be letters of thanks. You won't get one from me because I came by in person to thank you.'

'And you don't like writing,' Felix said as he gave Chivers a nod to let him know he could leave.

'Where is Grantley by the way? By now he's usually done his best to shoo me away.'

'As you sneaked in, Grantley no doubt believes I have been resting quietly in my room as per doctor's orders. No doubt, he will emerge shortly to ensure I am still all right.'

'Doc Morton ordered you to rest?'

'He didn't really need to tell me. I was so tired this morning I couldn't get up. But I had the doctor look me over last night because Grantley was so worried. I feared if I didn't he'd sit up beside me for the whole night and he really is too old to still be doing that.'

'What did the doc think of you holding a party?'

'Doctor Morton frequently surprises me. Unlike my staff and Aunt Lavinia, he had no objection to the party. He said once I get used to the idea, and don't get as excited before it has even started, that they shouldn't tire me the way last night did.'

'That's good to hear. Now, I suspect you could use a bit more rest and the chance to look at your post. I needn't guess who the smelly lavender letter came from.'

'Lady Giddings,' Felix said. 'It isn't the first I've had from her.'

'Well, enjoy. I shall see you again shortly,' Percy said and took his leave.

Felix was sorry to see him go. He felt like there was still plenty of gossip to be extracted from the party. But Percy had duties and other friends to see, and he couldn't hog him. Felix didn't want to be a clinging relative anyway. It would only give Percy a distaste for him. So he reached for the letters instead.

Celia sent a very gratifying letter saying how much she enjoyed herself. Lord Hounslow's was briefer but said he hoped to get better acquainted. Felix smiled at that, it would be nice to widen his circle of friends, and he could do worse than a man who wanted to marry into the family. He hoped that would progress well for all involved.

Professor Antrobus had unexpectedly neat handwriting and as, no doubt, he'd done for countless parties, he thanked his host for an enjoyable evening. To Felix's surprise, he also said he hoped they might meet again and he found himself wondering why. He had no wish to further any acquaintance with a love rival and surely any man might feel the same way but, apparently, Antrobus did not.

Now he had two letters left. He recognised the handwriting on both, having received notes from both ladies before. What surprised him was that he was more eager to read the letter from Miss Seaborn than from Lady Giddings. That gave him pause.

He held a letter in each hand and tried to work out why he had left both till last. One reason was to keep the best till the end, so he could savour it. But which was the best?

Why didn't he yearn to hear from Lady Giddings now as he had in the past? Was familiarity something that operated so quickly that merely seeing the lady three times had resulted in a cooling of his ardour? Or was it the uncomfortable conversations they'd had?

He turned back to those as he had all morning. It was strange the way they seemed to have nothing in common. It wasn't just that he was an invalid and therefore couldn't share in her interests, riding and shopping. No that was wrong, he liked shopping too, only he did it via the periodicals. That should have given them common ground, only… it didn't. Her taste in dresses was that same slightly off-kilter as her opinions.

He didn't like the way she dressed, he thought with a sigh. He'd been trying to ignore it, but he couldn't any longer. She'd looked distinctly odd in the sapphire blue dress she wore last night. It wasn't the colour, that suited her well enough, it was the odd cut. It was the height of fashion, but it simply didn't work on Lady Giddings.

Miss Seaborn, on the other hand, was wearing the same grey dress as before. She'd changed the accessories, and she looked neat as a pin, if somewhat severe. How he would love to give her free rein to let her be herself rather than the buttoned-up companion. She would look so much better if she could wear her hair in a more relaxed way.

'What nonsense,' Felix snapped and ripped open Lady Giddings' letter. The gist was the same as the others. She thanked him for a delightful evening, underscored. And a wish that she could see him again soon. It was odd that it only cheered him a bit to hear that Lady Giddings wanted to see him again.

'Am I that fickle?' he murmured and gazed down at the letter, trying to bring back the memory of the first letter he'd had from her.

That had thrilled him so much it left him feeling giddy. Now he just felt... she was still beautiful. He wanted to touch her, to hold her but... he no longer had any interest in speaking to her. How odd.

He added her letter to the pile and felt Miss Seaborn's envelope one more time. It was thicker than the other letters. It was also interesting that the two ladies had sent him separate notes. They always sent him separate notes. Living in the same household, they could easily have sent him a joint letter. It spoke to a remote relationship.

Felix slit open the last letter. He was surprised that it consisted of a large sheet of quite heavy paper, certainly more substantial than what one usually used for a letter. He unfolded it and found himself staring at a sketch.

'*Bazaar at Cairo,*' he read in the space below the drawing. He skipped to the top of the page. '*Dear Lord Peergrave, I wanted to thank you for a very pleasant evening. I have seldom enjoyed myself more. I enclose this sketch I made in Cairo. It was a sweltering day, and the man on the left-hand side of the sketch sold the most delicious mint tea. Drinking the tea with my father under the shade of a date palm is one of my abiding memories of him.*'

Felix examined the picture more closely. It was excellent, with a lot of detail. He wished Miss Seaborn could be there to tell him more about it. And having seen this one sketch made him want to see the others even more.

This brought on another sigh. He really didn't know his own mind at the moment. What he needed was to discuss this with somebody. 'I shall write to Celia,' he said.

Chapter Seventeen

F elix was feeling languid. His dilemma about Lady Giddings and Miss Seaborn had caused him a restless night, and he desperately needed a distraction. He found his gaze constantly drifted from the magazine he was flicking through to the fire. Its movement drew the eye, and he couldn't look away.

'Your grace, Mr Testwood is here again,' Grantley said emerging from the dressing room. Unusually, he didn't look disapproving.

'Good heavens, Grantley, could it be that you have come to accept Mr Testwood?'

'As to that, I wouldn't like to say, sir,' Grantley said with a sniff and waved a grinning Hieronymus in.

'What delights do you bring me this morning, Mr Testwood?' Felix said.

'Well, your grace, I have been considering your bath chair.'

'Have you indeed?'

'It strikes me as very cumbersome. I would like to make it smaller and more manoeuvrable and also perhaps give you the option of propelling it yourself, rather than being pushed or pulled by your staff.'

'Mmm, the thing is, when I am feeling so weak that I can't stand, I am in no great condition to propel myself about either. Although, having said that, it's always good to have the option.'

'I will look into it, your grace. The other thought I had isn't something I can do, but I was wondering... well, how do you get upstairs at the moment?'

'I don't. I stay on the ground floor. Hence the conversion of these lower rooms into my living quarters.'

'But if you did have to go upstairs, how would you currently do that?'

'I have a group of four burly footmen carry me up in the bath chair. I don't like it though. Partly because I don't like my people having to carry me anywhere and also because it feels precarious in the extreme. A most uncomfortable experience,' Felix said and examined his inventor more closely. 'You have an idea for that?'

'I thought you might like to see all of what you own and perhaps see more of London from your upper floors. Now there is a way to do that, especially in such a big house.'

'There is?'

'Have you heard of a lift, your grace?'

'A lift?'

'It's a device, much like a small room, that travels vertically through a building. It's operated by hydraulic pressure. One has been installed at the Grosvenor Hotel although I wasn't allowed in to try it.'

'They didn't allow you in?'

'I was told the tradesmen's entrance was round the back.'

'I see.'

'They've called it the ascending room, which is exactly what it is. It carries guests up effortlessly to all their floors.'

'How fascinating, I should like to see something like that.'

'Well, I have all the literature I could procure on the lift with me,' Hieronymus said.

He pulled a wedge of papers out of his coat pocket and laid it out on the table in front of Felix.

'You could have it put in while you're in your country house so it wouldn't even cause any inconvenience, although obviously, you would lose a room on each floor to the lift.'

'Mmm,' Felix said as he looked over the diagrams and accompanying literature. 'I will enjoy this. How goes the other matter you were looking into, the compressed air?'

Testwood flushed, in the same way as when he'd mentioned the Grosvenor, but he said, 'Mr Andrews was receptive but suspicious. It may take a while before I can win him round.'

'I see.' Felix examined Hieronymus more closely and said, 'I do believe, Mr Testwood, it's time you get a new suit. If you have no objection, Grantley can arrange something for you.'

'I don't understand, your grace.'

'It appears you have a problem with gaining access. This lift sounds very interesting, but these documents only take you so far. There is nothing quite like seeing the thing for yourself. For that, you'll have to deputise for me and take a proper look. It would be good if you go to the manufacturer too. Would you be willing to do that?'

'If you trust me to, then yes, your grace I will. I'm just not sure they'll let me in even in a better suit, which I do feel I should procure for myself.'

'You are doing this work for me, Mr Testwood, under any other circumstances you wouldn't need the suit, so it is therefore down to me to provide it. Grantley will know exactly how to fit you out as a man of business. In fact, it wouldn't surprise me if he's been itching to do it. If we combine the right clothes with a letter of introduction from me, then you will be able to get in anywhere. That sounds vainglorious, but it's a sad fact of life that a ducal crest can work wonders. I would be a fool not to make judicious use of that.'

'Oh, er, yes, your grace. I suspect your letter is the only reason Mr Andrews was willing to see me.'

'There you are then. I'll get Grantley to take you in hand,' Felix said and rang his bell. 'In the meantime, I'll get on with the letters.'

Felix spent a couple of pleasant hours going over the literature on the lift. It really was a remarkable device. It got his mind seething with conjecture about where he might place it in the house and how he could use it. He was so absorbed in his speculation that it was a surprise when Celia was announced.

'How are you feeling this afternoon?' Celia said as she dropped down on the chair opposite Felix. 'That dressing-gown of yours is quite spectacular by the way.'

'Do you like it?' Felix said and gave it a twitch to get a better view of the technicolour splendour of the embroidery. It depicted a river flowing through a sunset landscape dotted about with cherry blossom laden trees. 'It's my latest acquisition and in the Japanese style.'

'It is the most impressive garment I have ever seen. Is it silk?'

'Yes, quite a heavy one, but when it was offered to me, I couldn't resist.'

'I can see why. Now my dear, what can I do for you? Your letter was far too cryptic for me to work it out.'

'Before I tell you that, can I ask... Professor Antrobus?'

'Ah, I really am sorry about that. I thought of him, particularly when I heard you'd invited Pixie.'

'So Percy was right about that.'

'He guessed, did he? Well, I'm sorry about how it turned out. I really thought if anyone could resist the lures of Lady Giddings, it would be Antrobus. I have told him in no uncertain terms that he has no chance with her.'

'Because she's after money?'

'I'm sorry, Felix, but I do believe that to be the case.'

'As does everybody else.'

Felix waited as Danby brought in some tea and sandwiches. He placed them on the table between them and left with a bow.

'Neither you or anyone else has said so bluntly what you think of Lady Giddings till now.'

'It really isn't my place to do so,' Celia said and took up the role of tea pourer in chief. 'Besides, having been in the throes of passionate love myself, I know how pointless it is talking to the sufferer.'

'And now?'

'You will note, I have not warned you off. What you choose to do with Lady Giddings is entirely your own affair.'

'But you don't like her.'

'I'm afraid not.'

'Why not?' Felix said, surprised by Celia's reply. She was like her mother in her directness.

'Mainly, I suppose, because I don't like to be snubbed. Lady Giddings has no interest in anyone who isn't openly admiring of her. As a consequence, she tends to ignore women.'

'Does she?'

'Did you see her speaking to any of us at dinner?'

'No, I didn't,' Felix said in surprise. 'I didn't notice.'

'You had other things on your mind. Now, my dear, what can I help you with?'

'Ah, yes...' Felix wondered how to phrase this question because he was still so confused about it himself. He decided on a more neutral opening question. 'I was wondering what you thought of Miss Seaborn?'

'Miss Seaborn?'

'You were sitting right next to her.'

'On the other side of my husband. Who, incidentally, was very impressed by Miss Seaborn.'

'Was he?'

'According to him, she is more sensible than most of the young men who bring him reports from around the world. Which was the first I knew that his remit was so broad. But I digress, yes, Bellamy liked her.'

'And you?'

'I liked her too in as much as I got to know her over dinner,' Celia said. 'She held her own in a very high-status group. This when she is the mere daughter of a soldier who apparently dragged her everywhere he went. It isn't the best education for a young woman. However, it left her unflustered when she was placed between a duke and a peer of the realm.'

'I don't understand. As Lady Giddings' chaperone, she must surely have sat in similar surroundings before. Why would mine be exceptional?'

'Because chaperones usually get relegated to the end of the table away from the most important guests.'

'I see.' Felix was surprised at how little notion he had of the way society worked. He'd never even considered where a companion might sit, and it was never mentioned in anything he'd read before.

'So, am I to assume that you now prefer Miss Seaborn to Lady Giddings?' Celia asked gazing at Felix over the brim of her tea cup.

'I don't know.' Felix felt so foolish about making this admission. How could he not know his own mind?

'And that was why you wanted to see me?'

'I need more information, and Percy wouldn't be able to help. He'd just laugh and make a witty comment about my predicament.'

'There are other women, you do know that, don't you, Felix?'

'Other women... to ask?'

'No silly, to marry. It doesn't have to be Lady Giddings versus Miss Seaborn.'

'Mmm, the thing is, after my short time meeting young women... I know I should consider it again, but Lady Giddings was such a breath of fresh air. The other women were young, uninteresting shadows who obeyed their mothers and performed. I have a feeling I could sit with a hundred more of that kind of girl and never get to know any of them. Then Lady Giddings breezed in, and she was so beautiful, so very... alive, so very much herself. She came as a positive relief.'

'And you fell head over ears in love with her.'

'Yes.'

'But now you have doubts.'

'And I don't know why.'

'Don't you?'

Felix sighed and said, 'Things weren't perfect at the dinner. I enjoyed talking to Miss Seaborn more than Lady Giddings and then yesterday morning I got these,' Felix said, holding out the letters from the two ladies.

'And?' Celia said.

'Take a look. Tell me what you think.'

'Perfumed lavender,' Celia said with distaste as she took the two missives.

'I have the lowering feeling that Lady Giddings sends the same kind of letter to everyone.'

'By that you mean men, I doubt she'd send anything like this to a woman.'

'You are probably right.'

'And Miss Seaborn sent you a sketch, that is unusual.'

'I discovered at dinner that she drew. I said I would like to see her work. She didn't say it, but I got the impression she wouldn't be able to show me anything while she is under Lady Giddings' roof.'

'There's no doubt about that. Lady Giddings would be furious if you showed more interest in her chaperone than you do in her. Especially as she seems to have taken a rather proprietary view towards you.'

'She did behave as though she expects to marry me.'

'She probably thought she was being subtle, but I noticed it too.'

'I am afraid I may have led her on.'

'What, by being bowled over by her? Nonsense. You haven't made her any offers or promises have you?'

'None, but I doubt she'll see it that way. She seemed very clear about what she thought was going to happen next.'

'That young woman has never suffered a setback in her life. It will do her good to be rebuffed.'

'The thing is... I'm still not sure. Was I mistaken in Lady Giddings? Do I like Miss Seaborn more? What if I'm just fickle and will lose interest in both of them a week from now, or a month. This is all very confusing.'

'It is,' Celia said and took Felix's hand. 'But you don't have to worry. We all go through this. Things will become clear in time.'

'Are you sure?' Felix was embarrassed yet comforted to be holding Celia's hand. While at the same time feeling he should be more manly and clear about what he wanted.

'What you need to do is see them both again. You can't make a decision in a vacuum.'

'Another dinner? I don't think-'

'No, not a dinner, that's too formal. Do something only with young people or rather, unattached people, maybe a tea, with some games thrown in. Make it a light afternoon diversion.'

'Your mother won't like that.'

'No doubt, but this is your house and your life. So far you have managed mother without too much difficulty, but in this instance, you can leave her to me. I will make sure she doesn't kick up a dust.'

'You can do that?' Felix said and felt relieved he didn't have to fight this particular battle with his aunt.

'I suspect you prevail over my mother more often than I do, but in this instance, I have a trump card.'

Felix wondered what that was but decided he wouldn't like the answer so instead, he said, 'All right so... only the unattached people?'

'That's right, everyone from your dinner party excepting Mother and Father, Bellamy and me, of course.'

'I'm not sure, you would be handy and as for Professor Antrobus...'

'I'm afraid, as a married lady, I fit into the wrong category in this instance. As for Antrobus, I do think you could grow to like him and also... I got the impression Lady Giddings was intrigued by him. If she were in love with you, he wouldn't stand a chance.'

'You're deliberately trying to show her up.'

'Am I wrong?'

'No, but it will be a challenging afternoon. Also, what does one do at a tea? The only teas I've been to have been interminable affairs with our elderly relatives. And what kind of games? I don't want to be the odd man out, just watching as everybody else careens about the room.'

'It will be all right,' Celia said as she gave his hand a reassuring squeeze. 'You will have Percy, Juliana and Pixie there, who all know not to tire you. They can be primed on what you like and what you won't like so that they can make sure things don't get out of hand. Miss Seaborn is also a sensible young woman, and I get the impression she is unlikely to engage in high jinks. The same is undoubtedly true of Antrobus, who really will be the old man of the party. So with all of them, it's only Lord Hounslow and Lady Giddings to think about, and I believe they will go along with whatever the group does so it will be fine.'

'I have a feeling this is somewhat irregular. Surely an elderly relative should be present to chaperone?'

'That had better not be a ploy to get me to come along,' Celia said with a laugh. 'A group of cousins getting together with a few friends, one of which is a chaperone, it will be fine.'

CHAPTER EIGHTEEN

F elix dipped the nib of his pen into the inkpot and scratched
across the page finishing off the last invitation in his perfect
copperplate. He waited for the ink to dry and then folded
the thick paper carefully. It was an extravagance using such
heavy paper as the post would cost him more. But, these were
important invitations, so he felt the additional cost was worth
it. His lips twitched up as he considered what his aunt might say
to yet more irresponsible expenditure.

He hoped all his potential guests would be able to make it and
wondered how Lady Giddings would do. She had said on more
than one occasion that there was nothing she liked better than a
cosy afternoon spent around the fire with friends. His tea party
was for precisely that, so in a way, it was a test for her and for
him. He hoped she would pass it.

'Your grace,' Chivers said as he appeared in the room, 'There
is a Lord Overbrook here to see you. He is being most insistent
and says he won't leave before he has spoken to you.'

'Good heavens,' Felix said.

His initial inclination was to send the man away. He was
unknown and uninvited, but his curiosity wouldn't allow it.

'Help me to the drawing room, Chivers, and then you can show his lordship in.'

'You're going to see him, your grace?'

'I am,' Felix said as he heaved himself to his feet. 'But I want you to stand by at the door with a couple of footmen because we may just have to eject our visitor.'

'Forgive me, your grace, but if you expect trouble, shouldn't you just send the gentleman away?' Chivers said and maintained his sphinx-like expression as he assisted Felix across the hall and into the drawing room.

Felix admired him for that. He wished he could do the same. 'It would be best to deal with him now.'

'Very good, your grace,' Chivers said as he lowered Felix into his favourite chair. 'I will now fetch Lord Overbrook.'

'Take your time.' Felix knew Chivers would understand; he needed to get his breath back.

His wait was all too brief, but at least it left no time to regret his decision to see the earl.

'So you are the Duke of Morley,' Overbrook said as Chivers announced him.

Felix stood up but made no attempt to shake the man's hand, 'I am.'

He took his time looking the earl up and down. He was older than expected, gaunt and dressed in an old fashioned coat. It was frayed at the cuffs. Considering he was known to be extremely wealthy, it spoke to Felix of a miserly attitude. At the moment, he was banging his walking cane repeatedly on the floor in an unconscious gesture.

'I knew your father,' Overbrook said. 'You look like him.'

'Then I'm afraid you have an advantage over me as I am not familiar with you.'

'Didn't say I liked him, mind you,' Overbrook said.

'What can I do for you, my lord?' Felix said as he sat back down.

He didn't bother to offer the earl a chair. He didn't look inclined to sit down, and Felix was fast coming to the conclusion that he had no intention of encouraging him to stay.

'It has come to my attention that you are making Lady Giddings the object of your affections,' Lord Overbrook said.

'Has it indeed? And why, may I ask, is that any business of yours?'

'Lady Giddings and I have an arrangement.'

'Is she engaged to you?' Felix was pretty certain she wasn't.

'No, as to that, I haven't proposed yet. But I have given her a gift, a solitaire diamond on a necklace. She understood the meaning of it. You must understand it too.'

'I'm afraid her ladyship hasn't mentioned you to me at all,' Felix said, keeping his cool despite the man's incredibly rude behaviour.

'Well, sir, I am telling you now, Lady Giddings is mine. You would do well to remember that.'

'Until I see a notice of your engagement in the papers, or Lady Giddings tells me to leave her alone, I will do exactly as I please.'

'You will not. You will stay away from her, your grace, or before God, I swear I will destroy you!' Lord Overbrook hissed. He slammed his cane into the floor again, turned and left.

'Good God!' Felix said as he stared after him.

'Are you all right, your grace?' Chivers said.

'I am, make sure my visitor leaves, Chivers, and never allow him in again!'

'Very good, your grace,' Chivers said and hurried after the earl.

'The impertinence of the man!' Felix said to the empty room. 'How dare he?'

Felix was furious. He'd never been so angry in his life, and that was a danger. He took a deep breath and forced himself to calm down, to slow his breathing and keep his cool. It was difficult. He checked his hands, they were shaking. Still, he couldn't believe it. How dare anyone...

'Are you sure you're all right, your grace?' Chivers said, reappearing.

'I'm fine, but ask Mr Forsyth to come and see me please.'

'Right away, your grace,' Chivers said.

Mr Forsyth was deadly dull but rock solid. That was exactly what Felix needed. He needed someone who couldn't be shaken.

Someone who would carry on in his meticulous and monotonous way, putting one fact before the other. There was no high angst with Mr Forsyth. He would calm down if he were speaking to his man of business. He couldn't but do otherwise.

'You wanted to see me, your grace?' Mr Forsyth said as he entered on a bow.

He was as solidly built as his temperament and dressed in a neat pinstripe suit as befitted a man of business.

'Yes, thank you, Mr Forsyth. I have just had an extraordinary meeting with the Earl of Overbrook. I won't bore you with the details, but the gist of it is that he threatened to destroy me.'

'Destroy you, your grace?' Mr Forsyth said and even he was unable to hide his surprise. 'Why would he wish to do that?'

'The reason isn't important. My question is, could he do it?'

'Well...' Mr Forsyth said as he sat back and made a steeple with his fingers. 'I suppose it's possible. Did he mention what he was likely to do? Is he aiming for your reputation or your fortune?'

'I didn't think to ask.'

Felix felt a flicker of amusement. This was all absurd. Yet at the same time, he had to be careful. Overbrook's threat had sounded genuine.

'If he wants to destroy your reputation, he would have to spread innuendo and lies. It would be difficult. If he wanted to damage your fortune, he could use his own to try and undermine your business. He might bribe people to not serve you and draw suppliers away from your estate, that sort of thing.'

'And what could we do to counter that?'

'We will have to double our vigilance. You must rally your supporters around you for they will have to counter anything the earl says against you as quickly as possible.'

'My supporters?' Felix felt like he'd just landed in the middle of a melodrama.

'Perhaps you should seek the advice of Lord Bellamy, your grace. I understand he is accustomed to dealing with skulduggery.'

'Yes, perhaps I should,' Felix said. 'Thank you, Mr Forsyth, I will keep you informed.'

Felix concluded that Mr Forsyth was correct about consulting with Bellamy and lost no time in sending a note round to his place of work.

His lordship was gratifyingly prompt in his response, and a couple of hours later, he arrived in Belgravia.

'Forgive the lateness of the hour,' Bellamy said as he was ushered into Felix's room.

'I'm glad you came. I hope I haven't dragged you away from important business.'

'Not at all,' Bellamy said and took the indicated chair.

It gave Felix a moment to consider how to phrase his dilemma. 'I feel a little foolish about this,' he said.

'Professor Antrobus?'

'What? Oh, no, nothing to do with him.'

'Well, that is a relief at any rate. He is a very good, old friend. I wouldn't like to fall out with him, especially over a woman.'

'You don't like Lady Giddings?'

'She's not the sort of woman I like. There's no question she's a beauty, I just prefer something a little more... robust.'

'Like Celia.'

'Exactly,' Bellamy said on a rare smile.

'Did you fall instantly in love with her?'

'Love at first sight? No, not at all. I hardly registered Celia when she came out. She was just one girl amongst hundreds of other debutantes. Then Lady Littleton introduced us, and we stood up together for a dance. That was when I discovered that she was uncommonly straight-talking for a young woman.'

'She is.'

'It seems to be a family trait. She also has a sense of humour, and that too is a rarity amongst debutantes. I was intrigued. So I invited her to dance every time we happened to be at the same party, and I watched her fall in love with a military man.'

'Captain Roberts.'

'So she told you about him, did she?'

'Only to warn me off youthful infatuation.'

'I knew she wasn't entirely in love with me when we married, but I have tried to be a good husband, and I believe she is happy with me now.'

'Yes,' Felix said. 'So she tells me.'

'I am glad to hear it.'

'This also isn't why I asked you here but, what do you make of Miss Seaborn?'

'She is a sensible young woman and observant.'

'Is she?'

'Oh, yes. Many people can live in a place and know the names and faces of people, and their day to day business without picking up on the undercurrents. They would never know whether people are happy or oppressed, rebellious or content.'

'And you need to know that about South Africa?'

'Her majesty's government is keen to expand the empire. I wanted to know from Miss Seaborn whether the Boer Nations might oppose us. She was of the opinion they would and gave me some good reasons. Part of which is that by their very nature they are the adventuring kind of a people who will resist anyone telling them what to do. That was useful to know.'

'I see.'

'Now, if none of that was the reason you wanted to see me, what is it that I can do for you?'

'This feels... forward. I mean, we don't know each other well and...'

'Your grace, if it helps, I like you. I have always thought it a shame that we have seen so little of each other. I believe it is a good thing that you are widening your circle of friends. I might add that, infatuation aside, you might find a good friend in Antrobus as well.'

'Thank you, and infatuation is sort of the problem. You see I had an extraordinary visit from Lord Overbrook today. He is a contender for Lady Giddings' hand-'

'Yes, I am aware of that.'

'Well, he threatened to destroy me if I didn't leave Lady Giddings alone.'

Felix watched Bellamy closely. His response to this threat was important. If he laughed it off, Felix would be relieved.

Instead, he looked surprised and said, 'Good lord, did he?'

'I'm afraid so. Only I have no idea whether he's the kind of man who will follow through on his threat.'

'He is an argumentative man. He is always picking fights with the people around him. As a result, he has few friends left. I also seem to recall that he did ruin one of his former friends.'

'So his threat should be taken seriously?'

'As he has made it, he will attempt to follow through. I will make sure he doesn't succeed, however.'

'How will you do that?'

'I will let it be known, discreetly, what he intends and why he is doing it. You are known to be an astute businessman so he shouldn't be able to attack you from that side. If he does, you and Mr Forsyth can deal with him. In addition, if people know that they are not only up against you but the whole family, that will make them think twice before siding with Overbrook.'

'Thank you, Bellamy. I do appreciate this. I wasn't sure how to resolve the problem on my own.'

'There is no need for you to be on your own.'

'Sometimes, it doesn't feel that way.'

'Understandably.'

'I wasn't aware people thought me an astute businessman either.'

'Your estates are well managed. Those in the know have observed them going from strength to strength, particularly of late years. Mr Forsyth has been clear that he's following your instructions. He's a good man, many is the man who might leave people to assume they were doing all the work, Forsyth puts the credit where it's due.'

'Not entirely, he taught me a lot, and I respect his judgement.'

'That's as it should be.'

Chapter Nineteen

Felix spent a couple of days with Mr Forsyth shoring up his estate and businesses and ensuring that there were no weaknesses that could be exploited by Lord Overbrook. Felix also took the time to acquaint himself as thoroughly as possible with the earl's financial position and all the ways he made his money. The majority of the earl's income came from his vast estates that he farmed and the additional products that came from it. He owned a wool mill and had diversified into cotton cloth production too.

It was interesting to learn about business from this different angle. Up till now, all Felix had done was look at his own properties and products. After this, he thought he might spend more time learning about how some of the other estates ran themselves too.

For now, though, he concentrated on Overbrook. From what he could gather, the man delegated most of the day to day running of his estate to a manager. He seemed only to get involved when he was bent on ruining somebody. Then there was a pattern he followed, and Felix felt confident that they could block the people he usually used.

Hopefully, if he resolved his feelings about Lady Giddings, he might get a resolution with the earl as well. That was, after all, the point of the tea party.

'I'm glad you decided on an afternoon do this time, your grace,' Grantley said.

'Really?' Felix said, watching his valet via the mirror as he put the finishing touches to his hair.

'You will be less tired if you don't stay up past your bedtime.'

'My bedtime is ridiculously early for a grown man.'

'Your grace, you know you tire yourself out if you stay up too late.'

'Alas, I am all too aware of that.'

'So an afternoon tea is better.'

'Indeed,' Felix said and lapsed into contemplation. It was a fortnight since the dinner, and the wait had been interminable, but he couldn't have held it sooner. It would have been too much for his guests. As it was, he hoped he hadn't caused them to cancel other engagements to come to his tea.

The one person, strangely enough, that he had expected to come whatever other events she had lined up was Lady Giddings. In this, he was proved right. She'd answered his invitation within a day and expressed delight that she would be seeing him so soon.

He couldn't muster up the same enthusiasm. He still lusted after her. A part of him desperately wanted to still be in love with her, or infatuated, as he now suspected it was. But the rest of him hankered more after seeing Miss Seaborn.

It was always the same, he'd begin by wondering what it would be like to see Lady Giddings again. He pictured her beautiful face and amazing blue eyes, and then he remembered the dress, and his heart sank. She'd worn that odd blue dress and matched it with the red shawl he'd given her. As a gesture it was... he supposed it was meant to be gratifying, her showing how much she valued his gift, but they just didn't work together.

Then he'd find his thoughts drifting off to Miss Seaborn and how well she looked in her grey dress. His gaze flitted to the picture that he had propped up on his work table beside his sofa. He wished he could ask her more about it for it was remarkably detailed. Surely there was more than one tale attached to that single picture. He would have to ask her.

'Poole, please run upstairs and get the young ladies Juliana and Prunella. There's no sense in making them wait in their room when they can occupy the drawing room.'

'Do you want them there before you, your grace?' Poole said.

'Certainly, why not? You may tell them I'll be along shortly.'

'Very good, your grace,' Poole said and hurried away.

'Strictly speaking, he should have sent a footman up for the young ladies,' Grantley said as soon as the door closed behind Poole.

'True, but then I wouldn't have time to ask you how he's doing. He ghosts you so closely that I never have the chance.'

'He's doing very well, your grace. I've never trained a gentleman before, but I'd say young Poole is better than most. He pays attention, he has a good eye for fashion and good sense about cloth and clothes. In time he will make an excellent gentleman's gentleman.'

'Only in time?'

'There is much I still need to teach him.'

'Are you sure you aren't just delaying because you don't wish to retire?'

'Not at all, your grace. I didn't realise until I had to show somebody else, what a great body of knowledge I have built up over the years. In fact, I have started writing it all down. I believe there may be a useful handbook in all I know. A book that may benefit a great number of people and not just valets. Anyone who wishes to turn out to perfection or who needs to know the right way to treat garments to clean them, keep them in good order and, when needed, repaired.'

'Is that so?'

'It is indeed.'

'Well, once it's written I will gladly write a foreword for you. That should help when it comes to interesting a publisher.'

'You'd do that for me, your grace?'

'Of course, I would. The more I think about it, the more I like the idea of your book. I'm sure you are right, there will be a willing market, especially as it will be written by the valet to a duke.'

Felix was pleased to see that for once Grantley couldn't remain inscrutable. He positively glowed with pleasure. 'Now, shall we wait for Poole to reappear or should we head to the drawing room straight away?'

'We didn't need his help before, your grace, I'm sure we can do without it today as well. And if I may say so, sir, you are looking very well today. You have more colour in your cheeks than you have had for quite some time.'

'That's good to know,' Felix murmured as he rose to his feet. Taking only the lightest of grips of Grantley's arm, they headed for the drawing room.

'Cousin Felix,' Juliana said as she hurried down the stairs to join him, 'you're up!'

'So you see.'

'We shall have such a fine time,' Juliana said.

'And don't worry, mother has given us a fire and brimstone talk about not tiring you,' Pixie said with a broad grin as she made her way down the stairs at a more leisurely pace.

'Now, do you really think I would give you a similar talk?' Felix said.

'Not at all. You're a lot more easy-going than mother led us to believe.'

'And you're a lot more grown-up,' Felix said as he waved the two young women into the drawing room and followed after.

'This is perfect,' Juliana said. 'Have you decided what we'll do today, cousin Felix?'

'Aside from drinking tea and tucking into the finest selection of cakes I could dream up, you mean?'

'A whole selection of cakes?'

'And a few savouries for the gentlemen. It's rather gratifying that everyone from the dinner party has agreed to return.'

Felix watched Juliana for any hint that she might be more eager to meet one gentleman over any other.

She merely smiled beatifically and said, 'It will be good to see them all again.'

'Indeed,' Felix said and then caught Pixie's eye. She clearly understood what he'd left unsaid. 'How about you, Pixie, have you an interest in seeing one gentleman in particular over the others?'

Pixie did blush as she said, 'Maybe. But I'll tell you this, Cousin Felix, if I was it wouldn't be Professor Antrobus.'

'No?'

'No,' Pixie said firmly.

Felix wondered whether he should ask her why not when Chivers came in, opened his mouth and Percy loomed up behind him.

'No need to announce me, Chivers, we cousins don't stand on ceremony.'

'Percy doesn't at any rate,' Felix said.

'Quite right, how are you, old man?'

'Fine, thank you, quite well in fact. I see that although we are informal cousins, you have come dressed up to the nines.'

'Couldn't let the side down,' Percy muttered and gave the sleeve of his Horse Guards jacket a quick brush. 'Besides, you may not have a fancy uniform, but you're always the best turned out of the lot of us. Now, I must greet my other cousins. I have been unforgivably rude ignoring them for so long. Lady Juliana, Lady Prunella, it is a pleasure to see you both again.'

'It's wonderful to see you again too, Percy,' Juliana said. 'You are so droll, and we had such fun together last time, especially with Lord Hounslow.'

'He is rather a card, isn't he?' Percy said as he gave Felix a meaningful look which completely escaped Juliana.

Poor Lord Hounslow, Felix thought. At least Lady Giddings was aware of him, a little too aware really.

'Lady Giddings and Miss Seaborn,' Chivers said.

'Your grace,' Lady Giddings said as she swished into the room. 'It's always such a pleasure to see you again.'

'The pleasure is all mine,' Felix said as he bowed over her outstretched hand.

As he straightened up, he realised he was being examined closely by Lady Giddings. In fact, she seemed to be waiting for something.

'You look as ravishing as ever.' It cost Felix something to lie like that, but it clearly pleased her ladyship. He couldn't for the life of him see why she'd chosen to wear a canary yellow dress. It jarred against her ash-blonde hair. 'And Miss Seaborn, it's good to see you again too.'

'Thank you, your grace,' Miss Seaborn said, and there was... a flash of amusement on her face, that instantly vanished.

She knows, Felix though, she knows what I think of the dress, well, well.

'Lord Hounslow and Professor Antrobus,' Chivers said.

'Ah marvellous, everybody is here,' Percy said as he shook Lord Hounslow vigorously by the hand.

'Welcome, gentlemen,' Felix said. 'Thank you for coming. I look forward to getting to know you better.'

'It was good of you to invite us back,' Antrobus said as he shook Felix's hand.

'Not at all, I look forward to learning more about philosophy but not, I think, today,' Felix said as he took in the professor's brown velvet jacket. He was as scruffy as ever. Still, these clothes fitted him better and reflected his profession, so it seemed more appropriate.

'I come prepared to be generally entertaining,' Antrobus said as his gaze flicked across the room and paused on Lady Giddings.

Felix was interested to note that she was momentarily confused before she looked away.

'What a wonderful gathering, your grace,' Isolde said. 'I feel sure we will have an enjoyable time this afternoon.'

'I certainly hope so, Lady Giddings. Please do sit down, all of you, and I'll get in the refreshments.'

'Good idea,' Percy said as he sat himself down beside Felix which neatly ensured he had Pixie to his other side.

Lady Giddings took it as given that she would be next to Felix. She settled herself in the armchair to his right, which he found irritated him as he realised that he really wanted Miss Seaborn to sit next to him. Still, it was informative. For the time being, he could enjoy the spectacle of everyone else manoeuvring to their best advantage.

Lord Hounslow made a concerted effort to be beside Juliana, and Professor Antrobus made sure to keep his distance from both Lady Giddings and, Felix suspected, from him. It meant he landed up beside Miss Seaborn. *If only he realised how much I wish it were otherwise*, Felix thought.

'There's nothing like food and drink to break the ice of a gathering,' Felix said, as the footmen came in bearing a collection of silver salvers brimming with cakes, pies and sandwiches.

'Too right, old boy,' Percy said. 'I have been entertaining myself all morning trying to guess what delicacies you may have dreamed up for us today.'

'Then I hope I don't disappoint,' Felix said but was satisfied with the look of the spread. It was enticing even to him.

'Oh, tea cakes to toast, my favourite,' Juliana said.

'Allow me to put the tea cake on a fork for you, Lady Juliana,' Lord Hounslow said.

'Thank you,' Juliana said. 'But I want to toast it myself, mind, it's more fun that way.'

'How about you, your grace?' Lady Giddings said. 'Do you also intend to toast your own tea cake?'

'Maybe later. I prefer savouries over sweet, so I will start on the sandwiches. What about you, Lady Giddings?'

'Toasting is such a messy business, and I don't find crouching before the fire to be very comfortable, so I will have a slice of this beautiful cake.'

'It seems such a shame to ruin it,' Pixie said. 'Cook must have spent hours on the icing and making all those lovely butterflies.'

'Well, a cake is meant to be eaten, my dear. Why else would it be served up to us?'

'All the same, I see Pixie's point,' Percy said, joining in the fray. 'It must have taken hours to make, and with a single slice, all will be in ruins.'

'Not all, I will only be taking one piece.'

'Have as much as you like, Lady Giddings,' Felix said. 'Cook would be more offended if the cake went back to the kitchen untouched.'

'Thank you, your grace.'

Lady Giddings lifted a slice of cake onto her plate, with practised grace, stuck a silver fork into it and turned back to Felix with a smile. 'Lord Overbrook told me that he came to see you, is it true?'

'I beg your pardon?'

Felix was astonished that Lady Giddings knew of the visit and was apparently willing to discuss it in public.

'When did he tell you that?'

'Overbrook told me at the Summerville party last night.'

'Good heavens,' Felix said, aware that he had the attention of the whole room now.

'Was it not true?'

'No, it's true.'

'So he did issue you an ultimatum?'

'Is that what he told you?'

'He is frightfully jealous,' Lady Giddings said with satisfaction. 'What did you tell him?'

Felix glanced at Percy, who also looked astonished before he said, 'I told him that the decision should be yours, Lady Giddings.'

'You want me to choose between the two of you?'

Felix instantly realised his mistake. 'I don't think it appropriate for gentlemen to argue over the fate of a third person without that person's knowledge. It would be absurd, especially if neither man actually knew the wishes of the third party.'

'A philosophical conundrum if ever there was one,' Professor Antrobus said.

'Indeed,' Felix said relieved by the professor's intervention. 'And not a conversation for today.'

'Fine,' Lady Giddings said but without conviction. 'What else should we talk about then?'

'Anything you like. You sound as if you have been as busy as ever over the last fortnight.'

'I have, indeed. I had a lot to catch up on since my cold and a gratifying number of people said how much they missed seeing me.'

'Ah... how nice,' Felix said and found himself at a loss for anything else to add.

'How about you, your grace,' Miss Seaborn said, stepping into the gap. 'What have you been doing?'

'I have been investigating the installation of a lift,' Felix said as he gave Miss Seaborn a grateful smile.

'A lift? Is that one of those contraptions that can carry you to upper floors without needing to use the stairs?'

'Exactly right, Miss Seaborn. My inventor suggested I get one so I can make greater use of my house.'

'What do you mean make greater use of your house?' Lady Giddings said.

'Currently I live entirely on the ground floor, but the view from the top floor is good, and it might be nice to see it more frequently. Or I might even have my room higher so that I may have a better view in general.'

'I think views are overrated,' Lady Giddings said.

'Oh no, not at all,' Lord Hounslow said. 'Views are great muses. Think only of all the poetry that has been inspired by a magnificent view.'

'None of London, I'm willing to bet,' Percy said. 'All you'll see here is a million chimneys spewing out smoke.'

'That is true, but at the moment all I look out upon is a rather dismal winter garden,' Felix said.

'D'you know,' Professor Antrobus said, 'the discussion of a view has taken us away from a far more interesting point. That's the fact that you have an inventor, your grace. What do you need an inventor for? He is surely not inventing lifts for we already have those. At least, I understand there is one in London, and I saw one on show at the Great Exhibition.'

'What did you think of it?'

'Interesting, I suppose, if you are willing to risk your life in something that goes up and down a shaft. If it were to fail, you'd crash to your death.'

'They do have safety features.'

'No doubt, but I'm not sure I'd be willing to risk my life on such a new contraption.'

'The same was said about trains, and yet now they are treated as a commonplace.'

'You are a braver man than I, your grace, and clearly a lover of technology. Especially if you employ an inventor.'

'Mr Testwood is a new experiment for me. But he has already come up with a number of contraptions to make my life easier. I also like him for the window he provides into another world.'

'That of inventors?'

'That of the metropolitan working man. I am more familiar with the lives of my farm labourers in general.'

'I can't imagine why either would interest you,' Lady Giddings said.

'No, perhaps not, but I suspect Miss Seaborn would, as she shares that interest.'

'Does she?' Lady Giddings said and turned to glare at Honour. 'How would you know that, your grace?'

Felix cursed himself for being so stupid. The look of dismay on Miss Seaborn's face told him instantly he'd been a fool to bring her into the conversation. 'I merely meant that if she drew all the people and places she visited with her father, she must have an interest in their lives.'

'Do you, Honour?' Lady Giddings said.

'My drawings are a way of capturing a moment and the feeling of a place and time. But yes, I was interested in the lives of the people I drew too.'

'I see,' Lady Giddings said frostily.

Felix was surprised by her reaction. It verged on jealousy and didn't bode well for Miss Seaborn when she and Lady Giddings got home. He found himself wondering how precarious her life was in the Giddings household.

It was incumbent upon him to change the mood though so he said, 'I was wondering whether any of you fancied a parlour game?'

'What sort of a game did you have in mind?' Percy said.

'I leave that entirely in your hands.'

'Murder Wink then,' Juliana said. 'That's such great fun.'

'Murder Wink?' Pixie said. 'You're terrible at that, you never guess the murderer.'

'Well, who knows, maybe I'll be the murderer this time.'

'Forgive my ignorance,' Honour said, 'But what is Murder Wink?'

'The rules are easy, Miss Seaborn,' Professor Antrobus said. 'One of the party is allocated the role of murderer via a secret ballot. Then we all stare into each other's eyes. If the murderer winks at you, you have been killed. You need to wait about ten seconds before you declare that you have been murdered, and the rest of us have to try and guess who the murderer is, they can keep killing till they're caught of course.

'If you suspect someone, you put your hand in the air and say, "I accuse." A second person also has to accuse, then the two accusers must point to who they think the murderer is. If they both point to the same person, that person must confess if they are the murderer. But if you point to two different people, then the game continues, and the murderer is free to kill again.'

'Very well, I believe I can do that,' Honour said.

'Excellent, I had the paper strips and pen prepared as well as a bowl to mix all the papers together,' Felix said. 'Would you mind collecting it from the sideboard, Percy?'

'I am at your service,' Percy said as he jumped up.

'Oh I say it's frightfully clever of you to know we'd play Murder Wink, Cousin Felix,' Juliana said.

'Not entirely. I have several games prepared for. So once we've had our fill of one we can move to the next.'

'How wonderful!' Juliana said with a deep sigh of satisfaction.

Felix found her enthusiasm charming. She was very easy to please. Lady Giddings, on the other hand, looked out of sorts and like she might put a damper on the afternoon.

Felix remained in the drawing room after everyone had made their cheerful farewells, savouring the moment, content that Percy was still with him. It would be good to chew over the events of the afternoon together.

'You know,' Percy said, 'aside from when you, me and Arthur have spent time together at your country estate, I can't recall seeing you in a happier frame of mind. It makes me wish I'd introduced a few choice mates to you a long time ago.'

'That would have been nice, but I doubt Aunt Lavinia would have allowed it.'

'Even now I'm surprised at how far you've managed to get out from under her protection,' Percy said. 'To hold a tea party from which Aunt Lavinia was excluded is impressive.'

'That was Celia's doing. I don't know what she told my aunt, but she hardly raised an objection at all when I informed her about the party.'

'Considering that you look fine, and not as tired as you usually are, I pronounce that the whole thing was a roaring success.'

Felix smiled as he looked around the room at the discarded party games and salvers where only a few items remained.

Percy gave a satisfied sigh and put his feet up on a table so that the fire warmed the soles of his shoes.

'So are you satisfied?' Percy said, and took the last dainty sandwich on the plate at his elbow and swallowed it in a single bite. 'Did the tea party answer your questions?'

'What questions might those be?' Felix said, looking up from the fire, a smile playing on his lips.

'About who you prefer, Lady Giddings or Miss Seaborn?'

'How did you know?'

'Celia, she really can't help herself. But in this instance, I can assure you, I was the sole repository of her information.'

'And you have never liked Lady Giddings, have you?'

'I wouldn't exactly say that.'

'You had me fooled for a bit. But now I can see the difference between pretence and reality.'

'I don't know what you mean.'

Percy squirmed under Felix's sceptical gaze which confirmed what he already suspected.

'My dear man, I would have to be blind not to realise that you are quite smitten by Pixie. Looking back to when you were making that rather blatant attempt on Lady Giddings, there can be no comparison. You played interested and attentive, but it wasn't the same.'

'Damn your all too perceptive eyes,' Percy said with a lazy smile as he leaned further back in his chair with his hands locked behind his head.

'Not that perceptive. I completely failed to understand Lady Giddings.'

'With good reason. She is beautiful, and it takes a while for her nature to take the shine off her looks.'

'It was rather comprehensively removed today, I'm afraid.'

'Let me guess it was the dress. That was the final straw, wasn't it?'

'It didn't help,' Felix said with an introspective laugh. 'But no. It was her mentioning Overbrook.'

'Good Lord, yes! What the devil was that about? And why haven't you told me about it before? I was so determined to ask you the moment I had a chance that I can't believe I went and forgot! Did Overbrook really give you an ultimatum?'

'He told me to stay away from Lady Giddings, or he would destroy me.'

'The devil! How dare he? He has no business doing that. I have a good mind to track him down immediately and call him out.'

'Which is precisely why I didn't tell you about it before,' Felix said with an appreciative grin.

'No really, Felix, the man isn't to be trifled with. He's rich enough to be dangerous.'

'I am aware of that which is why I discussed the matter with Mr Forsyth and Bellamy.'

'Oh, they are a better choice than me with that kind of business.'

'They both gave me very sensible advice, and we are doing what we can to scotch the matter. The irony of it is that I'd happily hand Lady Giddings over to Overbrook. They would be a good match for each other. Only I don't think she'd go.'

'She does look very much like she intends to marry you.'

'She also made damn sure I didn't get a chance to speak to Miss Seaborn. That surprised me. I didn't think she would notice any competition. She seems very sure of her conquest, but something must be causing her concern.'

'It's an instinct, I suppose. One that drives her even when she may not be conscious of it.'

'Indeed, but it leaves me with a dilemma. I would very much like to be able to speak to Miss Seaborn away from the watchful eye of her cousin.'

'To work out what you really think of her?'

'I was so mistaken about Lady Giddings that I worry I might be wrong about Miss Seaborn too.'

'You don't feel the same way about her as you did at first about Lady Giddings, do you?'

'It is a very different feeling. I just have a sense of deep comfort around her, and we have things in common. We could have a meeting of minds. Aside from that... she gets prettier every time I see her.'

'That sounds more like it,' Percy said with a wide grin.

'So you approve, do you? Even though she's a penniless soldier's daughter in straitened circumstances and must also be interested in my wealth.'

'I have never thought ill of any young woman for marrying to better herself. I always just felt that Lady Giddings cared not one tuppence for you. That would not only be a shame but a danger to you.'

'You think she'd actively try to speed my demise? Surely she isn't that callous?'

'Isn't she?'

'I don't know,' Felix said with a sigh and gazed deep into the flickering fire.

'Miss Seaborn is different,' Percy said. 'She has no pretensions. She most certainly hasn't made eyes at you in the time she's known you.'

'Which presents me with another dilemma. I have no idea whether she even likes me.'

'Considering she sent you a drawing, I think she likes you. She probably has no inkling that things could go further between you. She's very proper, which Aunt Lavinia would approve of. She probably sees herself as so far below your station that she is in no way in the running to be your wife.'

'A quandary then.'

'Maybe not. There may be a way that we can carry off a meeting with propriety.'

'Really?'

'I saw Miss Seaborn in the company of a sergeant major a couple of weeks back at the George Hotel-'

'But, Percy, that isn't good news. Maybe she already has a betrothed. She's used to a life of adventure. She's more likely to want to marry a soldier than an invalid.'

'Whoever he was, he was no paramour. He was far too old and looked avuncular. Most likely, he was exactly what Miss Seaborn said he was, an old family friend.'

'And how does that help me?'

'I shall sound him out. If he's amenable, he may be willing to help arrange a meeting.'

'I don't know. I'm not fond of skulduggery at the best of times but now... it feels wrong.'

'It might come to nothing, Felix, but for the time being leave it with me and I'll see what I can do.'

'Mmm, I suppose you'll go ahead whether I agree to this or not.' Felix didn't know how he felt about the proposal. It was a reflection of his indecision in general, the more he thought about it, the less he was convinced getting married was a good idea.

'You know what I'm like when I have the bit between my teeth,' Percy said. 'But if you really don't want me to do anything, I won't do it.'

'I should warn you off, of course, but I have to admit my curiosity won't allow it,' Felix said.

CHAPTER TWENTY

Honour wasn't surprised when she got another invitation to tea with Sergeant Major Bruin. Although, she had expected that he'd wait a bit longer before getting back in touch. She only hoped that he wasn't intending on proposing to her again.

She had no wish to marry him, but his proposal had clarified more than that. Even though she'd felt comfortable at the George surrounded by soldiers, at the sergeant major's asking, the possibility of life as a soldier's wife became very real. At that moment she knew, without a doubt, that it wasn't the life she wanted.

The sergeant major was a soldier though, and not used to taking a loss. He was highly likely to renew his offer. Fortunately, he'd also looked panicked by the notion. Honour was confident, therefore, that if he did reiterate his proposal, she could rebuff him again.

She took her time getting dressed, arranged her beautiful grey shawl over her shoulders and secured it with a simple silver circular brooch. It was one of the few pieces of jewellery she'd inherited from her mother. All her more expensive pieces had been sold off one after the other by her parents when she was growing up. Money had always been tight but, vague as her memories were, Honour couldn't recall her mother regretting her decision.

She supposed that was what love did. No matter the circumstances, if you were with the one you loved, they didn't matter. Honour laughed at herself for being so sentimental. It wasn't like her to contemplate such things.

Satisfied that she looked as neat as a pin, she hurried downstairs. If she was quick enough and quiet enough, she might just make it out of the house without Isolde spotting her.

She had nearly reached the bottom of the stairs when Isolde said, 'What are you doing?' from the upper landing.

Honour sighed inwardly and said, 'I'm going to tea with Sergeant Major Bruin. Remember, I told you last night?'

'Did you?'

'He will be leaving for Guyana soon, and he invited me for tea. I told you all of this.'

Lately, Isolde had been very suspicious of her, and she wasn't entirely sure why.

'If you're just going to tea, why have you got such a big bag?'

'Because he said he fancied a bit of reminiscing and he used to like my drawings.'

'A likely story to be sure!'

'He is coming to fetch me, so if you don't believe me, you can ask him yourself.'

'How do I know you're not just going to run off with him?'

'Why would I do that? Besides, you'll not be needing me for much longer either so why would you care if I went off a bit earlier?'

'Because I still need you now.'

'Fine, but you don't need me this afternoon. You'll be with your dressmaker and for God's sake don't let her make you anything else in that hideous yellow silk.'

'What was wrong with the silk?'

'That bright yellow doesn't work with your complexion, dear. It's really best avoided.' Whatever Isolde might have said about that was fortunately forestalled by the sound of the doorbell. 'Sergeant Major Bruin, I have to go,' Honour said.

'I want to see this man,' Isolde said and hurried with Honour to the door.

Both ladies arrived just as the butler showed the sergeant major in.

'Oh,' Isolde said as she took in the sergeant major's greying ginger hair and portly frame.

'Sergeant Major Bruin, Lady Isolde Giddings,' Honour said. 'The sergeant major was a great friend to my father.'

'And he to me,' Bruin said executing a deep bow. 'For it was Captain Seaborn's kind offices that secured me my promotion to sergeant major.'

'I see,' Isolde said instantly losing interest in the man. 'Well, I'll see you later this afternoon, Honour.'

'Of course,' Honour said. She hooked her arm into the sergeant major's and said, 'Shall we go?'

Sergeant Major Bruin only waited for the door to close behind him as he hurried Honour down the steps and said, 'So that's the cousin, huh?'

'I'm afraid so. She's similarly uninterested in anyone who isn't filthy rich.'

'Yep, I gathered that,' Bruin said and steered Honour to a hack.

'What are you doing? The George isn't that far away, and I could use a nice brisk walk.'

'Well, the thing is, we might not be going to the George,' Bruin said as he helped Honour into the coach.

'What do you mean we might not be going to the George?'

'Get in, woman, and I'll explain.'

'All right, but I do so under protest.'

'Just as long as you do,' Bruin said with a grin.

He settled opposite her and gave the roof of the coach a thump to tell the driver to go.

'Now, what is going on?' Honour said and was astonished to see the sergeant major blush.

'That all depends on you, my dear. We have two options, and we'll do whichever you prefer.'

'What if I don't like either option?'

'Mmm... I have a feeling you'll like at least one of them. But rest assured, if you don't I can take you straight back home.'

'You are incorrigible,' Honour said with a laugh. 'Very well, tell me about my two options.'

'The first is the easier of the two. That's us doing what I said in my note to you, tea and reminiscing at the George.'

'Which sounded perfectly lovely, but fine, what is option number two?'

'Now that one, you see,' Bruin said and felt around his collar. 'That one I'm not even sure I know what to make of it.'

'You have to put me out of this suspense, it's too much.'

'All right, all right, the second is... you've been invited by some duke to tea at his house. Apparently, he'd really like to see your sketches.'

'The Duke of Morley?' Honour said, and she was truly surprised. 'Felix Peergrave conspired with you to get me to visit him alone?'

'Well, strictly speaking, it was his cousin doing the conspiring. Came slap bang up to me at the George and set it all up. I was that surprised.'

'Incredible!'

'Honour, it sounds to me like this duke fellow likes you. Might it not be a good idea? I mean, he does have a lot of money.'

'What are you talking about?'

'Like any good soldier, I looked into the terrain before venturing forth. I discovered that this duke is not only fabulously wealthy, he's also in search of a bride.'

'Yes, that's public knowledge, but he would never marry me, that's absurd.'

'Why not?'

'Because he's a duke! He wouldn't marry a penniless nobody.'

'Seems to me he might not see it that way. He's seen your cousin, who I have to admit is a corker, and now he wants to see you.'

'That's nonsense. He is fond of art and tales about travel. That's why he wants to see me.'

'Maybe, miss, but I'd be failing in my duty if I didn't look out for your best interests. It seems to me, marriage to a duke, even a poorly one is way better than becoming a governess.'

'You're impossible! But very well we will go and visit the duke.'

Honour was shaken by the idea and not as convinced as the sergeant major that Felix Peergrave was interested in her. Even if he was, she doubted his family would approve. But could Sergeant Major Bruin be right? Might the duke like her? If he did, might he fall in love with her? Or worse, fall out of love with her as quickly as he had with Isolde?

She wasn't sure she could bear that, and she pushed the thought away because it frightened her. Up till this moment, she'd kept a tight rein on her feelings. She hadn't even admitted to herself that there was much about the duke to be admired. She'd not permitted an instant of fantasy involving him developing feelings for her, and now this. Now the sergeant major seemed to think she had a chance. It made her feel ill to even contemplate him being wrong.

Honour had never been nervous about visiting the duke before. Today was different. Now that she'd been given the impression she might stand a chance with him. Was it foolish to think so? Either way, she'd never approached his front door with more trepidation.

The butler was his usual aloof self and gave nothing away of how he felt to be admitting her and an unknown soldier. He was sufficiently intimidating that Sergeant Major Bruin said nothing as they were led deeper into the house. His expression spoke volumes, though. His eyes couldn't get any wider as he looked about.

Honour had been impressed by the house the first time she'd seen it. Still, with new possibilities opening out before her, she found the large marble entrance hall and deep pile carpets just that little bit more intimidating today.

She didn't have much chance to think about it before they were ushered into the drawing room.

'Miss Seaborn, you came.'

Felix was sitting in the chair she realised he always used, but today it was drawn up to the bow window that faced the street rather than its usual place by the fire. Had he been waiting for her?

He pushed himself up onto his feet, held out his hand in greeting and said, 'I'm very glad.'

'Thank you, your grace,' Honour said and felt breathless in his presence as she took his hand in greeting and gave it a firm shake. At least she'd learned that he liked that.

He looked so pleased to see her that it was reassuring, and he seemed nervous. Irrationally, that helped her too. His breathing was fast and laboured, though, which worried her for other reasons.

'Should you be standing up?'

'I shouldn't really,' Felix said with an embarrassed laugh and lowered himself back into his chair. 'Forgive me, Sergeant Major Bruin, I haven't greeted you yet.'

'Not at all, your grace,' the sergeant major said as he hastily pulled off his cap. 'It's an honour to meet you, sir.'

'And I am very grateful to you. I expect it took quite some persuasion to get Miss Seaborn to come here.'

'It did a bit,' Bruin said. 'Honour was always a stubborn girl.'

'I was not,' Honour said. 'But I am curious to know why you thought I might not come, your grace.'

'Because it is a little underhanded and I thought you, like me, might find that distasteful. If I only had myself to consider, I would simply have sent you an invitation to tea. But I suspect Lady Giddings wouldn't like that and might make your life uncomfortable.'

'You surprise me in your quick apprehension of my cousin's character,' Honour said then bit her lip, she was being too forward. The duke didn't seem to mind, though.

Felix gave a rueful smile and said, 'It has taken me a while to understand Lady Giddings, I'm afraid.'

'She does have quite an effect upon men, but, I suspect the yellow dress didn't help.'

'It did not,' Felix said with an appreciative gleam in his eye. 'Now you must forgive my manners, please do sit down, you and Sergeant Major Bruin.'

'It's very kind of you, your grace,' Bruin said, tilting his head at the chair Felix had pointed him to. 'But if it's all the same to you I have no wish to play chaperone in the middle. If you're agreeable, I'll settle myself there by the fire while the two of you talk.'

'That is very kind of you, Sergeant Major,' Felix said. 'But I understand you will be leaving the country soon and I don't want to take away from what little time the two of you have left.'

'Ah, there will always be another time, it will be fine,' Bruin said, beaming at Honour as he spoke which caused her to blush. 'Might I take one of these papers?' Bruin said of the pile on the table beside Felix.

'Take them all with my best wishes.'

'Splendid,' Bruin said and rubbed his hands together enthusiastically as he settled in an armchair by the fire. 'Heh! Who'd have thought I'd one day sit in a duke's drawing room reading newspapers by the fire.'

Honour turned to the duke who was watching her with a warm smile that sent an uncomfortable quiver through her chest.

'Are you really wishful of seeing my sketches?'

'I am. I liked your picture of the bazaar in Cairo. I would love to hear more about Egypt in general, and everywhere else you've been.'

'That might take a lot more time than we have. Perhaps we should just start at the beginning. At least, from the point where my pictures begin to look halfway decent. I'm quite proud of some of my images of the Crimea,' Honour said and took out the oldest sketchbook she'd brought along.

'Perfect,' Felix said with a happy sigh.

'It was spring when we first arrived. The fields were covered in flowers and ran practically right into the sea. It was quite breathtaking.'

'It looks it,' Felix said, leaning closer to the page Honour held out. 'You don't use colours?'

'I do when I can, but we had to pack light, and my sketchbook and pen were my two luxuries.'

'I see. These sketches of flowers are quite remarkable. The detail you've captured makes them akin to botanical drawings. Do you know what they are?'

'I have no idea, I'm afraid. I like drawing plants and animals, but I didn't have technical works to refer to.'

'From what I've gathered of the natural world, far more of it remains to be discovered than we have already identified. I wouldn't be surprised if some of these plants have yet to be classified.'

'I hadn't thought of that. Perhaps I should seek out a professor of botany and see what he thinks.'

'If you don't already have somebody in mind, I'm sure Professor Antrobus could make a recommendation.' Honour laughed at that and Felix said, 'Why are you laughing?'

'I suppose writing to professors is easy for you. No doubt they would be honoured to receive a letter from a duke, but for one in my circumstances, and a woman to boot, well...'

'Ah yes, I see. I didn't mean to be insensitive. I'd be happy to help by making a connection if you needed it.'

'Thank you, your grace, that's very kind. I just... I've never considered doing anything with my drawings. They're what I do to keep myself occupied.'

'It would be a shame to let talent such as yours go to waste, Miss Seaborn.'

'Perhaps,' Honour said as new possibilities opened up before her.

'Refreshments, your grace,' Chivers said as he led in a pair of footmen weighed down with trays of food.

'Thank you, please take a selection over to the sergeant major as well.'

'What a wonderful spread,' Honour said. 'And this when you weren't even sure I'd come.'

'I planned as if you would. I couldn't have you turning up with nothing prepared.'

'But what would you have done with all this food if I didn't come?'

'I would have invited my cousins to tea.'

'Well, I'm sorry they are missing out today.'

Honour realised that most of the food consisted of the things she'd favoured at the last tea. Had his grace been watching her that closely? She wasn't sure whether to be flattered or alarmed by that.

'Tea, Miss Seaborn?' Chivers said his hand hovering over the teapot.

'Yes, thank you, milk and sugar, please.'

Honour watched the duke as the tea was poured. He'd gone back to leafing through her sketchbook. His head was bowed over a page, and he traced his finger along the line of one sketch. He was so absorbed by the pictures that it gave Honour a chance to examine him. She'd done that before, of course. As a chaperone, she'd had plenty of time to watch and listen as she wasn't expected to speak much. But today was different.

Today she noticed how long and slim his fingers were, how well his navy blue suit fitted him, and how it turned his normally grey eyes a deep blue. He also looked younger, and his aristocratic features and strong jaw caused another unfamiliar flutter in her chest.

'This is a magnificent looking creature,' Felix said.

It took a moment for Honour to register that he'd spoken. She hoped she didn't blush as she hastily switched her attention back to the sketchbook.

'That was the colonel's horse, Hero. He was the fiercest stallion in battle yet gentle as a lamb when he was around me. Father said he'd never seen anything like it. Do you ride, your grace?'

'I'm afraid not. I did try it once, I was convinced that as it looked like people just sat on a horse that I should be able to do it. Aunt Lavinia wouldn't countenance it though, so I talked Percy and Arthur into helping me.

'We sneaked down to the stables one sleepy Sunday morning when everyone was at church and Percy and Arthur helped me up. I was dizzy already from the excitement, so that didn't help. But it turned out you need more muscle power than I had to control even the docile beast I selected. I passed out and went crashing to the stable floor.

'It gave Percy and Arthur the most dreadful fright. They hoisted me up and rushed me back to the house, shouting for the doctor all the way. I was so ill after that I escaped my aunt's wrath. Percy and Arthur weren't as fortunate and got the caning of their lives. I have always regretted that.'

'You poor things.'

'I'm not very manly, I'm afraid.'

'I wouldn't say that.' Honour said aware that the duke's wry smile hid a great deal of shame.

'It's no matter,' Felix said, waving the subject away. 'Your life has been far more interesting. I hope you don't mind telling me about it?'

'Not at all, but we must make a bargain, a story for a story.'

'If you wish. I doubt I have much to tell you, though.'

'I don't think that's true, but we shall see.'

'Very well. It's a challenge, and I will rise to the occasion.'

'Then, this is my tale. This is a picture of the palace my father's regiment was billeted in when we first got to India. We were far in the north, and the palace was high in the greatest mountains you've ever seen.'

'The Himalayas?'

'The foothills at least.'

'Your drawings make even these foothills look vast.'

'They were. The air is so thin there that as we marched up the hill to the palace, men grew faint and keeled over. I was walking along beside a wagon and had to climb up onto the luggage for my lungs were working like bellows and yet I still felt like I wasn't getting enough air.

'In the end, the colonel made us halt, even though we were only halfway to our destination and could see it above us. Under ordinary circumstances, we should have been able to reach it in a couple of hours, but that day it was impossible. So we set camp, and we stayed there for a few days till our bodies grew accustomed to the peculiar air and we could finally climb the last bit and get to our billet.'

'Astonishing,' Felix said, looking from Honour to the picture and back to her again.

'You really like to hear these things don't you?'

'It's my escape. I have read many tales of explorers and adventurers. Still, it's nothing like hearing it directly from somebody who's been there.'

'Do you not travel at all?'

'Only twice a year. I go to my estate in Kent in the summer, and we come to London for the winter. Travelling days are the high point of my year. It's when I get to see the countryside flashing by on the train.'

'So you do go by train,' Honour said and helped herself to a rather tempting slice of cake.

'In a manner of speaking. My whole carriage gets hoisted onto the train with me in it.'

'Good heavens, why?'

'It reduces the amount of time I have to move. I go from the house to the carriage, and after that, the carriage moves rather than me.'

'So you don't have to walk to the train, yes, I see.'

'It also protects me from being jostled by strangers and most importantly, from the air of London,' Felix said with a grin that lit up his eyes. 'My aunt thinks that as long as I stay in the carriage with the windows tightly shut I'll be all right.'

'And are you?'

'For the most part, yes.'

'So... when you're in London you never go out?'

'I take infections very easily, and the pollution in the city seems to exacerbate it. So when I am in London, I stay indoors. It isn't that much of a hardship as in London people can come and visit me more easily and the weather is so foul that you wouldn't really want to be out in it anyway.'

'What about when you're in the countryside?'

'I go outside then. My room is on the ground floor there too. I spend a lot of time on the terrace or under a big old lime tree on the lawns. And when it's cooler, I like to visit the kitchen garden.'

'That sounds better.'

'You like the outdoors, do you?'

'I grew up outside more than inside. Sometimes I feel so cooped up in London that I want to kick off all traces and run and run.'

'Do you?'

'Sometimes... more often than not it's... it's my circumstances more than my location.'

'Ah, I understand. My aunt sometimes makes me feel the same way.'

'That you'd like to run away?'

'Less so now that I have control over my fortune and I could make her leave if I wanted to. But when I was, oh, fifteen and sixteen, there were moments when I could hardly bear life with her. It's unfair on my aunt. She's only doing what she thinks is best, but it did nearly drive me to distraction on occasion.'

'She is a very forceful woman.'

'She is indeed. Now, you owe me another tale of your life.'

'I do, don't I?' Honour said much struck by how the duke looked like a boy waiting for his next treat.

'How about this?' Honour flicked through her book to a page with an image of a ship at port. 'This is the ship in which we sailed to South Africa. I've never spent as much time at sea as then, and it was wonderful. It was a lot less tiring than going overland. I found myself a quiet spot on the ship and could spend hours simply gazing out over the water. It was the most peaceful thing you can imagine. The sea is so clear that it's like glass and the creatures that throng the waters are fascinating. Drawing them though, was a greater challenge.'

Honour turned over the page and put her finger on a line drawing of a fish, every fin and scale had been recorded, and she was particularly proud of it.

'You seem to have managed very well. These pictures would rival the work of any number of naturalist artists I've seen.'

'That was our dinner. Every evening the sailors would haul in a net full of fish, and I got a chance to draw some of the creatures before they went into the pot.'

'Oh, I thought ships take their own food onboard.'

'They have plentiful supplies, fresh water, flour, salted pork, limes, oil, sugar, eggs and such as can't be procured at sea. But, as with a protracted land journey, the sailors supplement their rations with whatever they can catch. In this instance, fish, seabirds, and the eggs of any ground-nesting birds we came across on the islands we stopped at. Not that there were many. Sea travel has progressed in leaps and bounds since the arrival of the steamship. It only took us a month to travel from India to South Africa. The captain told me it was possible to do it quicker than that if he really pushed the engines. Apparently, there is fierce competition amongst captains to beat each other's crossing records.'

'I imagine there is,' Felix said gazing down at a sketch of a pair of seagulls fighting in mid-air. 'It sounds like a wonderful way to travel.'

'Surely it would be possible for you to do such a thing, your grace? I mean, it's the most restful journey I've ever been on. And in the new passenger ships, I've heard the accommodation is quite comfortable.'

'Do you think so?'

'It looked like it when I travelled from South Africa back home. I was in steerage, which wasn't so comfortable. But I was also in shock from losing my father, so I didn't really notice.'

'No, of course... I'm sorry.'

Honour forced a smile, struck by how sympathetic the duke was. Nobody else seemed to appreciate her loss the way he did.

'It's the past. Now please tell me, who is Arthur? You mentioned him earlier, but he wasn't at your dinner or tea. So I've been wondering. He is... he hasn't died, has he?'

'Oh no, Arthur is fine. He's in India these days though so I don't see him anymore, but he sends me fabulous letters. In the last one, he included photographs which were quite astonishing.'

'I see, and he's a friend?'

'He's my cousin. He's the eldest son of my father's eldest sister, Anne. He is also my heir, although he never makes anything of that. He pretends I'll live forever and have children of my own, so he goes his own way.'

'Which included going to India?'

'Much to my regret, although I had a hand in that too.'

'I don't understand.'

'It's a long story. I suppose it started when I was, oh it must have been four or five. My father decided I needed some company. He felt that a child should have other children around. So he invited Arthur, who is a couple of months older than me, and Percy, who is a year older, but who both lived locally to come and visit. We couldn't play in the conventional sense. I stayed in bed most of the time, but we came up with things to do. We were always supervised by my father to ensure I didn't overextend myself.

'When we got a bit older we were schooled together which I liked for I excelled at learning. I did better than Percy and Arthur, even though they also went to a proper school. It was a boost to my confidence.

'It was as well my father introduced me to Arthur and Percy. My aunt would never have allowed them anywhere near me had she been in charge from the beginning. She did try to banish them after my father died. But I was in such a state at the time that she unbent and allowed them back to see me. Ever since then, they have been my two friends, and they are the best and most loyal people any man could have.

'Arthur did a great deal of soul searching about going to India, and I fear that was because of me. He didn't want to leave me feeling abandoned. So I had to step in and tell him to go.'

'So he wanted to go?'

'As any young man would, he yearned for adventure and to make his fortune.'

'Did he need to do that?'

'Possibly not as my heir, but as I said, he's never considered the title his. His mother married for love, not money, though. Her husband is the local squire to my estate. He's a good man, but not wealthy and now with a large family to support. So Arthur decided to join the diplomatic corps. With a mother who is the daughter of a duke, and my letter of recommendation, he easily found a position. Then he proved himself to be very able and was offered a senior place in India. Of late he has met and is engaged to an Indian princess.'

'I see. He sounds like a very fast riser for one who is just twenty-one years old.'

'He is bright and charming, and he has been in the diplomatic corps since he was eighteen, so his success isn't that surprising. I also suspect that Bellamy gave him some pointers and may well be using Arthur as an agent.'

'As an agent?'

'I believe he is a spymaster of some sort, although he has never told me so.'

'Oh! I suppose that explains the questions he asked me over dinner.'

'He was impressed by your answers.'

'Was he?' Honour said with a laugh. 'I'm sure I didn't tell him anything he didn't already know.'

'Possibly not, but you probably confirmed quite a bit.'

'Well, well, that is a surprise. Now, I fear you really are tired, and it's late, I should take my leave.'

Felix nodded and said, 'I had a very enjoyable afternoon, Miss Seaborn. After all this time I'm glad we've finally had a chance for a proper talk, and I hope... I hope we can do this again.'

'I would like that, your grace.'

'Forgive me if I don't get up,' Felix said.

'I understand.'

'Might I ask another favour? Would it be possible for me to hang onto one of your sketchbooks for a while? I promise I will get it back to you.'

'Oh yes, certainly, which one would you like to keep?'

'I find myself fascinated by India. Might I borrow the book with your Indian sketches?'

'You are welcome to it,' Honour said.

Honour was surprised that she was so reluctant to leave the duke, but it really was impossible for her to stay longer. The early winter sun was already setting, and Isolde would be waiting for her so that they could go to the opera.

'Hah, well that went well,' Sergeant Major Bruin said as they bundled themselves into a hack.

'Do you think so?' Honour said.

'Good heavens, girl, don't you?'

'I don't know what to think.'

'You just spent two and a half hours with a man where the two of you never stopped talking. You looked like old friends, so you did. As far as I'm concerned you have the duke in the bag.'

'And you think that's a good thing, do you?'

'Of course, it's a good thing. No more scrimping and saving for you, child. You'll be living in the lap of luxury. Hah, if only your father could see you now, he'd be cock-a-hoop. It always ate at him how your posh relatives wanted nothing to do with you. They were rotten to the core, he'd tell me. Never forgave them for turning your mother off neither. If you marry well now, it will be a turn up for the books. All those nasty people will crawl out of the woodwork. You send them the right about when they do. They never gave a hoot for you when you were poor, they don't deserve anything when you get rich.'

'You are more than jumping the gun, Sergeant Major. His grace made not one mention of marriage or anything of that nature. Thank goodness, because I'm not sure I could accept even if he offered it.'

'Have you completely lost your mind, girl!? Is it because he's ill? I can understand anyone could hope for a hale and hearty husband, but honestly, you never know what's around the next corner. Many's the man I've known started the day off fighting fit only to be dead come nightfall.'

'Of course you did, you're a soldier.'

Honour hastily grabbed onto the door of the hack as he took an unusually quick corner that nearly threw her to the other side of the coach.

'Anyone can take a fever and up and die at any moment,' Bruin said. 'Life is uncertain for all of us. And from what I heard, the duke's had his fair share of close calls. But he also manages the risks. And not to sound too mercenary, Honour, at least you know if he pops his clogs before you, he'll leave you well provided for. Which is more than your poor dear father did.'

'I don't want to be that mercenary, Sergeant Major. And I don't want to fall in love with someone who might not love me. He might just be fascinated by my stories. What if I give him my heart and he isn't interested?'

'Honour, no man, much as he loves stories, would spend as much time as he did with you if you didn't interest him.'

'Perhaps, but at the moment it would be more sensible to see the duke as a patron. He might help me sell some of my drawings and maybe even a book of illustrations. That would be a great help and might get me a modicum of financial independence.'

'Now you're just being stubborn, like your father. Why settle for being a poxy blue stocking when you can have so much more?'

'Maybe because I don't want to be a scheming and deceitful wretch like my cousin,' Honour said and dropped her voice to a whisper as the hack had just pulled up outside the house. It was silly, of course, Isolde would never hear them, but she couldn't help herself.

'There's no sense in this world in being noble, child. We all live by our wits. It's all that keeps bread on the table. When you are presented with an opportunity like this, you should grab it with both hands.'

'I just... I don't know what he feels. I can't do more before I know that,' Honour said, as she climbed out of the hack and hurried away before the sergeant major could really get to work convincing her.

She didn't want him to convince her. She was feeling dangerously close to losing her heart already. The slightest push would be all it took to fall head over heels in love with the duke.

Felix stared out into the road, deep in thought. He'd watched Miss Seaborn, and the sergeant major get into their hack. Then he kept staring at the patch the carriage had occupied till long after it was dark and he could no longer see a thing beyond the flickering street lights. He barely registered the sounds in the room till he realised with a start that someone had settled in the chair recently occupied by Miss Seaborn.

'Pixie! What are you doing here?'

'I wanted to know how your meeting went with Miss Seaborn.'

'So you know, huh?'

'It's impossible to keep a secret in this house.'

'By which I assume your mother knows too.'

'Almost certainly. There doesn't seem to be anything that mother doesn't know.'

'That has certainly been my experience.'

Felix examined his cousin more closely. She really did represent her name. She was small and delicate, curled up on the chair, her feet

tucked under her and her head cocked to the side watching him
as closely as he was watching her.

'So I assume, as I was allowed this meeting without the
insertion of a third party, that your mother approves of Miss
Seaborn.'

'Do you think so?'

'Almost certainly, for she always engineered a way for me to
not be alone with Lady Giddings.'

'I didn't know that.'

'There was no reason why you should.'

'On the other hand, I can see why she might like Miss Seaborn
more than Lady Giddings.'

'So you are with the rest of the female world in your opinion
of Lady Giddings, are you?'

'She dismissed me, and honestly, I found her tedious. She was
only interested in herself. She sees the world from the prism of
her own viewpoint.'

'Much as it pains me to say it, you are right. I regret that it took
me so long to see that. What do you make of Miss Seaborn then?
You may be as brutally frank about her as you were about Lady
Giddings.'

'I like Miss Seaborn. She's sensible and friendly, and I suspect
she has more of a sense of humour than she is usually allowed to
show. There were times during her last two visits when I got the
distinct impression she might laugh if she was able and her eyes
did twinkle in appreciation.'

'Yes, I noticed that too. It's a pity that as a chaperone and an
indigent relative, she has to be so mindful of how she behaves.
She was far more natural this afternoon.'

'So you took to her?'

'More than is wise. It took a great deal of self-control not to
let her see how very fond of her I am growing.'

'But why hide it, Felix?' Pixie said, and her astonishment
was reflected in her expression. 'How can she know you are
developing feelings for her if you don't let it show?'

'Because maybe I don't want her to know. She is such a vital energetic woman. She has lived so much of her life going from one adventure to another, it would be cruel to lock her up with me. I may as well bury her alive.'

'Oh!' Pixie gasped. 'Maybe that should be her decision to make. I know I would be happiest with the man I love no matter the circumstances. That must surely be true of Miss Seaborn's mother, who went off with a soldier despite being threatened with dire consequences by her family.'

'It isn't the same, Pixie. He was a fit and healthy man who could look after his wife and child.'

'Only while he was alive. When he died, Miss Seaborn was destitute. She made nothing of it, but I gather the only way she managed to get back to England was because she acted as a chaperone to three girls who were being sent to boarding school. At least if she married you, she wouldn't have to rely on the needs of others. She would have a security most women only ever dream of having.'

'It's wrong.'

'You clearly don't like her as much as I thought you did then.'

'No?'

'If you really loved her you'd say damn the consequences, I love her, and I will make her mine.'

'Maybe I love her too much for that. Maybe her happiness means more to me than my own.'

'Maybe her happiness relies upon you. If she loves you, her happiest place will be by your side.'

Felix sighed and said, 'I suspect you and I have both read far too many novels. The real world is harder to navigate.'

'I don't think so.' Pixie cast her eyes over the array of cakes that had been prepared for Honour and selected one for herself. 'I fully intend to marry the man of my heart.'

Felix paused and examined his cousin again. Her chin was tilted up in defiance, but it was insecure, a child pushing at a barrier that frightened her.

'Percy?'

'You noticed?'

'I would have to be blind not to realise that Percy had taken a shine to you. I wasn't so clear on your feelings.'

'I was being careful. I didn't want mother to suspect.'

'Mmm, no, she won't like it.'

'She has great ambitions for me that don't include penniless professors either. Mother was quite cross with Celia over Professor Antrobus. But it proves to me that Celia also believes happiness is more important than money.'

'Although she married a wealthy man rather than her soldier and she tells me she loves him now and wouldn't have it any other way.'

'Celia didn't really love Captain Roberts,' Pixie said and broke off a small piece of cake and popped it into her mouth.

'Are you sure about that?'

'She talked to us girls of how dashing and handsome he was and of how all the other ladies swarmed about him yet he liked her best. It was a triumph for her because you know she is a bit big-boned and ungainly. Mother was forever saying that men prefer petite, elegant ladies. Which is why she is so certain I will make a great match.'

'I see.'

'She has it set in her mind that I will marry the Earl of Bognor. Can you even conceive of such a thing?'

'I don't think I have ever heard of the Earl of Bognor.'

'That's because he's so young he hasn't been to town yet. He's scarcely older than me and, I hear, none too bright. But he is titled and wealthy, and that's all mother cares about. Even Celia agrees with me that we would not suit.'

'That is a dilemma, certainly.'

'But one you could help me with, cousin Felix.'

'Me? What could I possibly do?'

'I don't know exactly, but I feel sure you could do something. At the very least you could stand our friend in the face of mother's wrath.'

'Does Percy know any of this?'

'No, of course not,' Pixie said with a gurgle of a laugh. 'He's being frightfully noble and keeping his distance as if he thinks he's protecting me by doing that. The only problem is, I don't want him to keep his distance. And I definitely don't want him going off and seeking solace in the arms of another woman.'

'Mmm, I feel sure your mother would think this a highly inappropriate conversation.'

'I'm sorry, but... would you help us?'

'You are very young still,' Felix said, reflecting that the way she nibbled at her food made her look even more pixie-like.

'I am sixteen, very nearly seventeen. But I will make you a bargain. I will wait a year and if I still feel the same way about Percy then, will you help me?'

'If you wait a year, then I will do what I can for you.'

'Thank you, cousin Felix. I knew you wouldn't let me down!'

'We shall see. Now, as we are talking about matchmaking, tell me what Juliana thinks of Lord Hounslow.'

'Oh, that poor man,' Pixie said and leaned forward in her chair to share this piece of gossip. 'He keeps sending her poetry and Juliana calls him that sweet man, but she has no idea that he is quite smitten.'

'Have you told her?'

'Not yet.'

'Good heavens, why not?'

Pixie shrugged and said, 'Call it my mischievous side. I am curious to see how long it will take for Juliana to realise.'

'And when she does, do you think she will love him?'

'Yes, yes, she will.'

'How can you be so sure?'

'Because Juliana isn't very clever. I love her dearly, and there is nothing she wouldn't do for me or any of her sisters, but she's just sweet and biddable. If mother tells her to marry Lord Hounslow and he goes down on one knee before her and proposes she will fall instantly in love with him and never care about anyone else again. Sometimes it seems to me the world is a happier place if you aren't very bright.'

'I suppose so.'

'I believe mother is also happy with Lord Hounslow. He's a man with a good income and a good family name. What is more, mother won't have the expense of a come-out. In fact, she will probably be cock-a-hoop to have married a daughter off straight from the nursery. She will be the envy of every other friend with a handful of girls to marry off.'

'Well, that sounds quite settled. But I wonder, Pixie, whether the two of us shouldn't look around more. Should we both settle for someone we met early on before we have seen what London has to offer?'

'I don't know about you, Cousin Felix, but I couldn't fall in love with anyone else now that I've met Percy.'

'You see, that's exactly what I did. I thought I loved Lady Giddings, and now I think I love Miss Seaborn.'

'Does it feel the same?'

'No, my passion for Lady Giddings was... I shouldn't say this to you, but it was, well, raw. I hungered after her. With Miss Seaborn... it's more a sense of contentment.'

'Well, Percy makes me feel happy. When he's around, it feels like the sun has come out, and I don't want to lose that.'

'I suppose it's different for each of us. You know though, Pixie, if you really do want to marry Percy you should speak to your father.'

'Father? What could he possibly do?'

'Far more than you realise,' Felix said.

CHAPTER TWENTY-ONE

I t was a week since Felix had seen Miss Seaborn and never had the days passed more slowly. Nothing he did could distract him sufficiently to stop thinking about her. Every moment was a battle to prevent himself from sending her another invitation to visit.

His sensible side kept reassuring himself that he was doing the right thing by staying away. Miss Seaborn was an adventurous spirit who couldn't be tied down. She didn't even like London because it hemmed her in too much. How much worse if she were stuck inside one house

He found himself working out how much she could go out. Just because he had to stay indoors didn't mean she had to, did it? His uncle and aunt lived pretty separate lives. Uncle Marmaduke spent as much time in his club as he did at home.

Was that a solution, to send his wife out into the world without him? Would that be acceptable for a woman? Would she even want to do that?

It was unlikely. Women didn't go about on their own. People would find it too odd. He was just trying to avoid the horrible truth that she was the wrong woman for him. Well no, not the wrong woman. She was the perfect woman, if he was as healthy as Percy or Arthur.

Then they could travel together and have any number of their own adventures. That was a pleasant fantasy. The reality was that he couldn't travel. Never in his life had that realisation filled him with more gloom. It appeared to be obvious because Grantley and Poole were giving him more room and time alone than was usual too.

'Good morning, your grace,' Hieronymus said, breaking in on Felix's ruminations.

'Ah, Mister Testwood, thank God. Welcome back. You look very smart this morning,' Felix said taking in the brown serge suit and yellow waistcoat.

'Thanks to Grantley, sir. He got me this suit, and I have to say with this and your letter I have had no difficulties getting in to see anyone. In fact, the lift factory manager himself showed me around and talked me through all the specifications of how they work. He's very excited by the prospect of installing one in your home.'

'And what do you think, Mr Testwood? Should I trust my life and the structural integrity of my house to this contraption?'

'I liked it, your grace. I have now ridden in several lifts, and they have all been smooth and trouble-free. I'm convinced by the safety features. I have also seen several buildings that had lifts installed in them without difficulty. They're getting better at it all the time.'

'So you would recommend it, would you?'

'I would, your grace. It will make life easier for everyone, including the maids carrying hot water up the stairs at the moment. It will be quicker, and there will be less spillage.'

'I must admit that hadn't occurred to me as a benefit, but no doubt you are right.'

'I believe so, your grace. You should also know that I have been offered a considerable incentive by the lift manufacturer. They are convinced that once London gets to know a duke has installed a lift in his house, it will become all the rage amongst the well-to-do. I didn't take the money, but there might be a career in it for someone, to be a lift salesman.'

'You're not tempted?'

'I enjoy inventing too much to give it up and become a salesman. But I did use the suit to good effect. I went to the patent office with the designs for my hoist and the walking frame. I'm hoping something good will come from both. I've even worked out a way to make the height adjustable on the walking frame so that I could make a single model, but people could adjust it for their height whatever it may be.'

'That sounds eminently sensible.'

'Other than that, er... I haven't come up with anything new.'

'The compressed air device doesn't work?'

'It's more complicated than Mr Andrews and I first thought. While he can compress air, we have yet to develop a container that can store the gas. The device for compressing the air is far too big and cumbersome to be able to carry it around or set it up in your room.'

'But you continue to think about that and other inventions, do you?' Felix said and decided that he wanted to keep Testwood on. He provided a valuable diversion and a direction to his life that he needed at the moment.

'Oh yes, your grace. I have come to realise that many people find it difficult getting around or performing the most commonplace tasks due to illness, accident or deformity. They could really use some help. The only problem is... well, these people are the least able to pay for any of my inventions.'

'I see. I have to admit I never considered the plight of anyone else in this regard. But you are right, without a means of income, they also have no way of procuring that which might assist them. Perhaps a trust needs to be set up to aid people like me but with less money.'

'Oh, I hadn't, that is to say, I didn't mean to imply-'

'I like to feel useful, Mr Testwood, allow me this action. I will speak to my man of business about a trust, and you will remain on the payroll. Think of me as a patron to you and to the trust, together we will be able to make a difference.'

'Yes, your grace, thank you. It's very good of you.'

'Not at all,' Felix said and suppressed a smile at what his aunt would make of this latest way he'd conceived of spending money. 'Now, you will have to forgive me, I have another meeting. But speak to Mr Forsyth on the way out and tell him we're putting in a lift. I will want to see the plans before work begins. I'd like them to do it while I'm away during the summer.'

'So we're going to have a lift, are we?' Grantley said the moment Mr Testwood had left.

'We are, at which point I may well move upstairs.'

'And you'll let the staff use the lift, will you? All those maids carrying bathwater up and down, doesn't bear thinking of,' Grantley said with a sniff as he tidied away the magazines Felix had discarded. 'It will give them airs. Make them use the stairs, I say.'

'But why?'

'Because fancy things like lifts are for their betters which I'm sure is what her ladyship will say.'

'Quite possibly, but it isn't her house.'

'No, your grace, point taken. Now, are you ready for the visit from Professor Antrobus?'

'I am. I have to admit I'm curious to know what he wants. He's a very challenging man.'

'Just as long as he doesn't tire you out, your grace, especially not with Lady Giddings coming this afternoon.'

'It doesn't rain, but it pours, not so, Grantley? Quiet for a week and then three visitors in a day.'

'Indeed, your grace, although you didn't know Mr Testwood was coming. That man's a harum-scarum, coming and going as he sees fit.'

'I find him refreshingly different. Now tell me, where is Poole?'

'Pressing your jacket, your grace.'

'By himself?'

'He is making progress, your grace. This is a test for him, the first time he has pressed your jacket without my supervision.'

'Mmm, so your retirement draws ever nearer.'

'Not so near, your grace.'

'I fear we are both putting it off, Grantley. At this rate, you'll never get to enjoy your new house.'

'Well, as it happens, I've been to visit it a couple of times and have started furnishing it. Nothing vulgar you understand, and I was wondering... whether I might... take the odd half day.'

'Of course, that sounds like an excellent idea. That way, you can still be around to support Poole for a while and ease yourself into retirement.'

'That's what I was thinking, your grace.'

'Capital!'

Felix was relieved that his retainer hadn't spoken about leaving so that he didn't have to either. He was finding the change more of a wrench than he'd expected.

'Ah Poole, my jacket, it looks perfectly pressed too.'

'Thank you, your grace,' Poole said woodenly.

'No, don't hand it to Grantley, you help me into it,' Felix said as he stood up. 'Then you may as well accompany me to the drawing room for my next visitor.'

Felix had half an hour before Professor Antrobus was due, which gave him plenty of time to wonder why the man was coming to visit. Only he couldn't think about that because he found his mind drifting more and more to the reason for Lady Giddings' visit. He'd been surprised to receive her letter, informing him that she was coming, as he'd made no further move to contact her since the tea party.

He wondered vaguely whether Overbrook thought that a triumph. Did he imagine that he'd scared Felix off? He didn't like to think that. He didn't want the earl to believe he was that easily cowed, especially when the man had broadcast his threat to society in general.

Bellamy had let him know that the earl had made some attempt to interfere with one of Felix's feed suppliers, but that had been quickly and easily scotched. Mr Forsyth had also moved to shore up everybody else. Felix did wonder though, whether attack might not be the best defence. Perhaps that was better held onto should things escalate.

None of that explained Lady Giddings' approach and brought him back to wondering what he might tell her. He'd been scrupulous in not leading her on. He wasn't really sure why, when he'd been so bowled over by her.

No, that wasn't true. He'd not said anything to her for the same reason he hadn't said anything to Miss Seaborn. It was because he had serious doubts about his suitability as a husband.

He wished he had Aunt Lavinia's rock-hard conviction that he had to produce an heir. If he were sufficiently driven by that ambition, then his concerns would be irrelevant. But honestly, he wasn't that worried about the succession.

Perhaps his father's relaxed attitude towards it had influenced him more than he realised. He was perfectly happy to let Arthur and his descendants inherit the duchy. His dusky descendants, Felix thought, which had him grinning. Aunt Lavinia would definitely hate that.

Still, it didn't solve his dilemma: what to do with Lady Giddings. She had expectations which he was about to dash. It wouldn't bother him unduly except for the consequences it might bring to Miss Seaborn.

It wasn't her fault, of course, but he doubted Lady Giddings would see it that way. Then again, she was unlikely to suspect anything. So surely Miss Seaborn had to be all right, didn't she? What was it about Lady Giddings that made him so unsure of that fact?

Either way, perhaps it would be a relief. He'd put an end to what hadn't really even been an affair let alone a courtship, and he'd move on. Marriage wasn't for the likes of him and was best forgotten about. Odd that decision left him feeling very low indeed. The idea of spending the rest of his life alone was one he didn't want to face.

'Professor Antrobus, your grace,' Chivers said as he held the door open.

'Oh yes, of course,' Felix said, relieved to be pulled out of his melancholy reflections. 'Please, do come in, Professor.'

'Thank you, your grace, it's very good of you to see me.'

'Not at all, please sit down,' Felix said and indicated the chair opposite his. 'Your letter was rather cryptic, which had me intrigued.'

'Ah well, you see,' Antrobus said and pulled at his collar, but remained standing, 'I have a request to make on behalf of my college.'

'Do you?' Felix said, and the professor's unusually tidy appearance started to make more sense.

'No doubt you get any number of begging letters from all around the country.'

'More so now that I have reached my majority, and my name and wealth were splashed across the pages of the newspapers.'

'Ah yes, I suppose that's understandable,' Antrobus said and then looked at something of a loss on how to proceed.

'You don't do this very often do you, Professor?'

'Do what?'

'Ask for money.'

'You're right there, your grace! I've never done it before in my life, and I find it singularly distasteful.'

'So what has brought you to this pass?' Felix said and felt considerable sympathy for the man as he looked so uncomfortable.

'My college made some foolish investments that have severely affected their ability to pay their staff. We have all been sent out to try and make up the shortfall.'

'And if you don't?'

'I will most likely find myself without a job.'

'I see. What of the men who lost the money? What will happen to them?'

'Three of them have already been let go. The rest, I believe, are being kept on to make things right.'

'Mmm, it doesn't sound like a wise place to make an investment.'

'No, I don't suppose it does, your grace, you're right there. Please forgive my presumption. I shouldn't have come this morning,' Antrobus said and stood up.

'You're giving up, Professor? Just like that?'

'It wasn't the right thing to do. You have no connection to the college, let alone the state it's in now. It isn't right to expect you to bail us out.'

'Would that be the philosopher in you speaking?'

'I suppose it would be.'

'Please, sit down.'

'Your grace, I don't want to waste your time or tire you, and I know... I'm sorry, but you are not well, and I shouldn't burden you with this.'

'Sit,' Felix snapped. He was annoyed that his health had been brought into the discussion. 'Now tell me why you thought to ask me in the first place.'

Professor Antrobus looked startled to be ordered so brusquely and sat down with a bump.

'I'd been sent to London to meet with several former alumni. Most of them have been my students, and then I received your invitation to dinner. If it hadn't been for Bellamy, I'm not sure I would have come... No, that isn't entirely true, I was curious. Curiosity has always been my weakness. After the dinner, Bellamy also asked why I'd gone so I told him and he said I shouldn't shy away and I should ask for some money.'

'What reason did he give?'

'You think he gave a reason?'

'If I am any judge of the man, yes, he would have.'

'He told me you value learning, and you might like a philosophy professor at your beck and call for the occasional chat. Although, he didn't phrase it in those terms.'

'But you would feel beholden to me if I helped fund your college?'

'Yes, which Belly knows full well.'

'He is a good judge of character.'

'Too good.'

'And what of Lady Giddings?'

'Ah, your grace, I leave that field entirely to you.'

'You would give her up for the chance of some money?'

Felix was driving Antrobus hard, but he felt he was entitled to if he was expected to become a benefactor.

'You imply that I have something to give up. I wish I did, but it was clear by the end of the tea party that Lady Giddings had eyes for only one man.'

'Me?'

'Indeed, and if I may say so, you didn't look that thrilled by the prospect.'

'No. I'm afraid I'm more fickle than I realised and I no longer have an interest in the lady.'

'She is too cruel.'

Felix was surprised by that assessment. He'd thought Lady Giddings selfish but no worse than that. 'You think she is cruel?'

'Oh yes, there is no doubt about it. She would watch you die and not shed a tear.'

'And yet you still love her?'

'Like a suicidal moth to her beautiful flame.'

'I see.'

'I appal you, I can tell, but I have a melancholy streak, and Lady Giddings feeds it nicely.'

'It would be a curious romance. Especially as I got the impression, her ladyship isn't entirely impartial to you.'

'Unfortunately for me, I have no money. Otherwise ours would be a perfectly imperfect match.'

'That sounds like philosophy again.'

'Just a little bit.'

'What a curious dilemma. I am tempted to fund you merely to hear how you progress with Lady Giddings.'

'Alas, your grace, you and I both know she will move on to the next wealthy man, and I will have nothing to entertain you with.'

'I wouldn't be so sure of that. I may live cloistered in this house, but I read, and I am aware of more than one adulterous affair.'

'You counsel me to try and seduce a married woman?'

'Let's just say that I wouldn't be surprised if Lady Giddings was amenable to the idea.'

Felix was shocked by what he'd just said, but he genuinely thought it a possibility.

'Would that give you sufficient revenge on the Earl of Overbrook, your grace?'

'It might,' Felix said, a laugh surprised out of him. 'I was more angered by his threat than I realised.'

'No man should take a threat lightly.'

'Nor did I. Now, as for your college-'

'Oh leave that, your grace, it really wasn't appropriate and I-'

'No. You came all this way to ask, the least I can do is give you an answer.'

'Very well.'

'I won't fund the college. I have no confidence in them, but I will fund your position.'

'My position?'

'You are the chair of philosophy, are you not?'

'I am.'

'And that post could sit anywhere, couldn't it? Within that college or any other.'

'I suppose so, I've never really thought about it.'

'Well, the decision is yours, but don't necessarily take the easy way out of sticking with your current college.'

'What would you want in return, your grace?'

'Why, for you to come and entertain me on occasion of course,' Felix said with a wide grin.

Felix was just finishing lunch when Percy strolled into the drawing room and gave him a penetrating stare. Felix was used to it. Most people examined him just a little too closely.

'Percy, what brings you here?'

'What do you think?' Percy said with a shrug and a laugh.

'Aunt Lavinia,' Felix sighed. 'I suppose I should be grateful you didn't show up for tea with Miss Seaborn.'

'In which, don't forget, I played my part. But no, Aunt Lavinia described Miss Seaborn as an unobjectionable young woman.'

'Did she now?'

'She did,' Percy said, as he settled onto the sofa and lounged back. 'Now tell me, how was the meeting?'

'Honestly, the most enjoyable afternoon I can ever recall.'

'So why the look of gloom?'

'No reason,' Felix said, shrugging it off. 'I still don't see why you should be here. Aunt Lavinia must know I'm no longer interested in Lady Giddings.'

'Oh yes, she knows. I'm just here to make sure La Giddings doesn't make a scene when you give her her marching orders.'

'What makes you think I'm going to do that?'

Percy crossed one leg over the other and pretended to examine the gleam of his boots.

'Because, unlike other men who might just avoid Lady Giddings until she gets the message and moves on, you prefer to make things clear.'

'I dislike dishonesty.'

'Indeed, now as I see her coach pulling up, we'd best school our faces into something more complaisant.'

'You and your joking. At this rate, I won't even be able to keep a straight face.'

All the same, the situation was a serious one and Felix no longer felt like smiling by the time Chivers showed Lady Giddings in.

'My aunt, Mrs Sumner,' Isolde said as she swept in, trailing a dumpy old woman.

'Mrs Sumner?' Felix said, aware of a deep sense of disappointment to not see Miss Seaborn.

'I'm afraid so,' Lady Giddings said briskly. 'My cousin, Honour Seaborn, and I had a falling out, your grace.'

'You did?'

'It turns out she was a deceiving, deceitful wretch who took my kindness and repaid it with treachery.'

'I don't understand. What could she possibly have done to make you so angry?'

'Felix you should sit down,' Percy said and tugged his cousin down into his chair.

'What did she do?' Lady Giddings snapped. 'She lied to me. She told me she was going out to tea with that odd-looking Sergeant Major Bruin, and then she came here! My friend, Miss Downs, lives one block along from here and she happened to walk past your house and saw the two of you sitting as bold as you please in that bow window.'

'Ah, well you see,' Percy said leaping in. 'Miss Seaborn didn't know she was coming here that day. I'm afraid I played a trick on her.'

'You too, Captain Shawcross?' Isolde said. 'You would lie to me too?'

'So what happened to Miss Seaborn?' Felix said, cutting across the two of them.

'We had a blazing row, and the following morning I was informed that my cousin had left. She packed her bags, and without so much as a thank you, she vanished.'

'Where did she go?'

'I don't know, and I don't care,' Isolde said.

'You don't know where she went?'

Felix was astonished and frankly disbelieving. It seemed so out of character for Miss Seaborn to simply disappear.

'As I said, the ungrateful wench just walked out. I assume she went to live with some other relative. Or maybe she went to Guyana with Sergeant Major Bruin.'

'I see,' Felix said. 'Well, I'm sorry to hear that. I am also sorry to have deceived you, for you must know I played my part in inviting Miss Seaborn to visit. I was curious to see her drawings.'

'Her drawings? That's the same poxy tale she tried to spin me.'

'It happens to be the truth.'

'But why would you want to see her drawings? That's just preposterous.'

'Actually, they are very good.'

'What nonsense,' Isolde said and took a turn about the room. She appeared too angry to actually sit down.

'Did you ever look at them?'

'Why would I do that?'

'Why, indeed?' Felix murmured. 'No, I don't suppose you would be interested in anything other than yourself, Lady Giddings. Even now, you have come in here flinging accusations and making sure I know how hurt and angry you feel. So I have apologised, and that's where I draw the line. I don't see any point in seeing you now or ever again. Thank you for your visit, Lady Giddings, Chivers will show you out.'

'What?' Lady Giddings gasped, 'You can't throw me out.'

'Yes, I can.'

'But... but I'm going to marry you.'

'Whatever gave you that idea?'

Felix was stunned nearly into breathlessness that she was so bold as to say what she had so clearly assumed all along.

'You said-'

'I said nothing.'

'You sent me a gift.'

'At the same time as I sent Miss Seaborn a gift.'

'No, it can't be!'

'Good day, Lady Giddings,' Felix said and gave Chivers a meaningful look.

'If your ladyship will follow me,' Chivers said with a punctilious bow and showed her and her chaperone out.

'Good lord!' Percy muttered.

'Wait,' Felix said and held up his hand.

He listened to the strident sound of Lady Giddings' voice recede down the hall and out of the house. Then he watched as the two ladies hurried into their carriage.

'Are you all right, Felix?' Percy said.

Felix held up a trembling hand for inspection and said, 'Shaken, that's all.'

'That was a devilish nasty scene and no mistake.'

'Poor Miss Seaborn. What have I done to her, Percy?'

'She'll be all right, I'm sure.'

'Maybe, but it's my fault she fell out with Lady Giddings. She would still have a roof over her head if it wasn't for me.'

'Lady Giddings is bound to be right. She probably has just gone to another relative.'

'She didn't have any other relatives to go to. She told me that herself.'

'Well, that is odd then,' Percy said as he flung himself back into his seat. 'Especially as Sergeant Major Bruin said she was planning to go off and be a governess.'

'A governess? Really?'

'Apparently, she preferred that to going to Guyana with him. So the sergeant major said anyway.'

'She was planning on becoming a governess?'

'That is what I understood. I tell you what, Felix, you did damned well with Lady Giddings. I don't think I've ever been able to give a woman her marching orders quite so neatly.'

'She made it rather easy for me, don't you think? Coming in here to scold me. It removed any requirement for delicacy on my part.'

'All the same, old boy, she had me quaking in my boots, but you stayed as cool as a cucumber. I'm very impressed.'

'Don't be, I feel quite shaken.'

'It didn't show. I'll tell you something else, though... it's a damn good thing Aunt Lavinia wasn't here. She'd have been roaring back at Lady Giddings in your defence.'

'Indeed, but it's a small mercy. Just now, I am more concerned about what has happened to Miss Seaborn.'

'So, you do care about her, do you?'

'More than I wanted to admit to myself. I was really looking forward to seeing her today and the sense of disappointment when that other woman walked through the door, well... I don't know what to do anymore.'

'I thought you told Pixie that, like her or not, you would put her out of your mind.'

'You've been speaking to Pixie?'

'I sneaked in for a quick chat before I came to support you.'

'Mmm, well, she was right. I don't think it's fair to keep any woman chained to me, especially one who is used to being as free as Miss Seaborn.'

'It's not much freedom being tied to a family as a governess which seems to be the best Miss Seaborn hoped for. You wouldn't be tying her to you, you'd be freeing her from a life of servitude.'

'I don't know.'

'Well, I won't push you further. You've had more than enough excitement today.'

'That is something of an understatement. In fact, if you would be so kind as to support me back to my room, I'll have a little lie-down.'

'Are you sure you're all right?' Percy said sharply as he examined Felix's face more closely.

'Just tired, nothing more, I assure you.'

The day took such a toll that Felix decided to lie on his bed rather than on the sofa. Poole was on hand to help him out of his jacket and into his dressing gown. He arranged the pillows so that Felix could be propped up, then he removed his shoes, replaced them with slippers and covered Felix's legs with a blanket.

'Nicely done, Poole,' Felix murmured as the young man brought his magazines and placed them within easy reach on the bedside table.

Felix had intended to browse through the pictures for some distraction, but he was tired, and his eyelids kept drooping closed.

'Felix, Percy told me what happened,' Lady Lavinia said as she strode into his bedroom.

'I'm all right,' Felix said and forced his eyes open. He was more tired than he wanted to show his aunt and certainly more shaken.

'If I had only known she was going to create a scene, I would have shown her the door straight away.'

'As it was, Chivers did it for you.'

'Percy thought you did really well. He positively glowed as he related the whole episode.'

'Yes, he seems to have enjoyed it.'

'And you didn't. Well, I'm sorry, and I'm also sorry Miss Seaborn has fled. But you know there are plenty of other young women in London. I'm sure we can still find you somebody suitable.'

'I don't want anybody,' Felix snapped. 'I've had enough of all of this. I just want some peace and quiet!'

'Of course. I shouldn't have brought it up now. You need to rest. We will talk again tomorrow.'

'Heaven help me,' Felix muttered as the door closed behind his aunt. He had so hoped to put an end to all this, but now it was just a battle deferred.

CHAPTER TWENTY-TWO

F elix woke feeling tired. Sleep had been elusive, and he was haunted by fears of what had happened to Miss Seaborn. Everyone else seemed to think she had left of her own accord and that she wasn't coming back. The assumption then, was that he would also move on and find somebody else.

'But I won't,' he muttered for the hundredth time.

At least his sleepless night had resolved one question. He did love Miss Seaborn. He swore to himself that should he ever see her again he would ask her to marry him.

God, if he ever saw her again. What if he didn't? It didn't bear thinking of.

What made it worse was that he was partially to blame for her disappearance. If he hadn't been so underhanded in arranging to meet, she might not have fallen out with Lady Giddings. Then again, Lady Giddings would never have allowed them to be alone without her under any circumstance so they'd not had much choice.

The big question now was, where was Miss Seaborn? The more he pondered that, the more worried he grew. Lady Giddings, by both their admissions, was the only relative who was willing to take Miss Seaborn in, so how could she find somebody else?

The thought that she might have become a governess also sounded unlikely. For one, how would she get references? Lady Giddings certainly wouldn't give her any, and who else could she ask?

He might not know much about the world, but he'd sat in on sufficient family meals where his aunt went on and on about governesses to know all about how they were retained. It usually involved at least two references.

Finally, there was the sketchbook. It was a prized possession. Surely Miss Seaborn wouldn't leave it with him and never reclaim it?

Maybe she would, though. Maybe she'd write and ask for the book to be sent to her with a forwarding address enclosed. At least then he'd be able to write to her.

At the very least Miss Seaborn was owed an apology. And the rest... he would be able to speak to her, sound her out... ask her to marry him. He'd make a clean breast of it, let her know that he knew he wasn't an ideal man, far from what any young woman might dream of. He'd let her choose.

'Damn it, I have to find her,' he muttered and rang his bell.

'Yes, your grace?' Poole said as he hurried into the room.

'No Grantley?' Felix said in surprise. Since his seventh year Grantley had always got him up, and this was not a great moment for something new.

'He's feeling a little under the weather, your grace,' Poole said shifting uncomfortably under Felix's gaze.

'He's unwell?' Felix said as a shiver of fear ran through him.

'He said not to trouble yourself, your grace, he'll be fine in a little while.'

'The devil he did!' Felix snapped. 'Fetch Doctor Morley for him right away.'

'He won't like it, your grace,' Poole said, 'but I'll do it just the same.'

By this Felix gathered the lad was more worried for Grantley than concerned about getting a ticking off. He'd shot away too, no hanging about. That alarmed Felix even more, and he pulled on the harness to get himself upright. He had to see Grantley for himself.

'Don't you go getting out of bed, your grace,' Dr Morley said as he came striding through the room on the way to the dressing room. 'I knew you'd be up, but you can't go in to see Grantley, not till I know he hasn't come down with a nasty infection.'

'Well be quick then,' Felix said to the doctor's back.

What a devilish few days it had been, with no sign of improvement.

'The doctor's sent me out,' Poole said as he came back into the room. 'Are you all right, your grace? Shall I build up your pillows for you?'

'Yes, please do, we may as well use the hoist too. Grantley might not approve, but as it's just you and me this morning, he needn't ever know.

'Yes, your grace.'

'How are you settling in, Poole?'

'I'm doing fine, thank you, your grace.'

'Is it better than the stables?'

'Oh yes, sir, and mother is that proud. She's right cock-a-hoop.'

'Well, I'm glad to hear that.'

'I shouldn't have said that, sir, not in that way. Grantley is forever telling me I have to behave more proper.'

'It will come with time. How are the other servants treating you?'

'Fine, thank you, your grace.'

'Well that was perfect decorum, but not, I think, the truth.'

'I know you want the truth at all times, your grace, but honestly, I can solve my problems on my own.'

'I'm glad to hear it, Poole. However, should you happen to find yourself in too deep you may call upon me. For, you know, it is the duty of a master to have the needs of his servants always in mind.'

'Thank you, your grace,' Poole said blushing all the way to the tips of his ears.

Felix laughed and might have said more, but Doctor Morley came in and said, 'He's going to be all right, your grace.'

'Thank God for that. What ails him?'

'Nothing but a touch of fatigue. A day in bed and he'll be right as rain.'

'I see,' Felix said, he needed to know more, but the doctor was the soul of discretion. 'Poole, would you go and ask Mr Forsyth to come and see me at his convenience, please?'

'Yes, your grace,' Poole said and hurried away.

'Now tell me honestly, doctor, will Grantley recover?'

'He is suffering from old age, your grace. Rest is what he needs right now, and he'll need that more and more. He simply isn't as strong as he used to be.'

'I try to ignore it, but I have seen that for myself. I will get him to take more time off and make sure he actually uses it.'

'That would be for the best. Now how about you, your grace? I hear there was high drama yesterday including a lady being escorted from the premises.'

'There really are no secrets in this house, are there?'

'I heard it from my man. He saw the lady being shown the door. I assume it was Lady Giddings?'

'It was. I only pray the whole of London isn't half as well informed about this as my household is.'

'That all depends upon Lady Giddings I suspect, your grace. I doubt your staff will say anything to the outside world.'

'I hope you're right,' Felix said and nodded farewell as Mr Forsyth arrived and waited discreetly at the door. The doctor took his leave, and Felix said, 'Please take a seat, Mr Forsyth.'

'Thank you, your grace. What can I do for you this morning?'

'Two things, interrelated. First, I would like you to find out all you can about Lady Giddings and her father.'

'Your grace?'

'I need to understand them better. They don't have a country estate, just the house in the city. It's unusual.'

'Not that unusual.'

'No, but see whether you can find out a little more. I may need it for leverage.'

'For the second task?'

'Yes, I need you to find someone for me.'

'I see, who am I looking for?'

'Miss Honour Seaborn. I was told she has gone to stay with a relative, but not which one. All I know, at this point, is that she is no longer living with Lady Giddings. I'm sure I don't have to emphasise that discretion is essential.'

'You may rely upon me, your grace.'

'Thank you. And, Mr Forsyth, I am worried about her safety so please, find her quickly.'

'I will do my all, your grace.'

'Thank you,' Felix said and laid his head back down on his pillows.

Mr Forsyth left so silently that Felix didn't even hear the click of the door as he stared up into the canopy of his bed. He wondered, for the hundredth time, about what had happened to Miss Seaborn.

CHAPTER TWENTY-THREE

Felix flicked through Miss Seaborn's sketchbook listlessly and stopped at the picture of Rose Cottage. The drawing intrigued him for it seemed a peculiarly English house with roses growing over the front door. It didn't fit with the rest of the drawings that were all of India. Even the label was different. All the other images had a description in a plain neat handwriting, Rose Cottage though, was ornate, with twisting rose ornaments curled around each letter.

He desperately wanted to ask Miss Seaborn what it meant, but it was three days since he'd heard she'd left and still there was no sign of her. Worse yet, she hadn't written asking for her book to be returned. That seemed ominous.

He was worried sick but trying not to show it. He didn't want people to grow alarmed over his health or more irritatingly to fuss. But the worry was taking its toll. He felt exhausted, so tired he couldn't get out of bed.

'Your grace, would you not like to get up?' Grantley said as he slipped silently into the room.

'Grantley, you're better!'

'I am, your grace,' Grantley said and actually looked embarrassed.

'How do you feel?'

'Much improved, thank you, your grace.'

'You need to take it easy, old man.'

'So the doctor tells me, but it is not a thing I am accustomed to doing.'

'Well, take it from me,' Felix said with a laugh, 'it is always best to follow the advice of your doctor.'

'Yes. I... I hope you don't take this amiss, your grace, but these last few days... They gave me a better understanding of what you have had to put up with your whole life.'

'Ah, well. I am sorry you had to experience that.'

'It isn't easy, is it, your grace?'

'I have never had it any other way, so I suppose I am accustomed. I might have felt my illness more acutely if I'd had it come on after a life of activity.'

'All the same, your grace, I will try to nag you less. It is just quite irritating, isn't it?'

'I'm afraid it is.'

Grantley nodded deep in thought as he said, 'Dressing gown, your grace?'

'I believe I will,' Felix said as he was helped into his dressing gown and then onto his sofa.

He was about to return to his perusal of Miss Seaborn's sketches when there was a knock at the door, and Mr Forsyth looked in. 'May I speak to you, your grace?'

'Yes, come in,' Felix said, and his heart beat faster. Was Mr Forsyth about to deliver bad news? He was difficult to read, but he looked grave.

Mr Forsyth settled into the chair opposite Felix and took a slow deep breath. 'I have been doing as you asked, your grace and have looked for Miss Seaborn.'

'And?'

'As of yet, I have been unable to find her. I have gone through her entire family tree and located all its members. I have written to each of them enquiring after Miss Seaborn. They all claim not to have seen her. Those who were polite, and there were few of them, said that the last they heard she was still in South Africa and asking for somewhere to stay.'

'So she didn't go to a relative.'

'It doesn't look that way, your grace. I then followed up the possibility that she left with Sergeant Major Bruin. I managed to get a list of all the passengers that embarked on the voyage to Guyana. Miss Seaborn's name was not amongst that list. She may be travelling under a different name, but I feel that is unlikely. I did, however, check for a Mrs or Miss Bruin, but they were not on the passenger list either. All the other women on the list were clearly attached to one or other of the soldiers, so I believe it is highly unlikely that Miss Seaborn went to Guyana.'

'Good God, how could she have vanished so completely?'

'That was not the end of my investigation, your grace,' Mr Forsyth said.

'No?'

'I began to suspect that there was something odd about this whole business, so I made inquiries about Lady Giddings' household. I was able to ascertain that Miss Seaborn was allocated a maid from the house. I discovered her name and, very discreetly, took the young woman out to tea.'

'You did? Good heavens, you are to be commended for your tenacity, Mr Forsyth.'

'I'm afraid the young woman, one Doris Bramley, didn't know what had happened to Miss Seaborn either. She did think that the manner of her disappearance was strange, though. She said Miss Seaborn left overnight. She apparently went to bed as normal, and in the morning she was gone. The room looked like it had never been lived in. Doris was considerably surprised by that. She said Miss Seaborn wouldn't have left without saying goodbye.'

'Strange indeed.'

'Yes, your grace, it does look that way. Young Doris was able to tell me Miss Seaborn had been to an agency to look for work. After following her description, I tracked the agency down.'

'I get the feeling you got nothing from them either.'

'I'm afraid not, your grace. They were reluctant to tell me anything at first. But I was able to learn, eventually, that Miss Seaborn had been talking to them about becoming a governess. No position had yet been found for her, nor had she been in contact for a few weeks.'

'I see.'

'I now find myself at something of a dead-end, your grace. I cannot think what else we can do to find Miss Seaborn other than report her as missing to the police. That may cause some embarrassment to the young lady if she isn't actually missing though.'

'Some embarrassment?'

'She may have gone off with a young gentleman, sir.'

'No, I don't think so.'

'Do you want me to report her as missing then?'

'I doubt they could be more thorough than you have been, Mr Forsyth. I don't suppose... she might not have landed up in hospital, might she?'

'Not with all her luggage, your grace, but I did check the hospitals too.'

'This is very strange.'

'I'm afraid so, your grace.'

'Thank you, Mr Forsyth. If you think of anything else you can do, please look into it. I will also wrack my brains to try and solve this puzzle.'

'I will continue to look, your grace,' Mr Forsyth said and bowed himself out.

'Oh God,' Felix murmured. 'What has happened to you, Miss Seaborn?'

Whatever it was, it was his fault. He shouldn't have been so stupid as to try and sneak a visit. If Miss Seaborn and Lady Giddings hadn't fallen out, he felt sure Miss Seaborn would still be around. As it was, she had fled and somehow fallen into misfortune.

'Or something worse has happened,' Felix said.

'Something worse?' Celia said from the doorway.

'Celia?'

'Forgive me, I did knock, but you didn't hear me, and you seem very preoccupied.'

'Have you heard about Miss Seaborn?'

'Percy told me everything last night. I was so annoyed with him that he'd not said anything till then. I'd have been around sooner if I'd known. I'm so sorry, Felix, I know you liked her,' Celia said and straightened her skirts as she sat down.

'It's my fault. Lying never works out well and sneaking around behind Lady Giddings' back was stupid.'

'Well, I don't know what else you could have done. Lady Giddings would have cut up stiff at any time if you'd shown more interest in Miss Seaborn than her.'

'And now she's vanished.'

'Percy said she's gone to a relative.'

'No, I checked that. I can't find her anywhere.'

'You've been looking for her?'

'Mr Forsyth has been most thorough.'

'How thorough?' Celia said so Felix told her, and by the end she said. 'That does sound suspicious.'

'I'm worried. I can't shake the feeling that Lady Giddings is somehow involved. At the very least, she must know where Miss Seaborn is.'

'She is manipulative certainly, but this? What do you think she could possibly have done?'

'I don't know, and I have no idea how I could get her to tell me.'

'Her reputation is her weakness. Nobody looking at her out every night would guess that you and she are no longer linked. She made a big noise about the fact that you were interested in her. Even the bookies had stopped taking bets on the chance that the two of you would get married, and she hasn't done anything to back away from the rumours.'

'She put it about that we were going to get married?'

'Not entirely, I would rather say that she was so sure of you; she spoke as if it was only a matter of time. I would say that being rejected by you is a novelty for Lady Giddings. I doubt she has ever been rejected before. In fact, I wouldn't be surprised if she thinks she can still get you to come to heel.'

'That would take an astonishing level of arrogance.'

Celia smiled and said, 'I doubt she would believe that anyone could like her dowdy cousin above herself.'

'Miss Seaborn isn't dowdy,' Felix said stiffly.

'No, but no doubt, Lady Giddings thinks she is.'

'I have to speak to her.'

'She won't tell you anything, Felix. She's more likely to laugh in your face than admit she had anything to do with her cousin's disappearance.'

'So you would have me do nothing?'

'I would hardly call scouring the land for Miss Seaborn, nothing.'

'And yet, when I find she has vanished without a trace, which is altogether more alarming, you tell me my only remaining course of action will get me nowhere.'

'I don't know that it will help and the strain on you would be great.'

'So it comes down to this; I'm not man enough to rescue the woman I love.'

'Felix, I didn't mean that. If you are set on confronting Lady Giddings though, make sure you don't do it alone.'

Felix gasped in air and forced himself to calm down. He was getting too worked up and proving Celia's case for her. 'I should have Percy by my side, you mean.'

'Him or mother, or both. She won't be easy to crack for her pride is at stake, and we both know her pride is immense.'

'I suppose you are right.'

'I'm sorry. I did come round to try and cheer you up.'

'I appreciate that, thank you, Celia. Now, if you don't mind, I really need to rest.'

'Of course. Get some sleep, life always looks better after a nap.'

Felix nodded and watched as Celia left. She looked worried and that no doubt meant she was going to try and do something well-meaning. That would probably bring Aunt Lavinia down to see him and that, he couldn't take today.

He rang his bell, and as Poole and Grantley appeared he said, 'I don't want any more visitors today, lock my door, please, and tell everyone I'm asleep.'

'Yes, your grace. Shall we help you to bed too?' Grantley said.

'No, you can leave me here, just no visitors is that clear?'

'Very clear, your grace,' Grantley said and gave a nod to Poole who locked the bedroom door with a solid click. 'We will make sure you are not disturbed, your grace.'

'Thank you,' Felix said, leaned back and closed his eyes. He needed to think.

CHAPTER TWENTY-FOUR

Felix's sense that something was badly wrong grew throughout the day. He was sure he wouldn't be able to sleep unless he got some sort of a resolution. He was also aware that everybody else thought he was overreacting.

That meant that he was going to have to find out for himself what had happened to Miss Seaborn. For that, he had to be rested, so he forced himself to stay still and quiet on the sofa. He could do that for his body, but his mind seethed with speculation and led to an uncomfortable afternoon.

'Grantley, once you've helped me to bed you may as well knock off for the night,' Felix said when evening finally arrived.

'You aren't having supper, your grace?'

'I'll have some soup in bed. I'm far too tired to face my aunt this evening.'

'Very good, your grace, Poole can let cook know, while I get you into bed.'

'Thank you,' Felix said and leaned more heavily than usual on Grantley. Partly it was a ploy. He wanted his valet to think he really was exhausted. It wasn't far from the truth. Despite the day of rest, the restless night before and his sense of foreboding drained him. All the same, he would need his strength, so he used his valet, and he lay still in bed with his eyes closed till Poole came back with a bowl of soup and a freshly baked roll.

'Should I get Doctor Morley, your grace?' Grantley said.

'No, I'm fine. An early night will see me right.'

'Then I will take my leave,' Grantley said. 'Poole, be sure you don't forget any of your duties!'

'I won't, Grantley,' Poole said with a punctilious bow.

Felix smiled at him and said, 'You're getting the hang of this.'

'Thank you, your grace,' Poole said and blushed.

'You may leave me for the moment. I'll ring once I've finished the soup.'

Felix watched as Poole bowed himself out. Then he listened carefully to the voices coming from the dressing room. Last-minute orders from Grantley to Poole no doubt. That was followed by an opening and closing door and silence.

Felix checked the clock on the mantle. It was just past 6. It was still early, too early for his aunt and uncle to be having supper despite the fact they were due to go to the opera. It was the opening night of Verdi's Macbeth.

How he would like to attend something like that. It would be quite marvellous. The closest he ever came was the occasional string quartet his aunt got in for her tedious tea parties. The music was the high point of those events.

He shook that thought away. He had other more pressing matters to attend to now and no time to muse about opera. He rang his bell.

'Yes, your grace?' Poole said as he hurried in.

'Help me up, Poole, I want to get dressed.'

'Get dressed, your grace?' Poole said and couldn't hide his astonishment.

'Yes, dressed. Get out my black suit, it's the warmest and sturdiest of my clothes. I usually wear it when I travel,' Felix said, keeping his tone both light and firm. This was hurdle number one, and he didn't want a battle with his valet.

'I don't understand.'

'I'm going out, Poole, and you're coming with me.'

'Out... you mean outside?'

'Precisely, which is why I need something warm and hard-wearing. Now get a move on, I don't have all day.'

'Your grace, Grantley and her ladyship won't-'

'Be told,' Felix snapped. He didn't like to bully people, but tonight he had no choice, so he said at his most implacable, 'Poole, you work for me. You will do as I tell you and nobody else, is that clear?'

'Yes, your grace.'

'So we are going out tonight, you, me and a coach. You will order the small coach round. My uncle and aunt will be taking the big one to the opera. You will tell Havers you have an errand to run for me and you are to use the coach. Get them to back it up to the rear door of the house.'

'Your grace, please!'

'There will be no debate about this. You either obey my orders to the letter, or I will turn you off without a reference, do I make myself clear?'

'But if you die-'

'I have made provision for you. So you see, your worst option is to refuse my orders.'

'I don't want you to die, your grace.'

'Neither do I, Poole, but I have no choice this evening. I have to act, and so do you.'

'Yes, your grace,' Poole said, hanging his head.

'Good, now go and get my clothes,' Felix said relieved to have got this far. There was no chance he could have persuaded or bullied Grantley. He'd flat out refuse. Fortunately, Poole was currently more biddable.

'Here, your grace,' Poole said.

'Thank you. I will start on the dressing, you go and arrange the coach, we don't have much time.'

'Yes, your grace,' Poole said breathlessly and hurried away.

The poor young man was terrified, and Felix felt sorry for him, but he had an even greater fear driving him. He couldn't stop for anyone else.

He scrambled into his clothes and put his calling cards in his wallet. That was a novelty. He usually just enclosed a card in his letters, he'd never actually given one out at the door. He hoped they would work their magic though.

He'd just finished pulling on his socks when Poole came back. 'Did you have any difficulties, Poole?'

'No, your grace. The house is far too busy getting supper ready and preparing for Lord and Lady Doubtless's trip to the opera to pay much attention to me. Havers just grumbled that he was already busy. But he said he'd have the coach round in ten minutes.'

'Good, then we will be away well before my uncle and aunt come downstairs.'

'Are... are you sure about this, your grace?'

'I've never been more certain about anything in my life, Poole. Now you'd better get me a scarf. Make it a black one. I can use it to hide my face but also, hopefully, to protect me from the foul night air.'

'It's a right pea-souper outside tonight, your grace. The air's so thick you can practically eat it.'

'Is that so? Well, all the more reason for a scarf. And the top hat, it will be a bit of a novelty to wear it. It comes out of its box only twice a year too.'

'There you go, your grace,' Poole said as he eased Felix's warmest coat over his shoulders and did up the buttons. Then he stood and looked helplessly at his master. 'You're sure you want to do this?'

'Let's go,' Felix said firmly, in part to bolster Poole's courage and also for himself. 'Now we have to get out without being seen. So a bit of sneaking is going to be required.'

'I was afraid of that, sir,' Poole muttered.

Felix pulled his hat down low, wrapped his scarf about his face and gave Poole the nod for him to go. They crept down the corridor to the stairs, stepping into the shadows whenever they were in danger of being spotted.

If it weren't for the vital need to get out of the house, Felix would have found the whole situation wildly amusing. As it was, he clung onto Poole's arm and prayed they didn't run into anyone.

They were nearly at the back door when Danby slapped a hand on Poole's shoulder and said, 'What's all this? Who are you sneaking out of the house, Poole?'

'Mind your own business, Danby,' Poole said as he swung round.

'Not bloody likely. I should have realised you were the sort who fancied men, you with all your airs and graces. Wait till I tell his grace-'

Poole punched Danby square in the nose, and the footman reeled backwards and collapsed.

'I say,' Felix said, astonished by the turn of events.

'We didn't have time to talk him round, your grace.'

'Well, you can't leave him there.' Felix was more impressed by Poole than ever now. 'Is he all right?'

'He's got a broken nose, and he'll have a bad headache, but he'll be fine,' Poole said.

He shoved Danby's hanky into his mouth, tied his hands up behind him with his belt and pulled him into one of the small cupboards that lined the corridor that led to the back door.

'He'll be fine till we get back.'

'Do you do this kind of thing often?' Felix said, surprised by how efficiently Poole had disposed of his footman.

Poole took Felix's arm again, and as they hurried on to the back door, he whispered, 'Danby doesn't like that I've become your valet. He also thinks because I'm smaller and lighter than him, I can't hold my own. But I grew up labouring on your farm, your grace, and he just swans about the house.'

'I see,' Felix said and was rather pleased that he had Poole for this adventure.

A cold wave of air struck them squarely in the face as Poole opened the door, and it nearly took Felix's breath away. But he was bolstered by Poole's bravado so stepped out towards the coach that was partly obscured by the smog. Poole had been right about that too. Maybe tonight that would be a help.

Before they reached it through, a man in a suit emerged from the swirling fog, heading straight for them. He had a large brown-paper wrapped package hoisted under one arm. It took Felix a second to recognise him.

'Good Lord, is that you, Mr Testwood?'

'Your grace!' Hieronymus said, staggering backwards in surprise. 'What are you doing out of the house?'

'There's no time to explain,' Felix said worried that if they lingered here, he'd be caught. 'Get up into the coach, you may as well come with us.'

'Your grace?' the coachman said anxiously as Felix and his party approached.

'Yes, Finch, isn't it?' Felix said and gave the young man a friendly smile.

'Your grace, I can't-'

'Yes you can, Finch, and you will be rewarded handsomely for it. Now, no more delay; I'm in a hurry. We are going to Lady Giddings' house.'

Felix relayed the address and then had Poole and Testwood hoist him into the coach before Finch could think to argue.

'Make sure he doesn't bottle it,' Felix murmured to Poole.

'Yes, sir,' Poole said, leaned halfway out the coach and said, 'You've had your orders. What are you waiting for?'

'Thank you,' Felix said as the coach pulled off.

Felix sank into his seat, pulled the scarf tighter over his nose and mouth and tried to get his breathing under control. His lungs were working like bellows, and he felt dizzy, but he was also elated. He'd made it out of the house. Against all the odds he'd managed to sneak out and into the coach.

'Are you all right, your grace?' Poole said.

'I'll do,' Felix said and turned his attention to Testwood who was staring in wide-eyed surprise at him. 'What brings you to my house at this late hour Mr Testwood?'

'I have just this minute left the laboratory of Mr Andrews. We have successfully compressed and bottled some air, your grace,' Hieronymus said as he unwrapped his parcel. 'I was so excited that I hurried over to show you. I didn't expect to find you outside, though.'

'You've bottled air?' Felix said grateful for this distraction and the fact that he had another person to support him on his adventure.

'Indeed,' Hieronymus said and held out what looked like an iron bottle with an impressive stopper wired firmly in place. 'But... your grace, what are you doing out. Surely this isn't wise.'

'Probably not,' Felix said and forced a smile to encourage both Testwood and Poole. 'But it can't be helped, and I'll be glad of your support. If I am to succeed, I'm going to have to lean heavily on both of you.'

'Your grace?'

'I didn't want to bring your walking frame, it's too cumbersome. Which means that Poole was going to have to hold me up. If you don't mind, I'm sure he would appreciate your help.'

'Very well, your grace.'

'I can mostly manage on my own, but as the night progresses, I will get more tired. So it's best if I use you for support from the start to pace myself, so to speak.'

'Yes, your grace.'

Felix gave both men a satisfied nod and then noting Poole's still alarmed expression he said, 'You're doing well, Poole, keeping your cool. It's exactly what I need.'

Because he couldn't stand their worried stares, Felix looked away and out of the coach window. He wasn't used to seeing London from anywhere other than his room, and he'd never been out at night. There wasn't much to see through the swirling fog. Even in the coach and with his scarf, there was the strong scent of coal smoke, though.

He dreaded to think what it was doing to his lungs. He shrugged that thought away. He had a bigger trial to prepare for.

He'd already planned what he was going to ask Lady Giddings. He just hoped he could stick to that. He also hoped she hadn't left early. There was no way he'd be able to sneak out of his house a second time. Felix was pretty sure she'd be going to the opera, which hopefully meant she would still be at home getting ready.

'I think we've arrived, your grace,' Poole said as the coach slowed down.

It stopped before a house whose front door lamps were barely visible through the fog.

Percy cursed as he made his way up to Felix's front door. 'What a bloody awful night,' he muttered.

He didn't like it when the smog was this dense. Anybody could be lurking in it, and the first you'd know about it was when they bashed you on the noggin and took your money. Still, it couldn't be helped, he needed to rally round.

It had been a few days since the meeting with Lady Giddings, and he'd have come to visit anyway, but Celia had prompted him to drop in sooner than planned.

He'd been astonished when she appeared at Horse Guards Parade in her carriage and demanded to speak to him. His first, terrible thought, was that something had happened to Felix. Fortunately, that wasn't the case.

Celia, however, was worried about Felix and feared he might do something drastic to find Miss Seaborn. She'd even brought up that ridiculous misadventure from their childhood where Felix had attempted to ride a horse. They'd all had the fright of their lives then, and Percy was in no hurry for a repeat. So, knowing Felix might well take matters into his own hands, he came prepared to talk him down.

'Percy, good lord, what are you doing here?' Lady Lavinia said as Percy was shown into the drawing room by Chivers.

'Just thought I'd drop in on Felix,' Percy said. 'I hear he's feeling a bit under the weather.'

'He's been moping ever since Miss Seaborn went off,' Lady Lavinia said. 'I hope you can cheer him up. He pays me no attention at all when I talk to him about all the other young ladies he could still meet.'

'Yes, well I'm afraid he's become sincerely attached to Miss Seaborn, and that isn't easy to shake.'

'See what you can do. Marmaduke and I are about to have supper, you're welcome to join us if Felix doesn't want to listen to you.'

'Thank you.'

'And if you're going to the opera you may as well join us in our carriage. It isn't much of a night to be out on foot.'

'And rather a long walk. I was planning on taking a hack, so the offer of a lift is most welcome. Now I'd better see Felix,' Percy said and hurried across the hall.

He didn't bother trying the dressing room door this evening and went straight to Felix's door. He didn't want Grantley to intercept him.

'Locked,' he muttered. 'Felix is feeling worse than I thought.'

Percy toyed with the idea of giving up. That would mean two things though, supper with his aunt and uncle, and having to confess to Celia that he hadn't charmed Felix out of the doldrums.

So he took a deep breath and tried the dressing room door. To his surprise, that was also locked, and that had never happened before. He knocked loudly and got no response.

'Chivers,' Percy said loudly to get the butler's attention. He was still hovering in the hallway, 'Have you seen Poole or Grantley recently?'

'Grantley took the afternoon off, sir.'

'How about Poole, then?'

'I can't say I've seen him since he took a light supper to his grace.'

'Well, I can't seem to rouse either of them, and both doors are locked.'

'They're locked?' Chivers said, and a flicker of alarm crossed his usually inscrutable face. 'I'll fetch the master keys from my office,' the butler said and hurried away.

Percy watched the man go with a sense of increasing alarm. He went back to Felix's door and knocked as loudly as he could.

'Felix, Felix, if you're in there open up. We're worried.'

'What's wrong?' Lady Lavinia said as the noise drew her out of the drawing room.

'I'm locked out,' Percy said.

'The keys, sir,' Chivers said when he reappeared in short order trailed by Danby who looked considerably dishevelled and was holding a bloody hanky to his nose. 'But I don't think we'll need them. I think his grace has gone out.'

'What!' Percy and Lady Lavinia shouted.

'Poole knocked me out, sir,' Danby muttered through a stuffy nose. 'And he was accompanied by another man who was all bundled up so I couldn't see his face.'

'Felix?' Percy said momentarily so surprised he couldn't think of anything more to say.

Chivers, in the meantime, had unlocked the dressing room door and Percy pushed past him. Crazy as it sounded, he feared Danby and Chivers were right, and Felix had left, but he had to check.

Percy ran in shouting, 'Felix, Felix, are you here?' He dashed through the dressing room and into the bedroom. 'Nobody,' he said as he took in the unmade bed, half-eaten bowl of soup and barely touched roll.

'He really went out?' Lady Lavinia said as she arrived in the room. 'Oh God, he can't have gone out. Not in this weather!'

'Looks like the little fool has though,' Percy said.

'But where? He must be found.'

'I can think of only one place he might go,' Percy said. 'And that's to see Lady Giddings.'

'Lady Giddings, but why?'

'To find Miss Seaborn,' Percy said.

'Miss Seaborn, I don't understand.'

'I don't have time to explain,' Percy said as he hurried to the front door. 'Can I borrow your coach? I might just be able to catch up with Felix.'

'But how can you be sure you're right? This might be a wild goose chase.'

Percy caught a whispered and agitated conversation going on between Danby and Chivers and said, 'Well, do you have something to add?'

'It appears the small coach is missing, sir. Apparently, Poole asked for it to be brought round to the back door not half an hour ago.'

'There you are then. Felix went off in the coach.'

'Poole arranged this?' Lady Lavinia snapped. 'I will sack him for this, he-'

'There is no time for that, my dear,' Uncle Marmaduke said. 'Percy, take the coach. The opera can wait.'

'Thank you, sir,' Percy said and ran out of the house.

CHAPTER TWENTY-FIVE

'J ust a moment,' Felix said as they reached Lady Giddings' front door, supported on his left side by Testwood, who looked very anxious, and Poole on the right. 'I must get my breath back.'

He couldn't even hold himself upright he was so tired. Ye gods but this was going to be difficult.

He took another couple of deep breaths, straightened himself and said, 'All right, now.'

Poole pulled energetically on the bell, and they waited. A few moments later, the door was opened by an austere man dressed in a black suit.

'Good evening, I wonder whether Lady Giddings is at home?' Felix said as he pulled down his scarf and handed over his card.

'I will find out, sir,' the butler said as he peered at Felix, then Poole and Testwood and finally held the card up to his face to read it. 'If you would be so good as to wait here,' he said, showing them into the entrance hall.

'Thank you,' Felix said and gave the man a slight smile in an attempt to allay his suspicion. It would do nothing for his curiosity.

Fortunately, the wait was not a long one as Lady Giddings appeared almost immediately and rushed down the stairs towards them. She looked glorious done up to her best and even the overly ornate red and black dress didn't detract from her beauty. Felix felt a slight pang that her character didn't match her lovely face, then dismissed it. He was here for something far more important.

'Your grace, it's so nice to see you,' Isolde said giving every appearance of being sincere, which Felix found hard to believe. 'Have you come to apologise? You were very horrible to me last time you know,' she said with an arch smile.

'Apologise?' Felix said.

This was not what he'd expected. He'd expected tears or at the least cold contempt. Apparently, Lady Giddings was determined to win him back even if she had said something designed to offend him. He supposed if he was smitten he might have grasped it as the olive branch it was meant to be.

'Do I owe you an apology?'

'After the beastly way you treated me last time I saw you?' Isolde said, smiling coquettishly up at him. 'I think you owe me that, at least.'

'If I offended you, then I apologise.'

'There see, that wasn't so difficult.'

'Now, my lady, you owe me something.'

'Do I?'

'I would like to know what has really happened to Miss Seaborn.'

'Miss Seaborn? You came here to talk about Miss Seaborn?'

'I did,' Felix said and had to stop to take a breath. He'd had far too much excitement today, and it was starting to take its toll. 'I have looked for her, and she isn't with any of her relatives.'

'Then she's gone off with that soldier,' Isolde said with a shrug. 'I don't care where she is. She was a wretch to go sneaking around behind my back, acting as if she cared for me when all the time she was scheming to take you away from me.'

'She didn't do that,' Felix said. 'She behaved entirely properly. In fact, I doubt she even knows I care for her because I never told her.'

'And you never will,' Isolde snapped. 'Look at you. You can't even stand up on your own. How foolish I was to even consider marriage to a wreck like you. Why, I wouldn't be at all surprised if you had a heart attack right in front of me and I wouldn't lift a finger to help you. Not now, not after you betrayed me like you have.'

Felix stiffened and said, 'Do you even know how distasteful you sound when you speak like that?'

'Huh, now you sound like Honour, always pretending to be shocked by what I say. Well, you will never find her. I will see you dead before I tell you where she is.'

'So you do know where she is.'

'Much good it will do you. Now I'm going to the opera. You run off back to your bed and if you're lucky you may just live to see the morning,' Isolde said and turned to leave.

'Lady Giddings,' Felix said. 'If you don't tell me where I might find Miss Seaborn, I will go straight to the police and lodge a missing person's report. I will also tell them that I believe you have something to do with the disappearance of your cousin.'

'Go ahead,' Isolde said, swinging back to glare at him. 'You will never prove it.'

'I won't stop there. I will also let all of society know that you are responsible for Miss Seaborn's disappearance. There might not be any actual proof of nefarious activity on your part, but people will start to whisper. They will look at you differently. You will find your invitations dry up, society will distance themselves from you.'

'They would never do that, people love me!'

'Men love you, and not all men either. But, if that doesn't sway you, I will also tell the world what I have discovered about your father.'

'What about my father?'

'He isn't half as wealthy as he leads people to believe. I did wonder when I learned you didn't have a country estate. So I had my man of business look into your father. It appeared the stocks and shares he gambles with aren't performing half as well as you might think. With very little effort on my part, I could ruin him. Then what would you do, Lady Giddings? Your reputation in tatters and suddenly penniless. You'd be in a worse position than your cousin when you offered her a home.'

'Ah, but I did offer her a home.'

'And who do you think will offer you one when I put it about that you've done away with Miss Seaborn?'

'I haven't killed anyone, damn you.'

'Then what have you done to Miss Seaborn?'

Isolde chewed on her finger for a moment torn by indecision and snapped, 'I hate you.'

'No doubt, but I have the upper hand at the moment. Now tell me, where is Miss Seaborn?'

'She's in Bedlam, all right?'

'Bedlam?' Felix said, and he was so shocked he had to grip Poole's arm even tighter as the room swam about him.

'I know a doctor there,' Isolde said. 'Doctor Lamb, he loves me. I convinced him that Honour was a danger to herself and to me. So he came by with a couple of men and bundled her away.'

'You allowed a woman under your protection to be abducted from her bed and taken to an insane asylum?' Felix said, horrified by the audacity of it all.

'She betrayed me first.'

Felix stared at her in disbelief. Surely she couldn't be so dead to all human emotion that she felt that she was in the right? But apparently, she did.

'Come, Poole,' Felix said. 'I have nothing more to say to this woman.'

'Yes, your grace,' Poole said and discreetly half-carried him as they made for the door.

'Wait,' Isolde said. 'You're not going to tell people, are you?'

'That all depends on what condition I find Miss Seaborn in.'

'I hope she's dead!' Isolde hissed. 'I hope you both die!'

Felix shook his head and kept going. 'There's nothing more to be said here,' he murmured to Poole and Testwood.

If anything, the short trip back to the coach was harder than getting to the house in the first place. His confrontation with Lady's Giddings had been more of a trial than he'd expected.

But when Poole said, 'Where to now, your grace?' Felix had no hesitation in saying, 'Bedlam, we're going to Bedlam.'

'Shouldn't we go home, sir? We can send others to fetch Miss Seaborn.'

Mr Testwood nodded in anxious agreement, but Felix couldn't stop now.

'I daren't risk it, Poole. I wouldn't put anything past Lady Giddings. She might send a message to the hospital, and the unscrupulous Dr Lamb, to have Miss Seaborn moved.'

'She is quite an awful woman, isn't she, your grace?'

'I'm afraid she is,' Felix said and slumped back in his seat as the coach headed into the smog in the direction of the insane asylum.

Percy bounded up the stairs to Lady Giddings' house and hammered at the door. There was no coach in sight, nor had he spotted the coach going in the opposite direction returning home. He'd practically hung out the window on the way there, praying he would see it. He hoped he'd got this right and that Felix was indeed headed to the Giddings house.

Thankfully the butler of this household was quick to answer the door. With only a raised eyebrow, he took Percy's card and made his way upstairs. It wasn't usual for a butler to show anything so either the man was a bad butler, or something had already happened in the house.

Isolde appeared at the top of the stairs, looked down at him and said, 'You too, Captain?'

'By that, I assume my cousin has come and gone, Lady Giddings.'

'Never mention that man to me again!' Isolde snapped.

'Did he get what he came for?'

'He's an insolent pig, and I hope he dies.'

'Oh, yes?' Percy said and wondered whether he could get from her ladyship exactly where Felix was now.

'You are much nicer. I like you, I never liked him. I don't like sickly men. I'd much rather marry somebody strong and handsome like you.'

'I see,' Percy said thrown for a moment till he remembered the impression he'd given Lady Giddings that he stood to inherit. 'Would you tell me where my cousin has gone?'

'What does it matter? He didn't look well when he left, which means you won't have long to wait now for your inheritance.'

'All the same, I'd like to see him. For all we know he went straight home after seeing you,' Percy said, praying it was true, but he had his doubts.

'Oh no, I think he went after Miss Seaborn. She seems to have him wrapped around her little finger.'

'So you do know where she is?' Percy said, fighting hard to keep his cool. Yelling at this young woman would get him nowhere.

'What does that matter?'

'Humour me.'

Isolde stamped her foot and said, 'She's in Bedlam. It's where they both belong.'

'Bedlam?' Percy said and, despite his low opinion of Lady Giddings, he was astonished. 'You sent your cousin and mine to Bedlam?'

'So what if I did?' Isolde said. 'You're all going on as if it's something terrible.'

'Well, I hope you never find out whether it is or not, my lady,' Percy said. 'Although that's more than you deserve.'

CHAPTER TWENTY-SIX

F elix kept his eyes closed and rested his head against the back of the chair in the coach. At some point, his head slipped sideways onto Poole's shoulder, and he didn't have the energy to straighten it. He would need to hold onto what reserves he had for the next step of his plan.

'I don't like the look of this,' Poole said.

'I'm afraid I have to agree,' Hieronymus murmured.

Felix opened his eyes, struggled to sit forward and was grateful when Poole put his hand in the small of his back and gave him a light push.

An ominous dark building loomed out of the smog. It was difficult to make out more than the door that was lit by a single lamp.

'It isn't the friendliest of places,' Felix said. 'All the more reason to get Miss Seaborn away from here.'

'But what if they don't let you take her? What if these porters decide we're mad too and bang us up. We might never get out.'

'We'll be fine,' Felix said and hoped he projected more confidence than he felt.

He too, was intimidated. It was more by the beggars clustered around the front door and sleeping on the steps, though, than by what lay within.

Thankfully Poole didn't argue. He and Testwood helped Felix out of the coach and up the steps. Felix tried to ignore the pleas from the beggars, but it cut him to his heart. Really, he was too soft for this world. He doubted his aunt would spare a moment's thought for these poor people.

Poole pushed at the door, and it swung open to reveal a grim reception hall with a bare black and white checked tile floor. An unpleasant odour of disinfectant barely masked the smell of human sweat, vomit and urine. A couple of orderlies loitered at the bottom of the staircase that led into the depths of the hospital. A man in a grubby white overcoat occupied an office, secured against the outside world by a barred window. Around the room were several benches upon which sat a sorry collection of individuals, some of whom had the slack-faced look of the mentally disturbed. Poole took a firmer grip on Felix's arm which felt very much like the young man needing some reassurance.

'That one, in the office.'

Watched by everyone, Felix and his little entourage made their way to the barred window, and he pushed his card across the grubby counter.

'I understand there is a Doctor Lamb in residence in this hospital.'

The man in the white overcoat took his time examining the card. Then he apparently decided caution was the safest option and said, 'What would you be wanting with him, your honour?'

'I wish to speak to him about one of his patients. The matter is urgent.'

'Urgent, sir?'

'Yes, man, very urgent.'

'I dare say that's what everyone thinks of their own business, sir,' the orderly said.

'Do you have any money on you, sir?' Poole whispered in his ear.

It took Felix so much by surprise that he jerked back and examined Poole blankly for a moment. 'Money?'

'Yes, sir,' Poole said, inclining his head meaningfully at the orderly behind the counter.

'A bribe?' Felix said, and then felt stupid as the orderly turned crimson and set his face in as stolid an expression as he could. He hadn't repudiated the notion though, and Felix was willing enough to try anything that would speed things up. He pulled a crisp £5 note from his wallet and slid it across to the man.

'Will this be sufficient to get to see the doctor?'

Poole practically squealed in indignation. But the note vanished in the blink of an eye under the orderly's meaty hand.

'I'll get him down for you immediately, your honour,' he said. 'He won't be best pleased though, he's on his way to the opera.'

'Well I won't detain him for long,' Felix said.

'Five pounds!' Poole groaned as the orderly hurried away. 'You didn't need to give him that much, your grace. He'd have done the same for a guinea.'

'Possibly,' Felix said in an undertone, 'But that's all I had in the wallet. I didn't think to bring money. It's pure chance that note was still in there. I always have a little cash when I travel to and from London.'

'You mean you came out without money?'

'I didn't even consider it. I doubt I've actually ever paid out cash more than a handful of times in my life. Somebody else always does the paying for me.'

'Oh,' Poole said and shook his head.

'It will be all right,' Felix said and gave his man and Testwood an encouraging smile. 'We've got this far, haven't we?'

Poole was saved from having to reply as a sandy-haired young man came down the stairs two at a time. He'd evidently attempted to grow mutton chop sideburns but didn't really have a sufficiently bushy beard to be able to pull it off. It made him look scruffy despite his smart black and white evening dress.

'This card claims you're the Duke of Morley, is that right?' Doctor Lamb said.

'That is correct,' Felix said and forced himself to stand up straight. It took a great deal of effort.

The doctor looked back down at the card clutched in his hand and said, 'You'll forgive my scepticism. We have a dozen gods, seven Jesus's, a handful of emperors and any number of nobles in our facility.'

'Do you?' Felix said. 'None, I'll wager, who walked voluntarily in through the front door.'

'No, that is rather unlikely in fact.'

'Doctor,' Felix said, 'I have no interest in a verbal joust with you. I came this evening to try and find somebody, that is all.'

'We have hundreds of patients. I can't be expected to know each and every one of them.'

'No? I have been told you know this one. In fact, I would be astonished if you don't remember her. For, you see, you kidnapped her from her bed no more than a week ago.'

The doctor stiffened and said, 'I don't know what you are talking about.'

'Well, you'd better figure it out quickly, or my next call will be to your governors. I doubt they will look with favour upon any of their doctors so infatuated by a beautiful woman that he abused his power and imprisoned someone who is sane.'

'Lady Giddings told me that she was insane, mentally unbalanced.'

'Do you agree with her?'

'The insane rarely admit their deficiencies.'

'In other words, you didn't want to know. Did Lady Giddings tell you why she actually wanted Miss Seaborn out of the way?'

'I didn't ask.'

'She did it because I'm in love with Miss Seaborn and Lady Giddings was determined to marry me. So you see, locking up Miss Seaborn does away with any chance you might have to marry Lady Giddings. Which, I might add, is remote in the extreme as the lady is only interested in marrying a man of wealth and title.'

'At least I'm hea-'

'Don't even say it,' Felix said. 'Just tell me where I might find Miss Seaborn. I'm taking her home. If you are very fortunate indeed, I

may chalk your actions up to youthful indiscretion and not tell
your governors.'

'She's in the women's wing,' Doctor Lamb said as all defiance
crumbled. 'I will get one of the orderlies to take you there.'

'Thank you,' Felix said. 'Enjoy your opera.'

He didn't wait for a response just followed the orderly who
rattled his big ring of keys suggestively and set off down a dim
corridor with a big grin on his face. Evidently, Doctor Lamb
wasn't very popular with the staff.

'This way, your honour,' the man said.

'The doctor didn't have to tell you where to go?'

'No, your honour. I was in the detail that took Miss Seaborn
in.'

'And it didn't worry you that you were abducting a perfectly
sane woman?'

'She isn't the only sane person locked up here, your honour.
Loads of nobs get rid of inconvenient relatives in here.'

'Good God.'

'There's good money in it. It keeps the hospital afloat.
Otherwise, who would pay for the rest of them lunatics?' the
orderly said as he flicked a thumb in the direction of a row of
women variously lying and sitting against the wall.

One of the women was curled into a ball, moaning incoherently,
her hands gripping her loose frizzy hair in tight fists. Another
rolled about plucking at her clothes. Much to Felix's horror she'd
so far succeeded in pulling off her top and one of the other women
was trying, in a bumbling way, to cover her with a rag-like blanket.

'There has to be a better way to treat the sick.'

Felix felt as though he'd stepped into a painting of hell. It was
a sensation heightened by his exhaustion that made everything
swim before his eyes. If it wasn't for Poole and Testwood's firm
grip on him, he'd already have collapsed.

'How they get treated is not my problem,' the orderly said as he
stopped to unlock a door and made his way down a dim hall lined
on both sides with simple iron beds.

The women were all chained to their beds. Quite a few whimpered and backed away at sight of the orderly. He made his way to the end of the room and a young woman, sitting very still, wrapped in a blanket, gazing up at the single high small window.

'You're being released,' the orderly said and undid the manacle around Honour's wrist.

'Miss Seaborn, thank God!' Felix said as he realised with a shock who it was.

'Your grace!' Honour said and finally turned around. 'Good God, what are you doing here?'

'Rescuing you,' Felix said with an embarrassed laugh.

'What madness, look at you. You look deathly pale and your lips, they're turning blue.'

'I'll be fine, but what about you? How dare they treat you in this way? How dare they chain you to a bed, how dare they?'

'I'm all right, honestly.'

'You're shivering, and just in a nightdress... did they not even give you back your clothes?'

'I don't know what they did with my possessions. The last I saw everything was being thrown into my travelling trunk.'

'It's in the storeroom,' the orderly said. 'I'll go get it.'

'Thank you,' Honour said, but she spoke abruptly. Clearly, this orderly was no friend.

'Come, let's get you out of here,' Felix said and took a frantic gulp of air. It was getting harder and harder to breathe.

'You'd better lean on me too, your grace. You really don't look well. I think-' Honour stopped at the sound of an argument from down the hall. 'Now what?'

'I rather think,' Felix said, 'that it's the cavalry, and just in time too.'

'I don't understand,' Honour said examining Felix closely. 'You should sit down, I'm worried about you.'

'Not yet,' Felix said. 'But it's going to be all right.'

'Felix!' Percy shouted as he appeared in the doorway, dragging two irate orderlies who were hanging onto his sleeves. 'Let go of me, you sods!' Percy said and shook them loose. 'That's my cousin, and if I'm not very much mistaken, Miss Seaborn as well.'

'Percy, thank God,' Felix said.

'I've got you, old man,' Percy said as he pushed Testwood aside and wrapped a powerful arm around Felix's waist.

'I found her, Percy,' Felix said, and he grabbed hold of Honour's hand as he was pulled away from her and hoisted more onto his feet by Percy.

'So I see, old fellow. I can't tell you how happy I am to see you too, Miss Seaborn. But, by God, Felix, you look like hell.'

'I have a device in the coach that might help,' Hieronymus said.

'Mr Testwood?' Percy said. 'What are you doing here?'

'Never mind that,' Felix said through snatches of breath. 'Hurry and fetch it, Mr Testwood.

'Right away, your grace,' Hieronymus said and ran for the exit.

'Now let's get the rest of you out of here,' Percy said. 'Poole, you keep hold of his grace's left and let's get moving.'

'You're as managing as ever,' Felix whispered. He was so out of breath, it was the best he could manage.

'Can you walk, or should I carry you, Felix?'

'I can walk,' Felix said and cast a quick look at Miss Seaborn. He didn't want to appear so weak before her. She looked pale and gaunt and very tired, which instantly banished his own fears. 'You're safe now, Miss Seaborn, I promise.'

'I know,' she said and gave his hand a squeeze.

With the military precision Honour always appreciated from the army, Percy got the group out of the hospital, down the stairs and to the coach.

'All right, everybody in,' Percy said as he hoisted Felix off his feet and pushed him into the coach with Poole's efficient support.

Felix went, dragging Honour with him and collapsed into the far corner of the coach still holding her hand tightly.

'Feet,' Felix muttered.

'Elevate them, your grace?' Poole said.

'Yes,' Felix gasped, as Honour helped to prop him up against the cushion.

Poole lifted his legs and, laying him lengthways across the front seat, pushed a pillow under his feet.

'Thank you,' Felix muttered and coughed, gasping for air.

It worried Honour because he looked to be deteriorating. She couldn't do a thing about it but scrunch up to the end of the back seat.

'Your grace,' Hieronymus said as he scrabbled to untwisted the wire keeping a seal attached to a metal bottle. He held the bottle against Felix's bottom lip and said, 'Take a deep breath, your grace,' as he pulled the lid away. A hiss of air escaped the bottle and blew into Felix's face with such force that it scattered his hair.

At the same time, he took a deep breath and then a second. It appeared to help as his breathing eased for a moment. Felix gave a vague smile and murmured, 'It works.'

'Not for long enough,' Hieronymus said.

'You will fix that,' Felix said and took another deep breath.

For a moment, his hold on Honour's hand slackened, and it nearly slipped from his grasp.

'No!' Felix cried, 'Miss Seaborn!'

'I'm here,' she said and held his hand again.

'I found you,' he whispered. 'I found you.'

'Yes, you did.'

'Don't... don't leave me.'

'I won't, I promise,' Honour said.

'Time to go,' Percy said as he pulled the coach door shut behind him. 'It's going to be a bumpy ride, I'm afraid. I've told the coachman to get us home as quickly as he can.'

'It can't be soon enough, sir,' Poole said.

'I wouldn't be so eager if I were you, Poole,' Percy said as the coach rumbled out of the hospital grounds. 'You're not in her ladyship's best books.'

'I know it, sir.'

'You didn't have much choice did you, Poole?' Honour said as she kept her gaze fixed on the duke.

She was worried because it was growing increasingly difficult for him to draw breath.

'Not really, miss.'

'Well, no doubt Felix will explain all, won't you, old boy,' Percy said more loudly as he gave the duke's shoulder a squeeze.

'Not Poole's fault,' Felix gasped. 'I... forced him.'

'Well, I'll protect him against Aunt Lavinia's wrath then,' Percy said. 'You don't worry yourself, Felix. You concentrate on getting well.'

'So I can... be scolded?' Felix said with a slight smile.

It was such an act of bravado that Honour's heart swelled with emotion to see it. She was experiencing such a jumble of feelings at the moment that it was all she could do to not burst into tears. But the duke's determination to put a brave face on things fortified her own resolve.

She'd lived through a terrible time. She'd not thought anything could have been worse than the death of her father and finding herself suddenly adrift and unprotected in a harsh and uncaring world. Even though she was miserable living with her cousin, at least she'd felt secure. She also felt in charge of her own destiny when she was setting herself up to become a governess.

But she was ripped from her sleep, had a blanket thrown over her head and was carried bodily out of the house. She was chained to a bed in a room full of mad women with no explanation and nobody who would listen to her. She was struck by a brute of a man when she protested that she was sane and told to shut up. It was the hardest thing she'd ever had to endure. The worst of it was, she had no idea when or if it would ever end.

It was like a miracle when the duke appeared, more so because it was so unexpected. Her first flush of relief was washed away by a sense of shame that he was seeing her in that condition. Finding her in her nightclothes without any shoes, wrapped in a blanket.

That was followed immediately by fear, for he looked done in. The duke's attempt to find her was too much for his heart. Now she sat, clutching his hand as tightly as he was holding onto hers, terrified that he might die.

She was confused by what it all meant too. The duke had come for her and been so relieved to see her. He was also scared he might lose her again. Could that mean that he cared for her? It had to mean something, didn't it?

Yet at their last meeting, he'd been a bit distant. He'd been polite, engaged by her stories, willing to share stories of his own life but not... not amorous. Which was why it had felt so absurd when Isolde accused her of trying to seduce the duke.

Honour felt on solid ground and had said, 'If you'd seen him you would know he feels nothing for me. He was just interested in my tales.'

That hadn't convinced Isolde, clearly not, considering the lengths she'd subsequently gone to. Now it seemed Isolde was the one who was right. It looked for all the world as if the duke really did like her. It was confusing and wonderful at the same time and terrifying, especially because his current state was partially her fault.

'It's going to be all right, Miss Seaborn,' Percy said, leaning forward so he could see past Poole and Testwood sitting between them.

'Do you think so?'

'Felix has come back from worse.'

'I'm sure you are right,' Honour said.

But she wondered whether the captain was trying to boost the duke's spirits or her own. Perhaps even his. He had come after his cousin, after all, so he must have been worried too.

'How did he... I mean, why didn't he just come with you or... or send you to find me?'

'He should have done. Only the rest of us weren't as worried by your disappearance as Felix was. Your cousin told us you'd left to live with relatives and I'm afraid I believed her. We all did, except for Felix.

'He had a sense something was wrong and set out to find you. When his man of business came up empty-handed well... we still told him not to worry, and that was our mistake.

'Because then Felix decided we wouldn't help him. He took matters into his own hands. Why even tonight I only dropped in to try and cheer him up. That was when we discovered he was gone. That gave us all a shock, I can tell you.'

'Yes, I can imagine,' Honour said and checked on the duke. His eyes were open, fixed on her, but she felt like he wasn't taking them in anymore. 'Can't this coach go any faster?'

'Quite possibly, but I wouldn't want to risk crashing or overturning. Believe me, the coachman knows full well how important it is to get Felix home quickly.'

'I'm sure he does,' Honour said.

She tightened her grip on the duke's hand as she watched his breathing. It was as if she could see his airways fill with fluid as he coughed and gasped for air. Fear for him sat like a sick knot in the pit of her stomach.

'We're here,' Percy said as the coach pulled up outside a house that was lit twice as brightly as all their neighbours.

Footmen erupted into the night, ran down the stairs and yanked the coach door open.

'All right, all right, keep calm,' Percy said. 'Poole and I will get his grace up and out to you. You can take him from there.'

As Felix was lifted though, his grasp on Miss Seaborn's hand fell away. 'No!' he gasped. 'Miss Seaborn!'

'I'm right here.'

Honour hopped out of the coach, registered Mr Testwood clambering out behind her and then dismissed him from her mind as he hurried away into the night. Honour had more important things to worry about. She ran to keep up with the four footmen who'd hoisted the duke into the air and rushed him into the house.

'Don't vanish,' Felix said and reached out to her.

'I'm not going anywhere, I promise,' Honour said and hurried alongside him and the footmen.

'Felix, thank god!' Lady Lavinia cried as she emerged directly behind Doctor Morton from the drawing room. 'Where have you been? Oh, Miss Seaborn?' her ladyship said as she spotted Honour. 'So he found you.'

'Yes, my lady,' Honour said, and she ran into Felix's room. 'Please forgive me, but I promised his grace I would stay with him.'

'Don't worry about the clothes,' Doctor Morton said as the footmen deposited Felix on the bed and Poole attempted to get the duke's coat off. 'Just get rid of that stupid scarf.'

'Yes, sir,' Poole said and pulled the scarf away.

'And get him propped up. He can't breathe flat on his back.'

'Right away, sir,' Poole said and pushed all the pillows into a pile under the duke.

'Now I'm going to roll you over, your grace,' the doctor said and turned Felix halfway and bent him over his pillows. 'I'm going to try and clear your lungs,' the doctor said loudly and began to tap firmly up and down Felix's back with his fingertips. 'You know what to do, your grace. You cough all of that foul air you've been breathing up, and you'll start to feel a lot better.'

Felix coughed, but Honour wasn't sure whether that was on command or simply because he needed to. The doctor kept up the firm tapping for a while till he noticed Honour and said, 'Do you think you can do this?'

'The tapping, sir?'

'Yes that's right, the tapping.'

'I can do it.'

'Do you have much experience with looking after sick people?'

'My father was a soldier, sir,' Honour said as she took over tapping the duke's back. 'I helped out in the hospital whenever they went into battle.'

'Ah well, then you'll do fine,' Doctor Morton said. He fitted his stethoscope to his ears, pushed the duke's shirt up and pressed it against his back. 'Just hold off on the tapping for a second,' the doctor said and listened intently. He moved the stethoscope and listened again. 'His lungs are congested, keep up the tapping Miss... what is your name?'

'Seaborn, Honour Seaborn.'

'Well, keep going, Miss Seaborn. I shall return in a moment with an expectorant for his grace.'

CHAPTER TWENTY-SEVEN

Honour worked hard to look calm and competent while she followed the doctor's orders. It was difficult because the duke was struggling so much and she feared that each ragged breath he took might be his last. She couldn't bear the guilt and the loss if she were the cause of the duke's death.

After the expectorant and the tapping and a good couple of hours of continually taking the duke's pulse, Doctor Morton finally said, 'I have done all I can. Now we wait.'

'Will he recover?' Honour said. 'His breathing is still so laboured.'

'I have brought him back from worse,' the doctor said. He hesitated on his way out of the room and said. 'I assume you are the young lady his grace has taken a fancy to?'

'So it would seem.'

'You didn't know?'

'He kept it from me.'

'Well, Miss Seaborn, you appear to be a sensible young woman so I won't waste my time with platitudes. His grace is a very sick man. He was born with a weak heart, and I'm afraid that is incurable. He may well make it through the night. He may well survive his latest adventure. He has, in fact, astonished us all by reaching his majority. But you cannot expect that he will have a long life. And he can't go off gallivanting. It is suicidal to do so. If he is careful, though, then he may live a good few years yet.'

'I see.'

'I am only telling you this because you should be aware of the facts before you contemplate marriage.'

'Thank you. As the duke hasn't proposed, you may be premature in your assumptions.'

'Miss Seaborn, foolish as it was for his grace to go out in his condition, it was also nothing short of heroic. No man, be he a knight of the realm or a hero like Nelson, showed more grit and determination than the duke did when he set out to find you. He may not have said anything to you, but there is no doubt that he loves you.'

'Oh,' Honour whispered.

'And you have clearly been having a difficult time yourself, so I don't blame you if you hadn't noticed,' the doctor said, gave her a bow and left.

Honour blinked after him. She'd never come across such a straight-talking doctor before, and he left her feelings more up in the air than she'd thought possible. Had the duke really done something so epic? Right now, he looked pale and very ill, and that just filled her with dread.

'May I come in, miss?' Poole whispered from the doorway.

'Of course,' Honour said.

'I've brought you some soup,' Poole said. 'I thought you might be hungry. I doubt they were feeding you well in Bedlam.'

'Thank you, Poole, that's very kind of you,' Honour said.

'I've got your trunk down off the coach too if you're wanting to get dressed.'

'I would, but not yet. I can't leave his grace. I promised him I wouldn't.'

Poole shot his master a worried glance, gave an accepting nod and said, 'I'll bring your clothes here and make sure you're not disturbed while you change.'

'That's a good idea, thank you. I assume, as you're here, you have escaped Lady Lavinia's wrath.'

'The jury is still out on that one, miss. Captain Shawcross did what he could, but it all depends on whether his grace recovers now or not.'

'Doctor Morton is hopeful.'

'Thank you, miss,' Poole said with a slight smile hastily hidden and a quick bow.

The soup was wonderful. Despite her worries for the duke, Honour was ravenously hungry. It had been another torture of Bedlam that they didn't bother feeding their inmates properly. Their one and only daily meal consisted of a thin gruel made predominantly with oats.

She'd not been in much of a mood to eat it though. She felt so trapped and helpless and angry. She was enraged at Isolde for her cruelty and the doctors and orderlies for knowing full well she was sane but treating her like all the other inmates.

At first, the women she was locked up with frightened her. After a while, she realised they were more distressed than anything else, and the way they were being treated made their various illnesses worse rather than better.

She put her empty bowl down and examined the duke again. He was restless. A cough plagued him, and he moved from side to side, trying to get comfortable but failing. He was also muttering something. She wished she could calm him for surely he needed some proper rest.

As there was nothing she could do for him, she opened her trunk and took a first look inside. No care had been taken with her belongings. It was a great jumble of all she owned. She would have to take everything out and tidy it, but not this evening.

For now, she reached through the clothes for a dress. It was sadly creased but far cleaner than the nightdress she'd worn ever since her abduction. What she wouldn't do for a washstand and some clean water. Her feet were particularly dirty. Well, never mind, for now, it would do.

She was sorely tempted to throw the nightdress away as she pulled it off, but her sensible side intervened. She would need it, and after a wash, it would be as good as new. She slipped into her plain grey dress, wrapped herself in the shawl his grace had given her and pulled on some stockings and shoes. With that and the soup, she started to feel more human again.

The duke muttered in his sleep and coughed, and she went back to his bedside to check on him. He was growing more agitated.

'Miss Seaborn... Miss Seaborn, I have to find her. Where is she?'

'I'm right here,' Honour said and took the duke's hand.

'Something's wrong, I have to find Miss Seaborn,' Felix muttered. 'Miss Seaborn!' He cried, and his eyes sprang open.

'I'm here, your grace, you rescued me,' Honour said and squeezed his hand.

'Oh,' he murmured, staring vaguely at her. 'You're here.'

'Yes, you fetched me from Bedlam. Do you remember?'

'You're safe.'

'I'm perfectly safe.'

'Thank God,' Felix said and dropped back into sleep.

Honour watched his breathing closely. She wasn't sure what it meant that he was no longer restless. He seemed at peace now and instead of feeling reassured, she worried it meant his heart was about to give up.

She really didn't want that because his concern for her and his relief that she was there and she was safe brought back the doctor's words. He had been heroic to rescue her. It would have been heroic from any man. She would have been relieved if anyone had got her out of Bedlam. That fact that it was the duke, well... it meant more.

Maybe she could let her guard down too and let herself believe that he did love her. Maybe she could open her heart and love him back now without fearing he'd rebuff her. Or worse, look astonished that she might even believe he loved her. That would be terrible, to misread someone and see it only once you had shown your own feelings.

Especially with someone like the duke, someone who was, to be brutally honest, extremely rich and titled. It was a prize to be valued. She just didn't want him to think that was why she liked him.

Now, as she sat in the dark, holding his hand, she also had time to think. This could very well be the rest of her life spent with this man. She prayed he'd continue to surprise everyone and live a long time.

That was uncertain. But she had learned that nothing in life was certain. The duke himself had lost his father, by all accounts, a fit and healthy man, when he was seven. Would he live long enough to see his son reach his seventh year? Would she? That was, after all, when she'd lost her mother.

No, life wasn't certain. Illness, accident, childbirth, anything could happen to whisk away those you loved. The best thing was to live life as best as you could. To make a difference and... try not to leave anyone in the lurch if you did die before them. She didn't want any child of hers to face the same desperate situation she'd found herself in when her father died.

She looked back down at the duke, sleeping peacefully now. He was good looking, and a bit boyish still. When he was awake, he looked older. His intelligence showed through and gave him gravitas. Then again, he also found a lot to be amused by, and his lips would twitch a smile that put everyone at their ease. She liked that smile, and maybe now she would be able to tell him that, she thought, as she drifted off to sleep.

'Miss Seaborn? Miss Seaborn, are you all right?' Felix said.

'Oh, I dropped off,' Honour said as she sat up with a start and realised it was morning. A second realisation was that the duke was awake and examining her more closely than she was used to from any man.

'Have you been here all night?' Felix said.

'Well... I promised that I wouldn't leave you,' Honour said and scanned the duke's face to check how he was doing. He still looked very pale but better than the night before.

'I'm so sorry. You must be exhausted. When last did you have a decent night's sleep?'

'It has been a while, I own.'

'You must get some sleep! I've been so selfish,' Felix said and rang his bell. 'Oh, Grantley, you're here,' he said as his valet appeared.

'Yes, your grace,' the man said at his most wooden.

'Grantley, Miss Seaborn has had a hellish week and is in desperate need of a decent bed, some good food and... and probably a bath. Please make sure she gets it.'

'Your grace is very kind,' Honour said. 'But are you sure?'

'I've been unpardonably selfish after the terrible time you've had. Please, Grantley will make sure you are made comfortable.'

'If you will follow me please, Miss Seaborn,' Grantley said with a stiff bow.

'Of course,' Honour said and made her way through the duke's dressing room with Grantley.

'Miss Seaborn's box needs to be brought up, Poole,' Grantley snapped.

Honour was astonished by the rage coming from Grantley all aimed at Poole. Poor Poole had a hangdog expression that told her he'd been having a hard time of it for a while now. She felt bad for him and was determined to help where she could.

So, as they mounted the stairs and continued deeper into the house, she said, 'Is something wrong?'

'Not at all, miss,' Grantley said frostily.

'You do seem rather angry.'

Honour was familiar enough with servants to know that in the end, they did want to unburden themselves even if they kept the facade of propriety.

'What could I possibly have to be angry about, miss? Why would I be upset if his grace decides to go off gallivanting without me?'

'You didn't know he was going out?' Honour said as understanding began to dawn.

'He tricked me into thinking he was going to bed. He sent me away!' Grantley said, and his voice cracked. 'And he took that gormless Poole with him instead.'

'Ah.' Honour realised she was facing a very hurt and betrayed man.

'Not that I mind at all. I'm about to retire anyway. What do I care if his grace wants to go off and kill himself,' Grantley muttered as he pushed open the door to a sunny yellow bedroom. 'The guest room, Miss Seaborn. Would you prefer to sleep first or bathe first?'

'A bath, I have been dreaming of a bath for a whole week,' Honour said.

'Very good, miss. I will arrange it.'

'Before you go, Grantley,' Honour said and wondered briefly about the wisdom of getting involved. Then she shrugged it away, she would do what she could. 'Would you have helped the duke on his adventure last night if he had asked you?'

'Of course not. Begging your pardon, Miss Seaborn, for I know that you were indeed in need of rescue, but it was far too great a risk.'

'So you would have prevented his grace?'

'I would.'

'Which was precisely why he sent you home and bullied Poole, and he did bully him. He said so himself, he forced the young man.'

'His grace never makes an idle threat,' Grantley muttered, still unwilling to give an inch.

'So you do understand why he sent you away.'

'He should never have done it, Miss Seaborn. He should have sent someone else to rescue you. Captain Shawcross could have got you out.'

'He couldn't do that, Grantley,' Honour said, and really she only understood it fully herself now. 'His grace feels like he isn't a proper man because of his illness. He told me about the time he tried to ride a horse and failed. He was ashamed of that.

'Think how much worse he would feel if he sent someone else out to rescue me. He'd essentially be saying he couldn't do it. He'd also fear I'd feel beholden to Captain Shawcross for the rest of my life, and think less of his grace at the same time.'

'It wasn't sensible.'

'It was extremely foolish,' Honour said. 'But every man has his pride, and every man has a point where he will say, "this thing must be done on my own, or I must die trying." I have seen it many times from soldiers going into war. There is a moment where a man must be tested and succeed or fail upon his own merits. This was his grace's time. However, if he does ask me to marry him, I will make sure that he never does anything that silly ever again.'

'Oh,' Grantley said.

'I would scold him too if I could, Grantley, but this time he did come to my rescue.'

'Yes, I see.'

'So, will you unbend to both him and Poole?'

'Well, as to that...'

'They both look up to you, you know?'

'Ha!' Grantley said but looked considerably mollified. 'I will order a bath up for you, Miss Seaborn. It will only take a jiffy.'

'Thank you, Grantley,' Honour said, pleased that she had at least eased a part of his wounded pride.

CHAPTER TWENTY-EIGHT

F elix wondered, for the hundredth time, whether Miss Seaborn was all right. It was late afternoon, and it had taken superhuman effort not to fret and fidget, or demand that the footmen carry him up to see her. Poole was his secret intelligencer in this and brought back whispered updates on Miss Seaborn's condition. That hadn't changed for the whole day, she was still asleep.

As Doctor Morton had assured him this prolonged sleep was merely due to exhaustion, he had to accept it and rest himself. He wanted to be at his best again when he did finally see Miss Seaborn. In the meantime, he distracted himself by trying to solve another mystery.

'Are you all right, Grantley?' Felix said as he watched his valet tidying the room.

'Yes, your grace, I am fine.'

'Are you sure?'

Felix couldn't understand why he wasn't getting the cold shoulder or the wounded expression he should have received from Grantley. Surely he was hurt by being deceived. But no, in fact, earlier on he'd helped Felix into his Japanese dressing gown quite serenely, and he wasn't a fan of it.

'I am quite sure, there is no need to trouble yourself, your grace.'

'How about Poole, is he all right?' Felix said and waited for the frost to descend.

'Poole is also fine, sir. He is currently laundering the coat you took out on your... your rescue mission.'

'Is he?'

'Lady Lavinia has him in the dog house, but no doubt he will be fine now that you are up.'

'He will be,' Felix said. 'I told him I would send him off without a reference if he didn't help me and you know I would have seen that through.'

'Yes, sir.'

'Indeed,' Felix said even more surprised by Grantley's equanimity.

'Miss Seaborn explained everything, your grace. I understand why you had to do it. I wish you hadn't, but as it turns out you rescued the young lady, I suppose all's well that ends well.'

'Miss Seaborn explained, did she?'

'She could tell I was upset, your grace, and you were in no fit state at the time to talk to.'

'That is certainly true. Do you know how Miss Seaborn is doing?'

'I understand she is still asleep, your grace. Lady Lavinia has also made it clear to all the staff that she is an honoured guest in this house.'

'I'm glad to hear that,' Felix said. It certainly did relieve him of one of his concerns.

'If there isn't anything else, your grace?'

'No, no, I'm fine, thank you.'

'I'm glad you found her, your grace,' Grantley said and bowed himself out.

'And I must find out what magical thing Miss Seaborn told you,' Felix murmured.

Just thinking about talking to Miss Seaborn caused him to feel a flutter of nerves in the pit of his stomach. He desperately wanted to see her again and be able to speak to her properly. He'd been so exhausted and trying so hard to keep upright and conscious when he'd found her in Bedlam that he hadn't said anything much.

Then Percy arrived, and it had been all he could do not to pass out. Never mind providing comfort to Miss Seaborn after her ordeal. Quite the opposite, in fact. He'd clung to her hand, desperate not to lose her again.

Now he'd see... he'd discover whether she was too disgusted with him to stay. Or whether she could bear to live with an invalid. He prayed she didn't feel beholden to him, or worse, so straitened in circumstances that she thought she had no choice but to marry him. He wasn't sure he could rebuff her if that were the case, such was his need to keep her near him, but it would hurt.

'Your breakfast, your grace,' Poole said and set a tray down on the table beside Felix.

'So Grantley let you do this, did he?'

'Yes, your grace.'

'Fascinating,' Felix said. 'I was sure he would be more angry with you than with me.'

'He was, sir. I thought he might never forgive me. Then he went off with Miss Seaborn and when he came back... he didn't say anything about Friday night, but he's been normal towards me ever since.'

'Me too. Miss Seaborn appears to be some kind of miracle worker.'

'Yes, sir.'

'And I owe you an apology.'

'Oh no, sir.'

'Yes, I do. I detest bullies, especially those that bully their staff with the certain knowledge their people need the jobs.'

'Your grace-'

'No, let me finish. I truly am sorry I forced you into helping me. But I couldn't have done what I did without you, and I will always be in your debt. I'd also like you to have this as some small recompense for what I put you through,' Felix said, holding out a note.

'Five pounds? No, your grace it's-'

'I could hardly give you less than I gave that black-hearted orderly now could I?'

'It's a lot of money.'

'Your service to me means more than that, Poole. Now, I am aware you send a fair amount of your wage to your mother, that is your prerogative. But I hope you will spend this windfall on yourself.'

'Oh yes, sir, thank you, your grace,' Poole said, bowed and hurried away.

Felix hoped that he had at least in part made up for forcing the young man into a most uncomfortable predicament. If he'd died on his adventure, Poole would have been in a great deal of trouble indeed despite the note he'd left exonerating the young man.

'Your grace, I couldn't stop him,' Chivers said as Hieronymus forced his way through.

'Mr Testwood?'

'Please forgive this intrusion, your grace, but Mr Andrews and I were up all night and most of today filling this flask with compressed air. I thought you might need it,' Hieronymus said and held a metallic bottle out in front of himself like a talisman.

'All night?'

'It takes rather a long time to condense the air, I'm afraid. And it appears you are no longer in need of it, so I apologise for disrupting your day.'

'It's fine. I could use a distraction actually, and I am curious to see, or at least try, a bit more of that air. I was somewhat distracted last night, but it did seem to me that your air gave me a moment of relief.'

'I'm glad it helped. I realised that we needed to add a valve to the device as all the air rushed out at once, and it would be more beneficial if it could be administered slowly.'

'That is certainly true. Is your valve that complex-looking device over the mouth of the bottle?'

'It is, it also makes it easier to get the bottle open than the wired on cork we used previously. I worked on that last night while Mr Andrews compressed more air.'

'Remarkable,' Felix said, examining what looked like a rather primitive device still. He'd got to know Mr Testwood's methods well enough to know that he would refine and improve it over the coming days. 'I think it's time you have a proper chat with my doctor, Mr Testwood. He should be involved with this development of the compressed air and give us his medical opinion on the safety of it. But, I personally have high hopes that it will be beneficial.'

'Thank you, your grace,' Hieronymus said beaming from ear to ear. 'I'll take my leave of you then.'

'Come back soon. In the meantime, you can expect a bonus from Mr Forsyth as a thank you for your assistance last night.'

'It was unexpected, your grace,' Hieronymus said, 'but I was happy to be of service. I assume you and the young lady will-'

Felix shook his head to stop Testwood and said, 'That remains to be seen.'

'I'm sure it will all work out,' Hieronymus said, bowed deeply and left.

'I hope you're right,' Felix murmured.

Since he had nothing else to do, he examined his lunch. Obviously, everyone from the cook upwards had decided he needed feeding up after his ordeal. He couldn't face the food though, not till he'd spoken to Miss Seaborn. She must have been tired indeed if she hadn't woken up yet.

He selected an innocuous piece of toast and took a bite. He at least needed to make an effort or else he'd be nagged by everyone. At the same time, he went back to Miss Seaborn's sketchbook. He knew it very well now, but she drew such detailed images he was always finding new things within the pictures. They would have to keep him entertained until he could finally speak to her.

Honour slowly became aware of tapping at her door. It had seeped into her dreams and felt as though it had been going on and on.

She opened her eyes and vaguely took in the yellow walls and furnishings. The tapping stopped, was followed by the sound of whispering and then another more tentative knock.

'Come in,' Honour said and felt strange doing so. She was just a guest, could she actually keep anyone out if they didn't want to be kept out.

'Are you awake?' Juliana said as she poked her head into the room.

'Of course she is, you silly goose,' Pixie said as she pushed the door open and hurried inside. 'How else could she have spoken to us?'

'I am awake,' Honour said and pushed herself up in the bed. She felt stiff like she sometimes had after a long trek. She supposed she had just lived through a similarly trying time, so it wasn't surprising. 'What time is it?'

'What time? Better to ask what day?' Pixie said with a grin as she dumped an armful of dresses on the foot of the bed.

'What day?' Honour said vaguely. 'How long have I slept?'

'A full day and night. It's Sunday morning now.'

'His grace? Is he all right?'

'He's fine. He's up. Well, he's sitting on his sofa in his room, but not dressed. He's in his dressing gown.'

'I have a feeling that means something.'

'If he's feeling very poorly, he stays in bed. When he starts getting better, he moves to the sofa but stays in his dressing gown. When he's feeling his best, he gets dressed and sometimes goes to the drawing room.'

'I see.'

'Are you going to marry him?' Juliana said, clasping her hands together in a wistful way.

'I don't know yet,' Honour said. 'He hasn't asked me.'

'He will,' Pixie said. 'He told me he loves you.'

'Did he? When?'

'After the two of you had tea.'

'That's why we're here,' Juliana said. 'We've brought you some dresses. You can't be proposed to in that boring grey dress. It makes you look like a governess, and you're too young and pretty for that.'

'Thank you, Juliana, that's very kind of you, but I don't need a new dress.'

'You should have one though,' Pixie said. 'Or are you still in mourning?'

Honour sighed and said, 'Not really. Not officially. But I was still so sad at Lady Giddings' that I couldn't bring myself to go back to wearing colours. On top of that, it wasn't appropriate for a chaperone.'

'I'm not surprised you were sad at Lady Giddings',' Juliana said. 'She's horrible. I'd much rather be related to you than to her.'

'Thank you, that's very kind, but I can't take one of your dresses.'

'Yes, you can. I have loads. We'll have to do up the laces more tightly though because you have more of a waist than I do,' Juliana said wistfully. 'Besides, once you're a duchess you can give the dress back to me because you'll have plenty of your own.'

'Mmm,' Honour said. 'I really don't think I should be taking that for granted. Besides, what does your mother think of all this?'

'It doesn't matter what mother thinks if Felix has made up his mind,' Pixie said. 'You mustn't think he's easily browbeaten, because he isn't. Percy told me he also gave Lady Giddings her marching orders in fine style.'

'Did he? I wish I could have seen that.'

'Are you going to take her to justice for what she did to you?'

'I don't think I will anymore. When I was locked up in Bedlam I was so furious I would have done anything to see Isolde pay for what she had done. Now... She lost the duke you see, and that is going to be a terrible blow to her pride. That isn't even including who she lost him to. It will eat away at her that his grace loves me more than he loves her. That is punishment enough.'

'That's very generous of you.'

'Not really, and I have his grace in mind too. I wouldn't want to have his name dragged through the papers again, or have the possibility of having to go to court.'

'That wouldn't be good,' Pixie said. 'Well, there you go, we are halfway to being settled. You needn't worry about scandal attaching itself to you either. Mother has already said we will let it be known that she invited you to stay with us girls in the nursery as soon as it became clear you were to be a part of the family. So you see, she has already accepted you. She was never very opposed anyway.'

'Really? Even though I'm the penniless daughter of a soldier?'

'You aren't Lady Giddings,' Pixie said with a broad grin. 'Mother was so violently opposed to her that anyone else is preferable.'

'Well that is a relief,' Honour said.

'Dr Morton also put in a good word for you. Mother's primary concern is Felix's health and the doctor said you are sensible and capable. He said you could be relied upon in a crisis. I would say that was a clincher. Not that mother would ever tell you that.'

'Oh, I see,' Honour said. 'I hadn't really thought-'

'It's all mother really cares about. Now, let's try on some dresses, I can't wait to see you looking pretty,' Pixie said, and Juliana clapped her hands in enthusiastic agreement.

Honour thoroughly enjoyed herself trying on dresses. It was a strange and rather pleasant treat to have so many pretty frocks. She stood in front of the full-length mirror, critically examining herself. She had to admit she did look nice, and much younger, in the white muslin dress with a fetching wisteria-patterned lavender print. Her loose locks hung down around her shoulders, and Juliana and Pixie were holding a spirited argument over the best way to tie up her hair.

She let the discussion roll over her. She'd never owned such a frivolous garment before. All her clothes had been practical and hardwearing. Even the dress she'd worn to balls was a simple cream cotton affair designed to be packed and moved over continents rather than to show off her feminine charms.

'Miss Seaborn, I see you are up,' Lady Lavinia said as she came into the room.

'She is mother,' Juliana said. 'Doesn't she look beautiful?'

To Honour's surprise, Lady Lavinia actually appeared to give the question full consideration as she examined her from tip to toe. 'Yes, you will do very well,' she said. 'Now, my dears, I wish to speak to Miss Seaborn in private.'

'Yes, Mama,' Pixie said, gave Honour a conspiratorial smile and pushed her sister out of the room.

'Thank you for your kind hospitality, Lady Lavinia,' Honour said and hoped she wasn't about to be told off.

'I was appalled to hear what happened to you, Miss Seaborn. Your cousin is quite beyond the pale and needless to say I will cut her dead should I ever run into her.'

'I see.'

Honour wondered how much influence her ladyship had. If it was substantial, and it probably was, Isolde could well find herself ostracised from society. That would be harsh punishment, indeed. Honour couldn't find it in herself to try and talk her ladyship round though. Besides, she was more worried about what this fierce woman was going to say about her.

'By rescuing you, my nephew has made his wishes very plain.'

'Perhaps.'

'There is no doubt about it and no point in pretending to false modesty.'

'I am not being modest. His grace has yet to mention anything to me, and I don't wish to be forward.'

'Very well. However, I believe it is only a matter of time, so I thought I'd let you know that I approve. I would have preferred that Felix marry a young woman of means and title. However, your family is sufficiently respectable, so I have very little hesitation about accepting you.'

'Thank you, Lady Lavinia,' Honour said and wondered what the duke might make of his aunt's intervention. She suspected he would be amused.

'You will find it is quite a step up being a duchess. But I will guide you, and you will soon find your feet.'

'Thank you,' Honour said. She hadn't considered the reality of what she might be stepping into till that moment.

'Well, you'd best not keep him waiting. He'll be fretting till he finally sees you.'

'Oh er... now?'

'Did you have any other plans for the day?'

'No.'

'Well then, run along.'

CHAPTER TWENTY-NINE

F elix was staring unseeing out of his bedroom window, Miss
Seaborn's sketchbook resting on his lap when there was a light
tap at the door.

'May I come in?' Honour said as she stuck her head into the duke's
room.

'Miss Seaborn!' Felix said and scrambled to stand up as his
stomach gave a somersault of fright.

'Don't get up,' Honour said as she hurried over. 'Shall I sit here?'

'Of course. Please do. You look... you look very pretty in that dress.
The lavender really suits you,' Felix said and felt a fool for saying it.

'Thank you,' Honour said as she settled in the chair opposite him.

'I like your hair done in that more relaxed style too,' Felix said
and despaired of himself. How could he be talking about such
unimportant things when he had the most crucial question of his
life burning in his brain.

'Juliana and Pixie insisted that I not look like a governess,'
Honour said and smiled so warmly at him that it took his breath
away.

'How are you feeling after your ordeal?' Felix said.

'I am much better, thank you. I have never been happier to see
anyone in my whole life than when you arrived to rescue me. I'd

been trying for the whole week to work out how to escape, but to no avail.'

'You were planning an escape?'

'Of course, but two things hindered me. The first was how to get away. The second was what to do after that, penniless and in my nightdress in London in winter.'

'Yes,' Felix said struck by the enormity of the challenge. 'The mind boggles.'

'Mine did certainly, but in the end, I didn't have to worry,' Honour said and looked up at him.

She looked so happy, so... adoring it gave him the courage to take her hand as he said, 'Miss Seaborn?'

'Yes, your grace?' she said and wrapped her fingers gently around his.

'I'm... I'm not the most robust of men, as you know. And I'm sorry that in what was intended as a rescue, you landed up having to look after me.'

'I didn't mind that.'

'No, but...' Felix was at a loss. How did he say this? 'You... you are used to military men, and being able to march all the way across a continent, and to live life in its full rough and tumble and I... I can barely walk from one room to the next.'

'We all have different strengths, your grace. You are an intelligent man, and you make the best possible use of your talents.'

'That is very kind of you to say,' Felix said. 'I just, I... I love you, Miss Seaborn.'

'Oh!'

'I would very much like it if... If you would marry me but I know that might not appeal. I can't... I can't give you the life of adventure you are used to, and I fear you may not want to be trapped in just one house but-'

'Your grace,' Honour said and squeezed his hand. 'I never wanted a life of adventure. That was my father's life. I loved him, so I stayed with him, but it wasn't what I dreamed of.'

'It wasn't?'

'My dream was Rose Cottage.'

'That picture of an English-looking house in your sketchbook?'

'It was from a watercolour our regimental colonel had of his childhood home. When I saw it, I was struck by how wonderful it looked. You see, I dreamed of a pretty little place where I could make a nest. I didn't want to sleep under canvas anymore, or be woken by cannon fire, or walk for miles and miles for days on end or watch men have their limbs amputated.'

'Oh,' Felix said. 'But I don't have a small cottage. I have a rambling, rather uncomfortable country seat.'

'I am sure I could make it comfortable,' Honour said. 'All I really meant was I wanted a place of my own, where I could feel safe and protected.'

'I can do that,' Felix said, and he felt on more solid ground. 'And you... you will always be safe, Miss Seaborn, I promise. No matter what happens to me.'

'I don't want you to die,' Honour said. 'You must promise me you will take the greatest care from now on. Never ever do anything as foolhardy as you did when you rescued me.'

'Then you must promise never to get abducted,' Felix said with a laugh.

'I will never leave your side.'

'So... so you will marry me?'

'I will.'

'Honour!' Felix said. 'You have made me so happy. What a relief to finally be able to call you by your name, after so much time and formality.'

'Felix,' Honour whispered and tears rose to her eyes.

'Oh no, my dear, don't cry,' Felix said. 'Don't be unhappy.'

'I'm not unhappy, these are tears of joy,' Honour said and sniffed. 'Oh dear, I need a hanky.'

'Come and sit beside me,' Felix said as he guided Honour onto the sofa. 'I will deal with those tears.'

'Thank you,' Honour said as Felix gently dabbed at her face.

He couldn't resist, she was looking up at him, her lips so close, that he leaned down and kissed her. Instead of stiffening, she leaned against him, and he suddenly felt overwhelmingly happy.

'My love,' he murmured.

Honour sighed in contentment and snuggled up against him. Felix, feeling very manly indeed, wrapped his arms around her. He was astonished at how wonderful it felt to be sitting on the sofa with a woman in his arms. His woman.

'I love you,' he murmured as he kissed Honour again.

'I love you too. It's such a relief to finally be able to say it.'

'It is, isn't it?' Felix said. 'When did you first decide you liked me?'

'Oh, long before you liked me. I started falling in love with you the second time we met.'

'Only the second time?'

'When we first met, all I saw was yet another man fall victim to Isolde. By that time it had become wearingly familiar, and I had so hoped you would rebuff her. Not because I knew anything about you, just because I didn't want Isolde to have everything handed to her.'

'Well, she hasn't.'

'In a spectacular way. I wish I could say I was sorry for her, but I'm afraid I'm not.'

'She has brought her misfortune upon herself. But tell me, what changed your mind?'

'Captain Shawcross told me at one of the balls we both attended that you had noticed me. I didn't believe him, but after our second visit you sent me this gift,' Honour said as she twitched her shawl.

'I sent Lady Giddings one too.'

'I know, but in all the time I had been in her house, you were the only one of her gentlemen who ever sent me anything. Your solicitude touched me. At that point, I had already decided that I quite liked you and was trying hard not to let it grow into anything more.'

'But why not?'

'When you didn't love me? How could I bear it – to be in the same room as you when you only had eyes for Isolde?'

'I'm sorry I was so blind for so long.'

'It doesn't matter anymore.'

'I'm glad,' Felix said and wrapped his arms more tightly around Honour. 'So Percy talked to you quite early on too, did he?'

'I got the impression at the time he was trying to understand the enemy.'

'Lady Giddings?'

'I believe so.'

'Mmm, and I was so angry with him, but in the end, he was right.'

'He has done a great deal for both of us,' Honour said. 'We should do something to help him.'

'What do you suggest, my love?'

'Well, I don't know how we can do it, but I do believe he and Pixie are in love. Only Lady Lavinia is unlikely to countenance a match between them.'

'Ah no, she wouldn't like it, but as it happens, I have been considering the problem.'

'You have?'

'Pixie asked for my help. Percy, as yet, has no inkling of that.'

'Do you have a solution?'

'I believe so. I can buy him a commission. We can make him up to colonel or major, whichever is necessary to sway my aunt.'

'That's a splendid idea. When are you going to tell him?'

'Not for a while yet. I told Pixie she'd have to wait a year, but I might have to do something before then.'

'Well you know what's best,' Honour said and snuggled even closer.

'May I come in?' Percy said as he popped his head around the bedroom door to find Felix and Miss Seaborn together on the sofa.

'Percy,' Felix said, and a smile lit up his face. 'Come in, you are very welcome.'

'Not interrupting, am I? The two of you look like you were drifting off.'

'We are both still recovering from our ordeal.'

'That's understandable. Am I right in assuming that you are now engaged?'

'You are the first to know. It's true, yes.'

'Congratulations, I couldn't be happier for both of you.'

'Thank you, Captain Shawcross. I'm not sure we would have made it this far without your intervention,' Honour said.

'My meddling you mean, but as we are about to become cousins, you must call me Percy.'

'Gladly, Cousin Percy.'

'That has a good ring to it. So, have you decided on a date for the wedding yet?'

'We have just finished discussing that,' Felix said. 'We will send the announcement of our engagement to the papers tomorrow, and set the wedding for a fortnight hence.'

'So soon?'

'There is no reason to wait, and every reason to get it done quickly.'

'Well, I suppose as Honour has already moved in and hasn't got anywhere she could move out to, it is the most sensible thing to do.'

'It is,' Felix said, leaned down and kissed Honour.

'That's it then,' Percy said, 'the two of you are sorted,' and he laughed because neither Felix nor Honour were listening anymore.

Write a Review

Enjoyed this book? You can make a huge difference

If you are like me, you use reviews to decide whether you want to buy a book. So if you enjoyed the book please take a moment to let people know why. The review can be as short as you like.

Thank you very much!

Also By

Get all my books here:

MEDIEVAL HISTORICAL FICTION available ePub, paperback and hardback
Fraternity of Brothers, *Life of Galen, Book 1* – Cast out for a crime committed against him, his future looks bleak. Until an unexpected visitor gives him hope for justice. A fight for acceptance, absolution and friendship in Anglo-Saxon England.
Comfort of Home, *Life of Galen, Book 2* – Proven innocent, he's returned from exile. Can he recover all that he lost? A tale of friendship and return to a family he thought he'd lost, set in Anglo-Saxon England.
Kindness of Strangers, *Life of Galen, Book 3* – Trapped in a land plagued by vikings, can one small miracle be all they need to survive? A tale of miracles, betrayal and friendship while under viking siege.

The King's Hall, *Life of Galen, Book 4* – As if being commissioned to create a book to turn back the Apocalypse isn't enough, intrigue and romance threaten to destroy everything he's come to rely upon. Friendship, love and intrigue at the court of King Aethelred the Unready.

Restless Sea, *Life of Galen, Book 5* – Just when they thought they could go home, they're thrust into an adventure at sea. A journey that tests the bonds of friendship.

Friend of My Enemy, *Life of Galen, Book 6* – Captured by an implacable enemy, their future looks bleak. Will escape even be possible?

Road to Rome, *Life of Galen, Book 7* — A journey across a turbulent continent. Will Galen find the answers he seeks?

Eternal City, *Life of Galen, Book 8* — *Coming JUNE 2023*

AUDIOBOOKS with a human narrator

Fraternity of Brothers, *Life of Galen, Book 1* – Cast out for a crime committed against him, his future looks bleak. Until an unexpected visitor gives him hope for justice. A fight for acceptance, absolution and friendship in Anglo-Saxon England.

Comfort of Home, *Life of Galen, Book 2* – Proven innocent, he's returned from exile. Can he recover all that he lost? A tale of friendship and return to a family he thought he'd lost, set in Anglo-Saxon England.

Kindness of Strangers, *Life of Galen, Book 3* – Trapped in a land plagued by vikings, can one small miracle be all they need to survive? A tale of miracles, betrayal and friendship while under viking siege.

HISTORICAL ROMANCE: available ePub, paperback, hardback and audiobooks with AI narration

Sanctuary, *a sweet Medieval mystery* – He needs shelter. She wants a way out. Will his brave move to protect risk both their hearts? An optimistic tale of redemption with heart-warming characters and feel-good thrills.

The Duke's Heart, *a sweet Victorian romance* – His body may be weak, but his dreams know no bounds. Will she be the answer to his prayers? A disabled duke, a strong and determined woman and a slow-building relationship.

Duchess in Flight, *a swashbuckling romance* – She's on the run from a deadly enemy. He lives in the shadows of truth. When their lives merge, will their battle for survival lead to love? A reluctant hero, a woman and her children in distress, a chase to the death.

What the Pauper Did, *a body swap mystery romance* – How do you define yourself? Is it through your appearance, your memories or your soul? Intrigue, murder and romance in an alternate Lisbon of 1770.

CONTEMPORARY ROMANCE available ePub, paperback, hardback and audiobooks with AI narration
Scent of Love – Can two polar opposite perfumers be able to overcome their differences and create a unique blend all of their own? Love, intrigue and clashing values in the perfume houses of Lisbon.

Sky Therapy — A detective and the son of a serial killer. Is it safest to stay apart, or will they risk everything for love?

SCIENCE FICTION/ FANTASY available ePub and paperback
City of Night, *Eternal City, Book 1* – World-threatening danger, a female demonologist, an unwitting apprentice, a city in a single tower, a satisfying ending.

SHORT STORIES: available ePub, paperback, and AI narration
Living, Loving, Longing, Lisbon – A collection of short stories inspired by the city of Lisbon, written by people from around the world who live in, visited or love Lisbon.

FREEBIES: available ePub and AI narration
Shorties – My shortest works: futuristic, contemporary and historical.
White Rabbit of Lisbon – A whimsical short story. What will happen when a rabbit and a raven fall in love?
Scourge of Demons – How would you deal with your demons? A short story set in the world of the Life of Galen series.
The Greek Gift – A Christmas short story. At the gym he ignored her; will it be any different at the Christmas Eve party?
Christmas Fates – A Christmas short story. Aurora Dawn is about to learn the true meaning of Christmas and it has nothing to do with how many of the latest must-haves she can sell.

About Author

Marina Pacheco a binge writer of historical fiction, sweet romance, sci-fi and fantasy novels as well as short stories. She writes easy reading, feel-good novels that are perfect for a commute or to curl up with on a rainy day. She currently lives on the coast just outside Lisbon, after stints in London, Johannesburg, and Bangkok, which all sounds more glamorous than it actually was. Her ambition is to publish 100 books. This is taking considerably longer than she'd anticipated!

You can find out more about Marina Pacheco's work, and download several freebies, on her website: https://marinapacheco.me
Website: https://marinapacheco.me
Patreon: https://www.patreon.com/marinapacheco
Facebook: https://bit.ly/marinas-books
email: hi@marinapacheco.me

Printed in Great Britain
by Amazon

48587486R00209